P9-BTM-776

IT'S SUPERMAN!

IT'S SUPERMAN!

A NOVEL

TOM DE HAVEN

SUPERMAN CREATED BY
JERRY SIEGEL AND JOE SHUSTER

CHRONICLE BOOKS
SAN FRANCISCO

DIXON PUBLIC LIBRARY
DIXON ILLINOIS

ACKNOWLEDGMENTS

A great part of this novel was written in a tiny cabin on a small island off the coast of northern Maine. I would like to thank the Eastern Frontier Educational Foundation for making that residency possible, and Steve Dunn for his generosity, encouragement, and friendship.

© 2005 by DC Comics. Superman and all related characters and elements are trademarks of DC Comics. All rights reserved. No part of this book may be reproduced in any form without written permission from the publisher.

This is a work of fiction. Names, places, characters, and incidents are products of the author's imagination or are used fictionally. Any resemblance to actual people, places, or events is entirely coincidental.

Library of Congress Cataloging-in-Publication Data available.

ISBN 0-8118-4435-8

Manufactured in Canada

Cover design and illustration by Chris Ware
Designed by Brett MacFadden

Distributed in Canada by Raincoast Books
9050 Shaughnessy Street
Vancouver, British Columbia V6P 6E5

10 9 8 7 6 5 4 3 2 1

Chronicle Books LLC
85 Second Street
San Francisco, California 94105
www.chroniclebooks.com

For Margaret Hussey, whose fortunate son I am.

———

PART ONE

THE WPA GUIDE TO SMALLVILLE

Public enemy. Events at the Jewel Theater are recounted.
The baby that fell off a wagon. Science fiction.
Alger in Smallerville. Mr. and Mrs. Kent.

———

1

Our version of the story opens on the last Saturday of May 1935
with the arrival of Sheriff Bill Dutcher at the police station in
Smallville, Kansas. A craggy man with steel-gray hair and long side-
burns, he's wearing tan slacks and a barn jacket over a maroon polo
shirt. His star is pinned to the pocket. He brought along his pistol belt
and holster but leaves that in the trunk with his 12-gauge. Those won't
be necessary. When he got the call an hour ago, Dutcher was off-shift,
at home in Lyndon savoring his third highball of the evening and playing canasta with the wife and some neighbors. He could have been
easily in a fume, or worse, by the time he motored thirty miles through
drizzle and dust blow to this clodhopper town but no, not at all. He is
in fine spirits, especially once he discovers those federal glory hogs out
of Topeka haven't showed up yet. He shakes hands with two deputies
that meet him at the door, even clapping one of them on the shoulder.
Then he speaks privately with Doug Parker, the local chief of police,
both of them turning together to cast brief looks at the farm boy, seventeen years old and hunched low in a varnished chair near the chief's
desk. Judging by the kid's shiny eyes and heavy breathing and the tense
fist that he rubs back and forth on his thigh, any minute he'll put birdie
to his dinner plus whatever Jujubes or Raisinets he had earlier at the

picture show. "You might think of giving Sergeant York, there, a wastepaper basket," says the sheriff, "while I go and see Jiggs."

"Straight back. You can't miss him."

Beyond the lavatory door with its tractor calendar stands a long sawbuck table where Mr. Jiggs Makley, for some years a presence both on wanted posters and in rotogravures, has been laid face up. A chunk of that face, however, is blown off, and the rest of it, including a cheap theatrical mustache, is covered with blood, not all of it dry. His big eyes are open and staring.

Hands deep in his pockets, idly jiggling coins and keys, the sheriff stands alongside of the table thinking, Poor dead hillbilly son of a bitch, he looks completely flabbergasted. Thinking: Good pair of Florsheims. Hardly been worn. Brown pleated trousers, he thinks, but no belt. *That* figures. Dutcher removes one hand from a pocket and fingers the shirt collar away from Makley's neck. Essley brand. Size 16. Top, second, and third buttons missing. Plucked off, it looks like. And no cufflinks, either. Surprise, surprise. "Chief," he says realizing that he's been joined, "tell me again. *What* was it your boy said? The craziest gun?"

"Stupidest. He said Makley must've owned the world's *stupidest* gun."

"Meaning?"

"That it had to've fired backwards."

Dutcher laughs. "I know you told me his name, but—"

"Kent," says Chief Parker. "Clark Kent."

2

His left hand curls into itself and he keeps squeezing it like a slow pulse, but every time Clark thinks he might actually *open* his fingers and *look,* he feels another bolt of panic and changes his mind.

"How you doing, son?"

Clark's fist draws back to his waist, pressing there.

"Something wrong with your hand?"

"No, sir."

The man nods, a few times too many. "Bill Dutcher, Clark. I'm sheriff of Osage County." Grabbing a small chair, he twirls it casually and sits down, his thick folded forearms across the back. "Say, you wouldn't be related to the Kents live over to Osawatomie, would you? Own that big stove company?"

"I don't think so."

"My wife's cousin does their bookkeeping—or she did. Maybe don't anymore. Things being how they are." Dutcher leans forward. "Sounds like you had yourself quite an evening." He sits back, plucks out a hand-rolled from his shirt pocket. "So hows about you tell me what happened?" Dutcher holds the paper of matches in his right hand, tears off a match, and runs it across the friction strip with his left. And seeing that, realizing Dutcher is left-handed, same as he is, Clark relaxes a little. He feels an odd kinship with lefties. Just as he feels one with blue-eyed people or people with black hair. With fingernails shaped like his: square and blunt.

Finding people who are like him, even in the smallest ways, is always a comfort. It's stupid, he knows, but still it's *some* comfort.

"Clark," says Dutcher, "I surely don't mean to push you, son, but do you think you might tell me about—"

"Excuse me for just one second, Sheriff." Holding a cup of coffee, Chief Parker settles himself, carefully so he doesn't spill any, behind his desk. "Clark, you *sure* you don't want me to send somebody for your dad? It's no trouble."

"I don't want to worry him, with my mom and all. But thanks."

"Up to you." Earlier the chief offered to call Clark's father—or let the boy do it himself, of course—except the Kents don't have telephone service. Or electricity, either. Truth be told, they're lucky to have a roof still over their heads. Things being how they are. "Well, if you change your mind. And oh, Clinton drove your girlfriend home, she's fine."

"I just took her to the pictures," says Clark. He feels heat rise in his neck. "She's not my girl." The chair under him creaks. "But what about Alger Lee? He all right?"

"I'm sure he's fine," says Parker. "We told him to stick around, but he left. I expect he ran on home."

"Alger Lee?" says Dutcher.

"Colored boy I told you about, was there. I'm sure he just—I expect he ran straight on home. We can go fetch him now for you if you like."

Dutcher seems to consider the offer but doesn't respond to it. Just pulls at his cigarette and exhales. Then: "What movie you go see?" he asks Clark.

"We were *supposed* to see *The Werewolf of London*."

"Now, somebody told me about that one. It's with the guy plays Charlie Chan, right?"

"Warner Oland," says Parker.

"I bet it's good," says Dutcher, then he says, "Chief, could I bother you for some of that coffee? Sweet if you got sugar, no milk."

One end of Parker's mouth quirks up. Then he purses his lips slightly and smoothes them out again, and Clark figures all that pantomime is to let the sheriff know he's amused by the request, takes no offense, and sees it for the rank-pulling take-a-hike that it is. "Clark, how about you? Coffee?"

"No, thank you."

"Be right back, then."

"Take your time," says Dutcher. "This young fella's gonna tell me what all went on, and you heard it before. So Clark," he says, "what time the picture start?"

"Eight o'clock."

"Lot of other folks there tonight?" Dutcher asks. Then asks him again because the boy is getting more and more remote every moment. "Full house?"

"About regular for a Saturday."

"And what's about regular?" Dutcher finds an ashtray on the chief's desk and rubs out his cigarette. "Thirty people, fifty, a hundred?"

"I couldn't say. I guess half the seats downstairs were filled. I don't know how many that'd be."

"Uh-huh." Dutcher looks thoughtfully at Clark's face. Points. "You get whacked by something?"

Clark's right hand goes promptly to his forehead, tapping his fingertips around, playing dumb.

"You got a red mark, there, right there. Like something might've hit you."

"No, sir." But two hours ago, little less, Clark saw it himself, what the sheriff is squinting at now. A small welt barely an inch above his nose. He saw it when he leaned against a cigarette machine, *hugged* it, laboring to get control of himself. Saw it reflected in the panel mirror the same moment he saw the body of Jiggs Makley lying spread-eagled behind him on the Jewel Theater's fake-Persian lobby carpet.

"Son?" Dutcher holds up a wastebasket, offering it. "You going to be sick?"

"If they'd done it in the right order," says Clark, "this wouldn't of never happened."

"Done what in the right order?"

"Before the picture, it's always you got your coming attractions and then you got your cartoon and *then* you got your newsreel." Clark smacks his knee savagely with that doubled fist. "But oh no, tonight somebody had to go and do it different."

"What'd they do?"

"Showed the newsreel right after the coming attractions."

And it wasn't just the goofus running the projector machine, either. When you came right down to it, and Clark isn't *blaming* anybody, not exactly, it's just that . . . well, before heading into the auditorium, he *asked* Janey Laster if she wanted him to stop by the candy concession for a box of nonpareils or a chocolate bar or a drink, whatever she liked. He *asked* her, he *offered*, and if she only said yes. If only she said yes *then*. But she didn't. She said she was still too full from dinner. Thank you, though.

This was only Clark's second date, and his first with Janey Laster from his typewriting class. He'd expected to run into some kids from their high school, was *hoping* he would, since Janey not only was a pretty blond with the kind of figure people called "cute," but was known to be awfully picky about boys, which only could help Clark's standing with his peers. Although why in blue blazes he cared about *that* at this late stage of the game, he wasn't sure.

At school Clark is not actively disliked, he isn't *un*popular, he's just . . . there. There-but-not-there. You say hello, he says hello back. You don't, he doesn't. Overall, he's good-enough *looking*, but not what you would call handsome, either. His ears are too small for his head, and his crowded teeth crooked on the bottom. He's a quiet boy, a struggling B student, does all of his homework, and while it seems by appearances that he'd be strong, well-coordinated, quick—he has good shoulders and graceful legs—he has never gone out for athletics. And he was invited to by coaches any number of times. He reads a lot, but mostly the junkiest, dopiest pulps, the kind with tentacled green Martians on the covers. He likes movies, all sorts of movies, and often goes by himself. Even still goes to the kiddie show on Saturday mornings because he especially likes chapter-plays with cowboys and masked men, death rays and robots. And he writes—carefully, accurately, but with no special flair—for the school newspaper. He's okay. He's all right. In the opinion of his peers at Smallville High School, Clark is all right but nothing special. And Janey Laster was at the Jewel with him on a Saturday night, she went out on a date with Clark Kent, but nobody that he knew—at least nobody his own age—was there to notice.

"I think I should've gotten a Coke," said Janey during the preview of Katharine Hepburn's latest picture, something called *Break of Hearts*. Which didn't look so hot. "Do you mind?"

"Course not," said Clark, already on his feet.

"Oh, you know something? Forget it. I'm not really thirsty." She waved a hand in front of her face, then clucked for saying anything.

Clark sat down, wondering whether he should put his arm around her now, or wait.

A second preview played, for the new Mae West, then another, for a picture called *The Informer,* starring Victor McLaglen, an actor Clark recognized from some westerns he'd liked.

But when Mickey Mouse should have come on, instead it was *News of the World.* Not that it seemed any big deal at the time. In fact, it would've been okay with Clark if they skipped the cartoon entirely. He was never much impressed by that Disney stuff. Those things didn't make him laugh. Although he wished they did, since everyone else in the whole country, maybe the whole world, obviously found them hilarious, and whenever he would sit in the Jewel with a make-believe smile frozen on his face watching a bunch of cartoon animals play baseball or hot jazz, he'd just feel crummy—dumb and different and set apart.

He put his left arm around Janey's shoulder, and that seemed fine with her.

"That's when I first saw him," says Clark.

"In the theater?" asks Dutcher. "That what you're saying?"

Clark sighs and looks sadly up at the ceiling. "No," he says. "In the newsreel."

But first there was the May Day Parade in Russia, it looked like the entire Soviet Army was marching past the Kremlin with helmets on and bayonets fixed, Stalin not cracking a smile, not once, and then Hitler in the Reichstag shaking a fist, *both* fists, and screaming that he didn't care *what* the League of Nations said, Germany was set on building tanks and planes and submarines, whatever it wanted, and then came the funeral for Lawrence of Arabia, who'd been killed in England on his motorbike, and then it was back to the USA, and there was half a minute about the Boulder Dam, how'd they'd finished it finally. Then you got the running of the Kentucky Derby, and then farms buried deep in black sand dunes out in Texas and Oklahoma and western Kansas, then people on street corners selling dust masks for a dime, and families by the dozens leaving for California in rattletrap Fords, even on foot, and then there was a highway patrolman somewhere in Missouri pointing to a little grocery store that was all shot up, and to a wide dark stain on the ground outside near a filling pump that looked like motor oil but he said was blood. Then he said it was a massacre and for what? Far as he could tell the Jiggs Makley gang didn't get more than ten, fifteen dollars, at most, and—

"But when did you see *him?*" says Dutcher. He moves closer to Clark, bringing his face as near as six inches. "When did you see Jiggs?"

"Right after that highway patrolman finished talking. His picture came on. But if they showed the Mickey Mouse when they *should've—*"

"So you got a good look."

"Well, *yeah.*"

"Go on."

So next came Admiral Byrd and his men from the South Pole being congratulated by the president at the White House, and then—

Then Janey Laster hated to be such a pest, but would Clark mind a whole lot getting her that Coke now? Before the picture started? And if it wasn't asking too much, some popcorn?

Ahead of him at the concession was an elderly couple Clark recognized from the Methodist church he and his mother used to attend before she got sick. The Kemps. And as they bent forward together and pushed their faces nearer the slanted glass of the candy showcase, trying to decide if they wanted Sugar Babies or Charleston Chews and whether or not they felt like licorice tonight, Clark fidgeted and looked at his wristwatch. He glanced over their bobbing gray heads at lanky unsmiling Alger Lee patiently waiting for the Kemps to place their order. In one hand he had a paper sack he'd snapped open, and in the other hand an aluminum scoop.

Alger is a year or two younger than Clark but half a head taller. A good thirty pounds slighter, though. He wore a white uniform jacket, like a waiter's but with the red word "Jewel" stitched over the pocket, a ruffled shirt much whiter than the jacket, and a black bowtie pressed snug to his throat. When he noticed Clark, Alger nodded in that scant, almost formal way that he had. He said to Mrs. Kemp, for the third time, "Those are still a penny, yes, ma'am."

The usher had gone inside the auditorium, and the ticket taker was out on the sidewalk having a smoke. It was just the four of them in the lobby.

"And the gumdrops we sell by weight, yes, ma'am."

When Clark was much younger, Alger's father, Darron, worked on the Kent farm twice a year, once in high summer when they cut and put up the hay and then again in late summer when they brought in the corn. Clark well remembered Darron Lee both because he'd been an impossibly huge man—six-eight or -nine and as wide as a bear, a build his son hadn't inherited—and because he was the first colored person Clark had ever seen. He died, drowned, five years ago in a freak accident during a spring flood. Driving a team of horses to a hog farm west of town, he'd banked a curve and his cart turned over.

"And those, yes, are three for a penny, yes, ma'am," said Alger Lee.

Clark checked his watch again.

"Yes, sir," said Alger, scooping up a dozen malted milk balls and depositing them into the white sack. Then he scooped up and deposited half a dozen Bit-O-Honeys, and finally half a dozen Sugar Babies. "That all for you, ma'am? Sir? Then that'll be"—Clark watched Alger narrow his eyes, doing the math—"twelve cents, please." Then: "No problem at all, ma'am," he said and removed one Bit-O-Honey and one Sugar Baby, to bring the sum down to a dime. "Thank you, folks. Enjoy the picture. Next."

It made Clark uneasy when Alger, as usual, looked him straight in the eye and called him "sir." "What can I get you, sir?" Why'd he *do* that?

"Just a Coca-Cola and some popcorn."

"Small or large?"

"Large, I guess."

Watching Alger pump out the syrup and draw carbonated water from the fountain tap, Clark could hear tuba, banjo, and washboard music playing inside the auditorium—so he still wasn't missing anything but the mouse. Alger placed the fountain soda on the counter and turned to the popcorn machine. Clark was sliding a single from his money fold when Alger Lee clear out of the blue asked him, "How's your mother, is she feeling any better?"

For a moment Clark was too surprised to answer. "No, I'm afraid she's not," he said finally. "But thank you for asking," he said. "Alger."

With a short nod, Alger finished scooping popcorn into a red-striped paper box. He sprinkled it liberally with salt and added a wedge of butter. As he set the popcorn down on the countertop, Alger's eyes lifted slightly. Someone had just stepped up behind Clark and cleared his throat.

"Our friend Mr. Jiggs?" says Dutcher.

"Yes, sir."

"Wanted a candy bar, did he?"

"I don't know what he wanted," says Clark. "It never got that far."

"So how far *did* it get?"

"He started in calling Alger names."

Said, "You expect to find woolly-heads in Kansas City, but you got 'em *here*, too?"

Said, "Why somebody in these sad times got the *gall* to go and let a nigger work a job could be done by a white boy is just something that burns my ass."

Said, "And why ain't he wearing gloves, anyhow? Touching food."

Dutcher passes a hand over his eyes, gets up, and stretches. "That's what he said, huh? With no provocation?"

"He just started talking."

"How did Alvin react?"

"Alger. And he didn't."

Not at all. He merely looked back over at Clark and said if there was nothing else, that'd be forty cents, please.

"You ignoring me, sonny?" said the man.

"I didn't think you were talking to anybody in particular," said Alger, but he was still facing Clark, saying that like he was saying it to him.

A large bony hand clamped down on Clark's right shoulder. Brusquely he was shunted aside as the man stepped forward. He was drunk, Clark realized. *That* was no big surprise. What *was,* and it was a big *nasty* surprise that registered itself as a fluttering sensation in Clark's belly, was the man's face.

Clark knew it.

Had just seen it.

In a newsreel.

"Only the mustache was new."

"Master of disguise, huh?"

"Not really."

"So Alger mouthed off and Makley pushed you away to mix it up. That it?"

"Alger didn't mouth off. He just said he didn't think the guy was talking to anybody in particular."

"Funny boy, huh?"

Alger swallowed, but never blinked. Addressing Clark again, he said, "Your total's forty cents. Sir."

"You think you're a funny boy, *that* what you think? You come on out from behind there, hear me? And you, sonny"—the man Clark had recognized as Jiggs Makley was glaring at him now—"you go on back and take his damn place. I don't want to be waited on by no woolly-head thinks he's a funny nigger boy. Hey. What're *you* looking at?"

Clark said, "Nothing." But automatically—you stupid sack, he thought even as he did it—he raised his left hand, running the side of his index finger across his upper lip.

That's when Jiggs Makley grinned.

"Like he was flattered being recognized?" says Dutcher.

"I don't think so."

"I bet so. Be right in character, son. Vain little booger. Always strutting like a movie star."

"No, sir, I don't think . . . he wasn't too happy that I knew who he was."

"He say that?"

"He *grabbed* me. By the front of my shirt. And like he wasn't *about* to let go."

"You tell him to?"

"No."

"Curse him out?"

"No!"

"Well, *something* made him mad enough to want to shoot you, Clark."

"I guess I pushed him."

"You *guess?*"

"I pushed him, but not *hard.* I just . . ." He nearly opens his left hand, to demonstrate. At the last moment, though, he lets it fall. "I just pushed him a little so he'd leave. And he, um, hit the wall."

"And broke one of those big old glass picture frames with a movie poster inside, is what I heard."

"Yes, sir. But he must've lost his balance 'cause I never pushed him hard!" Clark's face turns red, and his eyes all of a sudden are shiny again. "It was only a little shove!"

"Hey, you didn't do anything wrong, son. Calm down. But do me a favor. Pretend where you're sitting right now is where you were stand-ing then, okay? Where's the movie poster?"

Clark draws a long breath, holds it, and swivels around on his chair. "I guess . . . where those deputies are."

Dutcher stares at Clark in disbelief.

The two deputies, speaking in hushed voices by the muster desk, stand a good twenty feet away across the station house.

"That was *some* little shove, Clark."

"He must've tripped. On the carpet."

"Okay."

"I'm just telling you what happened!"

"And I'm just telling you *okay.* He tripped and went flying and hit that frame hard enough to bust the glass—*then* what happened?"

Makley's lips separated, they *kept* separating, and it took forever. Then he was bellowing with rage, hurling curses, and his right hand reached behind him, and that took half an hour, a split second, no time at all. And then? He had a pistol, nickel-plated and long-barreled, and he straight-armed it, pointing, aiming, and the shot was the loudest sound Clark had ever heard, ever. It was a cannon, it was a plane crash, it was a planet blowing up.

"But somehow he missed," says Dutcher.

Clark looks down, looks up. Looks down. And nods.

"But then he fired again. Clark?"

"Yes."

"Did he say anything to you first?"

"No. He just—looked at me."

"Like he was madder at you 'cause he missed?"

Clark says, "Yes," but that's a lie. Makley looked across the lobby at Clark like he was scared. Not mad at him, scared of him.

"You told Chief Parker that Makley must've had the world's stupidest—"

"Gun. Yeah, I don't know why I said that. *That* was stupid. I just—I thought maybe the gun, you know, blew up in his hand."

"That's what you thought?"

"Well. I heard it go off again and the next thing I knew he was lying on the floor. So I thought—maybe the gun blew up."

"But you could see it hadn't?"

In his mind's eye now Clark watches himself clutch the right side of the heavy cigarette machine, be reflected in its mirror, discover that angry-red welt between his eyes, see Makley's body sprawled on the carpet, and notice the pistol, smoking but intact, lying a few feet away. "I saw the gun and it was—it looked all right to me. So it must've, the bullet must've ricocheted."

"Like they do off of them boulders in the cowboy pictures." Dutcher smiles pleasantly, but when Clark makes no complementary expression, no expression at all, he says, "I guess that's what *must've* happened. You got any ideas, though, what it might've ricocheted *off?*"

"No," says Clark with surprising vehemence, as though he'd been challenged. "None."

"Well, that's our job to find out, not yours."

They both sit there silently.

The front door opens, and three men dressed in suits and hats, all of them looking freshly shaved at half past eleven at night, file in. Dutcher groans. "Oh lord, my federal betters have arrived." He laughs and stands up. "I think it's time we cut you loose, Clark." He waits a moment, even seems to measure it out, then says, "Clark? You're a brave boy. You did good over there."

"I didn't do anything but see a man get himself killed!"

The sheriff looks down at him and nods. Then puts out his hand. Clark shakes it. Dutcher's attention cuts suddenly to Clark's other hand, still bouncing lightly on his thigh, still in a fist. And Clark is certain he's going to say open it. But no, all he says is, "Cufflink or shirt button?"

"What?"

Laughing, Dutcher says, "Let me get you that ride home."

"I have my truck. Sir."

"All right, then. Hope you get around to seeing that wolfman movie one of these days."

After he leaves the police station, Clark avoids going past the Jewel Theater by cutting down an alley behind the newspaper office and a mercantile store and clambering over a fence that lands him on a wheel-rutted sandy lane that curves away toward the tow mill. He follows that for a while, kicking sulkily at pop bottles and wadded cigarette packages, then veers off diagonally through an overgrown lot where the livery barn used to sit till it burned.

It is half past eleven and a light rain patters down, but at least the wind has quit so he can breathe without tasting dirt—topsoil—that's been carried east hundreds of miles from those same farms, probably, that he saw earlier tonight in the newsreel. Which he *wouldn't* have if they'd only showed the stupid Mickey Mouse cartoon when they were supposed to! And that's not *all* he wouldn't have seen.

But since it's a sad fool's pastime—as his dad is forever pointing

24

out—to compile a list of why-nots and if-onlys, Clark quits doing it, but right away finds himself doing the next worst thing, so far as his mood is concerned: toting up lies he told Sheriff Dutcher, starting with his pretense of having no idea, none, how he had gotten that small welt on his forehead, ending with the fiction that he drove himself to town and could drive himself home again. He didn't take the family truck. He walked. Well, ran. It's only seven miles. Ten minutes. Okay, *eight*. Seven or eight. It's not like he ever *clocked* himself.

He jumps another fence and begins to jog, running through vacant stony lots, putting on speed. A little more . . .

Nearing the perimeter of the Kent farm, he slows from a blur to a sprint to a dogtrot. His heartbeat is unhurried, his breathing as measured as a yogi's. His legs and calves feel springy. This year, and really for the first time, Clark has begun taking pleasure in his muscles and the ways that his body performs, in his changing relationship to the solid world and the so-called rules of gravity and physics. He's getting stronger by the week. And faster. Clearly faster. He's never had a scab. And he is pretty sure he never will.

Bouncing his left fist against the side of his leg, he walks the rest of the way home.

3

With his shoes off but dressed otherwise, Clark Kent's father is stretched out above the counterpane on his side of the bed, heavily asleep. Under the covers beside him, Mrs. Kent looks up from her poem book—the Sara Teasdale collection Clark gave her last Mother's Day. In the doorway, Clark pantomimes that he's going to bed, mouths Good night, Mom, I love you. But she squints in feigned rebuke and beckons him over. When he draws up a chair and sits down, she whispers, "Did you have a good time?"

Clark shrugs.

"You didn't like the picture?"

"It was okay, I guess. I don't know."

"Clark?"

"I'm fine, Mom, just tired." He slides the book from her hands, lays the green silk ribbon diagonally across her page. "And you should be asleep yourself." In the weak glow from the gasoline Aladdin lamp, her illness is not so evident as it is in the light of day. Even so, there is no mistaking her condition, how near she is to the end. She weighs scarcely eighty pounds. Six months ago, she weighed twice that.

Clark puts the book on the table, in among brown-glass medicine bottles and a framed family photograph, the smiling Kents posed stiffly outside in front of the gabled house. It was early summer and Clark was seven, and down at the right-hand edge of the picture, you can glimpse just a bit of the county road that passed by the property. His dad used to tease Clark when he was small, saying they'd found him in that very road, the baby that must've fallen off a wagon. Naturally, *we* didn't want you, he'd say, so we took you to the orphan asylum. But you were such a noisy fussbudget, they made us take you back. Oh Jonathan, that's enough. I'm only *kidding*, Martha, the boy knows that—don't you, Clark?

Of course he did, and he loved it. Loved it whenever his father caught the silly bug and you'd see one end of his mouth quirk up in a waggish grin. Yes, and Clark loved being the baby that must've fallen off a wagon, too. Where'd that wagon *go*? Clark, we're only funning you, boy. Oh sure, he knew *that,* sure, but still. Where'd that wagon *come from?*

Now Clark glances away from the photograph and finds his mother looking at his closed fist.

"What's the matter, son? You're not hurt, are you?"

"Mom," he says, "when was the last time *I* got hurt?"

He kisses her, then quickly leaves the bedroom and goes back downstairs.

With money earned raising his own brood of chickens, Clark bought a used Remington typewriter last year, intending to compose what his favorite magazine refers to as "scientifiction" stories. In school, English always has been his favorite subject, his themes invariably earning grades of B+ or sometimes even A, and whenever he reads anything, from a handbill to a prayer book to *The Hunchback of Notre Dame,* Clark pays scrupulous attention to grammar and syntax, punctuation, spelling, and vocabulary. He doesn't know if he means to be a *professional* writer when he gets older (he's afraid his imagination isn't as rich or lively as, say, Murray Leinster's or Jack Williamson's), but he does know that he wants to keep writing for his own satisfaction, that he enjoys it. It takes him away from himself, out of his body—his puzzling, uncomfortable, intimidating body. It's a pleasure to live in his head. To escape there, no matter how briefly.

Clark has tried to spend at least half an hour every evening at the typewriter. Cushioned by a bathroom towel, it sits on the maple-topped dining-room table where Clark also does homework and his father pays bills. Since getting the Remington, he's completed two short stories—or "yarns," as the pros call them—of roughly twenty pages apiece and has been working on a third. His first story was about a brain surgeon who discovers that people's "used thoughts" get stored in their hair, so in collusion with a big-city barber, whose customers include movie stars, bankers, theater lights, and politicians, he embarks on a doomed blackmail career. Clark titled it "I Hair You!"

His second story was about a robot named Cassidy who falls in love with a Model A Ford. He called that one "A Chassis for Cassidy." Both stories were rejected by every science-fiction magazine Clark mailed them to, and none of the rejections were of a personal nature or came with even the slightest encouragement. Nonetheless, Clark perseveres.

His most recent effort, which he began in early April, was inspired by a recurring dream he's had every few weeks since he was thirteen. The story (and the dream) is set in the distant future when the earth has grown old and is being wracked by earthquakes and tidal waves. The scientist-hero believes the planet eventually will blow itself to smithereens, but since he can't convince anyone to believe him or to act upon his warning, he sets about constructing, all by himself and in secret, a small rocket ship that will take him and his wife and baby to safety on Mars.

Up until last month, Clark had been making progress on the story, but his concentration fizzled after his mother's illness took a turn for the worse. He can't write when he's distraught, it's impossible.

Which is why it's such a stupid idea trying to do it now—does he *really* imagine he can work on his dumb old story after what happened at the Jewel?

No, but it sure would be nice to escape, for a while at least, into his head.

Slumped in a dining-room chair, Clark stares dully at the sheet of yellow paper, the cheap kind flecked with tiny bits of wood fiber, that he rolled into his typewriter more than two weeks ago. The sentence he was typing that evening when his mother thumped her cane twice on the bedroom floor, signaling she needed him, remains unfinished: *Giant orange flames* (it reads) *soared from great fissures and*

And? thinks Clark. *And?* And skyscrapers crashed down, shattering into dust. And the sky turned black. A terrible *rumbling* began, and grew louder.

Abruptly, he sits forward, remembering that dream, picturing it clearly in his mind, but as he raises both hands to the keyboard he sees with a pang that his left is still clenched.

Stupid story.

Stupid dream.

He gets up from his chair and goes out on the front porch, where he leans against the newel post and looks past the lilac hedge to the picket fence he and his mother painted last summer, then to the county road that just recently, and to his father's dismay, was macadamized.

"Surprised to find you still up, Clark." Mr. Kent catches the screen door with his hip and lets it close gently behind him and latch. "Can't sleep?"

"I ain't sleepy."

"I'm *not* sleepy."

"You neither?" says Clark, and they both laugh.

"Your mother thinks something's bothering you."

"She wake you up to say so?"

Mr. Kent smiles, steps closer. "Look, son, you shouldn't feel guilty about going out and having a little bit of fun. Your mother doesn't want you to stop doing things just because she's—"

"That what she thinks is the matter?"

"Well. Yes." He rubs his jaw. "It's not?"

Clark looks into his father's face—one cheek a tracery of red creases where it was pressed against the pillowcase—then glances away, back to the road.

"Son, what's the matter?"

Clark lifts his left arm, holds his tight fist in the air between himself and his father, then slowly opens his fingers. "This."

It glints on his palm.

"I don't understand," says Mr. Kent.

"It's a *bullet*, Dad. That somebody fired from a gun."

"I can *see* it's a bullet."

"I caught it. I put out my hand and I caught it."

4

Although technically part of Smallville, the place where Alger Lee lives is a good ways out Highway 75, three-quarters of a mile past the grain elevators that everyone generally considers the north edge of town. In the newspaper and in polite conversation, the community of forty or so board shacks facing each other across a dirt midway is referred to as "Smallerville," but otherwise it's called "Smellville." It is the "Negro Section," although several Mexican families have settled here too in recent years, migrants whose automobiles or spirits finally quit on them. Children outnumber adults, three to one. Dogs, stray dogs—nobody *owns* a pet—outnumber children. There is just one long-handled well pump that everyone uses, and normally you have to stand in line. But at ten minutes before three in the morning, Alger Lee has it all to himself.

Seated on an upended milk crate, he primes the pump, catches a burst of water in his cupped hands, drinks it quickly, wipes his palms dry on his pants. Then he reaches back into his candy sack, helping himself to some more chocolate-covered raisins, Mary Janes, and sugar dots, courtesy of the Jewel Theater.

How did Clark Kent *do* that? he thinks. What's he *made* of?

A scruffy yellow dog sidles over and pushes its nose into the candy sack on the ground between Alger's feet. "Go on, get outta here, you," says Alger, and the dog shies away, but only a short distance.

The dog sits, cocks its head, and watches Alger pick white and yellow sugar dots off a long strip of waxed paper.

I didn't see that no-account donkey shoot the first time, thinks Alger, but I sure as hell seen him shoot the second time. And he couldn't've missed. Well, he *didn't*.

I seen what I seen.

The dog whimpers now and Alger takes pity—throws a sugar dot that the dog snaps from the air. Alger throws a second one. Same thing. Great catch. But the dog isn't expecting the third piece of candy to come so quickly, he isn't looking, and it hits him between the eyes, then bounces back at Alger.

There you go! See that? Same thing, Alger thinks, same damn *principle*.

I seen what I seen.

But how'd that *happen?* How *could* it?

I don't know, thinks Alger, but I'll find out. One way or the other, I'll find out.

The dog trots over, sits on its hind legs, and greedily eats the rest of the sugar dots right off the paper.

5

Mr. Kent creeps back into the bedroom, but then his heart seems to freeze in his chest. Martha's breathing is so . . . quiet. He is not a believer in the way that his wife is, but still he finds it hard not to pray for a miracle, even when he knows it's—what? Hopeless? Hopeless. Nevertheless, he can *ask*, can't he?

And so he does, again.

Sitting down on his side of the bed and kicking off his shoes, Mr. Kent stretches out in his clothes again. A dull ache spreads through the small of his back. A bunion throbs on his left foot. A tiredness shudders through him.

He should sell the farm. Clark won't be staying, *he* knows that even if his son doesn't yet. Sell it for whatever he can get and move into town. And do what? Does he have to *do* something? Open a grocery store, then. Which is what he intended to do before he met and married Martha Clark. Their land, this land here, was her family's, just a parcel of what had once belonged to her father.

He shifts around, trying to get comfortable, hoping to ease the chronic ache in his back, then leans over, careful not to wake Martha, and blows out the Aladdin lamp. In the darkness he thinks again how foolish he was for not wiring the house for electricity when crop and pork and beef prices were high and he could have afforded that sort of thing. Not that electric light meant much to him, it meant nothing, but Martha would've enjoyed it. Her being such a great reader. It would've saved her eyesight. Was from reading all those books by gasoline lamp that finally gave her pretty green eyes a permanent squint. Green eyes. His mother had green eyes, too.

And thinking of his mother—whom he loved and who died in her thirty-ninth year, diphtheria—he can't help but remember his father, whom he did not love, though he tried to show the proper and natural respect, even when it was difficult, even when he was treated more like a slave than a son. His father working him on that miserable land near Tillerton that he leased from a suitcase farmer, working him from before sunrise till late at night. Working him half to death. A difficult man, Silas Kent, an angry, prickly, unlucky man, and finally a demented one who deliberately slashed himself across his abdomen with a butcher knife while standing in front of a mirror.

During the years when Martha, who so yearned to conceive, would sometimes cry out in dull anguish at the first sign of her monthly visitor, Mr. Kent would feel only relief; guilty, unseemly relief. He didn't know how to be a good father—he knew what it meant, was *supposed* to mean, but not how to be one—and feared he would become, over time, not just a disappointment to any children of his own, but also the object of their confused outrage and hostile pity. No. Better he was childless.

Then Clark arrived.

Mr. Kent pushes himself up in bed and wedges a pillow behind his back.

Oh Jonny, it's a miracle, isn't it? It was meant to be, wasn't it? Oh, look at this poor, poor beautiful baby boy. Oh Jonny, they can't have him back! You won't let them take him back, will you, Jonny?

"They." "Them."

No, Martha, they can't have him. If they come, I won't let them take him back.

"Back."

Back where?

Our son, Jonny! At last! God is good, God is great. God has blessed us!

But had He? Had He, really?

Clark changed their lives, filled them with new feelings, chances, and chores, glad ones mostly. There was no denying Martha was a good mother; born to it, as she'd always known. And Clark, no man and woman could have gotten a better son, even if sometimes—especially as a young boy—he seemed remote, unhappy, preferring solitude to the company of schoolmates, to the company of his parents. Catch him when he didn't know you were looking—his eyes fixed upon his

hands or his knees, a point on his bedroom wall or a knot in the table—
and his expression was inscrutably morose. He'd see you and smile, and
those were the times when Mr. Kent's heart came nearest to breaking,
because those smiles were so awkward and so pretended.

When Clark was four and five and six years old he rarely spoke,
just mumbling out a few words and shaking his head, yes, no, and holding his eyes down, chewing steadily on the side of his thumb or snapping his teeth around his thumbnail. Mr. Kent secretly feared that his
son might be slow or dull, "not right." He was afraid people in town
might be saying just that, quietly among themselves, pitying Clark the
way they pitied children with stutters or club feet or faces cratered
from the smallpox; pitying Clark the way they pitied, yet felt repug-
nance for, the mongoloid children or the polio children, or those children who would scream as though possessed and fling themselves
about and cut themselves and had to be kept indoors, locked away,
always. Even in a town like Smallville there were many such children,
and in those first years Mr. Kent sat awake all hours worrying that
Clark was afflicted in his own way, then feeling black waves of shame
for caring what other people might think or say about his son, despis-
ing himself for holding such vanity.

Eventually Clark outgrew what Martha always called "just a shy-
ness" and in time managed to hold his own with others outside the
family, to look people in the eye and speak for himself, always speaking
politely, finding the right smiles and small talk for most occasions. But
the boy never seemed fully comfortable in the world. But why was that
any surprise? The unnatural things he could do! And the natural things
that never happened to him, but should have.

Every town or region has its strongman, and for a long time Mr.
Kent could, and did, tell himself that Clark was just one of those rare
and lucky specimens. Extraordinary but not impossible, that effortless
strength of his. What he could lift, shove aside, knock over. Once, when
Clark was about seven, Mr. Kent saw the boy drive a nail into a fence
post with just his fist!

The other parts of it, though: *those* parts were harder to deal with. Never a scrape, never a bruise or a cut, never blood.

There were several occasions over the last dozen years when Mr. Kent had dropped what he was doing and run, expecting—and God forgive him, almost *hoping*—to find Clark with his leg twisted under him, a white bone showing, from a bad spill he'd taken off the binder, or with one arm cradling the other after he'd been kicked by a horse, or with his face and neck and hands erupting in twenty different places from hornet stings. But every time he would discover, with a pang of fear and confusion, that his boy, his son, was not only unhurt, but unshaken.

Outwardly, at least.

What must've gone through Clark's mind on those occasions Mr. Kent can't imagine, and because he can't, and because he can't bring himself to *ask,* he's afraid that he's failed the boy, miserably. Failed him as his father.

With broken bones or hornet stings, with sprained ankles, pulled muscles, measles or the mumps, the damn chicken pox, poison sumac, the croup, a *splinter* he would've known what to do. And done it.

Our son, Jonny! At last! God is good, God is great. God has blessed us!

Yes and no. Yes and no. Maybe and no.

He hasn't been a good father. *Tried,* but he just hasn't been a good father to Clark. He doesn't know *how* to be. Still doesn't. Not to the son he was given.

He never knows what to say.

It's a bullet, Dad. That somebody fired from a gun.

I caught it. I put out my hand and I caught it.

He just never knows what to say.

"Did you talk to him?" Martha's hand, dry and thin and nearly without substance, finds his.

"I'm sorry," says Mr. Kent, "did I wake you?"

"Not really. I was just resting my eyes. You spoke with Clark?"

"Yes."

"And?" When half a minute passes and there is no reply, she says, "Jonny, did you find out what's bothering him?"

"Yes."

"You're not going to make me *drag* this out of you, are you? In *my* condition?"

In the dark he turns to her and smiles, knows she is smiling back. He loves this woman so very much.

"Jonny."

"Yes, Clark told me what's bothering him and—"

"I worry so."

"I know it."

"I want him to be happy."

"I know that too. And he is."

"I wish I believed that. I'm so afraid Clark thinks . . . that he's *always* thought, that he's—"

"No."

"Alone."

"How could he possibly think that? He's fine."

"What did he tell you?"

Mr. Kent draws a long breath, lets it out. "It's just . . . oh, it's just as you said. The boy feels badly for going out when he could've stayed home and taken care of you."

"He's a good boy."

"Yes," says Mr. Kent, "he's a very good boy, our son."

6

Washed in moon glow, Clark Kent straddles his barn's peaked roof, staring out into the middle distance, seeing insects, bats, and owls in the blackness, and wondering uneasily what he's supposed to *do* with all of these crazy talents he just keeps finding out that he has. After a while he gets up jiggling that mashed wad of lead in his left hand. And flings it suddenly, hard as he can.

It climbs, keeps climbing, and doesn't arc . . .

A disreputable profession. Temper tantrum. The Berg family.
A young man and his camera. Breaking and entering.

———

1

Although she graduated college the previous June and was theoretically grown, Lois Lane (who skipped the fourth, sixth, eighth, and eleventh grades) still was only seventeen last August when she trained down to New York City from Monticello. She was moving there to take graduate journalism classes at Columbia University, and her father, concerned about her safety and virtue, had installed her in an old-fangled women's residency hotel. The Dolly Madison on East Twenty-seventh Street. Quite a distance from Morningside Heights, but lord knows he didn't want his daughter living in Harlem. Staying at the Dolly Madison was the one condition he'd set before giving her his grudging permission to pursue an ambition he felt was not just crazy and common, but dangerous.

Time and again Lois would remind him—gently, with a girlish smile; she knew how to handle the old man—that it was a journalist in Cuba directly responsible for making her father's reputation, which led—remember, Daddy?—to practically everything good in his uncommonly good life. From his hero's welcome home, to his Congressional Medal of Honor, to his rise in the marines and all of those plum postings, to his current position as first vice-president of the Hatlo Machine Company, *everything* had sprung from a newspaper reporter's two-hundred-word cable about a wounded young sergeant heroically wigwagging a makeshift flag under ferocious gunfire at Cuzco.

To all of that "Captain" Lane—he would forever be the "captain," though he'd retired from the corps in 1919—to all of that he would respond by saying yes, true enough, but Lois ought not to use Mr. Stephen Crane as a career model, the boy had been a brawling hothead and a drunkard, he'd smoked cigarettes like a fiend, married a divorced woman of questionable virtue, and died of consumption before he turned thirty.

Oh *Dad,* she'd say, I don't want to be a *war* correspondent, just a regular old reporter.

Regular old *reporters,* he'd scoff, are nothing more than Peeping Toms on a salary!

Oh *Dad* . . .

But if you simply *must,* I want you living at the Dolly Madison.

Which looked like a miniature Southern plantation and was run like a genteel sorority house with strict rules, including white gloves at dinner, a nine o'clock curfew, no smoking, no alcohol, and absolutely no gentlemen callers beyond the receiving parlor.

Lois stayed at the Hotel Dolly Madison, the dreaded Dolly, scarcely three months. Around the time she turned eighteen in late November, she checked out of there and into an automatic-elevator building on East Twenty-ninth Street, rooming with Betty Simon, an O.R. nurse at Roosevelt Hospital the boys had nicknamed Skinny because she was anything but.

When he found out about the move, the *fait accompli,* Lois's father stopped taking her telephone calls.

For about a week.

Oh *Dad,* she groaned long-distance, don't be such a worrywart. Real people don't live in *hotels.*

Your voice sounds husky—have you been smoking?

Of course not, she told him, quickly rubbing out a Lucky Strike.

And I hope to God you haven't started drinking.

Nope, she said, popping the *p* and then leaning over to peer into her cocktail shaker, chagrined to find it empty.

Lois, is that a *jazz* record I hear?

It's coming from the building across the way, Dad, she said, carefully lifting the phonograph needle off Fletcher Henderson's version of "Limehouse Blues." There, she said, I've closed the window.

Now, you have to promise me you won't let any men into your apartment.

Never, Lois said, meaning I'd never promise you *that,* then she pointed sternly at Willi Berg sprawled on the divan in his undershirt and boxer shorts, pointing at him so he wouldn't *dare* bellow something like Baby, we're out of gin.

I expect you to be a good girl, Lois, and behave yourself, said Captain Lane. I'm counting on that.

I won't let you down, Daddy.

And in her heart of hearts she hadn't. Maybe she drank a little, sometimes a little more than she ought to, but she could handle it. She never got *stewed.* Well. Once or twice. But the morning after she *always* remembered everything she'd done and said. And she smoked cigarettes, yes, but not every single *day.* Mostly she mooched, so that didn't count. And she bought records and danced to them, but how was *that* letting anyone down, even a retired captain in the U.S. Marine Corps? And she never allowed Willi Berg to sleep in her bed. At least not overnight. She was still a good girl. Her conscience was clear. But she was a *modern* girl too. And she *liked* being modern, being aware, being curious, unafraid of the new or the exotic (Willi was *Jewish!*). And one of these days those same qualities would get her what she fully meant to have: her own byline, her own column, in one of the big dailies. If Dorothy Kilgallen, that old sourpuss, could do it, then Lois Lane, pretty *and* smart *and* clever *and* talented, could do it too. Even Willi Berg, who was *such* a cynic—even *he* said complimentary things about her news stories, which, okay, were only class assignments, not the real McCoy, but still, good is good, correct? Good is good.

2

"You call this good?" Willi is saying now. "What's with 'incalculable'? 'The fire damage is *incalculable*'?" He tosses her class assignment down on the kitchen table. "Honey, the fire damage is ten thousand bucks or it's ten million, but it ain't *never* 'incalculable'!"

"All right," says Lois, "point taken. But what do you think of the story *overall?*"

"Dull. Dull, sister, dull."

"I hate you, you know that?" Does she really need a boyfriend? Does she really need *this* one?

"Got any dessert?"

"There's still some bread pudding, I think."

"From the other night? Don't you have anything fresh?"

At the sink counter she's been drying dinner plates (they had macaroni and cheese, light on the cheese) when a sudden impulse prevails upon Lois to smack Willi in the head with the wet dish towel.

Now she reaches over and into his shirt pocket, helping herself to his package of Chiclets gum.

"You could ask," he says.

She sticks out her tongue.

"But speaking of asking," he says, "I got to ask you a big favor."

"Oh no . . ."

"I'll pay you back tomorrow, I swear."

"How much?"

"Thirty."

"Rain on that! Where am *I* supposed to come up with thirty bucks? When I can't meet the rent, thanks to your flat-leaving old girlfriend."

"Skinny Simon is *not* my old girlfriend, she's just a friend. Number one. Number two, it was your decision not to find another roommate. And number three, you shouldn't blame the poor thing for falling in love—I never blamed you."

"The boy is delirious."

"Guaranteed you'll have the cash back tomorrow. Swear to God. By noon. Could be sooner."

"'Could be sooner.' Could be never, same as every other time I loaned you money like a real dope. No, Willi, and I mean it."

"Come on, Lois, I gotta get my baby outta jail."

"What?"

"I hocked my camera."

"Willi, that's how you make a living, you can't just hock it every time you want to play poker."

"How'd you know it was poker?" He gives her a loose grin.

"You're impossible. And a lousy card player."

"Not true."

"You're broke."

"True." He pushes back his cuff, glances at his wristwatch. "Honey, I really hate to banter and run, but it's ten past eight. If I don't get to the pawnshop by nine it'll be closed. So can I have that money? I'll try to stop back here later, okay?"

"I don't *have* thirty bucks."

"Lois, I *need* my camera. There's gonna be a factory fire in Canarsie."

"*Going* to be?"

"You know how it is with little birdies and such."

"Then go mooch off one of your little birdies."

"I know you can loan it to me."

Lois shakes her head. "And if I don't get it back, what do I do Saturday morning when the rent man comes?"

"You'll have it, I promise. I can sell ten pictures of this stupid fire. It's a *toy* factory, hon. With a *teddy* bear on the roof. Look, I'll pay you back thirty-*five* bucks, just for your trouble."

"Leave, okay? Just go."

"Oh come on, don't get mad. You mad?"

"Leave, I said."

"You really not gonna let me have it?"

"I *can't.*"

"Why, 'cause you don't trust me?"

Folding her arms below her breasts, she glowers at him across the kitchen table. "Right. I don't trust you."

That sets him off. Abruptly Willi bends over and sweeps an arm across the surface of the table, flinging the sugar bowl, the milk pitcher, an ashtray, the coffee pot, its trivet, and both of their cups and saucers through the air to shatter, splash, chip, and bounce on the linoleum tile. The pages of Lois's typewritten manuscript scatter, flutter around, skate in all directions.

With her back pressed to the sink, Lois stands transfixed, pale, frightened. Excited.

When he storms out, the door strikes the wall with such force that it bounces back and slams shut behind him.

Half a minute later when he emerges through the iron-and-glass apartment-house doors, Lois—who flung up her bedroom window and is leaning halfway through it—shouts down at the top of her voice, "I don't ever want to see you again, ever!"

Willi doesn't stop walking and he doesn't turn around and he doesn't look up, but he does sputter the razzberry.

It's Wednesday evening, the twelfth of June 1935.

3

Willi Berg grew up in cramped, dark, squalid apartments, always ones with dust-filmed windows, on the Lower East Side of Manhattan. Essex Street. Forsyth. Pike. Pelham. Division. He was the fifth of nine children (his parents actually produced twelve offspring, but—influenza, whooping cough, scarlet fever). Willi's mother, the epitome of the buxom, wide-faced, irritable peasant who spoke the kind of Jewish broken English vaudeville comics loved to build skits around, was born in the United States, in Baltimore. It was Willi's father who emigrated from a ghetto in central Europe, fleeing Russian-dominated Warsaw sometime in the mid-nineties.

During Willi's childhood, Papa worked what seemed dozens of jobs, sometimes as a pressman or cutter in the garment district, sometimes as a meat dresser at the East River stockyards; for a couple of years he worked as a laundryman in a commercial bathhouse. He made tile and paving bricks, sold carpets, sewed piecework, did construction (he mixed cement for the Woolworth Building), and one summer he lived away in Hartford assembling revolvers for Colt. The old man was a regular sweat-of-your-brow laborer. Without complaint, but without any pride, either. It's what you did. You worked. Hard.

Willi and his siblings were not close to each other or to their parents. On the other hand, friction at home was rare, but that might have been because once the boys were old enough—once they were of school age—they spent precious little time there. When Gene, Willi's second-oldest brother, was fifteen, he neglected to come home one evening, then stayed away three or four days. The evening he did finally show up again, their mother gave him her usual greeting—the slightest toss of her head—and never asked him where he'd been, what he'd been doing.

That small event, that *non*-event, had a profound impact on eleven-year-old Willi. Its significance crashed inside him like dishes. Mama hadn't been *indifferent* to Gene's absence, she'd *never missed him!*

Shortly after that, as a test, Willi took a weekend hiatus from the family, kicking around penny arcades and pool halls, sleeping overnight in Tompkins Square Park. And sure enough, no one missed him, either. He came back late on Sunday, sat down at the table, ate his reheated supper, and life went on.

Whenever he was present, he was taken into account, talked to, yelled at, and teased, but otherwise he was completely out of mind. How wonderful! How thrilling! *This*, Willi realized, was freedom, what "freedom" truly was, not that ponderous abstract stuff—Speech, Press, Religion, blah blah blah—that his boneheaded teacher Mr. Whoziwhatsis at P.S. whatever-the-number-was yammered about all the time in civics class. *This.* To vanish whenever you wanted, and return whenever—*if* ever—you felt like it. And nobody to give you grief for it. Suddenly the world seemed immensely more interesting, a better place, than it had before.

When he turned fourteen and it was legally permitted, Willi quit school to work. His parents approved. He would, he agreed, fork over three-quarters of whatever he earned. He found a two-dollar-a-day job pearl diving at a Village restaurant, but his hands got so chapped he quit after a month and found another one—general assistant at a passport-photo studio.

That was the first time Willi Berg ever had been around camera equipment, and it was love at first sight.

Ingratiating himself like crazy, Willi soon traded in his push broom and dustpan for an 8 × 10 view camera and tripod, spending his days touching off loads of flash powder, developing glass plates, making proofs by running outside and exposing paper to the sun. I can do this! he'd think. And in a short time he did it far more skillfully than his boss.

He moved on to a commercial house where he took pictures of merchandise for mail-order catalogs—pianos, brass beds, chandeliers, caskets. Occasionally he would rent one of his employer's 5 × 7 cameras for the weekend, lug it up to Central Park, and earn some money photographing children at Rowboat Lake, Belvedere Castle, Bethesda Fountain, the zoo. He had cards printed that read: Willi the Great/ "Photography like life." He gave them to parents, who were instantly charmed by his cockiness and subsequently pleased by the quality of his work.

Late one Saturday afternoon on his way back to the subway, Willi saw a man who'd just been shot dead lying half on the sidewalk, half in the curb, and a big Pontiac whizzing away. He set up his tripod and waited for a cop. When at last one came along, Willi took a picture of him stooped beside the body. He sold it that evening to the *Star,* and next day it ran on the front page, first three editions. That earned him ten bucks and a photo credit. He was flush, he was happy, and later that same week he turned fifteen. It was autumn 1929.

Crash!

It took a few months for the photography studio to fail, but eventually it did, and then Willi couldn't find more work. Who could? His father still had his job—rolling a push-boy through the Garment District—but he'd had to take a severe pay cut. Two of Willi's big brothers (Harry and Gene) continued to contribute to the family, but rarely more than three bucks a week. Freddy was an invalid by then, thanks to a fall from a scaffold, and half off his rocker. His older sister Ida could sew like the dickens, so she did all right, working a Singer machine. She gladly forked over eighty cents of every dollar she earned, but the rest she deposited into a piggy bank heavy as a cinder block that her fiancé "Murph" Silverman had won for her at Luna Park.

That damn piggy bank.

Using the edge of a butter knife to pry open the tin plug on the pig's underbelly, Willi started helping himself to a few dimes and nickels, a quarter, or a dollar bill now and then, then every day, using the money to rent a German Ica and buy darkroom time to develop his plates. Happening upon that freshly dead gangster on Central Park West had steered him to his specialty, showed him his true calling—he and the city's picture newspapers, the tabloids, were meant for each other.

Nights, he trawled the boroughs of New York, photographing auto wrecks and blazing tenements, husbands in bracelets grieving for wives they'd just murdered, the occasional live baby in an ash can. Rubouts in spaghetti joints, lady burglars being led from Central Booking, always between a robust matron and a grinning detective. He loitered around police headquarters, local precincts. He'd sell a picture and replace the money he'd "borrowed" from Ida. But then he'd borrow it back the next day, and maybe a little extra.

He rented a 4 × 5 Speed Graphic, faster, lighter, and no more plates. No more of that explosive flash powder, either! But then of course he had to buy flashbulbs and sheet film. Wouldn't it be great if he didn't have to *rent* his camera—if he could *buy* one? By then he'd saved up some money of his own, just not quite enough.

That damn piggy bank.

So with more of Ida's coins and cash, he purchased a secondhand Speed that the first owner—a Romanian who worked at the Empire City racetrack—had ingeniously adapted to use roll film. As soon as he'd sold some pictures that he took with it, he put the money right back into his sister's bank. Well, he couldn't put it *all* back, not yet. But he *would.* Eventually. Long before she needed it.

When he finally got his comeuppance (and Willi never denied he didn't *deserve* it) should have been a night to celebrate. In one twelve-hour shift he'd sold a picture of the vice-president of the United States picking his nose outside the Waldorf, a barge collision, a killer's old mother weeping at his arraignment, and a safecracker who'd been worked over plenty by the most vicious plainclothes cop in Brooklyn. He was whistling "Stardust" when he came home around six in the morning, walking on air. But as soon as he opened the door, it was uh-oh.

In the kitchen Willi's mother stood planted with her arms folded like the Golem of Prague. By the window, looking out as if contemplating a jump, his father pressed the heel of a hand against his forehead. His older brothers, even Freddy on his crutches, milled around drinking coffee. Quickly they all put down their cups. The little ones were either holding hands with great solemnity, or else bawling their heads off somewhere in a corner. And Ida, poor plain Ida, looked stricken. She sat at the table with her piggy bank in front of her, a measly pile of coins beside it.

Lucky for Willi he'd left his camera, as he always did, in a rented locker. Otherwise he might have had his head dented in with that too, not just the piggy bank. Harry did the honors. And then, except for his father, everybody kicked him while he was lying on the floor curled like a shrimp.

4

It takes some doing, but at last Willi convinces a cracksman friend named Patsy Cudhy to loan him a good set of picks, but under two conditions: that Willi is gone no longer than half an hour, and that he brings Patsy back a Buescher saxophone, preferably a True-Tone model. Tenor, not alto. And with the satin-gold finish, if he can find one in the dark. Patsy fancies himself quite the virtuoso on a gobble-pipe; his little apartment off Times Square is full of them.

But on his walk to the pawnshop—on Seventh Avenue in the high Thirties—Willi has second thoughts about the whole thing. Does he really want to do this? If he gets caught, he'll land in jail. With criminals! Is it worth it just to get his camera out of hock—well, off the shelf, off the *premises*—a couple of days sooner than he would otherwise?

Yeah, but I *really* want to shoot that fire, he thinks.

But what if some potsy strolls by checking doors?

By this time he's walked past the hockshop and the coast, damn it, is clear.

He pretends to study a window display of flatware, phonographs, trumpets, guitars, baseball mitts, paste jewelry, toasters . . .

His heart is racing, kicking.

Either do it, he tells himself, or go.

He turns to go, but then he does it.

And to his enormous surprise, he does it quickly, efficiently.

Second pick he chooses: *bingo.*

Now Willi is inside the pawnshop, the door shut, and his head is throbbing arhythmically. Get your stupid camera and blow, he thinks, carefully moving through the gloom toward the waist-high counter that runs half the length of a side wall. Behind it are deep metal shelves jammed with good and bad cameras and camera equipment, but Willi knows exactly where his Speed is. Yesterday he watched where Chodash the pawnbroker randomly stuck it. So just grab.

As Willi rounds the far end of the counter, his left foot collides with a solid object and the sole of his right shoe comes down in a puddle of something gummy and slides. A moment later he lands hard on his prat. What the *hell*? He scrambles to get up but keeps slipping. The seat of Willi's trousers is wet and so is one of his shirtsleeves, the cuff a sodden blotter. Both palms feel slathered with warm paste.

What's that *smell?*
Then all at once he knows.
And knows what he slipped in, as well.
"Mr. Chodash?" he says, reaching.

Good news. Gruesome discoveries. Willi plies his trade.
Trapped! Lois calls her mother to talk about men.

———

1

"*Lois?*"

"*Professor Gurney?* Oh my God, I thought you were someone else."

"Boyfriend?"

"*Ex*-boyfriend. And I'm so sorry—believe me, sir, I don't go telling everybody that calls to please drop dead."

"'Sir'? School is out, Lois. Call me John."

"There are still exams."

"You don't think we actually *read* those things, do you?"

"Professor Gurney, was there a reason . . . ?"

"As a matter of fact, there was. I have some very good news I thought I'd pass on. Lois, my star pupil, you are no longer speaking to an associate professor of journalism at Columbia University, you are speaking to the national tours editor for the Federal Writers Project."

"Oh my gosh! That's *incredible!*"

"Sought out by Harry Hopkins himself."

"You must be thrilled," says Lois.

"Can't say I'm crazy about living in D.C., but yes. To the gills. Play your cards right, my girl, and I'll get you a job writing for the American Guide series. Or better yet, I'll find one for your ex-boyfriend. In North Dakota. Say, is that a giggle? I love a girl that giggles."

"Professor Gurney . . ."

"I'm calling to invite you to a celebration. Tonight. Say yes."

"That's so thoughtful of you, but—"

"Stork Club."

"I really don't—"

"Harold Ross'll be there. Westbrook Pegler. George Jean Nathan."

"You're making that up."

"Lois! For shame. I'm a journalist, I don't 'make things up.' Hemingway might drop by. And Irving Berlin."

"Stop!"

"Lenny Lyons, Clare Booth Luce. Walter Winchell."

"Now I know you're fibbing. You *hate* Walter Winchell."

"It's a party, Lois! Grudges are buried, feuds forgotten. Morals forbidden."

"I wish you wouldn't say things like that."

"Like what? Oh, that. Lois, you're in New York City, not back home in darkest Poughkeepsie."

"I don't *come* from Poughkeepsie. And I thank you, Professor, but I won't be able to attend your party. It was kind of you to ask."

"'Kind of you to ask.' Don't polite me to death, darling."

"I should get off the phone. I'm expecting another call."

"From the Drop Dead Kid?"

"From my boyfriend. Yes."

"I thought he was the ex."

"Maybe I've changed my mind."

"Positive you won't come out?"

"I'm sorry."

"Well, then . . ."

"*Wait!*"

"Still here."

"Professor Gurney, you've . . . you've been a really good teacher."

"Obviously not good *enough*. So long, Miss Lane."

2

By the flame of a paper match, Willi confirms it: what he fell over was a body, what he slipped in was blood. Mr. Chodash and Mr. Chodash's. The pawnbroker's throat has been sliced open from ear to ear.

Willi shakes out the match, and despite being scared clammy he carefully stands and grabs a gooseneck lamp from the counter, squats down again, switching on the light, aiming it to create a dramatic clash of shadows. Then he finds his beloved Speed Graphic—thank God it still has film—and gets to work.

Following each exposure, he pops out the gooey flashbulb and fits in another.

Now for the unpleasant business—calling the cops, going through all of that. *I came by to get my camera, the door was open and there was poor Mr. Chodash—can I leave now?*

But the telephone wire has been torn from the wall. He wants just to leave, scram out, but he can't—because he can't sell any pictures without bringing in the bulls. They'll murder him if he doesn't. Is there another phone? In the back? Worth a go-see, Willi decides, and that's how he comes to find, in an aisle between floor-to-ceiling shelving, an open trap door. Half a dozen wooden steps lead to a cellar with lights burning.

He creeps down.

Willi has seen his share of handbook and wire joints, has even tagged along on a few gambling raids, thanks to his pull with a vice cop named Dick Sandglass (he used to play three-sewer stickball with Dick's kid, Spider), and they all look roughly the same, whether in a candy store, a dry cleaners, a social club, or a hockshop: you have your cashier's cage, your trestle table, your totalizers, your blackboard, your pencils, your sharpeners, your parlay slips, and your telephones.

There are a dozen here in the cellar, their cords all sliced.

This particular setup is slightly larger than most, to accommodate an inventory of pinball machines, punchboards, and nickel slots overlaid with bedsheets and jammed together at the far end of the cellar near a garage-style rolling steel door that seems like it could withstand an assault by a Whippet tank. Apparently the place is both a working house and a warehouse.

It's also a death house.

Five seated men with their faces turned left-cheek-down on the table in front of them like schoolchildren napping have been shot at very close range.

Definitely, Willi Berg owns the front page, the third page, *and* the centerfold tomorrow of whichever tabloid he wants, but right now he'd gladly settle for the fire at the toy factory, page six, and fifty bucks.

He's snapped off half a dozen shots when he hears mumbled voices in the alley behind the building, then a clasp lock snapping open. As the steel door rumbles up, Willi ducks under a pinball machine, reaching back to tug gently down on the bedsheet to give himself a tad more cover, praying he doesn't pull the whole *ferschlugginer* thing off.

"—pect you, sir, but I'm glad you came."

"Tell."

"It's pretty bad, sir, and I seen some stuff in my day."

"The boss said tell, he didn't ask you what you seen in your day."

So far, all that Willi can make out are trousered legs. Blue serge. Blue denim. But *some*body—presumably "sir"—is wearing a tuxedo.

"Oh Christ," says the tuxedoed man.

"I told you it was pretty bad." Blue Denim speaking.

"And you got here when?"

"Nine, little bit after."

"Where's Leon?"

"Upstairs, sir. They cut his throat."

"Go see if they took the records, Paulie."

"Sticky checked when he got here the first time, boss. They're all gone."

So Blue Serge is Paulie, Blue Denim is Sticky.

But what about the "boss"? Who is "sir"? Willi is certain he's heard the man's voice before. There's something about it. Something . . . "tony"? That, yeah, but not *exactly*, not Ivy *League* tony; it's not in the vowels or the sinuses, it's just . . . there's something *practiced* about it, and confident, like a radio voice you'd listen to if it told you to run out and buy Silvercup bread. Gingerly, Willi lifts the hem of the sheet, hoping to see a little better. No dice.

"I want all these men removed."

"Yes, sir."

"And disposed of. And I don't mean the river. Jersey. Or the Adirondacks."

"Sure, boss, no problem. But what about Leon?"

"Leave him. They'll call it a robbery."

"But they didn't take any money, sir."

"Then empty the register, Stick."

"And where do you want all this *stuff?*"

"Take it up to Inwood. But, Paulie, before you go sailing in there, check first. Make sure nobody's waiting for you."

"I'll take along five, six guys."

"Excellent. Very excellent, indeed," says the man in the tuxedo, and boom, Willi suddenly knows who it is standing not ten feet away and giving silky-voiced orders to remove five shot-dead bodies and a ton of illegal gambling equipment. And if he doesn't manage somehow to click a picture of him, he might just as well tear up all of those Willi the Great business cards and toss 'em off the Chrysler Building!

The trick of, course, will be to take the damn picture and live long enough to develop it.

3

"Your father wants to know if you're all right."

"I'm fine, Mother. Now tell him to go away."

"In case you forgot, Lois, he lives here."

"Doesn't he need to brush his teeth or something?"

"Hold on."

While Lois waits, she empties her ashtray into the wastepaper basket and lights another Lucky.

"Turtle? He's putting out the trash. What's going on?"

Turtle? All of a sudden Lois feels twelve again, the last thing she needs now. "Mom? How come men are such goofs?"

"For the love of mike! This is a long-distance phone call."

"How come?"

"Are you in trouble?"

"No!"

"Then I don't know what to tell you. How do *I* know about men?"

"I hate them."

"Your father's a man."

"Well, he's all right."

"'Goof,'" says Mrs. Lane. "I'm not sure I'm even clear what a goof *is*."

"I'd use a stronger term, but you're my mother."

"Thank you."

"Name me one that's not a sneaky, selfish, sponging liar. And Daddy doesn't count."

"Douglas MacArthur."

"Douglas MacArthur."

"You *asked*."

"No, I mean—"

"Will Rogers. Bing Crosby. Fred Astaire." Then she pauses for a moment and says, "F.D.R."

"Why are you whispering?"

"Because your father just came back, and you know how he feels about *him*. Oh Lois, honey, there are *millions* of nice men."

"I haven't met any."

"Was there anything else, dear? Because your father would like to close up down here and go to bed."

On her end of the wire, Lois sobs out, but then says, "No, nothing else."

"Did you love him?"

"Who?"

"The sneaky, selfish, sponging liar that broke your heart tonight."

"My heart is *not* broken, Mother. Where would you get *that* idea?"

"Then good night, Lois."

"Night, Mom."

"Lois?"

"Uh-huh?"

"Dick Powell. Dick Powell seems like a genuinely nice man. From what I've read."

"Okay."

"And what about your mayor? The little fat man? You like *him*, don't you? And what about that other one, the mayor's friend? You sent us that wonderful story about him, that you wrote for your class."

"Oh, you mean—?"

"The way you described *him*, he sounded like the cat's whiskers."

"I guess. But I'm not really talking about—"

"So we've established that there are many fine and good men in this world, and now we can both go to sleep with grateful hearts."

"Did you *really* like that story, Mother?"

"Of course."

"I did that one back in October. I'm writing much better now."

"Well, it was wonderful, and *you're* wonderful, and men—*most* of them—are perfectly wonderful too. And now, my darling Turtle, sweet dreams."

After Lois puts the telephone receiver back on its hook, she walks the floor trying to gauge whether her mood has been lifted or whether she's still wallowing in the Men All Stink Blues. She considers fixing a cocktail, but that's not what she wants. What she wants is for Willi Berg to call her now and say that he's sorry, horribly, wretchedly, *incalculably* sorry. And beg forgiveness.

Yes, but what she also wants, and quite suddenly, is to go dig out that news story she did for her Local Political Reporting class. She wrote it during her first semester, just before a special election to the Board of Aldermen was called in the wake of the previous office-holder's inexplicable suicide. It wasn't the *best* thing she ever wrote, but as she recalls it now it was pretty decent work.

She still has it, of course. She keeps everything, has always kept everything, including short stories, poems, themes, and diaries going back as far as the first grade, and clippings and tear sheets from all of her school newspapers, country day through college.

Her mother liked that story, did she? *That* silly old thing?

Without any trouble she finds the typescript in a folder on a shelf in the bedroom closet—she received an "A" for the assignment, natu-rally—and sits on her bed reading it through. As she does, Lois recalls the terror she felt "covering the story" that morning. Naturally, it wasn't an exclusive—after all, she was a mere journalism student. She arrived at the Commodore Hotel with Willi Berg, who blithely waved his press card, gripped her by an elbow, and shunted her into one of the ball-rooms. He left her then to find a good spot for picture-taking. The place was crowded, but somehow Lois managed to nab a seat in front.

When the candidate appeared finally for his press conference, she was electrified to see that LaGuardia himself had come along to lend support.

The mayor at her first press conference!

Could it get much better than that?

Yes. Yes, it could. Because practically the same moment she sum-moned the nerve to raise a hand, the candidate—"tall and athletic-looking," she would later write, "with a full head of wavy red hair"—pointed to her from behind his podium. "Yes, ma'am?"

Praying her face didn't look half as drained as it felt, and speaking in a firm, clear voice, the way Professor Gurney had taught her, she asked, "How would you rate your chances for election, sir?"

Lois smiles now, remembering.

How would you rate your chances for election, sir?

And of course she also remembers the candidate's single impudent wink and the beguiling way he looked at her, as if she were the only other person in the room.

"My chances?" said Lex Luthor. "Excellent. Very excellent, indeed."

An incriminating photograph is sought. Smoking condemned.
The sins of the father and the names of the son.
The humming alderman.

———

1

Over the last few months, Lex Luthor has had his picture taken more times, far more times, than in all of his previous life. But while surely that's a *good* thing, since it means his political career is flourishing, still Lex feels cold dread whenever someone points a camera at him. For the split second he's blinded by the flash light he has to quash an imperative instinct to cut and run. No matter who he is now, and he has worked hard to create himself, to build formidable identities both public and secret, at base he remains his father's son, and his father killed a man, then lived the rest of his miserable existence as a fugitive in constant fear of being recognized, seized, and punished.

Once, when the family—calling itself the Littles that year—was living in Ashland, Virginia, and Lex was eleven, a photographer snapped a picture of him parading on stilts at the town's July Fourth picnic. Next morning, it appeared on the front page of the daily newspaper, and there for all to see was Lex's father cringing in the background, one hand flung up to conceal his face. God, that look of sheer terror. Lex never forgot it. Or forgave it, either.

Now, decades later and just minutes after Willi Berg leapt out of nowhere and clicked a jeopardizing picture of *him,* of Alderman Lex

Luthor standing in a bookie joint with two known criminals and five murdered men, he wonders if his face looked as stricken as his father's had on that Independence Day. Jesus Christ, he *hopes* not.

But he will never find out—will he?—since that film is never going to be developed. *Is it?*

"No, boss. We'll find him."

"Yes, Paulie, we will."

"I don't know *how* he got in—"

"But we certainly know how he got *out,* don't we?"

"I thought Stick closed the door."

"Hey! *You* came in last, you shoulda closed it."

"Shut up, the both of you. And take a left here, Paulie. At Thirty-eighth."

"But how do you figure he'd go east, boss? He's some kind of news-hawk, right? So the closest paper'd be the *Times.* Or the *HT.* And they're a couple blocks up on—"

"He's a *tabloid* rat, Paulie. He'll head for the *Mirror* or the *Daily News.* East."

"But why do you think he took Thirty-eighth?"

"Because Thirty-seventh is closest, and he'd *expect* us to think he took it."

"How do you know he's on foot?"

"I don't. I'm hoping. And for your sake, Paulie, you'd better hope I'm *right.*" His eyes lock on the driver's profile and don't blink.

"I *thought* I closed it, boss. It musta stuck."

"Just drive. And Stick? When we spot him?"

"I'm out in a flash, sir, you bet. And I'll get you that camera, no problem."

"I expect you to get more than just the camera."

"Yes, sir. Goes without saying. That stinkin' little hebe is history."

"Stick, please. I don't want to hear that kind of name calling."

Then: "Paulie, speed up a little, I think I see him!" says Lex, think-ing if that picture ever *were* developed, which it *won't* be, he might look surprised, possibly shocked, but not terrified, not craven. Not *caught*. Not him. Never.

He's not his father.

"Stick! Now! Go, *go!*"

2

Not again. Lois feels as though she's wasted half the evening on the telephone—who's calling her *now*, dammit?

(Be Willi.)

"Oh, it's you," she says. "Flat leaver."

"Cut it out, Lo, and lis—"

"You really left me in the lurch, you know it? Moving in with your hotshot boyfriend, thank you so very much."

"Lois, Willi's been shot. They just brought him in."

"What are you talking about, *in?* In where? What are you saying?"

"I'm *saying*, Lois, that somebody shot Willi, and they just brought him into Roosevelt. I'll meet you down in Emergency."

"Skinny! That's not funny! *Skinny!*"

3

Seated in the rear of a gray Lincoln town car parked with the motor running on West Thirty-seventh Street, Lex Luthor idly jiggles a roll of twelve-exposure Kodak film in his left palm while observing a large-bellied cop at the Seventh Avenue corner smoking a cigarette.

Lex *hates* smoking, detests the *habit.* First thing, soon as he's the mayor? It becomes a felony. Smoking becomes a Class A felony—you get caught with those things, expect to do some hard time. Or maybe he'll have to wait till he's governor. Or president. Or king. But you smokers, all you nicotine fiends? Your day is coming. Gum chewers, too.

Hooking three fingers around the edge of the film container, he pulls, first bending, then cracking the metal. He tears out the sprocketed acetate. Then he lights it with a match and tosses it through the open curbside window, watches it burn in the gutter. A tune starts playing in his mind and Lex hums it. Just a month ago, a columnist at the *Mirror* stuck in a jokey little item about Alderman Luthor's "endearing" habit of humming half-aloud during soporific budget meetings—"When I Grow Too Old to Dream" was the tune the columnist specifically mentioned. That, and "Moonglow."

Now he's humming "Smoke Gets in Your Eyes."

A panel truck with its headlights off noses slowly from the alley just ahead but stops before it rolls into Thirty-seventh Street. That would be all the punchboards, the slot and pinball machines. The driver sets the brake.

Paulie gets out of the cab's passenger door smoking a cigarette. He walks over to the big Lincoln and smiles down at the still-burning tangle of film.

"All set, boss. The Ince brothers are in the back with the stuff, and that's Frank Wrobble at the wheel."

"All right," says Lex, "here's what you do. Tell Frank to go on up to Inwood without you—and remind him what I said about checking before just walking in there."

"I'll do that, boss."

"Mr. Luciano might not be entirely finished with his little games tonight."

"Is *that* who we're dealing with?"

"It's who *I'm* dealing with, Paulie. You're dealing with me."

"Sure, boss."

"What about the second part of the effort?"

"Boss?"

"The *bodies.*"

"Just finishing up."

"Who's driving?"

"Stan Elder."

"Make sure he knows he's driving upstate."

"Or Jersey, you said."

"Or Jersey. And tell him to call the police from a pay phone just before he leaves the city."

"Why would he do that?"

"Because he's a good citizen. Because he saw something suspicious going on here and wants the cops should take a look. Make sure he knows the address."

"Sure thing. Anything else?"

"Yes. Get rid of that cigarette."

"Why, boss? It aids digestion!"

"What'd I just tell you?"

Paulie removes the cigarette from his mouth, looks at it almost quizzically, and pitches it away, down on top of the gummy remains of the Kodak film.

4

No such person as Lex Luthor was in the public record anywhere prior to September 1923. Before that he was, serially, Alexander Bankton, Clay Alexander Plenty, Douglas Alexander Little, Alexander Todd Biggs, then Lex Robbins, then, following the death of his father, Luthor Dunn—Dunn being his mother's maiden name—and finally Lex no-middle-name Luthor.

When he registered at City College's School of Civic Administration and Business, it was the first time he had ever used the name or dashed off the signature. His high school transcripts were impeccably bogus, and, with the exceptions of his height and weight and his address at the time (he'd taken a small apartment on Fifteenth Street, near Union Square), every piece of documentation and each filled-in line of every standardized form was a carefully considered, always plausible lie. He even claimed to be twenty, when in fact he was eighteen.

His father may have been a gross disappointment, foolish and finally unmanned, but by example he had taught Lex both the rudiments and the nuances of creating, maintaining, and—if necessary—

60

sloughing off full-blown counterfeit identities. He, or rather the last fifteen years of his poisoned, fugitive life, also had taught Lex that violence without ruthlessness only made you vulnerable and weak, left you defenseless against self-contempt.

How could the dark-eyed gambler whose photographs Lex once discovered buried in a steamer trunk have turned into the chain-smoking, gum-chewing grocery clerk/factory hand/short-order cook who sneered at him, resented him, and probably would have beaten him three times to the month if his mother had not always intervened?

Yet the man Lex Luthor has become, is still becoming, that man, he has often mused, is undeniably the offspring of Wesley Bankton, who once cut a dashing, aggressive figure, taking options on thousands of acres in the Middle West, establishing towns—Wesley, Iowa; Bankton, Missouri; Wesdale, Nebraska—and serving as mayor of each one, at least till it failed or he grew bored or, in the case of Wesdale, he fled under cover of the night.

A thousand times during his childhood, Lex heard about Gorsline Easy, a wild-eyed Holy Roller who owned less than fifty acres planted in corn, a nobody, a shabby, drawling down-and-outer with a rawboned homely wife. Gorsline Easy. *Gorsline!* What kind of name was *that?* And what kind of fool was he to imagine he could win an election against Wesley Bankton? Not only that, what kind of *imbecile* was this *corn farmer* to think he could publicly accuse Wes Bankton of looting the town's treasury and get away with it?

On the ninth of September 1908, Wesley Bankton found this stupid nobody at work in his smokehouse and shot him dead.

Good. Lex Luthor would have done the same thing.

But then?

Then his father hastened away in darkness with his imperious wife and their three-year-old redheaded boy, and was ruined forever. It was not doing murder that changed him, unmanned him. It was the crushing fear that followed—fear of capture, trial, humiliation, imprisonment, execution. Fear was what a man could least afford. That was the only useful lesson that Lex ever learned from his father, the father he knew as Dick Plenty, Jerome Little, John Biggs . . .

The father whose memory continues to fill him with disgust.

"Well, finally!" says Lex as Paulie and Stick climb into the front of the town car. "I was beginning to think you boys were conducting funeral services."

"Sorry, boss."

"You said you wanted us to clean it up real good. Sherlock *Holmes* couldn't find no blood in there, sir."

The Lincoln follows a brewery truck to the corner of Seventh Avenue. When the truck turns left, heading south, Paulie asks, "Where to, boss?"

Lex checks his watch. No point going back to the Broadhurst now. Besides which, the play he was watching when he got the tap on his shoulder—phone call for you, Alderman, says it's an emergency—was a complete bow-wow. One of those phony jobs with a "cross-section of humanity" stranded together, this time in a Bar-B-Q on the Arizona desert, everybody speechifying like they were giving lectures at the Cooper Union.

"Boss?"

"Oh," says Lex offhandedly, "why don't you just run me up to Rockefeller Center and drop me off. Ray Noble's playing at the Rainbow Room."

Skinny Simon. Lois Lane, reporter.
Murder in the first degree. Insult to injury.

———

1

Betty Simon—the girl all the boys call Skinny because she is anything but—meets Lois Lane just inside the entrance to the Emergency Room. Taking her by a wrist, she leads her to a row of chairs. Nearby, a deli-man in a grimy apron hunches over, cradling a hand wrapped with a bloody towel. Despite his misery, he is unable to conquer the temptation to give a side glance at Skinny's extravagant breasts, hips, and rear end. Now, *that's* a nurse.

"Sit. *Lois?*"

"But what are they *saying?*"

"He's still in surgery."

"So why aren't *you* there?"

"Because I'm not. *Sit.* Do you want some coffee?"

"No, I don't want any *coffee.* I want to know if Willi's going to be all right!"

"We all do, Lois, okay?"

"Where did this *happen?*"

"I'm not sure—somewhere on the East Side. Had you seen him tonight?"

"We had a big stupid fight . . ."

"Listen, why don't I go check, see what I can find out?"

The deli-man lifts his eyes again to watch Skinny Simon leave, but when Lois glowers at him, he looks back down, abashed, at his bundled-up hand.

She begins to stride up and down the waiting room, oblivious to everyone who comes limping in or is called out for treatment or just sits there with fretful patience. But then she spots a cop outside speaking with a group of men who are obviously reporters. The pads, the pencils, the cigarettes fitted behind their ears.

". . . not too far from one of them university clubs," the cop is saying when Lois comes through the heavy glass door, "but nobody seen anything, is what I'm told. Nah, I don't know which club."

Scribbling as he speaks, one of the pad-and-pencil men says, "We heard his camera got smashed—that so?"

"Well, I can set you fellers straight about that. I wouldn't say it was *smashed,* more like it just fell and broke when the poor lad got it in the back."

Lois feels a cold pain move in her chest, crawling up from her sternum to the lower part of her throat.

"But you birds might like this. Seems our triggerman helped himself to the film."

"Any idea what was on it, Danny?" asks another reporter.

"Nope," says the cop. Then "You," he says to still another reporter.

"Where was he coming from?"

"Beats me."

That same reporter asks, "What's this about a set of burglar's picks?"

"Where'd you hear that?"

"So what about it? Willi have 'em or not?"

"No comment."

"Danny, Danny—what do you know about this stiff they just found in a pawnshop with his throat cut? That's only a couple blocks from where little Willi got shot. Any connection?"

"No comment," says the cop, then, "Yes, ma'am, you," he says nodding at Lois, who by now has dug out her own pencil and nickel pad from her purse and pushed rudely through the pack of newshounds.

Putting a sneer on her mouth, adding speed to her voice, and arching an eyebrow—the way Professor Gurney taught her to do it—Lois says, "So what are the doctors saying about his chances? This joe gonna make it?"

2

On Tuesday the eighteenth of June, Willi Berg finally opens his eyes again only to be told that a bill of indictment was handed down yesterday in the City and County of New York charging him with first-degree murder in the death of Leon Seymour Chodash.

Murder during the commission of an armed robbery.

There is the little matter of a claim ticket from the victim's place of business discovered in Willi's billfold.

Plus that kit of flagrantly illegal jimmies and picks stuffed in his jacket.

His fingerprints on the cash register, the counter, the telephone.

And if he wasn't stitched up and so full of drains, the two homicide detectives that arrest Willi in his hospital bed would show him exactly what they think of his cockamamie story about a bookmakers' parlor, a bunch of dead bodies—only *five?* Why not *ten,* Willi? Or *twenty?*—and the secret criminal career of Alderman Lex Luthor, the newest, youngest, and most popular member of the board.

"So who shot you, Willi? Have a little falling out with your accomplice? Didn't want to split the take?"

"*What* take?"

"Who shot you, kid?"

"I *told* you!"

"Yeah, yeah."

"Go to hell."

"Not us, you little mockie. You're the one's gonna have a hot date with the electric chair."

That same day Willi's picture runs on the front page of all of the two-, three-, and five-cent papers. Both the *News* and the *Mirror* refer to him as a "Mad Dog Killer." But that doesn't bother him half as much as what the *Planet* calls him: a "Would-be Fotog." Now, *that* hurts.

Sad day. An infidel in Smallville. Mrs. Kent's baking skills are recalled. Eighteen years ago. Clark takes a long walk in the woods and ruins a good pair of shoes.

———

1

Funeral services for Martha Clark Kent are scheduled for ten A.M. this morning at the Tomahawk Methodist Church, corner of Fourth and Union streets, Smallville, Kansas; Dr. Thomas B. Calais (pronounced: "Callus") will officiate.

Clark, however, isn't sure his father plans to attend.

It's not that Jonathan Kent is unreligious, or anti-religion, he just has no truck with *sectarianism,* with doctrine, with trifling dos and fiddling don'ts. Never has had. Not in his makeup. And he is not a Christian, either, although he is probably as familiar with the New Testament as anyone in town, "Dr. Tom" included. He's fond of the narratives, admires their hero, often quotes from the parables, and once told Clark that the bedrock of his personal philosophy—if an ordinary American farmer with an eighth-grade education ever could presume to use such a word or claim to *have* any such highfalutin' a thing—is the Sermon on the Mount.

Certainly Mr. Kent believes in God, in a conscious life after death, in the sodality of souls. After his own plain and pell-mell fashion he regularly ponders spiritual matters. Over the years of his life, particularly during the long winter nights of those many years, he has read a number of books with Judaism, Buddhism, Taoism, Islam, Hinduism, and even Spiritualism in the titles. And all of those paths, so far as he can tell, have their good points.

Beginning some time ago, however, Mr. Kent made the mistake of *sharing* a few of those good points. During the general gab at church suppers and picnics, he would casually mention something he'd come across in the Talmud or the Bhagavad-Gita, or something Mohammed or Mary Baker Eddy had said, but soon enough he realized it was just earning him a reputation as a contrarian, a crackpot. Dr. Calais's immediate predecessor once called him an infidel, but he did it with a tiny smile, so it didn't amount to anything serious. And since Mr. Kent could appreciate the social value of church membership, he might well have continued accompanying his family, at least semi-regularly, to Tomahawk Methodist services and functions had it not been for a couple of things he found impossible to ignore.

First was that damn temperance statue. Imagine spending the congregation's money to erect a seven-foot concrete skeleton of King Alcohol holding aloft a bottle of whiskey! It was plain foolishness, and Jon Kent let everyone know how he felt. Dr. Calais, though, had not appreciated the input, which included two long letters published in the *Smallville Herald-Progress.*

And then there was the unforgivable business with Dan Tauy. For Mr. Kent it was the last straw when that supercilious prig Tom Calais told the Chippewa handyman that while he could maintain—at a salary too low to be called even a pittance—the church building and cemetery grounds all week long, he and his family could not worship with the congregation on Sunday; they were not welcome.

That did it. Mr. Kent never again set foot in the Tomahawk Methodist Church.

Naturally, he wished Martha had joined him in his boycott, but he recognized that he'd put her in a difficult position. After all, it was her grandfather, R. H. Clark, who'd *founded* the church, back in 1879, when the original town site was platted out. So Martha continued to attend services, though sporadically, until her illness. Clark usually went with her.

And now, on the morning of her funeral, Clark suspects that he might be going into town alone. But just before nine o'clock, his father appears in the kitchen wearing his black Sears and Roebuck suit and shoes. They embrace without a word, then set off together in the slat-sided Ford pickup truck. Mr. Kent does the driving, of course.

"Will you be saying any piece this morning?" he asks.

"No. No, I didn't think I would. Will you?"

"No."

They ride in silence for a couple of minutes.

"I liked what you wrote about your mother in the paper, son. That was good."

"Thank you."

More silence.

"But it was '87, not '88 when she came back here from Dakota Territory with her little sister and her pa—just like you wrote."

"Mom told me '88."

"Trust me, Clark, it was 1887."

Silence again, for several miles.

"How come you didn't let me have a look at it before you sent that in?"

"I guess I forgot. I'm sorry, Dad."

They're in town now, coming up Union Street, half a block from the church, the cemetery with its small obelisks and listing headstones behind a black iron fence.

"Clark?"

"Yes, sir?"

"I was wondering why you put it in there that you're our *adopted* son."

"Because I am."

"It never mattered."

"I know that."

"She loved you like you were her own flesh and blood."

Clark nods.

"And you know I do too, don't you?"

Clark nods again.

"It was a fine piece of writing, son. I sure couldn't've done it."

2

She cherished her family, and baked the world's most delicious rhubarb pie. And her apple pie, too—the way she coated the crust with sugar, *that* you couldn't beat. Simply could not. And she was always there in your time of trouble, with a kind word, a smile, a sincere offer of assistance. She was humble. She was gracious. She wrote the loveliest, the most thoughtful Christmas letters. She had moral fiber, real pioneer strength of character. And. And did everyone recall that wienie roast just before the war, the summer Mary Agel was afflicted by shingles, and Martha, always the friend in need, always the selfless one, stepped right up and volunteered to—

Mr. Kent doesn't think he can stand too much more. Martha was all that everyone said, but she was also his wife of thirty-one years, his best friend, his soul mate, his *complement,* and she is five feet away from him now, confined forever in the plain wooden coffin she requested, and his heart is broken. Rhubarb pies! That woman made the sun come up. And he wants this ordeal to end, to go home, to *be* home, back in the house where her spirit is still present, will always be present, in the iron stove, the knotty pine wardrobe, the spoons, the handwoven draperies and pillow covers, the stair treads, the floorboards, their bed. In *everything.*

He wants to go home with his son and grieve.

To Mr. Kent's right, Clark sits hunched forward with his head bowed and his eyes closed. His knees are spread apart, and he's gripped the edge of the pew seat. Branching veins have risen on the backs of his hands.

". . . I can tell you, it wasn't just poor Mary Agel who was grateful *that* day, it was . . ."

Below the drone of this latest panegyric, Mr. Kent detects a slight fracturing sound. When he turns his head, his glance instinctively dropping, he sees, in the foot-wide gap between his son's curled hands, a split opening, breaching in the varnished oak-wood edging of their pew.

He touches Clark's left elbow. Clark's eyelids snap open. He flinches, jerks backward, and—

CRACK!

Aghast, Clark looks at the piece of broken wood in his hands, then blushes furiously as though discovering himself naked in public.

Calmly Mr. Kent takes the wood chunk, leans down, and sets it on the floor under the pew.

Behind them, Mr. Kent is well aware, the fifty or so congregants, town friends and neighboring farmers are all still looking, still craning, still wondering *what* in God's name . . . ?

It's time, he decides.

Martha, stay close. I need you.

3

Clark looks around unhappily, back toward the church where two women—Mrs. Kackle and Mrs. Kemp—have come outside from what parishioners call the "confraternity room" and where, an hour now since the interment, a solemn repast is still in progress. Mrs. Kackle lifts an arm and beckons. "They want us to come in," says Clark.

"I know it," says Mr. Kent. "But I don't think they'll raise a fuss if we don't, do you?" He slips into a trance of concentration, staring at the mound of rich brown earth in front of him. Then he shifts his eyes to Clark. "Take a walk with me? I want to show you something."

"What?"

"You'll find out."

They leave the cemetery by a gate wide enough for a wagon to pass through, and where a small fieldstone building is filled with the implements of grave digging. Dan Tauy, a large man of sixty with long swept-back gray hair and ropy, powerful arms, stands in the doorway as they pass by. He doesn't acknowledge them. Mr. Kent knows Dan still resents him for having made such a noise that time, years ago now, when the Indian was barred from worshipping in the church. He was humiliated by all the talk it caused, maybe even felt patronized. He didn't, and doesn't, need anyone to fight his battles. Well, so be it. Mr. Kent had done what he thought was right.

They walk down Union Street to Main, turn east there, and continue on. It is a warm summer morning, overcast and humid. On both sides of the exceptionally wide street automobiles are parked diagonally against the high curbs. Mr. Bleecher is out sweeping the sidewalk in front of his dry goods store. Where the Swede's bakery used to be, the plate windows are soaped over on the inside, swirling around a square yellow sign that reads: FOR RENT. Idly, Mr. Kent wonders whatever became of the Swede, whose name he can't recall now. He was Norwegian, really, but everybody just called him the Swede. Is he still in town? Maybe not. There are several more vacant storefronts. The radio repair, a lunchroom, even the shoe-and-boot repair: all of them gone.

Up ahead, Joe Diver, manager of the Jewel Theater, stands on a ladder affixing big letters to the bulb-ringed marquee. So far it reads: BRIDE OF FRAN.

Both Clark and Mr. Kent give wide berth to that ladder.

"Mr. Kent, Clark," Joe Diver calls down, "my condolences on your loss."

They both express appreciation for that.

Half a block on, Mr. Kent gestures to a pressed metal sign jutting out over the sidewalk: SMALLVILLE HERALD-PROGRESS. "I had an interesting talk with Newel Timmins the other week. He came out to the house to see your mom."

"Mr. *Timmins* did? Where was I?"

"Taking your examinations, I guess. He was saying how he thinks you're a pretty good writer."

"Told *me* I was fair."

Mr. Clark smiles. "He said he talked to you about doing some reporting for his paper."

"Yeah, he did."

"Proud of you, Clark. I think your mom would've got a big kick from your display of enterprise."

"He only wants me for maybe a day a week. I can still work on the farm."

"I'm pleased."

"Are you?"

"We'll manage."

"Be only a day or two a week. Maybe three. But I'll still work on the farm."

"We'll manage."

By now they've arrived at the daftly grand town hall, a marble-and-copper faux chateau built thirty years ago when Smallville had aspirations to being declared the county seat. With its vaulted ceiling, cavernous gloom, and the deep-resounding echoes that it makes of every footfall, the place puts Clark in mind of some ancient European library where never in a million years would he feel welcome. The Kents are greeted by Vernon Sisk, lobby guard here for the past eleventy-seven years. "Mornin', folks!" he says, then fixes a proper hangdog scowl on his lined old face. "I was very distressed to hear about Mrs. Kent. She was a fine lady. A *fine* lady. We always had a nice little jaw wag ever' time she came by to pay the taxes. She'll be missed."

"Thank you, Vernon," says Mr. Kent.

Mr. Kent starts up the central staircase. Clark hesitates a moment, then goes up too.

In between the offices of the Assayer and the Town Clerk and set flush against the left-hand wall are several long glass-topped display cases containing photographs of the first few clapboard buildings on Main Street, some arrowheads, and the yellowed front pages of old newspapers describing historic floods and locust infestations, as well as celebrated crimes, including two cases of incendiarism, a poisoning, and a daring 1897 bank robbery. There is the rope used to hang Del Slatterly, who smothered his wife with a pillow in 1901; several Mauser cartridges carried home from the Spanish-American War by Smallville's volunteers; the key to the original town jail; and assorted knives. There is a Kansas state flag the size of Clark's thumbnail made from dyed kernels of rice by Mrs. Lettie Segar, wife of Dr. L. Kipling Segar, and a jagged but vaguely fin- or rudder-shaped fragment of burnished green metal about the length of a man's foot, but just an inch or so thick. The hand-lettered card placed nearby identifies this particular exhibit as the "Mystery Alloy," and claims it dropped from the sky on June 5, 1917, landing on property owned by Millard "Ike" Cayhall. Later "metallurgic scrutiny," it says, failed to "discern" its "compositional properties."

"There," says Mr. Kent.

"*That's* what you want to show me?"

"That's it."

"What am I supposed to *see?*"

"All that's left of your wagon, son."

"My wagon."

"The one you fell off. Before your mother and me found you in the road."

4

They didn't find him *in* the road, of course, but in truth it wasn't too far *from* the road. Few hundred yards.

"Right about *there*," he tells Clark. "Or maybe . . ." Pushing through cornstalks, he squints for a moment. "No, right about there."

Clark tromps by, turning in circles, peering down, searching for— for *what* exactly?

"But the thing itself, *that* hit down quite a ways . . . over . . . there." When Mr. Kent stretches out his right arm, Clark eagerly sights along where his finger points.

"Who saw it first?"

"Your ma. I *heard* it, but she saw it coming in." He gestures up.

"From which direction?"

"That's my boy."

"What?"

"The reporter. 'From which direction?'" He turns all the way around. "From behind the house . . . to the front. So most likely from the southeast. And that's an excellent question, Clark, because your mom and I both wanted to get it straight. For when we talked to the army. Or whoever came."

"The army?"

"The *war* was on, Clark. We thought it was a bomb, from a zeppelin or some kind of airship. What *else* would we think?"

"A bomb."

"That's what it looked like, Clark. When we ran out here and saw it, the pair of us figured we were seeing the biggest, fattest bomb in the Kaiser's arsenal. Then we just rabbited back this way, thinking we'd been lucky so far but any second it was bound to blow up. And that's how we happened to find *you*. Naked as a jaybird. I nearly ran right *over* you."

Clark opens his mouth but just keeps looking *there,* then over *there,* then back to the house, then over its roof, to the southwest.

"Let's go inside," says Mr. Kent. "Hot as it is, I could use a cup of coffee."

It is about ninety-five degrees now. The heat bugs and crickets are loud, insistent, and Mr. Kent keeps slapping at mosquitoes as he trudges in silence next to Clark back through the corn, then across the road to the grassy yard, the porch, the house . . .

"So that piece of metal you showed me is all that's left?"

"*I* never found anything more. After it blew up, it was gone. Except for the chunk fell on Ike Cayhall's barn. I guess not *on* the barn, but pretty darn close."

"Who's Ike Cayhall?"

"Oh. He's long dead. He used to own what's Cure & Hurley's now."

"The *cannery?* That's ten miles from here."

"Or more."

Clark spoons sugar into his coffee and stirs. "So that's how come my birthday's June fifth?"

"That's how come. Though your mom said you looked at least eight months old, and the doctor in Tabor Lodge said you looked to be about a year. 'Course he also said you had the *strength* of a five-year-old. And the coordination, too. You grabbed hold of his eyeglasses and *crumpled* them." Saying that, Mr. Kent is reminded of his own glasses, which he removes and cleans with a napkin.

"By Tabor Lodge you mean . . . ?"

"The *orphanage* there, yes."

"I really broke his glasses?"

"That was the least of it. You were a holy terror. They'd put you in a crib and find you next morning two floors below in some classroom. Eating chalk."

"Really?" Clark can't help it: he grins. "Chalk?"

"Or—and your mother heard this from one of the nurses, the superintendent never told *us* about it, but *supposedly* you climbed some drapes and had yourself a grand old time hanging from the rod like Cheetah the chimpanzee. And when somebody climbed up to get you? You let go."

"And?"

"Clark."

"Right. And nothing."

"They started calling you the superbaby. Pass the milk? Please and thank you."

"But Dad . . ."

"*Why'd* we put you in an orphanage?"

"No. Well, *yes,* but . . ."

"Why didn't we *tell* anybody?"

"Yes, but—where did you and Mom think it *came* from? Where *I* came from?"

"Where did we think you came from. Well . . . after we decided you weren't part of a German bomb . . . since we figured no matter how savage we'd heard those Huns were, they weren't bad enough to bomb us with babies . . ."

"Or dumb enough."

"So we figured it was some kind of an airship, although Martha—your *mom* called it your cradle."

"My cradle."

"The truth? We thought somebody shot you off from someplace in Europe. Or South America. Or like . . . Kitty Hawk. And we expected to read about it next day in the paper."

"But why would anybody put a baby inside an airship?"

"That's what we wanted to know."

Holding his cup with both hands, Clark stares dreamily at the coffee.

"Clark, it took us maybe thirty seconds to decide that you were ours, that you'd been *given* to us." Mr. Kent clears his throat. "That's the *first* thing. We'd never been blessed with children—I was almost fifty-two and your mother was . . . a little younger. And some things it gets too late to happen. But here was this gift. Here was *you*. So that's the first thing you should know. We adopted you before we took you to any orphanage. As soon as we found you, that was it. You were our son."

5

Clark has been out walking in an uncleared wood that starts just beyond the Kents' Big Pasture and ranges cross-country over the next several miles till it thins out and skirts the Lang family's dairy farm. He's not sure who owns this wood, if anyone does; he never asked. He never asked about a lot of things.

He braces a foot against a blowdown in his path and pushes, intending to roll aside the big hemlock (actually, he most intended to vent some of the tension that crackles through him like electricity), but he pushes with too much force, and the tree snaps in two with a burst of dust, chips, and bark. *Now* look what he's done! Torn the sole raggedly off his shoe and the leather upper to ribbons. Likewise a good sock.

Although the sun set a while ago, darkness has not yet brought any relief from the heat and humidity. Heat never has bothered Clark (or cold, either), but he suffers whenever the humidity climbs and the air becomes saturated. Okay, not like other people suffer, but it makes him irritable. He feels that way now, but considering the day he's had it's probably not the humidity.

He buried his mom today.

He buried himself today.

And not six feet deep, six *miles,* and now he's trying to claw his way out.

But which way is *up?*

Clark wonders what his father is doing right this second. Resting? (Mr. Kent doesn't "nap," he "rests.") Maybe Clark shouldn't have left him home alone, the man buried his *wife* this morning, but—

But Clark needed to get away, to think.

So far he hasn't done too much of *that.* He's tramped around all jittered up and ruined a good shoe. *That* he's done, but think? No.

He sits down on a slab of granite jutting from the bank of a dry streambed. A coarse rind of lichen—the stuff looks like Wheaties—crackles under him.

The wood is utterly quiet. How can that be—in June? But it is, it is silent and still, and he is alone in that.

He is alone, period.

"Of course you're not alone," his father said to him earlier, after he'd told him the *why* of the orphanage ("Be pretty hard to explain you at our ages, son. So we left you at the doorstep, like in one of those cartoons you see. And so what? We always intended to come back, and we did") and the *how* of his adoption ("It maybe wasn't the only time your ma ever lied about her age, but for darn sure it was the only time she ever put a drop of color in her hair. I used it myself. So we got you, nice and legal. But if they'd said no, we'd've found some way to *steal* you back").

"Of course you're not alone, how could you even think such a thing?"

"Easy. *You* try coming from another planet."

"Clark. For goodness' sake. You read too many of those magazines."

"It was a *rocket,* Dad."

"It was an airship."

"Okay. Where from?"

Mr. Kent didn't have an answer.

"Dad . . ."

"You're not from outer space. You'd have four tentacles and a nose like, I don't know what—a horn."

Clark stood up from the table. "I need to go out for a while."

And now, after quitting the tangled undergrowth, he limps back out of the wood, returning to where he entered it. He stands in high bluestem grass, with a light breeze carrying a scent of hay across the meadow, and looks south, beyond the Big Pasture, the calf pasture, the broomcorn, the barn, back to his house bathed in the milky light of a near-full moon. He puts back his head, breathes in, and looks up at the stars.

Around him all the noises of an early summer night erupt again, dissonant and perfect.

New York City. Pressing municipal matters. Dick Sandglass.
Lex visits his mother. A pleasant evening with Governor Lehman.
Adventure in the hospital.

_____

1

Lex Luthor can't believe it. He *watched* Stick fire three shots into that sneaky little bastard, into his *back*—how could he survive? And now, according to the papers, Willi Berg is expected to "make a full recovery."

Misdialing twice because of trembling fingers, Lex makes several phone calls. Each calms him down a little bit more. Okay. All right. It's going to be fine.

The cops like the kid for Leon's murder . . .

Excellent. Very excellent.

But once he comes *off* the dope and starts to talk . . . ?

The thing to do is to make certain he never comes off the dope.

Within an hour that becomes Paulie Scaffa's job. "And Paulie? See that he doesn't sprout another wound. You know how to use a hypodermic needle?"

Hard as he tries, though, Paulie can't get close to Willi Berg's room at Roosevelt Hospital. If it's not his skinny girlfriend hovering over the guy, it's some blond nurse with a Jean Harlow chassis times ten. Then suddenly there's an armed bull posted outside his door around the clock.

Lex has considerable sway with the New York City police department, and in ordinary circumstances it would be simple enough to scrounge up some narcoleptic potsy and stick him in the hospital midnight to eight, the only time safe to do this thing. But it turns out that a plainclothes dick working out of Headquarters' Detective Division down on Centre Street, someone named Dick Sandglass, reputedly clean and apparently not a brownnose, either sits guard himself at Willi Berg's door overnight or else selects others for the job.

Lex's hands have begun shaking again. For long periods of time he has to keep them held in his pockets. And he's started to notice that clumps of his hair come out whenever he brushes or combs it.

Calm down, he tells himself. It's going to be all right.

It's going to be okay.

But why should he have to worry about this idiot Willi Berg when he has so many *other* things on his plate? Such as the careful awarding of contracts easily worth twenty-five million dollars for the construction of playgrounds, promenades, and ball fields between the Hudson River and Riverside and Fort Washington parks. Such as the brokering of deals for the expansions of subway trunk lines in Brooklyn and the digging of a new Sixth Avenue subway in Manhattan. *That* construction alone will run in the neighborhood of sixty million dollars. If Lex plays his cards right, cements certain friendships and eliminates certain gadflies, he can see clear to pocketing two or even three percent of the final budget.

So many things to do.

Not the least of which is the destruction of Lucky Luciano's alliances and various enterprises by means both legal and illegal.

Everything's going to be all right.

It's going to be okay.

But why has he suddenly started losing his hair?

And why the *hell* is this Dick Sandglass character taking a personal interest in the Willi Berg case?

2

"I appreciate you coming here like this, Mr. Sandglass," says Willi.

"No problem. I don't know how I can really help you, kid, but you were always a good pal to my son and that's worth something. He never had it easy, having a cop for an old man." You can say that again. And not just a cop, a real Dick Tracy who never takes so much as a free sinker and a cup of coffee. He is a good guy, though, and when Spider and Willi were young, Dick Sandglass would take them both out to Yankee Stadium two or three times every season, and on one memorable occasion, in 1926, to the World Series. It's how Willi got to see Grover Alexander strike out Tony Lazzeri in the seventh game with bases loaded.

As a kid, Willi used to wish that Dick Sandglass was *his* pop, despite all of Spider's complaints about the old man. No, really—what *other* dad used to be a drummer in a dance band? On summer evenings he'd come outside with a pair of sticks and beat hell out of the tenement stoop like he was still hunched behind skins on some nightclub stage. Yeah, and he owned a terrific Victrola he'd crank up for spinning disks by Red Nichols and Pinetop Smith, Louis Armstrong, the Goofus Five, the Ipana Troubadours. Willi's musical education started in Dick Sandglass's little front parlor. "Ida, Sweet as Apple Cider." "Boogie Woogie." "Sugar Foot Stoop." A real good guy, Spider's dad. It used to be said the reason his wife left him was because she'd got fed up by his honesty. A bull's wife was *expected* to own some jewels that weren't paste, a seasonal wardrobe, her own Ford motorcar, and a summer cottage in the Catskills.

"So what's Spider doing these days?"

"Three to five in Dannemorra," says Lieutenant Sandglass. "Atrocious assault."

"And you couldn't—?"

"I *wouldn't*."

Oh.

Sandglass sends Willi a look that wipes the hopefulness right off his face. But he reaches a hand out and pats Willi's knee through the bedcovers. "Spider's holding his own, like I know you will." He looks at the small radio that Lois brought over yesterday and that's playing softly on the night table. "Well, I'll be." He twists the volume knob. It's Mildred Bailey singing "Heaven Help This Heart of Mine." Sandglass listens with obvious pleasure. "Old Mildred," he says. "The pipes on her!"

Willi just nods.

"That's Buck Clayton on trumpet—you hear that? You couldn't miss *him*."

You couldn't? Willi could.

"Who's on drums, kid? Can you tell me who's on drums?"

"Cozy Cole?"

"The Coze don't play with Mildred Bailey! Where you been? That's either Maurice Purtill or Jo Jones, and I'm leaning toward Jo Jones." He listens a few more seconds, then lowers the volume.

"Hey. Kid. I really am sorry you got yourself in such a jam."

"You and me both, Mr. Sandglass. And like I said, thanks for coming. Thanks for *being* here. Those other cops today, jeez, I thought they were gonna tear out my stitches and stick their *hands* in there."

"They won't rough you up, Willi. I promise. But they won't lay off, either, not till you start telling the truth."

"I swear to God, Mr. Sandglass. I *am*. Why would I make up something like that?"

"Maybe it was the first dumb thing that popped into your head. You remember when you and Spider got caught roaming around that Catholic school on Thompson Street? You remember what you said?"

"I was thirteen!"

"You said four nuns grabbed you and locked you both inside till you promised to convert."

"I was *thirteen!*"

"When somebody comes by tomorrow to ask you more questions, tell the truth."

"I *been!* I swear on my mother!" Who hasn't visited Willi in the hospital, incidentally. His father, either. Or any of his brothers and sisters. What, they're going to waste their time on a no-goodnik like him? "I swear on my sweet mother! It was Lex Luthor!"

"Please." Dick Sandglass turns to leave.

"And somebody named Paulie and somebody called Stick. The three of them. I seen them there, believe me."

"Stick? Stickowski? *Herman* Stickowski?"

"I don't know any Herman Stickowski, I'm just telling you Lex Luthor was there. I *seen* him there, him and a guy called Stick and a guy named Paulie."

Dick Sandglass rubs his jaw. Then he says, "Ah, you've always been full of it, Willi. But I'll see they treat you right."

"I'm telling the truth!"

"I'll be outside."

"What, I'd kill somebody for my lousy camera?"

"Willi, from what I hear, you'd kill *anybody* for your lousy camera. Good night."

3

"Happy Independence Day, Mother." He let himself in with his key and finds her alone on the terrace in her unnecessary invalid's chair.

"I just had a *feeling* you'd come by today. Do I get a kiss?"

Lex bends down and lightly brushes his lips against her flaccid cheek, then straightens back up with pressed powder and face paint clinging to them like grit and glue.

Despite the broiling glare of the midday sun—her apartment's terrace faces west with views of the Palisades, the Hudson, and the high conical roof of Grant's Tomb—Lex's mother has on a black woolen dress from Arnold Constable's. Around her shoulders she's draped a fringed maroon shawl. Her legs are covered with a plaid blanket. She's tucked it snugly around her hips.

On a small glass-topped table within easy reach stands a small, squat glass filled, Lex knows, with Kentucky bourbon. Beside the glass is a candy dish containing prescription tablets, barbiturates entirely.

Around the clock she keeps that dish near to hand, but every time Lex pays her a visit there are more pills in it. He can't estimate how many there are at the moment, but fifty at least.

"Sit down, Lex. Are your hands shaking?"

"No, Mother."

"They certainly look it. And for heaven's sake, will you please stop humming."

"I am not *humming*, Mother."

"I beg to differ, Lex. You were just humming 'Isle of Capri.'"

"Then I beg your pardon."

"Sit, child."

He does, directly across from her. She seems smaller than she did even last week, more wrinkled, more crabbed and forlorn, more deeply deranged. "And I think you're beginning to lose your hair. You should see a doctor. Or else shave it all off. You have a nicely shaped skull, which you can be sure you inherited from my side of the family. My dear father had a skull shaped like the *world*. Excellent. A very excellent skull. He was not, however, bald. *None* of the men in the Dunn family, to my knowledge, ever were bald. You should do something, Lex. It looks *spotty*."

Lex grunts.

"How are you coming along with your engineering studies?"

"I haven't *begun* them yet, Mother. I haven't had *time*."

"Then see that you *make* time. You know how I feel. Politics are all well and good, but look where they got your father."

"My career is quite different from his."

"Let us hope. But the future belongs to the engineers, son."

"So you say."

"So I *know*. Oh, do what you like, I won't be around long enough to see what becomes of you anyway."

"Mother . . ." Brows furrowed, he stands up. Just below his diaphragm, his stomach begins to ripple in little fluttering spasms. Bracing both palms on the terrace rail, he looks out over the dark blue

Hudson. Firecrackers are exploding somewhere off to the north, probably in Fort Washington Park. "I wish you wouldn't talk like that. You're not even sixty-five years old."

"Am too. I'm seventy. Seventy-one."

"Mother! And for all these years . . ."

"Liar, liar, pants on fire," she says, then leans over the small table, her nose hovering above the glass of bourbon, shifting six inches to hover and twitch above the dish of pills. "What shall it be today, oh what shall it be . . . ?"

"*Must* we go through this every time I come?"

"The bourbon? Or the barbiturates? Bourbon? Or barbiturates? Eeeny, meeny, miney, moe . . ."

"I should be going."

"You only just got here!"

"Have to show my face at a parade or two."

"Do you enjoy all that?"

"No."

"Then *why?*"

"I have plans, Mother."

"And what might those be, Alexander?"

"I don't think I *need* to tell you everything I'm doing."

"No. You don't *need* to. But I'd hoped you might *want* to."

"All right, Mother. I've decided to take over all of the criminal rackets in New York City—that's all five boroughs—and with the money from that . . . well, I'm not quite sure yet."

"Oh Lex, really. I don't find this at all amusing. Now, sit down!"

He smiles and remains standing.

"I'd always thought we had a special bond, you and I. Seeing what we went through together. Fifteen years of hell. But no matter what, I always had you. And I liked to believe that you had me."

"I did. I still do."

"But you don't love me. You've never loved me."

"Mother, that's not fair."

"Ha! Fair." She plucks out a dark green pill from the candy dish. "Barbiturate? Or bourbon?"

"For God's sake!"

"Bourbon," she says and takes another sip. "I was thinking just earlier today, don't ask me why—but do you recall that pot-metal spaceship, that toy I got for you once at a Woolworth's in Madison, Wisconsin?"

"Columbus, Ohio. And it wasn't a Woolworth's, it was a Kresge's."

"You remember it? Red and yellow with tiny little portholes?"

"Of course."

"Do you also remember how I was so despondent one day, feeling so worn out from everything, all the running, and your father was already sick, hardly ever working—do you remember?"

"You were *always* feeling worn out, Mother."

"Oh Lex, you haven't grown up to be the kindest man, have you?"

"You were *saying?*"

"That I found you on the rug this one day playing with that little spaceship and I got down there with you . . . you remember that?"

"No."

"No. Well, I said, 'Honey, wouldn't it be nice if we could both just climb into that spaceship and blast off—go to another planet, just you and me?' I was sick of *everything.*"

His hands, Lex realizes, are trembling again.

"I said, 'Let's just you and me get in your spaceship and blast off!' And you said, 'I'm sorry, Mother, but there's only room for one.'" She laughs. "'I'm sorry, Mother, there's only room for one.' You really don't remember?"

"I really don't remember."

She nods. "Always the solemn little boy."

"Practical."

"*And* practical. Yes. Well, run along, my solemn and practical little boy, you'll be late for all your picnics and parades." She scoops up several pills and, with a tiny wince, puts them all in her mouth. Washes them down with bourbon. "And happy Independence Day to you too, Lex," she says, turning away her face, then tipping it back, full in the sun.

4

On Tuesday evening, July 9, 1935, Governor Herbert H. Lehman of New York has dinner in Manhattan with Alderman Lex Luthor at the Hotel Brevoort, Fifth Avenue and Eighth Street. Afterward they go by town car to the Booth Theater on West Forty-fourth Street and take in a musical revue (not especially tuneful, but Jimmy Durante and Beatrice Lillie are quite good). Later, they have drinks at Versailles, a nightclub at 151 East Fiftieth Street, where they are joined by Public Works Commissioner Robert Moses, golfer Gene Sarazen, and wrestling promoter Jack Curley. Later still, they huddle privately for an hour in the Wedgwood Room of the Waldorf-Astoria, Park Avenue and Forty-ninth Street. They conclude their evening in the governor's suite. Shortly after two o'clock on the morning of July 10, Alderman Luthor is picked up by his driver.

Early in the afternoon of July 11, Governor Lehman confers in his downtown office with the district attorney of New York County, William C. Dodge.

On the morning of July 12, D.A. Dodge meets with Thomas E. Dewey, an impeccably dressed prosecutor with black wavy hair and a thick mustache. The discussion lasts until noon.

The following Monday, July 15, promptly at eleven A.M., it's announced to members of the press assembled below the steps of the Old County Court House on Chambers Street that Mr. Dewey enthusiastically has accepted a position as special deputy assistant attorney general, charged with conducting a thorough investigation of citywide vice and racketeering before an extraordinary grand jury.

Although he is not mentioned by name, everyone there knows the target of that investigation is Charles ("Lucky") Luciano, the undisputed "czar of organized crime."

Or at any rate the *presumably* undisputed czar.

5

On Thursday, the first of August, Willi Berg is informed that his doctors have deemed him sufficiently recovered to be moved from his bed in Roosevelt Hospital to the hospital ward in one of the new fire-proof brick buildings constituting the model penitentiary on Riker's Island. The transfer will take place sometime within the next twenty-four to forty-eight hours, once the paperwork is completed.

Later that morning, Dick Sandglass tells him, "I'll still try to keep my eye out for you, kid, but it won't be quite so easy from here." Removing a 3 × 5 deckle-edged photograph from his billfold, he inches forward in the chair, closer to Willi. "Recognize this guy?"

"No."

Sandglass sits back, looking disappointed and beginning to put away the snapshot.

"Who *is* it?"

"I thought you might've told *me* . . ."

"Is that Stick? Is that Herman Stickowski? Let me see it again."

"Willi . . ."

"I didn't get a good look at the guy's *face,* I seen his *legs!*"

"But on the other hand, you saw Lex Luthor's face clear enough."

"I did! And if they hadn't stolen my film, the other two guys would've been in the picture. You woulda seen!"

"'Woulda.'"

"I'm telling the truth!"

"Sure, Willi . . ."

Early that afternoon, a lawyer from the Legal Aid Society who stopped by on two previous occasions informs Willi that he's been unable to convince a judge to set any bond, then suggests that he hire a criminal attorney for his trial defense. "Sooner," he says, "rather than later."

According to hospital admitting records, at three-thirty P.M., a male Caucasian, weight 240, height 6′3″, date of birth 5/12/95, occupation left blank, is assigned a private room two doors down from Willi's. His chart gives his name as Sidney n.m.i. Marsden and claims he is suffering from diverticulosis. He is not. He is in perfect health, although he does remember to groan occasionally, as he's been instructed, and to complain, but not too *much,* about his discomfort. In between his groaning and his complaining, he entertains himself by reading stories in a year-and-a-half-old issue of *Argosy.* It's a tribute to his professionalism that he resists ogling and mashing Betty Simon, one of the nurses on duty. *Madone,* the lungs on that broad! His name is not Sidney Marsden.

At a quarter to seven Lois Lane arrives at the hospital. Because her pocketbook holds a little zippered manicure kit containing a metal nail file and cuticle scissors, she has to leave it with the posted guard, this evening a young blond-haired policeman-in-tunic named Ben Jaeger. He apologizes when he divests Lois of her bag. She thinks he's cute.

Eighteen months ago, Officer Jaeger, still a rookie on traffic detail, arrested Spider Sandglass outside of McSorley's Old Ale House, 15 East Seventh Street, for assaulting an acquaintance Spider claimed owed him a small amount of money.

Clearly, Spider's father doesn't hold that against Officer Jaeger. On the contrary.

When Lois comes into Willi's room, she discovers him standing at the window, looking down nine stories to the street. "You shouldn't be out of bed."

"They're sending me to Riker's tomorrow!"

"Get under the covers—please?"

"I can't go to jail! I'll go nuts!"

"What about Detective Sandglass," she says in a measured, patient tone, "can't he—?"

"Feh! He still thinks I'm lying. *Everybody* does!" Willi hammers the crown of his head against the window frame. "*You* don't think I'm lying, do you? Lois?"

"Willi, I don't think you cut anyone's throat, of course not."

"*But?*"

"I think maybe you saw somebody who just *looked* like the alderman."

"I should just stick my tongue in a light socket and be done with it."

He looks around for a lamp, follows the cord to a wall, the plug—there! He might as well do it now! Save everybody a lot of trouble.

"Willi, you need to calm down. Now listen. I did some calling around today and I think I may've found you a lawyer. His name—"

"I can't *afford* a lawyer."

"I can help."

"Oh sure, *now* you can. *Now* you can loan me some money! Thanks a whole heap."

"Don't start."

"If you'd loaned me thirty bucks when I *asked* you for it . . ."

"So this is my fault?"

She expects another explosion of Willi's pique and a fresh fusillade of blame laying, name calling. Instead, his shoulders sag. "I'm scared, Lois."

"I know," she says, "I know." She's eager to hug him, but also reluctant: she doesn't want him to cry out in physical pain. But suddenly Willi hugs *her*. "It's going to be okay," she murmurs. "It's all going to be just fine."

But with the situation the way it looks, Lois has no idea *how*.

At ten minutes to eleven, a tall and buxom middle-aged nurse that Skinny Simon has never seen before briskly passes her by, absorbed, it seems, in making chart notations on the run. For a moment Skinny considers chasing after the woman to remind her it's against hospital regulations for nurses to wear perfume on the job. She is going off duty, however, and besides, she's not the shift supervisor. So instead she goes to check on Willi, not knowing what she could say to him; do you wish someone *well* when they're heading off to jail?

But she needn't have worried: when she peeks in, he's pretending to sleep (an R.N. can always tell). Skinny shuts the door, bids good night to Officer Jaeger (he's adorable), clocks out, rides an elevator down to the lobby, and leaves the building.

Out in the muggy summer night, she feels blue all of a sudden. Her live-in boyfriend, Charlie Brunner, is in California and won't return till

91

God knows when. Maybe September, but maybe not. He's a trumpeter with Benny Goodman's orchestra, which was on the verge of disbanding as recently as two months ago when the boys and their canary, Helen Ward, left New York on a last-ditch cross-country tour. Now they're packing in audiences night after night at the Palomar Ballroom in Los Angeles. Lucky Charlie! Poor *Willi.* Poor guy, she thinks, recalling the two or three, three or four, certainly less than *ten,* times they made love, just for the pure fun of it and nothing more. How could he have killed someone? She doesn't believe it. She believes it. No, she doesn't. Then she thinks, *Imagine* that nurse coming on the floor drenched in perfume! And cheap, awful stuff at that! Skinny stops, inexplicably bothered by something that has nothing to do with perfume. But *what?* She gives a tiny shrug and runs to catch her bus.

Meanwhile, the atrociously perfumed nurse is removing a vacuum thermos filled with strong coffee from a leather bag she stowed in one of the linen closets when she arrived at the hospital. She glances at her wristwatch, which has no second hand. She is anxious to get started, but it's still too early. Another forty-five minutes to an hour, at least.

Replacing the thermos in the bag and the bag at the back of a lower shelf, she closes the closet, looks up the hall at the policeman sitting in his tipped-back chair (she hates pretty boys), and then, to make herself scarce, goes and has a smoke on the concrete fire stairs between the ninth floor and the eighth.

The narrow square bar pinned to her uniform reads: TIBBELL. If anyone happens to ask her, she'll tell them her first name is Rosemary, and that it's *Mrs.* Rosemary Tibbell. But she hopes no one asks her.

Her name isn't Rosemary Tibbell, and she isn't married.

At a few minutes past midnight, now the second of August, Ben Jaeger is stifling a yawn and feeling the first cricks move through his shoulders and lower back when a nurse appears and offers him coffee. "You're an angel!" he tells her. He peers above the square yardage of her bosom to her name bar and adds, "Miss Tibbell."

"*Mrs.,*" she says.

"Thank you, Mrs. Tibbell."

As she unscrews the deep cap from her thermos, he has to turn away his head slightly and squint his eyes. Perfume has that effect on Officer Jaeger, causes his eyes to sting and water. Soon, if nurse Tibbell sticks around, he'll be sneezing his head off. But she doesn't. She fills the cap with hot coffee, watches him take an appreciative gulp, and says, "Why don't you just hold on to the thermos? You need it more than I do." She gives him a motherly pat on his wrist and pads away on her rubber-soled shoes, past the room where a new patient called Sidney Marsden is getting dressed in the dark. She doesn't notice that his door is closed.

It's locked, too.

Marsden finishes tying his shoelaces, then goes back to the closet and removes his overnight bag. It requires a key and he uses it. The bag contains a full set of men's clothes: underwear, trousers, shirt, and shoes, everything purchased only yesterday, the sizes estimated from newspaper photographs. Jeez, they forgot socks! Well, too bad. He rummages past the clothing, feels around and finds a small bundle, the newspaper wrapping spotted with gun oil. He takes it out and sets it down on a chair.

It's half past twelve by the radium glow of the bedside clock.

He was told "not before one."

Damn, though, he's been twiddling his thumbs for going on ten hours already!

But if he rushes and does this thing too soon, he'll get outside and there won't be a car waiting. Exhaling a long sigh of disgust, he sits down on the side of the bed.

By ten of one, Rosemary Tibbell is beginning to feel anxious. Even though she has been ducking into different rooms and utility closets up and down the ninth floor, hiding briefly, emerging, then hiding again, she has, she knows, been noticed by some of the other nurses working the shift. She caught three of them whispering together and looking queerly at her. Even worse, a freckle-faced Irish nurse has gone over and started flirting with the baby-faced copper—who hasn't, so far as Rosemary can see, taken even a *sip* of coffee in the last twenty minutes.

This better happen soon, she thinks.

She pats the slit pocket in her uniform skirt and feels the short loaded syringe there.

More than fifty blocks to the north, Lex Luthor's mother, "Mrs. Wesley Dunn," a widow, puts the last two pills from her candy dish into her mouth, below her tongue, and despite being logy by then, and nauseous, she rinses them down with the end of her bourbon. Vaguely, so vaguely, she hears the bells at the Cathedral of St. John the Divine ring the hour. One o'clock.

At the same moment downtown, on West Twenty-third Street, not far from the Hotel Chelsea, an explosion rips through a nineteenth-century brownstone residence that was converted five years ago into a workingman's brothel. Windows blow out, followed by flames.

From the steps of the nearby YMCA, Herman Stickowski, called Stick, watches the fire with a satisfied grin on his face.

Under the wheel of a Packard 8 parked just across the street, Dick Sandglass watches Herman Stickowski for a few moments longer, then jumps from his car and runs toward the burning brownstone. It is two minutes past one.

At three minutes past, on the ninth floor of Roosevelt Hospital, Officer Ben Jaeger slumps to one side, lets out a fluttering breath, and immediately begins dreaming.

At five minutes past the hour, Rosemary Tibbell, having consulted a piece of notebook paper scribbled with instructions, flips several toggles on a little wall dingus that looks much like a fuse box. Immediately, up and down the ninth floor, paired blue and red bulbs start flashing an emergency sequence. She watches all of the other nurses respond: they drop everything and rush in a pack toward swinging doors at the opposite end of the hall.

At six minutes past one, Mrs. Tibbell enters Willi Berg's room.

Stopping suddenly, she draws a sharp breath, then leans over Willi, who is fast asleep but whose legs are kicking under the covers. Carefully she pushes back the left sleeve of his pajama top and pulls out the plunger from her syringe.

She feels something cold touch her neck.

"Put it down, sweetheart."

Maybe she would have and maybe she wouldn't have, but Sidney Marsden, impatient beyond any further endurance, simply chops her across the windpipe with the edge of his hand, then punches down hard on the back of her neck. If he didn't think Mrs. Tibbell was a real nurse, thus a good egg and deserving of continued life, he surely would have struck her with blows guaranteed to kill.

She crumples, he catches her and eases her down to the floor.

Willi Berg flinches awake.

"Get dressed," says Marsden tossing him the overnight bag.

"Who the hell are you?"

"You want to get out of here?"

"Yeah, but who—?"

"Then get dressed."

Taking the stairs, they leave the hospital together about a quarter past one and by twenty past are riding downtown in a Dodge touring sedan. By one-thirty they are crossing the Brooklyn Bridge.

DIXON PUBLIC LIBRARY
DIXON ILLINOIS

National mourning. Further reports of arson.
Lex Luthor's shocking new appearance. Clark Kent, reporter.
Willi becomes a chainsmoker. His shocking new appearance.

———

1

The major story in newspapers published on Friday, August 16, 1935, is the plane crash near Point Barrow, Alaska, that ended the lives of Will Rogers and Wiley Post. After Charles Lindbergh, Post was the country's most touted aviation pioneer, and Rogers, of course, the universally beloved comedian, radio broadcaster, syndicated columnist, and movie personality, the Cherokee cowboy with a ready wink. He never met a man he didn't like. The two friends were on a flight to Russia. It's unbelievable. It's horrible. It's a national tragedy.

That same day readers also learn President Roosevelt has signed into law the Social Security Act, and Italy's Primo Carnera, who recently lost the world's heavyweight boxing championship to American Negro Joe Louis, has had his passport canceled by Achille Starace, Secretary General of the Fascist Party. "Carnera's showing," he says, "is a dishonor to Fascist sport."

And in New York City news, for the fifth time in two weeks a house of ill-repute allegedly operated by associates of indicted racketeer Lucky Luciano was destroyed last night in a blaze that fire marshals are calling a clear case of arson. Three lives were lost, but, according to an officer from the Eighteenth Precinct, they were just prostitutes.

Two weeks after his brazen escape from a guarded room at

Roosevelt Hospital, Ninth Avenue and Fifty-eighth Street, William Jacob Berg, twenty, the so-called Foto-Fugitive, still remains at large.

Meanwhile, (Miss) Catherine Barton, a woman of a certain age, was released yesterday from police custody. A cafeteria hostess from Woodside, Queens, who had originally given her name as Rosemary Tibbell, Miss Barton was discovered on the morning of August second lying bruised and unconscious in Mr. Berg's hospital room. She was dressed in a nurse's uniform rented from a costume store on West Forty-eighth Street. Although initially dubious of her claims to being romantically infatuated by the young murderer after seeing his photographs in the tabloid press, police finally charged the woman with simple trespass, allowed her to pay a small fine, and set her free.

In all the New York papers that day it is also reported that while Fred S. Gropper, vice-president of Amalgamated Gas & Electric, was being paid an annual salary of $60,000, AG&E President Howard H. Sloan had been charging the system's many holding companies an aggregate of $150,000 per annum for their respective shares of Mr. Gropper's services. Apparently, Mr. Sloan, whose whereabouts remain currently unknown, has been pocketing the $90,000-a-year difference.

Upon hearing of these revelations, Alderman Alexander Luthor, a personal friend of Sloan's who benefited from the financier's advice and monetary contributions during his recent election campaign, expressed shock and dismay but gently reminded members of the fourth estate that, in America at least, a man is presumed innocent until proven guilty.

During his press conference at City Hall, Alderman Luthor was asked by reporters to comment upon his startling new appearance. Running a hand over his recently shaved and polished skull, he laughed and said, "It kind of resembles the world, doesn't it?"

Leaving the rostrum, the alderman was overheard to hum a few sprightly bars of "I'm Just a Vagabond Lover."

In the funnies today, Winnie Winkle finds a handbag full of jewelry, Dagwood runs smack into the postman, the Lone Ranger and Tonto are ambushed in a gulch, Pat Ryan kisses the Dragon Lady, and Daddy Warbucks is still being held prisoner in a lunatic asylum by a quack doctor in the employ of a rival tycoon.

"You know something, boss," says Paulie Scaffa after he's finished reading *Little Orphan Annie*, "you kind of *look* like Daddy Warbucks now. Especially since you both wear tuxedos."

Whereupon Lex boxes Paulie's ears. "Mind telling me why you're sitting here reading the comics, is that what I pay you for?"

"Just give me something to do, boss, I'll do it."

"Find Willi Berg."

"Boss, we've *looked*. He just *vanished*."

"But how? Who helped him?"

Paulie shakes his head.

"I'm late for a meeting with Fatty Arbuckle," says Lex, referring to Mayor LaGuardia, a public friend he privately loathes. "We'll talk more about this tonight. And bring Stick with you when you come back."

"Sure, boss, and in the meantime, I'll keep looking for the kid."

"You do that."

As soon as Lex has gone, Paulie raises the windows in his boss's large, bright kitchen and lights a cigarette. Retaking his seat at the table, he continues to page through the *Daily News*. In *The Gumps* cartoon strip, Andy is griping to his wife, but there are too many words crowded into the talk balloons, so Paulie reads *Dick Tracy* instead. He knows he shouldn't like *Dick Tracy,* but he does.

He likes how whenever somebody gets shot, you can see the bullet go in one side of the guy's head and exit the other in a sinuous dotted line.

2

There is no paper published in Smallville, Kansas, on August 16. The *Herald-Progress,* eight broadsheet pages in a tombstone format, comes out just once a week. There will be a new edition next Tuesday. In the meantime, most town and farm residents still keep this past

Tuesday's edition on hand. They'll wait until the next one is delivered before putting it in the outhouse or using it for peelings. That's because Newel Timmins, at considerable expense, includes on the next-to-last page of his newspaper a complete seven-day program listing for all of the radio stations you can pick up in southeastern Osage County.

In Smallville, Newel Timmins is considered a crackerjack business-man and a genuine public servant, although Jonathan Kent thinks he was a real boob to support Herbert Hoover in the last election. Other-wise he's a decent enough fellow, for a Republican, and he certainly has been good to Clark. Even gives the boy his own byline if something he's written—the story about the seven Amish families, for example, that just pulled up stakes and moved to Pennsylvania—runs in excess of two columns.

In the still-current number of the *Herald-Progress*, Clark's name appears below "Ewing L. Herbert Celebrates 95th Birthday," "History of Basketball to Be Topic at S'ville Study Club," and "Farm Growth Since '31 Is Epic of Toil." In addition to reporting those long stories, he con-tributed several unsigned squibs, about a sawmill boiler explosion, the proposed teachers' contract for School District No. 43, and the robbery at a farmer's cooperative in Paola, over near the Missouri line, being attributed to members of the Jiggs Makley gang.

The final sentence reminds readers that Jiggs Makley died right here in Smallville, killed last May by a freakishly ricocheting bullet fired from his own gun.

Clark's father scowls over that last item prior to taking up scissors and cutting it out of the paper. Most of his son's other stories from the current edition, clipped out and neatly trimmed, are spread over the kitchen table, where there is also a jar of mucilage and a scrapbook. Mr. Kent keeps every story Clark writes, even those not amounting to more than public notices. Well, he can't help it, he's proud. And Clark, who claims to be embarrassed by the sheer thoroughness of his dad's new hobby, is deeply touched by his diligence.

It is ten o'clock in the morning and Clark is slathering two thick slices of bread with mayonnaise, piling on ham. He carefully cuts the sandwich in half on a diagonal, wraps it in paper, and sticks it in a carry-all he bought at the mercantile store with his graduation money. In the carryall, which he can either sling over a shoulder or wear like a back-pack, he keeps two notepads, a clutch of pencils bound with a rubber band, a cheap pencil sharpener, and a book he borrowed recently from the public library—the collected journalism of Richard Harding Davis. His interest in the science-fiction pulps has waned, may have even lapsed entirely. He no longer feels compelled to write that stuff, either.

"I'll be back sometime this afternoon," he says buckling the flap on his carryall.

"Whenever'll be fine."

"I think I got all my chores done."

"I'm sure you did."

"But I can help you with that sump later, if you like."

"Alger and I'll take care of it." As soon as he says that, Mr. Kent detects an ambient shift in the kitchen air, a chilling-down. He lays aside the mucilage brush and looks over a shoulder, meeting Clark's gaze. "You can't do everything, son. Well, maybe you can, but there's no need to. Alger's a good kid."

"I'm not saying he's not."

"No, I don't think you are. But don't be jealous of him, either. Okay?"

For almost a month—ever since Mr. Kent learned that Alger Lee's mother left suddenly for Detroit because her husband had been injured during a strike at the Ford plant—the boy has been helping around the farm three days a week. Sometimes four. Five, occasionally.

"Dad, come on. 'Jealous.' I just don't—I mean, can we afford to *pay* somebody?"

"Let me worry about that," says Mr. Kent. "So what's the scoop today?"

"Ah, big doings. Nellie Colman is donating her collection of col-ored postcards to the Smallville Library."

"Sounds like a slow news day."

Clark makes a face hitching his carryall onto his left shoulder. "They all are," he says.

3

In Washington, D.C., where buildings and monuments shimmer like mirages in the swampy heat, Willi Berg and Lois Lane are disagreeing about hair dye.

"I'll look ridiculous with blond hair! You want me to look like Buster Crabbe?"

"Believe me, cookie, nothing's gonna make you look like Buster Crabbe." She puts a hand to her forehead and it slides across the moisture there. Her blouse clings to her back and there are embarrassing half-moons of perspiration below her breasts. She desperately wants to take a cold shower, but there is no shower, no *tub,* in this suffocating little room they've rented. "So not blond, *what* then? Red?"

Despite their physical discomfort and cramped surroundings, despite even the constant dread they've been living with—Lois since Willi called her yesterday morning from a telephone booth in Jersey City, Willi since this whole bad dream started almost two months ago—despite that, they burst into laughter. Feels good.

"That's it!" he says. "Willi Berg the Irishman!"

"Straight from the Old Sod."

"Willi O'Berg."

"Leprechaun Willi."

Lois is enjoying this, but it's not getting them anywhere. "Maybe you should just shave your head."

Wrong thing to say.

New York dailies are scattered around the room, on the table, the floor, the narrow studio couch where they slept last night. In the *Mirror,* the *Post,* and the *Planet:* pictures of the newly bald and lustrous-pated Lex Luthor.

"I'm sorry," says Lois, "I wasn't thinking."

101

Willi twists open the cold-water tap on the tiny sink basin. Water trickles out warm. To hell with it, he splashes some on his face, then slicks back his hair. Lifting his eyes, he peers into the shaving mirror. "Maybe I should just get some Brylcreem, go for that Valentino look. Nobody'll recognize me then." He savagely twists off the tap.

"You really want to do it red?"

"I don't care, I don't care, I don't *care!*" Willi throws himself down on the couch and moans at the ceiling grooved with cracks and missing chunks of plaster. He flops out one arm and grabs his package of Camels. "I'm dead anyway."

"Cut it out. You're luckier than you know."

"Oh yeah?" He rolls onto his stomach. "How you figure that?"

"Right now you should be sitting in a cell on Riker's Island. Or did you forget?"

He strikes a match.

"Or lying on the bottom of the river with two buckets of cement on your feet."

Touching the match to the end of his cigarette, Willi inhales, then lets smoke jet through his nostrils. "They weren't ever gonna dump me. They liked me."

The driver of the Dodge sedan that took Willi Berg through Manhattan and across the Brooklyn Bridge was named, or called, Dakota. "Like the states," he said, actually reaching back to shake Willi's hand while they were stopped for a light. The man who'd snatched Willi from Roosevelt Hospital introduced himself as Carol, which sounded like a girl's name, unless it was spelled C-a-r-r-o-l-l and was his last name. Willi didn't feel he should ask.

"Dakota, you think we should stop and put a blindfold on this bird?"

"Should we? I dunno." Willi sensed Dakota was not a man who liked the burden of decision making.

"If you want," said Willi, "I'll close my eyes."

"What do you think, Carol?"

"All right, kid, close your eyes."

Willi closed them, kept them closed, and they rolled through the streets of Red Hook. The car finally stopped. Dakota helped Willi from the back, then he and Carol walked him to a door that somebody else opened from inside.

They brought him to a room and said he could open his eyes. The third man, the man who'd let them all in, was small and fat with sparse sand-colored hair combed in strings across the top of his head. There was a card table and several chairs, that's all. "You're gonna wait here," said Dakota.

Willi nodded. He wanted to ask for how long, for *who?* But didn't.

"You hungry?" asked the fat man, whose name Willi never got. "We could bring you something."

"No, thanks."

"Thirsty?"

"A little."

The three men went out and locked the door. Willi sat down, bewildered, elated, terrified. He had no idea what time it was. Did it matter? He was running a low fever.

Soon the fat man returned with a half-filled bottle of red wine and a glass that once contained jelly and was stenciled with pictures of Popeye the Sailor and Olive Oyl and Wimpy.

He hadn't meant to, but Willi finished the bottle, and what with all the tension of the evening he had a real buzz going by the time the door opened again and Meyer Lansky walked in with Joe Adonis and Benny Siegel.

"Did you recognize them all right away?" Lois asks him now as she cuts Willi's hair preparatory to washing and coloring it. She can't imagine what he'll look like with red hair! She loves it glossy black.

"Sure. I even seen Adonis once before, down at police headquarters. I might've taken his picture, as a matter of fact."

"Did they have guns?"

"I *guess.* Although Meyer doesn't pack, I'm told."

"Oh, it's Meyer, is it?"

"Well . . ."

"I'm just teasing you." She drags a comb through Willi's hair and snips again with the scissors. "Did they sit down, or—what?"

"Lois, I told you all this before."

"I need details."

"You 'need' details? What for? You gonna write up the story?"

"I might."

Willi twists around. "Don't even joke!"

"I don't mean *tomorrow.*"

"Never! Are you crazy?"

"Do you want this haircut or don't you?"

"You can't ever write about this."

"Okay."

"No, I mean it. Promise me you won't ever write about this."

"I promise," she says, but to herself she defines "this" as *right now,* as the *haircut* she is giving Willi, and she can promise, without hesitation, never to write about it.

She resumes carefully trimming around his right ear. "So. Did they sit down with you? Or stand?"

"Lansky sat. The other two stood."

"You don't have to call him Lansky just for me."

Meyer Lansky was short and coarse-featured, but unlike his companions, whose eyes stayed frosty even when they smiled, even when they *laughed,* he could express amusement with his whole face—lips, eyes, nostrils—and Willi felt it was genuine, that here was a guy who could enjoy himself and didn't believe you had to be sour to be a good mobster.

Meyer removed his homburg and sat down at the card table. He picked up the wine bottle and tipped it over Willi's empty glass. Not a drop left. "Can I get you more?"

"No, thank you, Mr. Lansky."

"Ah. So introductions are not in order. You know my associates?"

"Not personally." That was the wine talking, and Willi wished it would shut up.

Meyer smiled: mouth, nostrils, eyes. "We've heard some things you've been saying, supposedly saying, and thought we should hear them confirmed or denied directly by you. That's why you're here."

"Yes, sir."

"Do you know which things I'm talking about?"

Willi was in a panic now. It was like sprays of chipped ice had spumed through his upper chest and down his legs. He had to slide his hands from the table and sit on them. Was Meyer Lansky hooked up with Lex Luthor, was *that* it? Had Lansky heard about the story Willi told the cops? Oh God, he didn't want to be shot again. "I didn't kill Leon Chodash, if that's what you mean."

Meyer frowned. "I know you didn't kill Leon Chodash, Mr. Berg. *He* did."

Joe Adonis, a thick, sloppy-fleshed man in an exorbitant gray silk suit that glimmered when he moved, raised a hand—doing it in a comic manner, like a schoolchild who knew the answer to a question.

"We're only interested," said Meyer Lansky, "in who you saw in the basement of Mr. Chodash's establishment."

"I saw *three* men."

"Okay," said Meyer rubbing his palms together. "If you think you're being coy, we'll be glad to show you that's *not* the thing to be."

"I'm not coy. I'm scared."

"No need."

"And a little drunk."

"Jeezus Ka-rist," said Benny Siegel, "is this sheik for real?"

Meyer smiled again, taking out a package of cigarettes and a box of matches and putting them down in front of Willi. "Smoke. It'll sober you up."

"I'd rather not, if you don't mind."

"Smoke!"

"Yes, sir." With fumbling hands Willi lighted up.

"You need an aspirin?"

"No, I'm fine."

"Good," said Meyer. Then following a long pause, he said, "Lex Luthor."

"Yes."

"Yes?"

"He was there."

"You saw him?"

"I took his *picture.* That's why they came after me."

"And this picture is gone?"

"I wouldn't be in this mess if it wasn't."

"None of us would, Mr. Berg. How's that cigarette?"

Willi had not been smoking it, just letting the tobacco burn to an outcurving ash, but now, fixed by Meyer Lansky's no-longer-amused gaze, he took a long drag. "It's fine, thank you," he said.

"Keep the pack." Meyer pushed his chair back.

"Thank you, but I really don't—"

"*Keep* it."

"Yes, sir."

Now as he sits in this airless rented room with a towel wrapped in a turban around his head, Willi Berg lights a fresh Camel from the coal of the one he just finished. He never smoked before in his life, and now he's a nicotine fiend. A chain-smoker. And these things aren't cheap, either. Nickel a pack. Thank you, Mr. Lansky. Thank you very much.

"It's incredible," says Lois. Dressed only in her brassiere, bloomers, and a garter belt, she stands with her back to Willi, shaking clouds of talcum powder over her chest and stomach, along her arms, down her thighs and calves. She begins to smooth it in. "Just incredible."

"What is?"

"That they didn't even know who their rival *was.*"

"Until I showed up. Yeah, it is."

Willi is fascinated by the little bumps of her spine, and by the satin tag that sticks out below where fastening hooks secure the narrow band of fabric across her back. Last night he read the tag: 34B. What does *that* mean? he wanted to know, and she explained that it's how they're sizing these things now. Oh.

"When are you meeting this guy?"

"Five."

"Trust him?"

Lois slips into a clean blouse. Buttoning it up, she turns around to Willi. "I can handle John Gurney."

"He ever put the moves on you?"

"He was my *college professor.*"

Willi says, "Mmmm." He watches her sit down and roll on and secure her nylon hosiery. She stands again and steps into her skirt, tucks in her blouse, zippers up the skirt. She rummages through her handbag and takes out a small cylinder.

"Lip paint?"

"Oh stop. Do you want to be safe or not?"

"Yeah, but—"

"Then hand me my hairbrush and shut up."

He does.

"How do I look?"

"Too good."

"Thank you." She glances at her watch. "I still have time."

"For what?" He walks up behind her and puts his arms around her middle, his cheek to hers, and cinches hard.

"I'm glad you're all recovered, but don't you dare." Pushing him away gently, Lois tosses a couple of flat pillows off the studio couch, carefully smoothes the seat of her skirt, and sits down. Pats a place beside her. As soon as he joins her, she touches his face. "Willi . . . ?"

"Yeah?" he says nuzzling her hand, enjoying the touch.

". . . do you think Meyer Lansky and those others will try to kill the alderman?"

Disgruntled, he leans away. "Why not? But who knows?"

"You must've heard them talk."

"Not really. Meyer came back only once. The very next day, with Mr. Luciano . . ."

"'Mister' Luciano."

"Politest guy you ever heard, makes Amy Vanderbilt sound like Tugboat Annie."

"He came with Meyer Lansky *and . . . ?*"

"I told him the same story. And let me tell you, Mr. Luciano forgot his good manners for a minute there."

"But you didn't hear them say what they might do?"

"Sweetie, they weren't about to make their plans in front of *me*. And besides, I wasn't feeling so great by then. At first the little fat man gave me some aspirin. But when I got worse, that's when they moved me out of there."

"Why do you think they did it, Willi? I mean . . . ?"

"Instead of just letting me croak?"

"Yeah, instead of that."

"I don't know." He goes and gets his cigarettes. "Maybe 'cause I did them a favor or maybe they wanted something more from me later. I don't know. And I hope I never find out."

"God. So what was this 'clinic' like?"

"Lois, aren't you supposed to go meet somebody?"

"I still have time. What was it like?"

For the first several days he was there, it was like *nothing* since he lay in a constant state of delirium, the bacterial infection that had run wild through his body spiking Willi's temperature so high he was lucky his brains didn't braise. But eventually whatever it was the Egyptian doctor kept injecting him with had an effect. The fever broke, and Willi finally got sleep that wasn't frantic.

Some of his strength returned, then his color, then his appetite. And when he finally was focused enough to notice a few things, he noticed that everybody—Dakota and Carol, who came twice to check on Willi, the other "patients" recuperating in their own beds on the ward (mostly they were gunshot cases, although one guy had been shellacked with a baseball bat), and the orderlies, all of whom looked like stevedores—everybody called the doctor "Ali Baba." A gray-haired, dark brown man of sixty or so, Ali Baba would race around his secret dispensary, zipping from bed to bed with both a desperate urgency and the slapstick giant-steps of Groucho Marx. He even moved with his torso nearly parallel to the floor.

As long as Willi was there he never lost a patient.

In time Willi realized the ward was just the top floor of two side-by-side brownstone houses whose dividing wall had been broken through. Looking out the window near his bed one morning, he noticed that the buildings faced a small park. By squinting he could read the name of it on a sign by the entrance. More importantly, he read: "Frank Hague, Mayor."

So he was in Jersey City.

Until he left Ali Baba's clinic—until he crept out of there sometime around three A.M. yesterday morning—Willi had no idea how much time had passed since Brooklyn. If he had to guess, he would have said a week. Actually it was a week and five days.

He wandered around downtown Jersey City collecting pop bottles for the deposits. When he had five, he found a grocery store that had just opened for the day, cashed them in, and used the dime to call Lois Lane. "Don't talk, just listen. I need you to rent a car . . ."

"You'd better get moving," Willi is saying now. "It's twenty past four."

"Wish me luck."

"You think this guy'll go for it?"

"I have no idea." Lois takes a deep breath, exhales, then turns like a cadet and goes out.

He waits till he hears her get all the way down the creaking stairs before he unfurls the turban in front of the little mirror.

Touching his still-damp hair, he cocks his head to the left, to the right.

Ay-yi-yi.

Willi the Red.

Miss Colman. Courage. Homicide in the cemetery.
Lois begs a favor. Secret of the Sherpas. Good catch.

———

1

Nellie Colman, proudly eighty-seven, is one of Smallville's most cherished eccentrics. She brews tea from gnarly roots and dried sea grasses guaranteed to stimulate everything from appetite and regularity to mental telepathy, believes in supernatural visitations, conducts séances whenever she can find enough believers to fill the seats at a table, and claims to hear the midnight moanings of Corley McKinley and his oldest son Deet, lynched back in 1891 from a linden tree now part of her property. Weekly she writes to the *Herald-Progress,* complaining about taxes, locusts, and the insolence of youth, which she blames on radio. And she is forever finding "interesting relics" in her garden and side yards—usually chunks of rusted metal, Indian implements, Civil War bullets, the heel from a cavalryman's boot. But once she clamed to have unearthed bones that proved *some* dinosaurs were as small as dogs. Miss Colman feels it is her civic duty to share all of these finds with others in the community not fortunate enough to live on property quite so full of wonderment.

Her neighborhood is on the west side of Smallville, with all of the largest homes, built in high Victorian style and situated deep on four-and five-acre lots. Long ago some wag dubbed this part of town "Bigville," and that's how people still refer to it, although naturally not by anyone who lives there on streets named after railroad men, bankers, merchants, and land developers, some of whom are still alive.

The street Clark is walking along now, shortly past one o'clock in the afternoon, is the only one named after a tree: Maple. Nellie Colman's house is number 88, on a corner lot. Miss Colman's late father fought under General Nathan Lyon at the battle of Wilson's Creek and later operated a livery stable on Jayhawker Street, over on the far East End. James Dram Colman once ran for mayor of Smallville and another time for a seat in the state legislature. He lost both races, which might explain why the street is still called Maple rather than Colman.

Clark knows these things. He *likes* knowing these things. This is his hometown, and he always imagined he would live here forever.

Lately, though, he's begun to wonder about that, seeing as how he is so talented and all. And it's not just those *big* talents, either. He's been thinking that he might, with diligent application and stick-to-itiveness, become in time far too skilled a reporter for a dinky paper like the *Herald-Progress.* Is that vanity? Or self-knowledge? Good old American stocktaking? Or self-importance? At his mother's knee Clark learned that misplaced ambition is Lucifer's reel, but does he truly want to spend the rest of his life writing anniversary stories about the Sacrament Christian Church and reporting on the town council's latest efforts to restore the old log stockade out on Highway 75? Does he honestly want to spend this steaming but gorgeously blue August day listening to Miss Colman talk about tinted postal cards?

In this curious mood—a little nostalgic, a bit cranky, somewhat full of himself, vaguely at loose ends—Clark ambles along Maple Street. As he nears the Colman place, he stops, noticing a hopscotch pattern sketched with blue chalk. In one of the numbered squares lies a plump brown sparrow. Clark frowns and continues on. But a quarter of the way up Miss Colman's front walk, he stops again and goes back to pick up the dead bird, deposits it in one of the old spinster's trash cans. There is a short muffled airburst, then another sparrow—no, a finch, see those yellow tail feathers?—drops like a plumb bob into the street. Clark looks around, seeing no one and nothing out of the ordinary. He walks into the street and picks up the finch. It's warm but dead, with a tiny bleeding hole in its belly.

The sparrow, Clark discovers when he goes back to the trash barrel, has an identical wound. Why didn't he notice before? Some reporter.

He is still standing at the foot of the walk, a dead bird in each hand, a quizzical expression on his face, when the big glassed front door opens and Miss Colman steps out onto her wraparound porch. Before he can explain, she marches down the steps, shaking a fist. With her fluffy white hair, tiny crabbed face, almond-shaped spectacles, and old-fashioned swishing black dress, she reminds Clark of pictures of Carry Nation invading a saloon. "You devil!" she says.

"Miss Colman, I—"

But she isn't hollering at Clark or even looking at him. Charging off across her green trimmed lawn, she comes to a halt directly below a thick-trunked leafy oak. "You little devil! Do they teach you on the radio to murder God's gracious little creatures? Well, *do they?*"

From high in the foliage a voice calls down, "Don't you yell at me, you old witch!"

Branches shake, then a blond boy's head appears, followed by the barrel and stock of a BB rifle.

"Donald Poore, get down from my tree this very minute, you radio heathen!"

"Old witch, can't pay her taxes, don't you yell at me! Why don't you just go pay your taxes, 'stead of yelling at me, old witch, old witch!"

"How dare you!"

"My father says if you don't pay your taxes soon you won't be living here with the people that *do*, come nineteen hundred and thirty-six." Donald Poore's father, F. H. Poore, owns the Smallville Bank and is the wealthiest man in town. Poore is rich: a common quip. "Old crazy witch!"

Miss Colman is livid, trembling with rage, but curiously now unable to speak.

Clark says, "Donny, do what Miss Colman tells you."

"Don't have to!"

"Yes, you do."

"Clark Kent, this is *my* property, thank you very much." Miss Colman has found her voice again. "I'll handle things here, if you don't mind." She raises her wizened face and calls up at Donny Poore, "I'm going inside right now to telephone your father, you insolent little heathen!"

"Don't care if you do!"

Setting her jaw, Miss Colman turns and trudges back across the lawn. The heels of her sensible shoes clonk on the porch steps. She pulls the door shut behind her.

"Donny, I advise you come down now while you have your chance."

"Go away and maybe I will."

"All right." Carefully, Clark sets the two birds down on the ground near the tree trunk. "And you might consider taking your game with you."

Donny shinnies lower, crouches on a branch about eight feet above the ground, his Daisy rifle in a small fist. He is nine years old, dressed in new dungarees with the cuffs rolled twice and a polo shirt sprayed with red, yellow, and green comets and planets. Most of the planets have rings around them like Saturn. "Go on, don't stand close."

"All right." Clark ambles back across the lawn and up onto the porch. Little Donny Poore tosses down his rifle, then drops to the grass. Snubbing his nose at Clark, he tears off without taking the birds with him.

Donny lives directly opposite Miss Colman in a white-and-blue Italianate-style mansion with narrow tall windows, ornamental iron-work, and fish-scale siding. In the side yard is a peaked garden house where the boy is heading now, clutching his rifle by its breech.

Clark shakes his head, wondering how come Maple Street hasn't ever been changed to Poore Street. Wondering if Miss Colman will be in any mood now to grant him his pointless interview. Wondering if he has outgrown Smallville.

2

Lex Luthor's mother was buried two weeks ago in Moravian Cemetery on Staten Island. There had been no wake or funeral or burial service, but Lex paid for the plot and the interment. Anonymously.

This afternoon he is climbing the cemetery's neatly terraced acres and laboriously winding his way past and between headstones. Covering nearly eighty acres, the place is a packed-crowded city of death, and even below the merciless glare of the sun the long shadows crisscrossing helter-skelter from all of the gravestones, needles, crosses, crypts, and monumental angels make it seem weirdly dusklike.

He finds himself in the oldest part of the cemetery, where the graves dating from the eighteenth century are segregated by sex according to Moravian custom. No women *here,* no men *there.* Lex stops and wipes his forehead with the back of a hand.

Where's his damn mother?

He has half a mind to chuck the wrapper of flowers he's carrying and just drive back to Manhattan. Nonetheless he strikes off again in a new direction.

Now he is at a little fieldstone house with a push mower leaning against one side, heavy bags of lime stacked below a window, and, visible inside through the half-open door, sundry picks, spades, and shovels. But no one to ask for directions. Lex removes his suit coat, drapes it over an arm, and humming a catchy tune he can't identify but that has been stuck maddeningly in his mind for the past hour, he tramps on.

He doesn't know why he's here. Drove all this way. He finished his discussions with the mayor before noon (the talk had centered upon a variety of upcoming federal works projects, which Lex felt presented ample opportunities for looting), then went on to a fairly pro forma meeting of the Board of Aldermen, finally put in a brief appearance at the Salmagundi Club's summer art sale. Returning to his Graham 8—he drives the supercharged model—he found himself driving south on Seventh Avenue toward the Holland Tunnel. Yes, all right, he told himself, I should probably scoot over to Hoboken, check on things there. He meant at the commercial printing facility that he owns on Washington Street. Before Lex took it over, purchasing it under the name of Clay Alexander Plenty with cash "left over" from his election campaign, the company's four large Hoe presses had printed Saturday rotogravures and all of the two-color work for *Time* magazine; now they printed money. Beautiful $10 and $20 counterfeit bills. Lex passed a sheaf of them last week at the Saratoga racetrack.

Even before he went through the tunnel, he realized there was no good reason to visit the shop in Hoboken today. What was the matter with him? He was off, somehow. He lifted a hand from the steering wheel and ran it over the top of his smooth skull. Personally he thinks he looks good, certainly better than he looked once his hair started falling out. His skull *does* resemble the globe—anything wrong with that? Isn't the globe a symbol? It is. It's a symbol of wealth and power, a symbol of *everything.*

In Jersey City he stopped the car at a florist's, bought some calla lilies, then got on Hudson Boulevard. He followed that south through Bayonne and across the silvery new bridge that spans the Kill Van Kull to Staten Island. Then onto Richmond Road and over to Todt Hill and the Moravian Cemetery.

Bewildering, really. He never dreamed he would be the sort of man to visit his mother's grave.

But life is full of surprises.

And here's another one now: the gravesite he's been looking for.

After tossing the wrapper of lilies on the still-fresh grave, Lex eases down on a small ornamental iron bench. "You know," he says, "I was recalling the last thing you ever said to me—you wished me a happy Independence Day. I wonder if after I left you realized it was just too good an exit line to waste. Was *that* it? I mean, for heaven's sake, Mother, what a thing to do!" He waves a hand in disgust. "I suppose you'd been crazy for a long time, so there's no blame, of course. Certainly not from *me.*" He slowly shakes his head.

Somewhere not far off a car door slams, followed by another, then another. Lex vaguely registers the sounds as he gets up and stands at the foot of his mother's grave. "I'm very disappointed in you—not that I believe you can hear me tell you so. We don't believe in that stuff, do we?"

He sits down on the bench again.

"I won't be coming back, Mother."

His hands are shaking badly. He looks at them in horror.

Springing to his feet again, he paces up and down.

"No, I *didn't* love you, is that such a crime? Love! If you wanted *that,* you should've given birth to Irving Berlin, not me. I gave you something far better than love!"

Even as he says it, Lex isn't sure what he means, or what the "something far better" might have been—*himself?* His personality, his drive, his retaliatory nature? But as it turns out he won't have to finish his speech, he doesn't have the chance, because from the corner of an eye he spots three hatted men in inappropriate black raincoats walking quickly toward him, wending around headstones and monuments.

One of the men reaches inside his coat, and that's enough for Lex. He ducks and runs. And running, he suddenly and absurdly recalls the title of the song he's been humming half the afternoon: "These Foolish Things Remind Me of You."

A moment later gunfire cracks behind him, bullets glancing off granite, punching into limestone.

Lex pivots, swinging his head around, assessing the possibilities. When more bullets whistle past he dives behind a fenced monument to Richmond County sailors killed during the Spanish-American War. "They Made the Ultimate Sacrifice." He scrambles away on all fours, his breath chuffing in his ears.

Both Stick and Paulie had urged Lex to carry a weapon, but how could he do that? He's an elected official! An elected official who—

Is not afraid, he realizes. Three gunmen are chasing him through a deserted cemetery, he's unarmed, hobbled by ungiving shoes better suited to ceremony, and yet—

He is unafraid.

Crouched behind the pediment of an archangel with outspread wings, he looks at his hands.

Not a tremble.

Lex raises his head an inch or two, searching for his pursuers. He sees one of them just as the man spots Lex.

"Dakota! Over here, over *here!*"

Lex sprints again as more gunfire snaps off behind him.

At the groundsman's shed he kicks open the door and grabs a pickax from the workbench. Dragging it, he runs back outside, pulls the door shut, then ducks around behind the shed.

"Where? Where *are* you, Carol?"

"Follow my voice, for crissakes," says the gunman who saw Lex crouched behind the alabaster angel and is now less than twenty feet away. He has unbuttoned his raincoat, and it flaps around his legs as he moves forward in a heavy jog.

If the second man, or the second and the third man, arrive before Lex can get to this first one . . .

Well.

Whatever happens will happen.

Relaxing his stomach muscles, he breathes in deeply, feeling a long, buoyant thrill of pride.

When Carol stops in front of the shed, Lex clasps the ax handle with two hands, one fist around the base, the other below the head.

Now!

Gun in his right hand, Carol is reaching for the door latch with his left.

Lex drives the chisel edge through the back of Carol's skull. It punches out through his mouth.

The second man is calling Carol's name again, which gives Lex a direction. He snatches up the dead man's gun—it's a revolver—and follows the sound of Dakota's whining voice, walking steadily and straight-backed, swinging both arms like a commuter moving purposely across Grand Central Terminal but with plenty of time to catch his train.

When Dakota straggles off a grassy hill, Lex shoots him in the temple.

If he comes upon the third man, fine, but now he is going back to his car. The happiest man in the big wide world.

A minute later, Lex is nearly to the cemetery gates when he notices a hat bobbing up and down about twenty yards off to his left.

He shrugs and walks over there and shoots the third man, who is fat and lost and perspiring. He shoots him in the cheek and then in the stomach and then in the groin and then in the middle of his forehead.

The little fat man dies on a gravesite bearing the epitaph of Colonel Nicholas Howat, dated 1743.

On the long drive back to Manhattan, Lex turns on the car radio and listens to *Make Believe Ballroom*.

Man, he likes that Benny Goodman Orchestra. Those guys can *swing*.

3

"John."

"*John*. I know I'm asking a big favor, John . . ."

"I'd say so, yes." Gurney takes another sip at his cocktail—he is on his second rye and ginger ale. Lois so far hasn't touched her first. "A very *large* big favor."

Dressed in a pale tan summer-weight suit, he arrived half an hour ago, twenty minutes late, carrying a Panama hat by the crown. He placed that finically on the seat of the empty chair beside him.

"This friend of yours isn't in any *real* trouble, is he? With the police or anything like that?"

"No!" She can't meet his eyes. "No, of course not, it's just—it's like I told you, he's got himself into some, well, I guess you'd call it *family difficulties*—"

"Back home in Poughkeepsie."

"Monticello."

"And you've known this boy since *when*?"

"Oh, practically all my life. We were in school together. I can vouch for him, Professor Gurney."

"John."

"And he's a really good photographer, John. It's not like I'm asking you to give a job to someone who's not qualified."

"Of course not. Lois, are you lying to me?"

"I swear, no." She tries to laugh, but it sounds breathy.

"You came all the way down to Washington just to ask me to find some work for this old schoolmate of yours. You could have *phoned.*"

"Well. I thought it would be nice to see you again."

He sits back in his chair. "Well, it's nice to see you, too."

"So can you do this?"

"I really don't know."

"I remembered that night you were joking with me, remember? And you said you could send my boyfriend to North Dakota? So I thought . . ."

"Uh-huh. Whatever happened to your boyfriend, by the way? Wasn't he a photographer, too?"

"No, he wasn't. I wonder where you got that idea."

"I must've mixed you up with some *other* beautiful ex-student of mine. Though how I could've done *that* . . ."

Lois says, "Would you excuse me for just a minute, Professor?"

"No."

She looks startled.

"Not till you call me John."

With a weak smile she rises to her feet. "I'll be right back."

Her legs are rubbery as she crosses the floor of the hotel bar. Everything here is mahogany or brass, the banquettes are sumptuous leather, the tablecloths starched linen, the people middle-aged, successful-looking, assured of themselves, and Lois feels thoroughly, hideously conspicuous. Like the brainy wallflower she'd been at her first boy-girl dance.

The bartender nods to her politely as she goes out into the lobby.

A bellboy walks by with a straining Pekinese on a leash.

Lois spots the powder room door.

On her way there, she passes a sign framed under glass and propped on a painter's easel standing outside the entrance to the hotel's Café George Washington. The sign is pink, the size of a theatrical three-sheeter, and the lettering is in flamboyant script glued thickly with silver and red glitter. *APPEARING NOW: HARRY SELTZER'S CARBONATED RHYTHM ORCHESTRA. FEATURING SIGNE GREENE ON VOCALS. COMING IN SEPTEMBER: LEO REISMAN . . . LITTLE JACK LITTLE . . . DOLLY DAWN!*

Lois goes into the powder room, finds a stall, sits down, and closes her eyes. She lets her shoulders sag. Breathe in. Breathe out.

This is so ridiculous! She's a grown woman—well, nineteen—on a desperate mission, and she's behaving like some nervous Nellie, some *kid.*

Lois told Willi Berg she knew how to get him away from New York, far away, where he could be safe till they found some way out of the mess he's gotten himself in.

She didn't *promise* Willi anything, but she owes him her best shot. She does? Oh, does she? Why does she owe him anything?

Breathe in . . .

Breathe out . . .

Re-entering the cocktail room, Lois sees John Gurney's head snap up, which causes her knees to become gelatin-like. Instead of returning immediately to the table, she veers to her left, excusing herself as she squeezes between the backs of two occupied chairs at two different tables, and sits down at the long polished bar. The young barman appears with a clean rag and a fresh coaster. He is perhaps five years older than Lois, thickening around his middle, dressed in a vested white shirt and black trousers. She asks him if by some chance he has a cigarette she can borrow.

"You going to pay it back?" He smiles, already fishing into his vest pocket.

"Very next chance I get." He smokes Raleighs, and after Lois selects one he snaps open a flat gold lighter. "Thank you."

"You're quite welcome. Get you anything else?"

Lois turns and holds up a hand, twiddling her fingers at John Gurney: be right there. "Let me ask you a question, do you mind?"

"Is it personal?" says the barman.

"I guess you could say it was. I'm sorry, forget it."

"No. No, go ahead."

"Okay. Do you have a girlfriend?"

Going playfully big-eyed, he leans back and grins.

"That's not really the question," says Lois. "That's just the *start* of the question."

"Oh."

"And I'm not trying to pick you up."

"Ach, I knew those things only happened in books."

"So, do you?"

"Yes. Say, why didn't you ask me first if I was married?"

"No ring."

"Sure. Right."

"I'm an eagle-eyed reporter."

"*Are* you?"

"Yes," she says. Then: "Okay, though, here's my real question. If your girlfriend got in really big trouble, and I mean *really* big, would you do anything you could to save her? That's stupid. Let's forget I ever said anything." She tamps out her cigarette. "I should go."

"Hold on, let me answer. What do you mean by 'anything' I could do to save her? Including . . . kill somebody?"

"No. Everything up to that."

"You mean things that could get me into trouble."

"Yeah, or that you'd be ashamed of if anybody found out later."

"Okay. I got it. And no. For this girlfriend I got now, probably not. But we haven't been seeing each other that long. But for my *last* one, the one that got away? Oh definitely, I'd've done anything. *Including* kill somebody."

They laugh together, Lois nodding, nodding.

"Thank you. Thanks a lot," she says sliding off the bar chair.

"How about you? Would *you* do anything?"

"I don't know."

"Bet you would. My name's Lenny, by the way." He puts out his hand. "Lenny Boring. But I'm really not."

"Lois." No last name.

"Nice to meet you, Lois." Lenny winks, then notices that a solitary drinker at the far end of the bar is gesturing for his attention. "Hope to see you in here again sometime."

"Oh, I doubt that," she says. "Bye, Lenny."

The perfect gentleman, John Gurney stands up as Lois returns to their table. But he's glowering.

Breathe in, she thinks, taking a breath. Breathe out . . .

"I thought you were ditching me for the bartender," Gurney says once she takes her seat. Then he sits.

"I was just asking him for directions."

"Where to?"

"Back to the highway."

"You *drove* down here?"

"Yes."

"Alone?"

"Yes, alone."

He picks up his glass—it is nearly full and the ice cubes are large, so that's another one, a fresh one; his third? "Why do I feel that nothing is quite kosher about all of this? Can you tell me?"

Lois chooses to ignore that by asking a question of her own. "Can you help out my friend?"

"You want me to find a job for this old chum of yours who's got himself into a fix at home and needs to get away. That's it in a nutshell?"

"He's a *good* photographer."

Gurney smiles. "Okay. All right. Cards on the table. For a dear friend . . . a dear *friend*, mind you, *not* a former student . . . for a dear friend like you, yes, I might be able to find something. Yes."

"Thank you."

"Don't thank me yet."

"Oh."

"'Oh'? And what does *that* mean?"

"I'm not sure. Should I be?"

"You haven't touched your drink."

"And I don't intend to. Regardless of what happens."

His face is suddenly harsh. "I probably should run."

"I'm sorry—does your wife have dinner waiting?"

Gurney seems amazed, expressions of annoyance and amusement clashing on his face. Amusement stays. "You're quite a different person from the smart little girly I used to know." He removes a long billfold from inside his jacket and lays a ten on the tablecloth beside his glass. "I really have to run. It was good seeing you."

She nods, feeling on the verge of tears, on the verge of apologizing, of begging. Obliging.

Breathe in . . .

As he stands up, Gurney hands her a small white embossed card. "Tell your friend to call this gentleman here. But give me time to write a short memo first."

"Are you serious? John, I don't know what to say . . ."

He touches her fondly on the cheek, sighs, and moves off, lurching once but then catching himself and squaring his shoulders.

"Lois?"

She turns on her chair.

"I'll need your friend's name."

"What?" Her entire body from the crown of her head down to her insteps turns cold.

"His name. What's your friend's name?"

She opens her mouth.

"William."

"William . . . what?"

"Boring," says Lois. "William Boring."

4

Clark knocks. You don't just barge in on people. "Miss Colman?" Opening the front door about a foot, he calls her again. Finally he goes inside. Keeps calling but gets no reply. He thinks he might find Miss Colman still on the telephone, so he tiptoes into the high Victorian front parlor.

The room makes Clark feel claustrophobic. It contains two brocaded divans, a half dozen overstuffed chairs, intricately carved side tables, a piecrust table, a threadbare Persian rug, an embroidered fire screen, and a green-and-white-tiled fireplace mantel with porcelain figurines ranged along the top. An electrified chandelier descends from a medallion in the ceiling. And by the window there is a moth-eaten stuffed owl on its own pedestal. Through that window, closed and hung with sheer curtains that need laundering, you can see the Poore mansion. "Miss Colman? Miss Colman?" No Miss Colman.

He finds her at last in the kitchen, filling a glass from a brown bottle whose label is bordered with mysterious pictographs.

At first, she looks over at him, then sets down the bottle and drains her glass. For half a minute she winces and blinks. "Is that insolent monster still in my tree?"

"No, ma'am, he's gone. Did you call his father?"

"His father?" Returning the brown bottle to a cabinet shelf, Miss Colman takes down another. Dark blue, without a label. "Why would I call his father? We don't *speak*. He's an *awful* man. And I'll tell you something else: he wears *toilet water*."

After rinsing her glass at the sink, she fills it again from the blue bottle. Standing in the doorway, Clark can smell its alcohol content.

"Do you know the Sherpas, Mr. Kent?" she asks.

"No, ma'am."

"They live up in the Himalayas"—she pronounces it Him-AHL-yuhs—"and they live practically forever and have terrific strength and the most perfect lungs." She raises her glass slightly. "This is what they drink. I'd offer you a sip, but you're too young."

Miss Colman takes two short pulls, then carries the glass with her while she leads Clark back up the stairs and down along the hall—hung with oval family portraits, everyone unsmiling—and into the front parlor. She sits facing the window, and Clark takes the chair opposite her. He opens his carryall for his notepad and a pencil. "Shall we begin?" he says, noticing that already Miss Colman has produced from somewhere—the table beside her?—a small flat packet of hand-tinted postcards, the Grand Tetons on top. She begins to untie the packet but stops for another sip of her Himalayan nostrum.

"As I told Mr. Timmins," she says, "I've arranged for a display of my collection at the public library, but I thought. I thought." She yawns, her eyes begin to water. "Now, this one . . ."

Clark watches her shoulders droop, her eyelids close and stay closed. "Ma'am?"

She begins to snore.

"Miss Colman?" he says rising slowly from his chair, eyes fixed on the old woman whose head has plopped onto a shoulder. As he reaches to take the postal cards from her hands before they can spill all over her lap, the old woman springs up like she's been shot off the chair by a broken coil, colliding with Clark and shouting, "My God!"

"Miss Colman, I'm sorry, I'm really sorry!"

Her eyes are as big as eggs, but she is looking *past* Clark out through her front window.

She grabs him by his arm and points.

Across the street little Donny Poore, still with his rifle in hand, is walking, foot in front of foot, along the roofline of his house, a good sixty feet above the ground.

Clark has no sooner registered that sight than the boy slips. His rifle flies off in a wide arc, and Donny goes sliding down the inclined roof, bumpeting over the blue scaly shingles, his sneakers dislodging pieces and flinging them into space like skeet.

He rolls off the edge, grabs at a gutter.

But that tears free and then he's falling . . .

Later at dinner Mr. Kent says, "I figure something like that must've taken, what, five seconds, all told?"

"I don't know, Dad."

"But you caught him."

Clark grins. "I caught him. Yes I did. By the time *he* got there, *I* was there."

"Lord have mercy."

"Yeah, well, even *he* couldn't have done it much faster, if I do say so myself."

"Whoa there, cowboy."

"Only kidding, Dad."

"Uh-huh. And Miss Colman saw all this?"

"Sure did."

Mr. Kent rests his forehead on the cup of his palm.

"What? What's wrong, Dad?"

"Nothing." He pushes the heel of his hand up his forehead, making wales. "So I guess that means everybody is going to know about you now."

Clark's expression, which had darkened for just a moment at his father's distress, turns suddenly waggish. "Don't worry, Dad, she thinks I sneaked a drink of her patent medicine."

"You're kidding me."

"And did she ever bawl me out about it!"

They both laugh.

"But you should've seen that catch, Dad!"

Mr. Kent gets up slowly from the table and taps a hand on Clark's shoulder as he goes past, knowing he'll stay up long past his usual bedtime tonight, remembering Clark's adventure and the starry gleam in his son's eyes as he recounted it. And worrying, just worrying.

Photography in the rustic districts. Willi and Clark.
Out of gas. A kidnapping in Smallville.

———

1

In late August 1935, the administration of Franklin D. Roosevelt allocated $6,288,000 to the Writers Project, a branch of the Federal Arts Project, itself a branch of the monolithic Works Progress Administration. Part of the money was paid out in salaries for hundreds of career writers on the public dole. These men—some women too, but mostly men—were given a few days' training and then dispatched in groups of five or six to drive government Fords, a whole fleet of Rolls Roughs, around the forty-eight states, collecting raw data for a planned series of motoring guidebooks. Not that anyone in official Washington believed such things were *needed*—honestly, how many people were itching or able to take scenic automobile trips during a depression? The project primarily was a way for some idle citizens to earn ten or twelve dollars a month. Particularly a special category of citizens you had to figure wouldn't be much help building dams and bridges.

Each carload of fieldworkers included at least one academic who knew something about demographics, survey taking, and interviewing techniques; the rest could be fiction writers, ad copywriters, jingle writers, gag writers, playwrights, poets, or radio scripters. And there was usually a professional photographer, although sometimes one of the writers would be tapped for the role and issued a box Brownie.

Among the five fieldworkers covering the territory of eastern Kansas late that summer was a photographer who knew what he was doing even though he usually groused about doing it.

A redhead named Willi Boring. (Lois couldn't pick a better alias?)

The team assembled in Kansas City, Missouri, on Wednesday, the eleventh of September, Willi having trained out there from Union Station in D.C., his ticket—as well as his safety razor, a package of blades, two pairs of white socks, and a blue shirt—purchased with money borrowed from Lois Lane.

On his way to Missouri all of the papers he read were filled with stories about the assassination of Senator Huey Long in Baton Rouge. Although Willi had no love for Huey Long, who had always struck him as a little dictator with a gumbo drawl, he felt sorry for the poor slob, his sympathy connected, he realized, to the fact that he'd been shot himself recently and that only luck had saved him from sharing the Kingfisher's fate. In the same papers it was also reported, but with far less coverage, that Lucky Luciano, charged in August with sixty-two felony counts of "compulsory prostitution" (the best the Dewey commission could come up with), had had his bail revoked by New York's Governor Lehman and been confined on Riker's Island. In a funny sort of way Willi felt even sorrier for him than he did for Huey Long. Luciano had those good manners and hated Lex Luthor.

In Kansas City, Willi mailed Lois a nostalgically tinted picture-postcard (horse-drawn streetcar, men in derbies, pink clouds at dusk) and then didn't write her again.

What could he say? Once he was on the road he could itemize his complaints, tell her how much he loathed this stupid job, but that would be too . . . boring. Plus it would sound ungrateful. She went out on a limb for him. It wouldn't be fair now to turn around and *kvetch*.

No, but—damn it, he was taking pictures of *mile markers,* of mile markers and *fence rails,* water towers and Main Streets, all exactly the same! Eastern Kansas! Subsistence farms, poor little towns, nearly every place the site of some atrocity committed before, during, or after the Civil War. And wherever his team went they heard the same stories from amateur historians, the oldest living widow, the butcher at the Piggly Wiggly, the same dopey legends, local lore, and tall tales. Lem Blanchard. Jesse James. Big Nose Kate. Carry Nation. Butternut squash the size of glacial boulders. The ghosts of massacred Free Staters groaning on the wind. The superbaby in the orphanage.

But whenever Willi finds himself buzzing with discontent he still can hear Lois's voice whispery in his head: It's not better than Riker's Island?

So it's better than Riker's Island.

Okay, all right, but *still!*

While his companions read leisurely in county libraries or talk to leathery old-timers, Willi clomps around snapping the kinds of pictures you'd find in the dullest geography textbooks. Some grassed-over stop along the original Pony Express trail, lambs fattened for the State Fair, So-and-So's mansion, that Grecian Court House, this land-grant college, those cement silos.

Today—Saturday, October 12—in the town of Tabor Lodge (816 alt., 1,249 pop.), Willi passes half the morning taking pictures of buffalo troughs and a war memorial, then hikes back to the house in town where the team has rented a couple of rooms.

He shares the attic with Dave Nero and Studs Dillon. Their names make them sound like pulp-magazine writers, but in fact they are partnered-up playwrights working in the light-comedy mode. Nero is quick with the one-liners, Dillon is the plot man. Their plays, which have gone unproduced over the last several years, are set on the Philadelphia Main Line or in some Manhattan penthouse, worlds of money and pedigree Willi cannot imagine they know about firsthand. They resemble a couple of stew bums, dressing identically in dingy white dress shirts and cheap gray trousers. Dillon has a dead leg, wears a stirrup around his left elevator shoe that connects to a brace strapped to his calf. Maybe he had polio. Willi wonders about it but never asks. Early on he decided it was best not to get too chummy with his traveling companions. He doesn't have his new autobiography worked out enough that it could stand close scrutiny.

When he comes in this morning a little after ten, the superheated attic air is oppressive. Instantly Willi feels cranky. If this crazy unseasonable heat wave doesn't break soon . . .

Nero is pacing. Dillon sits at the typewriter.

"'. . . taken all of the bruises from that beast that I intend to,'" says Nero. "Hey Willi. Okay. 'Taken all of the bruises from that beast,' et cetera. And *then* she says, 'Metaphorically speaking, of course, darling.'"

Dillon stops typing. "I don't like it."

"You're mad! It's a guaranteed laugh!"

Willi lays his camera and paraphernalia on his cot, then changes into a clean shirt. Sits on a chair and reties his work boots. He is wearing dungarees rolled twice at the cuff. "I seen the car down in front," he says. "Be all right if I took her out for a couple hours?"

"You'll need a fill-up," says Dillon. "And get a receipt."

"Yeah, all right. See you guys later."

Nero says, "Willi—hold on. Before you go. Would Candace let herself be *actually* bruised?"

"Which one is Candace?" In the car (riding west, riding south, riding east, riding south, riding west, riding . . .), Nero and Dillon usually read new scenes out loud to Willi and the other two guys, Whitey Wolverton and Floyd Price. The former is a greeting-card poet, the latter a laid-off lecturer in sociology who also writes but rarely publishes English-style detective novels under the pen name Abigail Lyric. Everyone has agreed that *Never Too Tired* is a pretty good play. It's about soul mates, marriage, monogamy, adultery, and divorce. "Is Candace the ghost?" Willi asks.

"No, the actress!"

"Oh, she's pretty tough. Nah, the actress wouldn't let anybody *really* bruise her."

"Did you hear Willi, did you hear what he just said? Smart guy."

Dillon says, "All right. But somebody else says that same line, 'metaphorically speaking,' in the first act. I forget who."

"Amanda," says Willi.

"Amanda," says Dillon.

"Oh damn," says Nero.

Willi says, "See you guys later."

Outside it is hot as blazes, but driving with the windows rolled down he can at least catch a breeze. Bedraggled fields of stripped cornstalks press against both sides of the concrete highway. The occasional crossroads are marked with arrow-shaped signs: 7 miles to Parris, 10 miles to Tillerton, 14 miles to Smallville. Smallville! Right away Willi imagines an animated-cartoon village, everybody tiny, an elf with a high, chirpy voice. He'd be like Gulliver.

I'm losing my mind, he thinks.

Just beyond a bridge that spans a slow river comes Parris. It doesn't seem like it's even a town anymore—the few clapboard houses look abandoned—but when Willi sees a filling station on his left he steers off the road. He stops alongside of the two Perfection Gasoline pumps before noticing that both the office and garage bay windows are swirled over with glass wax. Out of business. His gas needle jiggles above empty. Maybe he should turn around and go back. But according to the last sign it's only a few miles to Tillerton. With any luck he can find a station open there. Willi is about to release the hand brake when he changes his mind, opens the door, and gets out. Here's as good a place as any to relieve himself.

He walks on around to the back of the small white building and waters the ground. As he rebuttons his fly, he glimpses a carport up a slight incline. It's slat-sided, decrepit, and jungled over with crispy vines, but there are gaps enough to glimpse an automobile parked inside. A DeSoto woodie, he discovers when he takes a closer look, the body filmed with powdery dirt, a headlamp shattered, and not much tread on the front tires. Once upon a time, though, it was a nice machine.

Willi's heart jumps when he comes back around to the front of the station and discovers a wide-shouldered older man standing in front of the government Ford, one foot braced on the fender. The man is dressed in overalls heavily spotted with grease. A yellow cigarette dangles from his bottom lip. One cheek is badly waffled with acne scars. His high bush of curly brown hair is shaped like a footballer's helmet.

The office door stands partly open now, and Willi has the feeling somebody's in there.

"I was hoping to get a fill-up," he says.

The curly-haired man stands there scowling. Then he tosses away his cigarette and points at the smeared windows. "Look open to you, mope?"

"Guess not." Willi decides to move again but stops when the man abruptly kicks the Ford's license plate with the heel of his shoe. "So you a guvmint man, are you?"

"Me?" Then he catches the reason for the question: impressed into the plate, right above the mix of letters and numbers, it reads: US GOVT. "Nah. I'm just taking some pictures for the WPA."

The man lifts his foot from the fender and sets it back down on the ground. "Pictures of what?"

"Whatever they tell me. But if you want I'll take a picture of you. Standing over there in front of your station. If you want."

"I don't want."

"Well, then I won't." Definitely somebody else is watching from inside the office; Willi registers a slight but distinct movement there, a shadow flicker, and it gives him the creeps. Time to boil. "Would you happen to know if there's a filling station in Tillerton?"

"Tillerton?"

"Isn't that the next town up the road?"

Elaborately offhanded, the man gives a shrug, which only makes Willi a little more nervous. He gets back under the wheel and slams the door. The man doesn't move. Willi pushes the ignition button, shifts into gear, fully intending to back out of there in another two seconds, but finally the man steps off to one side and lets the car pass.

Turns out, in Tillerton there is no filling station either, but at a milk-and-bread store Willi asks the counter woman if there's one in Smallville. She thinks there might be. Seems to recall there is. She looks groggy, unsteady in the store's damp heat. "Well, I'll give it a shot," says Willi. And if there isn't one, soon he'll be walking.

On the outskirts of Smallville, a Hooverville sprawls randomly in a scrub field. Most of the camps are constructed of blistered interior doors, but some are made well of planed boards or good logs and look fairly permanent. On an impulse Willi steers onto the grassy berm, stops the car, and sets the hand brake. Grabbing his camera, he walks back to the place that's called "Smallerville Pop. 147," according to a staked hand-painted sign, or "Smellville" according to another, cruder sign whitewashed on a tree and underscored with a blaze.

Near the roadside Willi sees a young fellow about his age wearing a cheap suit and writing in a nickel pad while he talks to a little colored girl at a lemonade stand (an upended wooden soda crate). She has pig-tails and wears a shapeless blue dress. A dinner plate across the top of her pitcher keeps out the bugs. There is a single Dixie cup.

"Got a thirst, mister?" she asks as Willi approaches.

"I guess." He nods to both the girl and the young guy in the suit.

While she carefully pours Willi a cup, he puts down his camera and pats his trouser pockets for coins. Then gives her a nickel.

"I don't got change."

"That's all right."

"You can have three drinks."

"One's plenty." You can say that again: it's sour and full of pits and stringy pulp. "Could I take your picture, honey?"

She beams, flattered to be asked.

"No, no, just be yourself," he says glancing over at the guy who steps back and watches, smiling. "You don't have to pose. What's your name, sweetheart?"

"Rose."

"That's pretty." Click, he takes her picture. Advances the film and, click, takes it again. "Is there a filling station close by? I'm sure hoping the answer is yes."

"About a mile ahead," says the young guy.

Willi nods his thanks, then strolls off into Smallerville. Behind him, he hears the guy says to Rose, "So that makes *how* many customers you've had today . . . ?"

Asking permission first but taking the scantest shrug as a yes, Willi photographs several old black men in Big Smith coveralls talking on rope-bottomed chairs; a woman offering her baby water in a Coca-Cola bottle that has a rubber nipple squeezed over the lip; and two young brothers who stare anxiously at his camera like it's a school-master with a hard question and a mean disposition. He also photo-graphs a mangy yellow dog that appears with a stick in its mouth, wanting to play.

At a trudging sound behind him, Willi turns his head.

It's that young guy in the cheap suit again, saying, "Hiya."

Willi nods.

"Would you mind my asking your name?"

"I might. Why?"

"I just . . ." He holds up his pad, waggles it. "I thought I could put it in the story I'm writing. If you don't mind."

"Story you're writing."

"I'm sorry," says the guy, "I'm Clark Kent. *Smallville Herald-Progress.*" When he flips his pad to a clean page, Willi laughs out loud.

"You really got your own newspaper in a dinky place like this?"

The guy's face turns red but he smiles, snapping his notebook shut like he's probably seen it done in the movies. "Thanks anyway," he says and walks away.

After lighting a cigarette, Willi calls after him: "Hey!" Running lithely, he catches up. "I didn't mean anything," he says falling into step beside Clark. "Was only a joke. So. You write for the paper?"

Clark glances at him but keeps going.

"So what're you writing, you writing about that little girl?"

Clark stops. "I'm writing about kids selling lemonade during this heat wave, she's just one of them."

"Oh. Hey. Interesting."

"No, it's not," says Clark, "but that's what I'm doing."

"They let you run stories about colored people in your paper? Must be pretty advanced little town you got here."

Clark's mouth moves fractionally, lips pushing out. For a moment it seems as though he might say something. But he doesn't. He starts walking again, heading for the highway.

"Wait! Hey, wait! I took a picture of that little girl—think your paper might be interested? Could run with your story."

"We don't run pictures."

"None?"

"Sometimes we run drawings, but nobody around here can draw too good, so it's mostly just stickmen."

"You serious?"

Clark laughs, hiking along the edge of the highway now.

"Jeez, I thought for a minute you were serious. Stickmen. That's pretty good." Willi watches him go. "Hey! You want a lift? I'm going into Smallville."

"No, that's all right."

"Come on, I'll give you a ride. What's your name again?"

"Clark."

"That your last name?"

"First. First name Clark, last name Kent."

"And I'm Willi . . . Boring."

Clark grins.

"Yeah, yeah, get in the car."

They go scarcely a hundred feet when the engine coughs and cuts off, and the sedan rolls slowly to a stop. Making a fist, Willi punches the steering wheel, then flings himself back against the seat.

"Want me to take a look under the hood?"

"Don't bother. I'm out of gas." He punches the wheel again, this time striking the horn, and it blows.

"The filling station's not a mile up the road."

"I don't have a gas can."

"What do you need that for? You steer, I'll push."

"Yeah, sure."

Walking around behind the car, Clark braces himself on his toes, stretches out his arms, palms against the trunk. "Ready?"

"Get off of it—you said a mile?"

"You *ready?*"

The Ford starts to roll . . .

"Enough," says Willi, "let's just—"

. . . and picks up speed.

Willi has to grip the wheel.

Especially once the sedan accelerates, the speedometer needle arcing steadily to the right: 15, 20, 25 . . .

As Clark gets ever smaller in the rearview mirror Willi hunches further over the wheel, clutching tighter. Taps on the brakes. Then tromps on them when he sees a Red Crown station coming up fast on the right.

The Ford rolls to a gradual stop beside one of the two round-topped pumps. Overhead a canopy stretches to the front door of the little glazed-brick office. Gas is nine cents a gallon, a penny more than it cost the other day in Lyndon.

Willi's hands drop to his lap. That, he thinks, didn't happen. Whatever just happened? Didn't.

"Fill 'er up?" A white-haired old man in gray shirt and trousers lifts the hose from a pump. At the same time he gives the side crank one half turn. "And check your oil?"

"Yeah. Please." Willi feels dazed. Sits there frowning while the attendant raises and braces the hood, reads the dipstick.

"You're okay for a while." Slam! He goes to check on the progress of the fill-up. And now: "Hiya, Clark, how's the boy?"

In disbelief Willi watches as Clark Kent comes scuffling off the road and, whistling tunelessly—being deliberately nonchalant, show-offy—heads for the car.

"Fine, Mr. Thayer—yourself?"

"Oh, I guess I'm doing all right. Say, Clark, that was a nice story you wrote there about Geraldine Natwin's birthday party."

"Why, thank you."

"Only thing, son, it was her *tenth* birthday, not her twelfth." Mr. Thayer hitches back the hose, replaces the gasoline cap, and tells Willi that'll be ninety-two cents.

Looking sullen, cheeks darkly pinked, Clark climbs into the passenger side and pulls the door closed. "Can we *go* now?" he asks Willi. Adding *"Please?"* when Mr. Thayer speaks to him again through Willi's open window, saying, "And you know that softball game at the Church of Christ . . . ?"

Willi drives.

"You want to tell me how you did that, Hercules?"

"I pushed you downhill, big deal."

"*What* downhill? What *hill?*"

2

Now that Jiggs Makley is dead and four of the other boys have headed off to Mexico, Ike—Curly Ike—Kelting is boss of what's left of the old gang: Milt George and Claude Draper, both of them, like Curly Ike, natives of Okfuskee County, Oklahoma.

Before the Depression Curly Ike worked as a cowboy and a wild-catter. He was married and raising three small children. He was a thirty-third-degree Mason. But after things went bust he was reduced to stealing just to feed his family. Well, and to enjoy a few small luxuries. Hunting rifles, ammunition, flabby girlfriends. It all worked pretty well, for a time. He would get word he'd be welcome to help rob this office or burgle that house and take away from each job at least twenty bucks.

Then Jiggs Makley passed through town. They met one day at a ranch where Curly Ike was rustling a few head of beef cattle, and Makley invited him to join his gang. It seemed a good deal. Two months on the road robbing banks, three months at home enjoying life. Regular work.

Unfortunately at his first bank job, in Pawnee, Curly Ike was identified by someone in a teller's line who used to live several houses away from Ike when they were both kids. If only Ike had noticed *him!* He could've shot the bum and continued on the way he'd been. But no, suddenly Curly Ike was a wanted man (with his own wanted poster!) and he stopped going home. *Had* to. For a while he regularly mailed his family envelopes full of cash. Eventually, though, he convinced himself that his wife had taken up with someone else, and he quit sending money.

He left home for the last time in late March of 1932. More than three years ago. He's tired now and near broke, and his right shoulder is a constant agony: he was shot there ten months ago robbing a bank in West Plains, Missouri. The bullet just ruined the muscles.

Soon as he has a decent stake, a few thousand bucks, Curly Ike plans to move to Canada, Toronto maybe. Rent an apartment, find a big soft woman, and start life over again.

He is looking forward to Canada so badly that whenever he thinks of it and about how many things can go wrong so he'll never get there, his belly seizes up like he has a bad appendix.

Right now in Smallville, Curly Ike is suffering that kind of agony. He sits behind the wheel of a silver-green and dark-green eight-passenger Cadillac Fleetwood limousine parked up the street from the white clapboard Church of Christ. He's wearing a chauffeur's cap but not the complete livery. That would have been too much of a production. Overalls will do.

Twenty minutes ago Curly Ike, Milt, and Claude staged an automobile breakdown near the corner of Maple Street and North Watkins. When the Poore family's chauffeur got out to help, Claude knocked off the dummy's cap, as he'd been told to, and shot him twice in the brain. After they dragged his body into some hedges, Curly Ike drove the limousine to the church. Claude and Milt followed in the gang's last remaining vehicle, a 1931 DeSoto woodie.

It is almost two o'clock, and within a few minutes the little Poore snot should be leaving Bible school, conducted in the basement of the church meeting hall.

Time for a quick smoke? Probably not.

Already some children are heading his way along the sidewalk.

Curly Ike lurches from the limo and runs around the hood, pulls open the rear curbside door. Then he tears back and gets behind the wheel again. He hopes Claude and Milt are paying attention. Posted near the church's bulletin board, they are both pretending to read the daily worship times and the title of the upcoming Sunday sermon: "Manna From Heaven . . . Or A Comet?" Curly Ike wonders what the hell *that's* all about—manna from a comet. He has an abiding interest in religion, Ike does, especially miracles.

He hopes he doesn't need one today.

Here comes the kid.

Curly Ike averts his face, turning it toward the street so Donny won't notice he isn't the regular driver. The privacy window is up between the front and the rear with the curtain drawn. Ike can't see what's happening back there, but the car lists suddenly to the right— someone climbing in—and now the door slams shut. And here's Claude hunched down and peering through the passenger-side front window while he thumps twice on the roof. The kid is inside, and Milt is too.

Curly Ike pulls out of his parking space and drives slowly to the corner where a Bible-school teacher is acting as crossing guard. A dozen children walk slowly in single file in front of the Cadillac. He breathes with relief when the woman waves him through.

As the car is rolling past her, the privacy window bursts into pieces. He knew it! He just *knew* this wasn't going to go smoothly.

"Milt?"

"He *bit* me!"

"Put him under!"

"I'm trying to!"

For the next half minute there is a lot of thumping and terrified screeching back there. Then abruptly it gets quiet.

"Milt?"

"I'm bleeding all over the place!" He puts his face near the broken glass. Ike glances at him, then back at the road. Milt's cheeks are raw with long red scratches.

"But he's out now?"

"Cold."

"Make sure you put the cap back on the chloroform."

"Okeydokey, Ma."

Two miles beyond Smallerville, Curly Ike steers the limousine into a belt of trees they selected as their rendezvous. Claude drives up a minute later, and he and Milt drag Donny Poore, limp and anesthetized, from the limousine. They dump him into the DeSoto's trunk. Last night they drilled air holes in it.

"All set?" says Curly Ike, now behind the wheel of the DeSoto.

"That went okay," says Claude.

"Easy for you to talk," says Milt. "I'm all scratched up. Look at me! If I was that kid's daddy, I wouldn't pay no ransom."

"Well, you're not his daddy," says Curly Ike.

3

"Hello?"

"It's me."

"Oh my God—Willi!"

He pulls shut the bifold door of a telephone booth on the corner of North Main and Schaffenberger streets.

"You okay?"

"Yeah, I'm fine. What's going on there?"

"My classes are all pretty good, but you wouldn't *believe* how much work I have—"

"Dammit, Lo, I mean *what's going on?*"

"Well, there's nothing about *you* anymore in the paper if that's what you mean."

"That's what I mean. And don't get snippy. How would *you* like driving around Kansas?"

"That cop you know came by to see me. Twice."

"Dick Sandglass?"

"He said if I was ever to hear from you, I should tell you to call him. I think he wants to help."

"Oh, sure. And what's going on with our favorite alderman?"

"I don't know, but Lucky Luciano's in jail, and Meyer Lansky and Benny Siegel both took off for California."

"I'm sunk!"

"Just hold on tight, honey. It'll work out. I promise. Hey, where are you calling from?"

"Lois, I should go."

"Write? Please? Once in a while?"

"What if the cops are checking your mail?"

"Then send it to General Delivery."

"Okay," says Willi, "I'll try."

"I miss you."

Willi says, "Yeah, me too," and prongs the receiver.

Stepping from the booth, he looks up and down the street. Which way? Does it matter? He starts to walk. After a few minutes Willi spots that same kid again—Clark something—that he gave a lift. He's coming out of a storefront—ah, the venerable *Herald-Progress*. Hailing him, Willi trots over. "Hey, let me ask you a question. Anything interesting I should take a picture of here in town?"

Clark thinks. "We got a pretty impressive town hall."

"Yowsah," says Willi, and rolls up his eyes.

When he rolls them down again, Clark is gone.

Solid gone.

If he were the type to scratch his head, Willi would be scratching it now.

What's *with* that guy?

With a shrug, he starts back to where he parked the car (he's already decided to pass on the "impressive town hall") when a Smallville police car pulls over to the curb.

His impulse is to cut and run, but he doesn't. You're Willi Boring. You work for the WPA. It says so in your wallet.

Nevertheless he is immediately handcuffed and placed under arrest, shoved roughly into the back of the cruiser, and driven straight to the city jail.

4

From the holding cell where he stands at the steel bars, Willi can look directly across the muster room at a batch of wanted posters pinned sloppily to a bulletin board. And his—Willi Berg's—is among them. If he squints he can read his alleged felonies (Murder, Burglary, Interstate Flight) and see the two small mug shots but not whatever is printed below. Does it say that he's armed and dangerous? Urge extreme caution? God, this is torture! Torture that one or another of Smallville's finest—thankfully, there aren't many here right now—might happen to glance at the poster, and torture as well that his vital and criminal statistics are out of reading range. He *always* read about himself in the New York papers, which stoked both his vanity and his outrage. But he has to be careful no one catches him now, peering at those wanted posters. So it's a relief when the other WPA guys are all marched into the Smallville police station and locked up along with him. "Hey, it's the rest of my kidnapping gang," says Willi.

Nobody thinks that's funny.

After a while he is gladly distracted by the poker game Nero suggests. They wager with cigarettes, Life Savers, and sticks of chewing gum.

Willi keeps losing.

It is almost five o'clock.

Two federal agents in gray fedoras and dark suits bustle in, followed no more than ten minutes later by a large man in a white cowboy hat and wearing a western-style lawman's star. Sheriff Dutcher, Willi hears one of the deputies call him. The sheriff! And a couple of G-men. It's like two kinds of Saturday-matinee movies colliding before Willi's eyes. Which is almost funny except that the more police that fill up the place, the more anxious he becomes.

When he realizes that he's staring at those wanted posters again, he shakes his head, looks down at his cards—another dismal hand—and folds.

"Say, you can't gamble in there!" It's one of the townie cops that arrested Willi because he was a stranger and so probably a career kidnapper. He's standing at the cell door barking at the card players. "Hand over the deck."

"Surely you jest," says Whitey Wolverton. "First you lock us up for no good reason, then you treat us like we're in a girls' school?"

"Give," says the townie cop snapping his fingers.

Everybody throws down their cards, and Floyd Price gathers them all up and decks them.

"Let the boys play, for pete's sake." One of the FBI agents. "You people here. No wonder you're still a dry state."

"That's our business," says the cop.

"You're right, it is." The G-man looks at Floyd. "Give him the cards."

Floyd passes the deck through the bars.

"You boys WPA?" says the G-man. "That what I heard?"

Everyone says yes, WPA. Eager to display their common federal origins.

"Ah, don't worry, nobody thinks you done anything. We're pretty sure who took the kid."

"Yeah?" says Willi. "Who?"

But the G-man doesn't reply. Instead he locks his attention on Willi's face, staring so intently that Willi begins to fidget.

"Do I know you?"

"I don't think so," says Willi. His voice doesn't wobble—does it?

The agent slowly rubs his jaw. "New York?"

"Jersey," says Willi. "Hoboken."

"You look familiar."

"Nah."

"Ah, give it up, kid," says Studs Dillon, "it's all over." Cupping a hand around one side of his mouth, he pretends to speak confidentially. "You got him, G-man, this is Machine Gun Boring, public enemy number nine."

And now it's like all the atoms of Willi's body are fizzing off into space, it's like he's dissolving. But everybody laughs, so he does too.

"That must be it," says the federal, then he raps on the bars with his wedding band—shave-and-a-haircut-two-bits—and walks away. He joins his colleague in conversation with the sheriff. The three of them stand only a few feet away from the wanted posters but with their backs to them.

"Why'd you say that?" says Willi turning on Dillon.

"It was just a crack."

"Yeah, well, keep your stupid cracks to yourself."

5

By six o'clock both the Cadillac limousine and the dead chauffeur have been located, miles apart, and F. O. Poore the banker has received two telephone calls from the kidnappers. The first announcing the fact of his son's abduction, the other setting the ransom at twenty-five thousand dollars in cash. Between the time he parks his father's truck and walks a block to the police station in the early-evening light, Clark hears the same news at least five separate times from small groups clustered on sidewalks and lawns.

The murdered chauffeur's name was Pete Santella. No, it was *Louis.* Louis Santella. No, it wasn't either, it was Pete, Pete *Santo.* Whatever his name was, nobody ever met him. *Seen* him a few times. Driving around. Filipino, supposedly. Poor little flip. And Donny! Donny Poore! Good kid. Bit of a scamp, though. Think he's dead? *Hope* not. Think he *is?* Clark knows most of the people, but when he realizes the ones he doesn't are probably out-of-town newspapermen, he feels an aggressive, proprietary quickening through his chest. Digging out his press ID, he pushes his way up the steps to the police station. They'd better let him in! He is ready to argue. That proves unnecessary. The officer posted at the door turns out to be Janey Laster's older brother Merle.

"Hiya, Clark," he says. "How you been?"

"Pretty good, Merle. And hey, congratulations on your engagement."

"Thank you kindly. Was it you wrote up that announcement in the paper? Nice job."

"Appreciate that."

"But Amy don't work at that seed company no more like you put, she's over at Peterson's nursery these days."

"'Scuse me, Merle," says Clark squeezing past him.

The station house is mobbed and noisy—telephones ringing, fans buzzing on file cabinets, everybody talking—and he can't find the chief. But he does spot Willi Boring looking pale and wretched inside a holding cell with several other men.

"Get us out of here, Clark, can you?"

"What are you doing in there?"

"Your Keystone Kops arrested everybody they didn't recognize. And now they forgot about us!" Willi's eyes dart left and right, then focus on something. When Clark turns to see what, all he sees are a bunch of uniformed cops and two men in dark suits and blue ties and a cork bulletin board covered in wanted posters.

"I'll see what I can do," says Clark. But he has no intention of doing anything. What can *he* do? And why should he even *try* to help that patronizing city slicker?

With his notepad in his back pocket and a pencil in his left hand (he really ought to get a pen, but the cheapest you can buy costs a buck and they tend to leak), he wanders around, excusing himself to cop after cop, pardoning-me to the vice-mayor and a selectman, clearing his throat beside the young town attorney huddled in conversation with the Poore family's gray-haired lawyer. But nobody will speak with him on or off the record. He feels scorned and clumsy. And not sure what he's supposed to do.

Yet again Clark wishes he were smarter, lots smarter, that his polish was as marvelous as his body's capacity to perform. He's no dope, he knows that, but neither is he anything special in the brains department. He wishes he were smarter, had a better vocabulary, didn't mispronounce words and use bad grammar, and he wishes above all else that he knew how to *be* in the world, that it came as easily as running.

It's seven o'clock. It's ten past. Half past.

There is an electric percolator on a small table, and he goes over there and pours himself a half cup. Drops in three cubes of sugar.

It's twenty of eight.

It's five till.

"Clark." Sheriff Dutcher is standing next to him now fixing coffee, blowing across the surface, taking a sip. "How've you been, son?"

"Fine, sir, thank you." Then he feels compelled to explain: "I'm working for the newspaper now. Part-time. That's why I'm here."

"Well, good for you. Good for you."

"So . . . is there anything you can tell me, Sheriff?"

"Probably not. You understand."

"Yes, sir."

"But if I *could,* I might tell you there's a good chance we're looking for a 1931 or '32 DeSoto woodie with a busted headlamp."

Clark is so astonished—he's *talking* to me!—that it takes the sheriff's prompting gesture, an index finger flicked toward his notebook, to realize that he should probably write it down. "Thirty-two or '33?"

"Thirty-one or '32."

"Right." He scribbles. DeSoto. Do you spell *woodie* with a "y" or an "i-e"? Clarks spells it with a "y." "Thank you, Sheriff."

"For what?" Dutcher drains his cup, then half turns away, burying a yawn in his shoulder. "Excuse *me,*" he tells Clark. But tired as he may be, the sheriff is alert again the moment two federal men step out of the police chief's office. He watches one collect his hat and duck out by a side door while the other—slight, pale, and fussy-looking—struts this way across the station house. "Agent Foley," says Dutcher.

Clark can tell Foley would just as soon keep walking. But with the briefest tightening of his mouth, he comes over. "Sheriff."

"Excuse me again, Clark," Dutcher says and moves away with Foley.

Speaking together, they both lower their voices.

But to Clark they might just as well be a pair of console radios with the volume knobs turned all the way to the right.

"We'll be taking the kid's father back to his office in a couple of minutes," Foley tells Dutcher. "To wait for the call."

"Just let me know, I'll head on over there with you."

"That won't be necessary, sheriff."

"Oh no?" says Dutcher. "And why is that?"

"Because it won't." Foley comes back to where Clark is still loitering, glances at him, glances away, and picks up the electric percolator. Shakes it. Making a disgusted face, he pours the last sludgy drips into a cup.

It is six minutes past eight.

Here's what happens before it is seven past.

Foley swallows his mouthful of coffee and rubs the back of a hand across his lips. Then, raising his eyes, he looks straight ahead at a wanted poster pinned to the corkboard.

Foley's heartbeat sounds to Clark like a baseball card clothespinned to a bicycle spoke, the bike flashing down a hill.

Clark looks up at the same poster.

Murder, Burglary, and Interstate Flight.

"Son of a bitch!" says Foley. "I *knew* I'd seen that guy's face!"

Dutcher says, "What guy?"

"*That* guy!" says Foley, turning and pointing to Willi in the cell across the room. "Look," he says turning back to the corkboard.

"At what?"

"You blind?" says Foley, and tap-taps the wanted poster with an index finger. Tapping till he says, "What the *hell?*" And freezes with his fingertip pressed to the mug shot of a Negro male with a shaved head and a thick mustache, Edward Thomas Burt, 45, 6′2″, 230 to 250 pounds, occupation truck driver, wanted for theft of government property. "But I saw it! It was right here."

Dutcher cranes an eyebrow.

Foley randomly skips his glance from flyer to flyer. "I saw it," he says. But very quietly.

It is now seven minutes past eight.

Without another word Agent Foley walks away, past the muster desk, out through the front door.

Dutcher shakes his head. After he is unable to suppress a grin, he winks at Clark. And strolls off, a man with nothing at the moment he can think of to do.

Willi is standing with his arms stretched up and his hands gripping the bars of his cell. Face clammy white as new butter.

Clark won't look at him.

At eight minutes past eight Clark opens his left fist and stuffs the crumpled wanted poster into his back pocket behind his reporter's notebook.

A DeSoto woodie. In the heart abides the truth.
Curly Ike tries to make a telephone call. Collision course.

———

1

"So they let you go, did they?"

"Finally."

"Where're your friends?"

"*Who?*"

"Those other men in the cell?"

"Oh. They're just guys I work with. They took the car and went home. But I thought I'd stick around, might be some good picture taking later. If anything happens."

Clark hasn't bothered looking up from his typewriter since Willi Boring walked into the newspaper office two minutes ago and found him at his desk. Now he asks, "What are you doing here?"

"Thought I might go buy a hamburger sandwich. Split it with you?"

"No place you can buy a burger this time of night. Not in a dinky little hick town like *this.*"

"What's the matter, you mad or something?"

"We're putting out a special edition. So if you don't mind . . . ?"

Across the room Newell Timmins has stopped reading proofs and is looking this way.

Willi says, "Okay, I just thought . . ."

"So long, take care, sayonara."

"Hey, what's with the cold shoulder?"

Clark reaches and picks up his notebook, holds it in front of his face, and scowls at his miserable scrawl. A dozen years of doing Palmer exercises, all of those margin-to-margin loops, swirls, zigzags, and ellipses, and he *still* can't read his own stupid handwriting half an hour after he wrote it. A '31 or '32 Dodge *what? Dodge?* Willi grabs the notebook from his hand, leans down close, and whispers in his ear, "What happened to that wanted poster?"

Clark snatches back his notebook, plonks it down beside him. "What are you talking about?" He drops his left pinky on the A key, lets his other fingers automatically find their proper places along the keyboard, then types, "Police are searching for a 1931 or 1932 Dodge woody they belie—" But he breaks off to say, "You wanted to get out of jail, you got out of jail. So now don't you think you should get out of town?"

"*You* took it. Didn't you?"

"Took *what?*"

"Hey! Clark, how's it coming over there, son? I'll need your copy in twenty minutes."

"You'll have it, Mr. Timmins." He turns to Willi. "You'd better leave."

"How'd you take it down?"

"I just did."

"Why?"

Clark shrugs: he doesn't know.

Willi leans over again, whispers, "I didn't do any of that stuff, Clark."

"So how come you're on a wanted poster?"

"Clark! We have a paper to get out. I'm going to have to ask your friend to leave."

"Clark's friend is leaving right now," says Willi speaking to Newell Timmins while looking at Clark. But now he looks past him at the copy paper rolled in the big Underwood typewriter and his eyes widen. "You sure it's a *Dodge* woodie? Not a *DeSoto?*"

For a moment Clark's brain goes blank—*what?* He grabs up his notepad, squints at his chicken scratch, and Willi says, "By the way? You spelled *woodie* wrong."

2

Ten minutes later.

"So you're just going to walk in there and tell them where to find that car? Then what? Just wait for them to come back and tell you what happened?"

"I expect I'll go with them."

"You expect that, do you? Think they'll invite you along? Oh, and here's a gun for you, Clark, just in case?"

They are sitting in the cab of Clark's truck, parked within sight of the police station. It is half past ten, street lamps are on, and a handful of people are still hanging around outside.

"I'm wasting time, Willi." Clark opens his door. "There's a little boy's been kidnapped."

"I know that. Just thought you might want to be a real honest-to-God reporter, that's all."

"You're a pain in the ass."

"Newsman worth his salt, he'd just phone in what he knows, then make for damn sure he was at that filling station with a front-row seat when the cops come charging up."

Clark slams the door behind him. "If you're not coming in with me I'll see you later." He checks for traffic before starting across Central Street on a diagonal.

"Clark!" Willi leans across the seat. "You can't say how you found out."

"Don't worry about it."

"Clark!"

"*What?*"

"I may be a pain in the ass but I never killed anybody."

Clark gives him a slight and placid nod but knows now—from

Willi's unchanging heart rhythm, its steady beat—that it's true: Willi Boring ... *Berg* ... never killed anybody.

And is that ever a big relief!

He *likes* this smart aleck, a lot, although *why* he does ...

He digs out the crumpled wanted poster from his back pocket and lobs it underhand through the truck window. "I'd eat that," he says, "if I were you."

Crossing the street, Clark tells Merle Laster, still manning the front door, that he has to see Chief Parker, it's important. Really, really important. But the chief isn't there, he's still over at the Smallville Bank waiting on a telephone call. "Merle, listen up," he says, but then spotting Sheriff Dutcher on the telephone he races past the deputy and halfway across the station house.

Dutcher's conversation abruptly ends when a spot along the telephone cord smokes suddenly and out pops a little flame.

Clark just hates doing that thing with his eyes, it makes them feel so *gummy*.

But this is an emergency.

It is exactly ten minutes before eleven when Sheriff Dutcher jumps into his county car, giving Clark firm, clear instructions to run right back and tell Merle Laster what he has just told him about that filling station in Parris, the one near that little bridge over the Sin River.

"But can't I come with you?"

"Clark—do as I say, boy."

It is not until the sheriff's car has peeled off, spraying gravel behind, that Clark looks across the street and discovers that his father's truck, and Willi Berg, are gone too.

3

A short-barrel defensive revolver is lying on the car seat next to Curly Ike, and he swears to God if he can't find a telephone booth in the next ten minutes, the next five minutes, he is going to pick it up and shoot himself. See if he doesn't.

Flecked with bits of gravel, the palms of his hands sting like blue blazes, and his right shoulder where that bank guard in West Plains shot him last December is throbbing again—all thanks to a nasty spill taken earlier tonight from a chain-link fence. And his stomach feels like it's full of cancer and broken glass. *I shoulda stuck to banks.*

Since eight-thirty, Curly Ike has been prowling the countryside and one dark hick town after another in the gang's big DeSoto. He expected to be gone no longer than an hour—he could trust Milt and Claude to watch the kid for that long, *hoped* he could, but here it is after ten! What kind of kidnapper can't find a public telephone?

In the late afternoon, Curly Ike had driven from Parris to Ozeana, seventeen miles, and used the phone in a drugstore there to call Donny Poore's father at the Smallville Bank. (Oh sweet Jesus, it's *Saturday!* He won't be there! He was there.) The call took scarcely half a minute (we have your son, we'll be in touch, don't contact the police). After he hung up, his nickel dropped—providentially, Ike thought—back into the coin return. He scooped it up and put it in his shirt pocket, then used it again an hour later when he called F. H. Poore the second time, from a phone booth just inside the main gates of a cement factory in Wisdom. Your boy is fine—so far. You want him back, it'll cost you twenty-five grand, in fives, tens, and twenties. Old bills. No cops. No feds. No funny business. We'll be in touch again tonight. Nine sharp. Have the money ready and a car gassed up to go. You're driving, Dad. And no riders. Click.

That time Curly Ike was on the wire for nearly a minute. Longer than he'd liked. And the damn phone kept his lucky nickel.

Still, everything was hitting on all six.

Kidnapping wasn't so bad after all. He was beginning to see its beauty.

Returning to the service station in Parris shortly after five with a few groceries (Lorna Doones, Goo Goo Clusters, Pepsi-Cola, and 7-Up), Curly Ike checked on the boy. Down in a mechanic's grease pit, he was still gagged and trussed up and struggling like some wild animal.

Claude and Milt were antsy, edgy, eager to get this all over with, pocket their heavy sugar and move on. So was Curly Ike. Canada, he kept thinking. By Tuesday. They sat around eating cookies and candy and drinking soda pop till it was time for Curly Ike to go back out and make his third and last telephone call.

That's when things got all balled up.

He was almost to Ozeana when he realized he'd forgotten to take along the sheet of paper with the drop-off instructions. And he'd spent half the day yesterday motoring around the county, meticulously jotting down left-hand turns and right-hand turns, making sure that country road numbers were correct, checking the odometer, citing landmarks (". . . nine-tenths of a mile past the Fisk Tires sign, you'll come to the Green Bottle tourist court . . ."), and *then* what happens! He forgets the damn piece of paper! It was too late to turn around and go back, so Ike decided to dispense with the winding route he'd so cleverly mapped out for F. H. Poore and just tell the banker his final destination: Pampa Lake Reservoir. On the phone he'd just say drive to the Pampa Lake Reservoir and throw the bag over the fence at the gate nearest the pump house, then turn around and get back into your car and go home.

Originally, the idea was to predetermine Poore's route so that Ike and Milt and Claude could intercept him on the way, thereby removing any possibility the cops or the feds might get to the reservoir first and set a trap. But what the hell. Life was full of risks, no matter what you did.

Damn, though!

As if that wasn't bad enough, when Ike got to the Rexall drugstore in Ozeana, it was closed for the night—he hadn't thought about that! He stood at the front door shaking the knob, peering inside. Twenty paces to the pay phone, but it might just as well be on the moon! It was full dark by then, and Curly Ike didn't see anyone on the street (the café directly opposite was also closed), so he balled a fist and gave a short chop to the glass. Even before he could reach inside to unlock the door, an alarm clanged. At first, Ike was stunned immobile. A burglar alarm—*here?* Who could afford a burglar alarm in a pissant place like this?

Back in the DeSoto and leaving town, he heard a police siren and cut the wheel sharply, turning into what he expected would be an alley that passed straight across to a parallel street. Turned out, it ended twenty yards ahead at a broad-plank fence. Stupid, stupid, stupid! And if those cops had seen him hang that left it would be all over now for Ike Kelting and his criminal career. But they hadn't—their car shot past the mouth of the alley and kept going.

Ike's stomach was clenching and spasming by the time he backed out the DeSoto and headed for Wisdom, ten, twelve miles cross-country.

By the time he arrived at the cement factory it was five minutes past nine and already the caper was off schedule: he'd told Poore he would call at nine sharp.

The cement factory was also closed, the fence gate wrapped with a chain secured by a padlock, but at least the telephone booth was outside. And if Curly Ike couldn't climb a ten-foot fence—him, a guy who'd rode steers for fun and clambered up and down oil rigs—then he should just pack it in. But he failed to remember his bad arm, and by the time he was halfway to the top, he was gritting his teeth, wincing in agony.

Then came the watch dogs, a pack of mastiffs, running from around behind the factory, barking explosively, their legs kicking up puffs of the white cement powder that covered the ground. They leapt, hitting and bouncing off the chain link, working themselves into a murderous frothing rage. Ike hung on, but then one of the animals jumped high enough to snap at the toe of his shoe as it poked through one of the diamond chinks. Instinct hurled him away, and he landed hard on his coccyx, scraping his palms raw.

On the other side of the fence, the dogs continued to hit and bounce, hit and bounce.

He thought about shooting them, every single one of them, but finally just limped back to his car, threw himself in, and drove off.

All he needed was a stupid public phone! That's all! Why was this happening to him?

It was twenty-five past nine when Curly Ike got to Somerset, due east of Temple and a place he'd never been before. He drove slowly around, looking for a pay phone. At the end of the shuttered business district, he spotted a lighted booth next to a stucco building occupied by a motor company selling Ford and Hudson-Essex cars. At the moment, the booth was enveloped by a group of high-school-aged boys horsing around while one of their friends talked on the phone. Ike parked at the curb and waited. They all noticed him, of course. He looked at his wristwatch. Nine-thirty-five. Nine-forty. He glared at the boy in overalls who was still inside the booth, still jabbering on the telephone. Ike decided to drive around and come back. How long could they stay? But if they were still there when he returned, he'd chase them. Even brandish his gun if he had to!

Soon he found himself driving through residential neighborhoods, completely lost. He kept passing the same boxy little houses, or perhaps they all just looked the same. When he finally got back "downtown" and to the motor company, another half an hour had passed. But at least the kids were gone! He dug out a nickel and trotted to the phone booth, pulled open the bifold door—then froze. Not only had those damn delinquents pried open the money slot and looted the phone, they'd torn the earpiece off the box! There it was, down on the floor. He picked it up, held it like a club, and whacked the horizontal coin shelf till it was vertical.

In the town of Reedville, four miles from Somerset, he found another booth, only to have it take his nickel, sound a gong, and go dead.

That's when Curly Ike gave himself five more minutes, five minutes and not a second more.

Either he finds another phone, one that works, in five damn minutes or he is going to blow off his own head.

He has turned the car around and is heading back in the direction of Tabor Lodge, Parris, Tillerton, and Smallville, driving on a two-lane concrete road past fields bristling with cornstalks. Clouds move away from the moon and—providentially, Ike thinks—silver a telephone pole about twenty yards ahead on the left. Now it dawns on him: why does it have to be a *public* telephone? Easing his foot off the gas, Ike lets the DeSoto come slowly to a stop. After setting the hand brake he climbs out.

With his eyes, he follows the telephone wire from the pole to a farmhouse with lighted windows up a curving dirt access road. A single RFD mailbox sits atop a short pole, the only such mailbox in either direction as far as Ike can see.

There is also a little wooden sign shaped like a parchment scroll that says in fancy script: "Clara's Creations."

Ike drives up to the house.

In the yard is a weird hodgepodge of functional pottery—bowls, cups, vases, and plates set out on planks straddling sawhorses—and dozens of three- and four-foot-high ceramic sculptures carelessly glazed. Dutch windmills. Log cabins. A fairy-tale castle. Charlie Chaplin as the Little Tramp. Felix the Cat on a Grecian pedestal. Will Rogers swinging a lariat. Underneath a lean-to at the far side of the front porch stands a potter's kick wheel. Beyond that, a kiln.

Curly Ike sits in the DeSoto, mesmerized. That Will Rogers is pretty good. Chaps and all. And he especially likes how the lariat is frozen midair in a big loop. Look at that! He can't imagine how you'd *make* such a thing.

A white-haired and bearded man, bearded like Santa Claus, comes out of the house and stands at the top of the steps with his hands in his dungaree pockets. Ike gets out of the car.

"Why don't you come back tomorrow when you can see better?" says the old man.

See better? Ike doesn't know what the guy's talking about. "I see fine."

"I thought you were here to take a look at my wife's pottery."

"Nah. I need to use your phone."

The old man removes his hands from his pockets. "You got some kind of emergency?"

"Could say that, yeah." Ike sticks his arm straight out so that Santa Claus can see the gun.

The old man takes a few steps back from the edge of the porch. Ike comes rapidly up the steps. "Just show me where your phone is, grampy. And don't tell me you don't got one. I seen the wire."

"We got one, we got one." He raises his hands like outlaws do in Harry Carey oaters. "It's right in the parlor."

"Show me."

The telephone rests in a semicircular niche built into the wall, and Ike is surprised to find it is one of those new-style models he's seen only in Kansas City—a sleek and chunky metal body with a Bakelite receiver. It comes with a side crank *and* a rotary dial. Finally, some luck! He doesn't have to go through Central. He can dial the bank himself.

"Stand over there, where I can keep an eye on you," says Ike. After he points to the upright piano and the old man does as he's told, Ike sets his revolver down on the shelf next to the telephone.

He's memorized F. H. Poore's number. Which is another lucky thing, since the number was written on the same piece of paper he left behind in Parris.

But as soon as he lifts the receiver, Ike can hear voices on the wire, one saying, ". . . laugh to split a gut," and the other saying back, "Uh-huh, uh-huh, oh, that Sapphire's some battle-ax, uh-huh!"

"Ladies," says Curly Ike, "get off the line."

"Who's that? Who's talkin'? Where's your manners?"

"Why should we?"

"Ladies, please, this is an emergency."

"Says who?"

"Says the police, that's who," says Ike. "And if you don't want me taking down your names . . ."

There are two clicks on the party line.

As he is dialing at last, something, maybe God, causes him to glance over at the old man in time to see his eyes widen. Dropping the phone, Ike grabs up his gun, spins around, and she is almost on him—a gaunt gray-haired woman moving swiftly, both arms up, elbows bent and jutting, a footed urn that must weigh twenty pounds raised above her head.

She lets it fly the same instant he shoots her in the cheek.

The urn misses Ike, explodes against the papered wall. The woman staggers but doesn't go down. She whips her head from side to side as if to clear it, then spits out blood, bits of teeth, a piece of her tongue, and the bullet. The sight of that fills Ike with such bright terror that his trigger finger instinctively flexes two, three, four more times. Her eye, her throat, her breast, her arm. Blue smoke churns in the parlor, especially above the lampshades. Ike is breathing hard. Then his feet lift off the floor and he's choking.

The old man's arm, wrapped around Ike's throat, squeezes his windpipe so tightly that his eyes pop. The air in front of him wriggles with sizzling threads of black and magenta.

Like he's trying to find a stud in a wall, Ike reaches behind him and pokes with the gun barrel till he's sure it's pressed up against the old man's side in between ribs. Then he pulls the trigger.

Nothing happens.

Ike is about to lose consciousness.

If the gun is empty he's finished.

But if it was a misfire, which isn't out of the question, the revolver being a piece of junk made in France by frogs . . .

The gun goes off, the flash bright, its report muffled. The old man shudders. His forearm drops away from Ike's throat as he topples backward over a piecrust table.

Collapsing onto the piano bench, Ike draws a long breath and exhales.

Would you just *look* at this mess!

Returning to the telephone, he picks up the receiver, jabs his index finger toward the rotary dial—and for the life of him can no longer remember the bank's exchange. He's just too rattled. So he uses the side crank to call Central, who asks, "Number, please?" and Ike says he doesn't *know* the number but he wants the Smallville Bank.

"I can't understand you, sir. Could you repeat that?"

The Smallville Bank, dammit, the Smallville *Bank!*

"Sir, I'm very sorry but I still can't understand you."

Of course she can't: words are not coming out of Curly Ike's mouth, *croaks* are.

That old bastard damaged his larynx!

The Smallville Bank. The Smallville Bank! The Smallville Bank!

Central disconnects.

Slumping against the wall, Ike tips his head back and gazes at the ceiling.

Somewhere a clock chimes and he counts along: eleven.

Out on the porch he leans over, places both hands flat on his thighs, and takes another deep breath. Another. By the time he straightens up he is sure of two things. That he isn't going to get any part of twenty-five thousand dollars or ever make it to Canada.

Beyond that he isn't sure of anything.

No. No, he *is*, he is sure of *three* things.

He is sure that he has to have that ceramic Will Rogers, *has* to, it's just too good to leave behind.

So he hefts it off the grass, lugs it to the woodie, and loads it in, setting it right down on the front seat beside him.

Nosing the big car down the dirt road, Curly Ike turns right on the two-lane and heads back to Parris . . .

He wonders if Milt and Claude will shoot him.

But how could they shoot him? He's the boss. You can't shoot the boss.

They might.

The drive back from the potter's house to the failed Perfection Gasoline station seems to take no time whatsoever. When Curly Ike sees the sign announcing the Parris town limits he flinches as if surfacing from a dream, the kind that's instantly and utterly gone. It spooks him for a second. He could have had an accident. But then looking over at Will Rogers propped on the seat, Ike laughs, feeling a bubble of joy burst in his chest. That is some beautiful piece of art, that is.

But remembering he shot the woman who made it, shot her not just once but five times, his joy all but vanishes. She was going to brain me, what *else* could I do? Still. He's not just an outlaw, he thinks, he's not just a bad man, he's a *bad* man. But how did that *happen?* Look at old Will Rogers there. Did you ever see such tears when the poor guy died? Everybody loved him. *I* loved him. But you know something? I could've *been* him! I could've. Me and him both were Oklahoma born, born the very same year, 1879. Both of us worked the longhorns, threw the lariat. But he turns out the hero and I turn out the bad man. Why do things happen like they do? How does it work? It's like—it's like that Bible story, it's like Moses. No, listen. His old lady puts him in a basket, sends him floating down the Nile River, and then what? The Pharaoh's daughter finds him in some reeds, plucks him out, and takes him home. Look what I found, Daddy! Great for Moses. Good for him. But what'd he *do* to deserve it? Another mother just as nice could've put *her* little baby boy in the same kind of basket, exact same day, gave it a little shove, let it drift, and twenty minutes later, what, he's crocodile food. It doesn't make sense. How can it? When it's all just a matter of who does or who doesn't find the little damn baby in the basket. I don't *feel* like a bad man. I don't. I don't feel like a bad man at all.

He slows down to cross the bridge over the Sin River, but even so every thumped plank sends vibrations pulsing up through his feet, his legs, his groin.

Curly Ike is so preoccupied thinking his thoughts that he's rolling into the filling station, coasting to a stop, before he realizes that the rollaway door is missing from the service bay—no, not missing: torn off and lying crumpled on the ground beyond the pump island.

And there's a big gaping hole in the tiled wall between the service bay and the office.

The office window is shattered, glass strewn everywhere and—

A red-haired kid is pointing a box camera at Ike's car and—

And—

A craggy-faced man with a sheriff's star pinned to his jacket is cradling a limp and bloody-faced Donny Poore in both of his arms.

Ike shifts down, steps on the gas, and the woodie lurches forward and—

From somewhere—left side? right side? *above?*—a dark-haired slender boy, white shirt and gray trousers torn and filthy, thrusts himself in between the sheriff and the plunging DeSoto.

He sticks out his arms and splays his fingers and—

In the last moment before the car's teardrop-shaped front end crumples, the big straight-eight engine calves up through the hood, and Curly Ike (along with the Will Rogers statue) catapults through the windshield, he sees (and it will be the last thing Curly Ike *ever* sees) the expression in the boy's wide-open blue eyes.

It isn't, as Ike would expect, a look of terror. It's one of crushed and absolute hopelessness, the blackest of black despairs.

Gene Autry at the Jewel. Sheriff Dutcher again.
An expression of gratitude. Serious conversations in the barn.
Samson, Goliath, and Paul Bunyan. Good-bye to Smallville.

———

1

Every Saturday, beginning at eleven in the morning and concluding around three-thirty, four o'clock in the afternoon, Smallville's Jewel Theater presents a full-blown kiddie matinee: two B-pictures, a dozen cartoons, various short subjects, and a sixteen-minute installment of a Republic or Mascot chapter-play, all for a dime.

Today the features are *Mystery of the Wax Museum* and *Island of Lost Souls,* both of which Clark has seen before. But that's all right. He's not here for the pictures. It doesn't bother him the soundtrack is gargly, the focus blurred, and the projection misaligned, nor is he fazed by the candy boxes bleating like cornets, the fleets of paper airplanes crashing into the screen, the boys firing peashooters and the girls getting up in packs to change their seats fifty times. Clark has come here to think, and when he wants to, when he concentrates, he can block everything out.

He knows he shouldn't be here, though, not at a *kiddie* show, he's too old, too *tall.* But where *should* he be? That's one of the things he needs to think about. Where *should* he be? And what next? What comes next? That's what he ought to be thinking about. But all throughout the Bosko and Farmer Al Falfa cartoons, the coming attractions, the first short subject (magic you can do at home with a milk bottle, a sewing needle, and a hard-boiled egg), the Popeye cartoons, and the inevitable Mickey Mouse (*Mickey's Man Friday*), the only thing that Clark does think about, *can* think about, is the fixed stare in Donny Poore's eyes. The fixed stare in Donny Poore's dead eyes. The blood on his face and his crumpled-in skull. A week ago tonight.

How could that have happened?

Gene Autry, Radio's Singing Cowboy, in *The Phantom Empire*.

How could somebody just pick up a wrench and *do* that?

Chapter 3: "The Lightning Chamber."

As the recap legend quivers beneath a fake-looking futuristic city ("Murania, located thousands of feet under the earth, is rich in radium deposits . . ."), Clark puts his fingertips to his temples, pressing hard. His eyes seem to burn.

Five days ago, for the first time in his life, he vomited.

Three days ago he discovered what a migraine feels like.

On the movie screen, riders dressed like Roman legionnaires gallop across an American prairie, dodging tear-gas bombs dropped from an airplane. A rider topples from his horse and rolls. It's Gene Autry, but he's okay. Smiley Burnett comes along playing his harmonica. Meanwhile, down in her subterranean kingdom, Queen Tika orders an execution. Square-headed robots clank lugubriously around her. Back on the surface Gene's young friends Betty and Frankie Baxter climb through an open window, searching for evidence that Professor Beetson killed their father. And there it is! A rifle hidden underneath Beetson's mattress!

But Betty and Frankie's father wasn't *really* murdered, it's just a story, a dumb movie serial, and Donny Poore was buried Tuesday morning following a funeral Clark was still too heartsick and troubled to attend.

He sits blank-faced through Robert Benchley's *How to Sleep,* a comedy short he must have seen half a dozen times, then through the first reel of *Island of Lost Souls.* By now, his eyes throb like hearts and the din around him has grown so loud and exclamatory it's almost painful. It *is* painful: *that's* never happened before. Enough, he thinks. This isn't working. Nothing is.

Clark gets up and leaves, with Good & Plentys, jawbreakers, and peanut shells raining down on his head and shoulders from the balcony as he trudges up the aisle to the exit.

After zipping his jacket up (the weather broke on Monday and it's been cold ever since), he extracts his cloth cap from a vent pocket, unwads it, and puts it on. He is tugging the brim low on his forehead when Sheriff Dutcher comes out of the auditorium behind him. He steps up alongside of Clark and touches him gently, almost gravely, in the small of his back. "Your dad told me where I might find you. But I wasn't expecting you to leave for three more hours."

"You were going to *wait* for me?"

"Well, you paid your dime, I didn't think it'd be polite to interrupt your entertainment." He pushes open a door, then follows Clark out into the open air. "And I was enjoying the Charles Laughton picture."

"I don't mean any disrespect, sir, but I don't want to talk to you. I don't want to talk to anybody."

"So your dad tells me. Tells me you've been in the bushes all week. And I can't say I blame you." Dutcher shrugs. "But how about we go someplace and sit down?"

"I'd rather not."

"Clark, I drove all the way here. And it's not official business."

The nearest place to eat is in the next block, Freundlich's, with an electric signboard, café curtains, and the menu white-painted directly on the front window. They sit at a table. Most of the others are unoccupied but at the lunch counter every high stool is taken. Saturday lunch crowd, farmers mostly. They all look over at Clark and the sheriff, to nod or smile slightly, and then—encountering an awkwardness they couldn't explain—turn immediately back to their franks and kraut, their hash, their oxtail goulash, coffee, and pie. And like it's suddenly broadcast over a loudspeaker, Clark hears a confidential whisper from twenty feet away: "I thought he got hit by a car."

"That your favorite kind of picture?" says Dutcher, clipping a cigar.

"What?"

"That horror stuff. First time we met, I recall you were going to see a werewolf picture."

"Yeah, I like that kind, I guess."

Dutcher lights the cigar. "How come you left early?"

"I have a headache."

"Sorry to hear it." Dutcher smiles at Mrs. Freundlich as she appears with two glasses of cloudy water and sets them down. She is a large round woman, wide-hipped, wearing an out-of-date NRA blue eagle pinned to her apron. She says hello to Clark and, obviously not recognizing the sheriff (he isn't wearing his uniform or even his star), greets him as "mister." She asks if they're ready to order, offering the information that the veal chops are especially good today. "Tasty," she says. Well then, veal chops it is for Sheriff Dutcher. Clark asks for a hamburger sandwich, no onions.

"I probably should've got that myself," says Dutcher after Mrs. Freundlich has gone.

"You can have mine. I'm not hungry." Clark takes a sip of water. Puts down the glass. Picks it up and takes another sip.

The sheriff puffs on his cigar.

When their food comes, Mrs. Freundlich serves Dutcher first. As she is sliding the second plate down in front of Clark, she says, "I hope the paper intends to do another story this year about the Arkalalah Halloween Festival. It's coming up fast, you know, and I'm on the committee."

"Well, I hope so too, Mrs. Freundlich, but you'd have to ask Mr. Timmins about that." He purses his lips, nodding to himself. "I don't work for the paper anymore."

"I'm sorry to hear that, Clark, you always wrote such nice stories."

"Thank you, ma'am."

She asks if there's anything else either of them needs. When they tell her there isn't, she returns to her stool behind the cash register at the end of the lunch counter.

Dutcher tamps out his cigar coal. "Clark. Look at me, son."

"I got a bad headache, I should go."

"You know why I came here today?"

Clark shakes his head, but tentatively.

"I came here to thank you for my life," says Dutcher slowly and quietly. "I came here to thank you, son, from the very bottom of my heart."

"I didn't do anything."

"I think you did. And it was the bravest damn thing I ever saw."

"If he hadn't cut his wheel when he did . . ."

"Clark . . ."

"And thank God there was no gasoline in those pumps." Clark is speaking in a numb monotone. "That would've been. That would've been . . . bad."

"Son, that car hit those pumps *after* it hit you. I don't care what you wrote in the paper. I was there."

"That guy turned his wheel . . ."

"Now, why would he do that?"

"Maybe because he wasn't . . ."

"What? Wasn't what?"

"All bad? Maybe at the last second he had, I don't know, a change of heart."

Dutcher sits back. "That car hit you."

Clark picks up his sandwich but then puts it down. And mumbles something.

"Excuse me? I didn't catch what—"

"I said you're welcome. You said thank you and I said you're welcome." Clark shrugs.

For the next two, three minutes they sit there and look at their food.

"We're not going to eat any of this, are we?" Taking out his wallet, Dutcher extracts a dollar bill and lays it down beside his water glass. "Let's go."

Everybody watches them leave.

"Why don't you let me drive you home?"

"That's okay, I got my dad's truck."

"No, you don't."

Clark turns and looks at Dutcher.

"I was at your house, remember? And there was your truck sitting out in front. Come on, I'll give you a lift."

Dutcher's car—and it's the sheriff's own machine, not the county's: a 1932 cream and blue Pontiac 6 coupe—is parked across the street from the Jewel. "Just throw all that stuff anywhere," he tells Clark, pointing to folders and clip binders piled on the passenger's side of the front seat. But Clark just gathers it all up and holds it on his lap.

Leaving the center of town they pass by the Herald-Progress building, which causes Clark to frown and the sheriff to ask, "So why'd you quit?"

"The farm keeps me busy enough." Clark pats his shirt pocket, finds his Black Jack chewing gum. Takes out a stick, unwraps it, folds it into his mouth.

They don't speak again till they reach the farm.

Dutcher turns the car into the gravel driveway, stops it halfway between the county road and the Kent house, and sets the hand brake. "What do you hear from your friend the photographer?"

"Willi? Nothing," says Clark, holding his voice steady and his gaze calm. "He took off with those guys he was traveling with. And he's not my *friend*. I just met him."

Dutcher is shaking his head. "We caught up with those WPA boys yesterday in Neosho Falls, and your pal wasn't with them. He went off to take some pictures in Aliceville Thursday afternoon, they told us, and never came back. Where do you think he went?"

"I wouldn't know."

Dutcher reaches over suddenly and tugs a sheet of paper from under one of the clip binders on Clark's lap. After unfolding it he holds it up. It's another wanted poster bearing Willi Berg's name, photos, felonies, and a caution that he may be armed and should be considered dangerous. "That federal man—Foley?—sent me this on Wednesday."

"And you said this wasn't official business."

"It's not."

Clark levers open his door. "I have to go."

"One last thing. I can't imagine how you'd ever need it"—Dutcher grins—"but if by some remote chance you ever do need my help, with anything, at any time, you call me. You call me, you write me, you send me a smoke signal, and I'll drop what I'm doing. Promise."

Clark nods and climbs out of the car. Then he bends from the waist, looking back in at Dutcher through the open door.

"Willi didn't kill anybody."

"Know that for a fact, do you?"

"Yes, sir. I do."

"Good enough for me," says the sheriff. "But I'm just one cop—so if you *do* see your pal again? Tell him to grow a mustache or something, would you? That red hair wouldn't fool a Boy Scout." He picks the wanted poster off the seat and passes it out to Clark. "Souvenir?"

After watching the sheriff back out his Pontiac and drive away, Clark skims the wanted poster again—Murder, Burglary, Interstate Flight—before crumpling it into a chunky ball and lobbing it straight up into the air.

He watches it—more like glares at it—till the paper bursts into flame, dissolves into granular soot, and quickly disappears.

Same as always, Clark's eyes are left feeling syrupy, almost liquid, like the waterglass that his mom would make in the summertime to preserve surplus eggs. But the sensation passes in less than a minute. And it's a small price to pay for such a—

Gift?

For the first time in a week Clark feels the muscles flex up at both ends of his mouth. It's not *much* of a smile but for now it will have to do.

He needs to speak to his father.

He needs to tell him good-bye.

2

Last night.

When the knock came at the back door, Alger Lee was complaining again about how much time it took to play a game of Monopoly while simultaneously counting out scrip to purchase six houses for even distribution on his green properties—Pacific, North Carolina, and Pennsylvania avenues. Mr. Kent, still scowling for having been assessed for street repairs by a Chance card, looked at the clock on top of the dining room bookcase. Ten minutes to ten.

The knocking was repeated, more insistently. Alger started to rise from his chair, but Mr. Kent shook his head. "Clark! Somebody's at the kitchen door." Although Clark finally had dragged himself out of bed around half past five that afternoon and come downstairs to sit with his father and Alger while they ate supper, he'd gone directly back up to his room once the dishes were done and put away. "Clark! You want to go see who's there?" While sympathetic, Mr. Kent felt he shouldn't indulge his son's melancholy. Martha, you could bet, never would have allowed him to lay in bed all day staring at the ceiling. *"Clark!"*

Alger said, "Why don't you let me go see who it is?"

"Keep your seat, Al. Clark! The back door!"

The first few times Mr. Kent called Alger "Al," the boy had looked startled—nobody had ever called him *that*—but by now he'd gotten used to it, almost, and come to like it. Yeah, it wasn't bad. *Al.*

Alger carefully positioned two wooden houses on North Carolina Avenue, two more on Pacific. "Your roll."

"Excuse me, Al. *Clark!*"

At last they heard his heavy footsteps on the stairs.

Clark shuffled into the dining room stifling a yawn. His shirttail dangled. His hair stuck out in fifty places. He looked sulky and irritated.

"Somebody's here," said Mr. Kent. "Would you mind seeing who?"

Clark nodded, went to answer, pulled open the door, and discovered Willi Berg finishing a cigarette on the short back porch. "Can I come in?"

Clark opened the door wider, indicating the kitchen with a toss of his head. He wasn't glad to see Willi but he wasn't not glad either.

Willi had a green duffel that he dragged in behind him. Like Clark he hadn't shaved in days. The beard coming in was black and it made his hair look redder, almost comic.

"How'd you get here?"

"Hitched. Walked. You know." Willi was looking around for an ashtray. Clark passed him a teacup to use. He took it and sat down at the table.

"What happened to those guys you were with?"

"I don't know. I left."

"Why?"

"Felt like it." He rubbed knuckles up and down his bristly cheek.

"You want something to eat?"

"No, that's okay." Willi noticed them first: Mr. Kent and Alger Lee standing in the doorway, Alger tapping his lips with a light blue property deed.

"Dad. Alger," said Clark, "this is Willi."

"The photographer," said Mr. Kent. He seemed untypically guarded. "Good to meet you."

"Likewise." Willi moved scantly forward on his chair, then decided against standing; just waved hi and smiled instead. "Sorry to drop by so late. But I just, you know, hit town." He gave a nervous giggle: he was tired, sagging tired.

"Did Clark offer you something to eat?"

"Yes, he did, sir. He surely did. But I'm not hungry. Thank you."

Alger leaned toward Mr. Kent, and using the property deed to cover his mouth, began to whisper something. Mr. Kent deflected him curtly. "How about some coffee?"

"Sounds good, but a place to sleep sounds even better—if I can impose on you."

"Well, we're a little short of beds in the house"—and that was because Alger Lee had moved in and was using the guest room—"but if you don't mind sleeping on the couch . . ."

"I was kind of hoping I could sleep in the barn." A grin inched up one side of Willi's mouth. "So I could say I done it."

"*Did* it," said Mr. Kent. "And that's completely up to you. But it's a cool night."

"I'll be fine," said Willi slapping his duffel. "I got a blanket." In fact he had two: each one stolen from a boardinghouse.

"Then Clark'll get you set up."

"I appreciate this, Mr. Kent. Well then," he said rising from the table. "Why don't I go on out there now and let you all . . . get back to whatever you were doing." He turned to Clark and their eyes met. "Walk me?"

Clark struck a match and lighted the kerosene lantern hanging on a nail just inside the barn's great door, then he carried it down the feed passage and up the ladder to the hayloft, which sloped hard toward the back wall. Willi clambered up behind him. He flung down his duffel. "Can you smoke in a barn?" he said, and Clark looked behind him and found an old milking pail that had been up there to catch leaks before he and his father repaired the roof and the weatherboarding.

"Just don't burn the place down, all right? And give me one of those."

As Clark was firing a cigarette, Willi dug through his duffel bag. He drew out a small, flat bottle of bootleg whiskey with a hand-lettered pasted-on label that read: "Aug. 2, 1928." He offered the bottle to Clark.

"No, thanks."

Willi unscrewed the cap and took a long swallow.

"Tell me something. Why are you on a wanted poster?"

So Willi took another long drink, then a short glug, twisted the cap back on the bottle, and told the story. Not the *whole* story, but nearly: he neglected to mention he'd used burglar's tools to get into the pawnshop. In this version, the front door was unlocked and he had merely walked in.

It took twenty minutes to tell, and when he was finished Clark said, "Could you be mistaken about the alderman? Maybe it just *looked* like him?"

"Why would you ask me that?"

"It's just hard for me to believe that a man like that—he's a public *servant,* Willi!—could be a gangster."

Willi stared at Clark with dismay and near contempt. "What *planet* are you from, Clark? Politicians are *always* crooks. It's their *job.*"

"That's just city talk."

"You need an education, my friend. A degree in what's what."

"Is that right? You're so smart, what are you doing with your picture on a wanted poster and that stupid red *dye* in your hair?"

"I was framed!"

"You and the Count of Monte Cristo." Clark frowned. Then he stretched out his left arm, wiggling his fingers at the bottle. "Let me try some of that."

For half an hour they sat under the ventilator with their backs to the hay door, smoking cigarettes and drinking colorless whiskey but not speaking. At last Willi said, "I need to show you something."

"What?

But as soon as Willi had scrambled his hands through his bag and brought out a large mustard-yellow envelope, Clark knew *exactly* what he was going to be shown. He'd probably known it from the moment he opened the door and found Willi on his back porch.

Photographs.

One second Willi was holding the prints in his hand, the next they were gone and Clark had them.

Going rapidly through all of them—a series of nine prints—Clark would glance at one, slide it to the bottom, glance at the next, slide it to the bottom, the next, the next, the next . . .

When he came to the last one, though, he sucked in and held his breath and let them all drop from his hands. They swished down, glided and scythed, a few to scatter free on the plank floor, the rest to overlap near his feet.

Willi said, "They're kind of . . ."

He said, "They're pretty grainy but . . ."

He said, "Still you can see . . ."

Clark's shoulders moved up and down.

Willi said, "I'm sorry, I didn't mean to . . ."

He said, "I thought you'd want to . . ."

He said, "I haven't showed anybody else."

"Why not?" Clark's eyes were red-rimmed but not wet.

Willi said, "I didn't think . . ."

He said, "It didn't seem . . ."

He said, "I wish I knew."

Stooping, Clark picked up one of the prints. The image was grainy, as Willi had said, and poorly lit, but not so poorly you couldn't see it was an image of Clark hoisting above his head a service bay door, the rollaway kind.

Willi said, "Hey!" when Clark tore the print in half. As Clark tore it into quarters he said, "I still got the negative."

Clark looked at another print on the floor, the one that showed him twisting an iron jack around both wrists of a man lying face down on the ground. A pencil notation on the back read: "CK & Claude Draper."

Willi stooped and picked up one of the prints. He held it in front of Clark's face. "Those damn bricks almost *hit* me when you came busting through that wall." Willi dropped the print, snatched up another. In pencil on the back it read: "CK & Milton George."

"When you hung that moron on the tree, did you fly up there or jump?"

"I'm not sure."

"You're not *sure?*"

"Jumped. I think. But maybe not. I haven't had much practice."

"Then we should do something about that."

"*We* should?"

Willi shrugged. "What do old Claude and Milt have to say about everything?"

"Nothing."

"At all?"

"They still don't know what hit them."

"No kidding. But . . ."

Clark hitched an eyebrow.

". . . you worked them both over pretty good."

"They deserved it." Clark was staring down at a print that had slid to the front edge of the hayloft.

Willi walked over there and looked to see which one it was. Oh. That one. "The kid was *how* old?"

"Nine."

Clark kept staring until a pinprick-size hole, faintly smoking and brown-edged, appeared in the photographic paper. Yellow points of flame struggled up, followed by a heavier scribble of smoke.

The hole widened out, chewing at the picture.

Willi moved to stamp out the fire. Clark pushed him away. When there was nothing left of the photograph but wafers of delicate ash, he ground those to soot and scraped it over the edge of the loft with the side and the heel of his shoe. Then he sat down with his legs dangling in space.

His eyeballs felt gummy.

Then they didn't.

"Why don't you come with me?" Willi dropped into a squat. "Why don't you?" He'd *thought* he was going to ask: How'd you *do* that? "Come on, Clark: haven't you ever thought about hitting the road? Seeing what's going on?"

Clark turned his head. "You make me tired, you know that?"

"What else are friends for?" He laughed. "At least think about it, would you? We could have some fun and you could, you know—*practice.*"

"Good night, Willi."

"Night, pal."

The moment Alger saw Clark leave the barn he said to Mr. Kent, "Here he comes." They were in the kitchen, Alger standing at the back door with his arms wrapped around himself, Mr. Kent seated at the table cleaning his eyeglasses. They'd put away the Monopoly game half an hour ago, neither of them much interested in playing after Willi's arrival.

"Why don't you go on up to bed?"

"You want to talk to him alone?"

"Something like that."

"Okay. Then I'll be saying good night to you."

"Good night, Al, sleep well."

Clark came in a few moments later.

"Well?" said Mr. Kent. He smelled cigarette smoke and liquor. But that was the least of his worries.

"He's leaving tomorrow."

"And?"

Clark opened his mouth, then shut it. "Nothing. He's just . . . leaving tomorrow."

After his son went to bed, Mr. Kent remained in the kitchen, eventually getting up and opening the cutlery drawer, gently touching some of the forks and spoons with the coarse pads of his fingertips. He opened the stove door and took out the saucepan and the iron skillet, looking at those and then putting them back, opening the cupboard door and reaching down a particular coffee cup with a chipped handle, turning it, blowing out the dust, replacing it on its shelf, then picking up from the windowsill a five-and-dime-store ceramic shepherdess-and-lamb. Something's happened, Martha. Something's different. Something's changing.

Something's changed.

Opening the sink tap, he rinsed grit and house dust from Martha's little figurine, dried it with a flour sack he'd been using as a dish cloth. At last, he trudged upstairs and got ready for bed, the worst part of his day. He read a few pages in *Spoon River Anthology*. The last poem he read (and he didn't actually finish it) before he closed the valve on his Aladdin lamp was the one titled "Ernest Hyde," the one that begins, "My mind was a mirror: It saw what it saw, it knew what it knew."

That all happened last night.

3

Today. Twenty past one in the afternoon. The hayloft. Neither Willi Berg nor Alger Lee meant to go flapping their jaws about Clark, about what he could do, what he might be: it just *happened.* They're both feeling vaguely guilty about it, too, but still. It's been an interesting conversation.

"I figure he's a hoodoo man."

"And what is that, exactly?"

"I'm not sure," says Alger. "But don't *you* be smirking at me. I suppose *you* know what he is?"

"A freak of nature, my friend. Merely a freak of nature."

"Oh yeah, that explains everything! You're full of hops, you know it?"

"Didn't you ever read the Bible? Never heard about Goliath? What about Samson? You ever hear of Paul Bunyan?"

"Paul Bunyan's not in the Bible!"

"I know *that.* I was just giving you some *examples.* Every so often, like maybe every hundred years or every million people, there's somebody that's born a freak of nature. You can't *explain* it. But that's all there is *to* it."

"Paul Bunyan was a giant—Clark is three inches shorter than I am!"

"Doesn't matter," says Willi. Then he says, "Excuse me," and shakes out one of his blankets, beats off some clinging bits of straw with his hand, then folds it quickly and squats down to stuff it into his duffel bag.

"I never heard about bullets bouncing off *Samson's* head." Alger taps his index fingertip against his forehead, then flings it off, way off, to pantomime a ricochet. "Seen it myself."

"In your hat."

"I seen it!"

Willi looks down at his feet. "You ever see him . . . fly?"

"Fly?" Alger laughs. "Naw, he can't do *that.*"

"Yeah?"

"What do you mean: *yeah?*"

"Nothing." Willi jams in his blankets and cinches the duffel. Then he takes a tab of paper—it's been folded again and again till it's the size of a matchbox—and hands it to Alger. "Don't forget to give this to him."

"I won't forget. But why do you got to leave before he comes home? I think you should wait."

The thing is: so does Willi. So then why is he rushing to leave?

He wishes he knew. Baloney. He *knows.*

All it would take would be a few hours more with this Boy Scout, this *Cub Scout,* and he could have himself a new best friend. His *first* best friend. Not that Willi *wants* one, necessarily. Acquaintances have been always more than enough. Friends, he feels pretty certain, are nothing but a nuisance. But this kid, this freak of nature, this Clark: *well.*

He could be Willi's Get Out of Jail Free card.

It was the scheme he was hatching all week long, the hope he's been flush with and the reason he walked to the highway in Aliceville, stuck out his thumb, and hitched an erratic series of short rides back here to Smallville.

But overnight he changed his mind.

It sounds stupid, it seems gloppy, but he really likes the kid.

"Well, let me get out of here if I'm going."

When Alger pushes open the great door, Clark has to jump back from the apron onto the service court so it doesn't strike him in the chest.

In his left hand he is holding a Gladstone bag that his mother used as a young woman moving to Kansas from the Dakota Territory with her widowed father.

Beaming at his new best friend, Willi Berg says, "If you're ready, let's go."

Open-mouthed, Alger watches them walk off together. Then he half turns back toward the house. And there's Mr. Kent at the kitchen door. They look at each other with frail smiles—Alger's frail and baffled, Mr. Kent's frail and full of sorrow.

"Al?" he calls after a minute. "Join me for some lunch?"

With a nod Alger starts back across the dooryard. He is almost at the porch when he remembers Willi's letter. He stops, pulls it from his dungarees, unfolds it, and reads: "Dear Clark, I burned those other prints this morning, along with the negatives. If you don't believe me, see for yourself. I burned them in the barrel over by that I don't know what you call it, where you keep the chickens. You're an amazing guy. Be careful or people will eat you for breakfast, if you know what I mean. Good luck. I'm glad I met you." He signed it Willi Boring, but then struck that out and wrote: Willi Berg.

Today is the twentieth of October 1935.

PART TWO

—

WAYFARING STRANGERS

Dear Father, how are you? Good, I hope. I am fine . . .

———

1

From Smallville, Clark and Willi tramp cross-country till they reach a railroad division point where freights stop to change engines and crews. There they jump into the first open and empty boxcar they find and catch out before long on a hotshot that takes them upstate, then across the Missouri River bridge into the Argentine yards.

Between them they have seventy-five dollars, but they want to be frugal. Even so, the two nights they stay over in Kansas City (jazz, barbecue, the stockyards, the War Memorial) they splurge and stay at the YMCA. On the morning following the second night Clark wakes to find his wallet stolen. Suddenly their joint resources are less than thirty bucks.

In the afternoon they catch out on a freight headed west, sitting in the side-door Pullman watching the scenery till the cinders and the steam blowback get to them both (yes, both) and they claim a corner of the boxcar. There are eight or nine other riders, a motley collection of old bindlestiffs.

Clark is certain he made a mistake, leaving home. What did he think he was doing? Going off in search of his fortune, his fate, *what?* "We're just *going,* Clark," Willi tells him. "It's an adventure. You're not a farmer."

"How would you know?"

During the footloose first days and weeks it *is* a great adventure. But there are moments of anxiety too, even terror. Fourth day out Willi loses his footing while they're riding back-to-back on the ladders between boxcars, and if Clark didn't snatch him he would have been crushed. Railroad bulls are on them sometimes before they even see the bastards, and always there are crazy raving hobos to watch out for.

Days turn into weeks . . .

They travel by rail and by thumb and by foot. Stay in hobo jungles and squatters camps, sleep on scraps of carpet in corrugated paper shacks, eat beans, fried dough, oatmeal mush, and drink oceans of boiled coffee.

In Shawnee they work briefly at the railroad yards, unloading soft coal from tenders, twenty-five cents a day, then motor around the Oklahoma panhandle in a pale-green Buick that belongs to a Frenchman (the first one of *those* Clark has ever met) named Paul Darcy who rents dilapidated theaters and taprooms to show a grind house film about venereal disease. For a dollar a day (show days only) Willi and Clark cover the towns with handbills and posters. They also run the projector.

Clark can't *believe* what that disease can do to your brain. Good thing to know.

Weeks turn into months . . .

The constant clackety-clack of train wheels, the creaks and groans of boxcars, the smell of steam mixed with hot oil. The loneliness of a concrete highway at two in the morning. They buy sacks of breakups for a nickel at the back doors of bakeries, elbow their way to the Free Food Dump, sit for hours on piles of switch ties in a drizzle. They trudge through dust blizzards, meet girls, go out dancing in a dozen different roadhouses. And naturally they talk. On slow freights moving west across the brown plains they stretch out on crushed gravel in gondola cars, and they talk. Sometimes eighteen hours a day.

Saying, "So who's better, Gary Cooper or James Cagney?"

Saying, "Who do you like, Detroit or Chicago?"

Willi saying, "Dracula!" Clark saying, "Get out of here—Frankenstein! You can't beat Frankenstein."

Clark saying, "Do you believe in God? Me neither. What about an afterlife? Me neither. What *about* God, though? Do you think there *could* be one?"

Willi saying, "Jews don't believe in an afterlife. Well, they do and they don't. It's complicated."

Clark saying, "What, you never chopped off a chicken's head?"

Willi saying, "I bet if you squeezed this lump of coal, you'd end up with a diamond as big as a chicken egg." Clark saying, "Yeah? I bet I'd end up with a handful of coal dust."

Willi saying, "Try it," and Clark saying, "Can we talk about something else?"

*Dear Father, today we are riding courtesy of the Fort Worth–
Pacific railroad company. I am fine. How are you?*

They are traveling in an empty Chicago Great Western box with a buzzard named Tiny Montgomery on his way to Texas to chop winter cotton. Tiny keeps warm, as warm as possible, with old newspapers stuck inside his jacket and down the legs and seat of his dungarees.

Willi and Clark have blankets.

It is around dawn when the Big Boy locomotive pulls its three dozen freight cars into Ardmore, Oklahoma. Willi wakes up freezing. And finds himself looking down the barrel of a Colt revolver. Tiny says, "You and your friend are dropping off here, get it? Wake him up."

Willi shakes Clark, who also has lost his blanket to Tiny Montgomery but hasn't noticed the cold. "Clark, hey Kent, get up."

Just at this moment the train stops with a loud screech. Bumpers and couplings clash, their boxcar lurches, and Tiny's revolver discharges. The slug bounces off Clark's front teeth and puts a hole through the metal roof. Willi uses Tiny's immobilizing awe to kick him in the nuts.

Tiny crumples, his fingers splay, and the gun drops, clattering and skittering across the plank floor. Clark rolls open the door, picks Tiny up by the waist of his trousers (newspapers sluice out), and flings him down a gravel incline. Then he boots Tiny's sack out after him, the open neck spewing a round mirror, a shaving brush, and a stamp collection bound in leather.

Next day they quit the freight in Dahlgren, Texas. Hitchhiking, they catch a few rides past cotton fields that stretch forever on both sides of every road, pickers out there bent over, dragging long muslin sacks behind them—Negroes and Mexicans, Filipinos and East Indians, and either Japanese or Chinese or both. Neither Willi nor Clark know how you're supposed to tell the difference.

Now it's late afternoon and they haven't had a lift in several hours. An automobile is coming up the road behind them—really zooming, a sand-colored Plymouth going seventy. Because they do it for every passing vehicle, they stick out their thumbs. But that driver isn't slowing down for anybody.

After the Plymouth tears past they follow it with their eyes for the next two, three miles on the dead-straight road. It gets smaller and smaller, then disappears over a slight misted rise.

Clark says, "I sure wouldn't mind owning a car like that."

"Well, if you'd squeezed that damn lump of coal like I *said*, we could be riding in one this very minute."

This could easily be the start of yet another one of their regular quarrels (Willi implying that Clark has made no effort to develop his talents, Clark saying he doesn't appreciate being made to feel like a performing seal, and besides, didn't he start a cook fire with his *eyes* yesterday morning, wasn't that *enough* for a while?). But the quarrel never develops. Instead they're distracted by a fleet of Ford A's full of men in American Legion caps that roar up from behind and streak by.

"Guy had a rifle," says Clark. "In that last car."

A county black-and-white pulls off the road just ahead of them. A tall rangy lawman climbs out, halting them both with his glare and then reaching back inside the vehicle for his white John B. Stetson hat. He wears smoked glasses, a creaking leather gun belt, khakis with insignias on the shirt sleeves, and cowboy boots. "Afternoon, fellas," he says, all twang. "You live around here?"

Willi says, "We're just walking to Fort Worth," and Clark cringes: Why can't he learn to call his elders and his betters "sir"? He could at least *pretend* some respect. He's a *fugitive,* for crying out loud.

"Uh-huh. And if I was to ask each of you boys to show me your wallets, would you have at least five dollars apiece? Because I tell you what, you'd be vagrants if you don't, and vagrants serve thirty days on the county farm."

Willi says, "We got money, you need to see it?"

"I most surely do." He looks at Clark, back to Willi. "What business you boys have in Fort Worth?"

Clark answers: "My uncle lives there, sir. He's going to give us both work in his butcher shop." So far they've used Clark's imaginary uncle (who lives in a number of different cities) half a dozen times with cops, train firemen, yard bulls, even Holy Rollers at the Sally. Folks are more likely to say yes or leave you alone if you seem to have an ultimate destination.

After examining each of their wallets, the county cop passes them back and says, "Why'n't you fellas get in, I'll give you a ride up through Garretson."

Clark and Willi exchange uneasy looks—do they have a choice? no—and climb reluctantly into the back of the radio car.

A few miles on, the road is barricaded by two local police cruisers parked crosswise with their grilles touching. And there's that nice tan Plymouth and all of those Model A's. Three legionnaires take turns using sledgehammers on the Plymouth's engine, slaughtering it. Others slash the tires, break the glass. While still others, over in that ditch, beat the devil out of a suit-wearing burly man.

Clark winces at the steady thuds and the gasps that follow. He tries to muffle them, filter them out, but neither mental commands nor repeated swallowing does the job.

Willi presses his face to the side window and watches intently.

An old wrinkled man with a limp hobbles up to the county car, stoops beside the driver's window. "Afternoon, Diebold. Told you he wuddent gonna serve no injunction." Then he turns to look back at what's still happening in the ditch. "Looks to me like that ACL-Jew lawyer won't make it to the courthouse by four."

"Jim—just so long as I don't have a corpse on my hands, is that understood?"

There is a sudden crash, a jolting vibration, another crash, as the Plymouth is rolled onto its side, then rolled onto its roof. The legionnaires all laugh and hoot like it's some big event at the state fair.

When Diebold the county cop drives on, skirting the roadblock, nodding to the local cops who stand together smoking, Willi slaps the mesh that separates the front and back of the car. "You're just gonna let them beat that guy up?"

Diebold peers at him in the rearview mirror.

He drives slowly through the town of Garretson, where people have assembled and are still assembling, Mexicans and whites, all men, and too many Texas Rangers. A loudspeaker truck blares warnings: do not, do not, do not. Congregate. Interfere. Obstruct traffic. Half a dozen scowling cops are lugging typewriters, bundled pamphlets, file folders, and a mimeograph machine from a square brick building. A crowd in the street jeers.

"The county line is two miles out. I'm putting you boys over it. And of course I don't want to see either one of you back here again."

Willi doesn't say anything.

Clark says, "Yes, sir."

And now they stand on the other side of the Leaving Garretson tin sign, watching Diebold's cruiser execute a U-turn and drive back toward the town.

Willi scrapes out his cigarette packet from his shirt pocket.

"I wish you'd quit smoking."

"And I wish you'd quit acting like some farm boy swallowed Amy

Vanderbilt. I don't know what you are, Kent, but if I had what you have . . . ?"

"Yeah? What?"

"I'd've done something to help that guy back there."

"What was I supposed to do? Beat everybody up?"

"For starters."

"You give me a headache," says Clark.

Dear Father, belated happy birthday to you! Hope you had a good one. I miss you and think of you all the time. I miss our farm, I miss my old bed, I miss . . .

After the events on the road to Garretson, Clark seems different. Older. *Changed.* For the first time since going on the bum, he plucks yesterday's papers from trash barrels and reads them all the way through. Reading about shoemakers striking in New Hampshire, watchmakers striking in Illinois, boatbuilders striking in Connecticut. Reading about Japs in China, Italians in Abyssinia, Reds in Spain. Reading about lovers who drank poison. He'll say, "Listen to this!" and then read something out loud. Willi scarcely listens. He hates being read to, and besides, Clark always picks the most gruesome stories. He'll put down a newspaper, shake his head, and ask Willi, "You have any relatives in Germany? I sure hope not." He's not the same guy. And now he walks with his hands clenched.

In a town called Safford they hook up with a singing cowboy named Plato Beatty and travel with him farther into east Texas. The reason he's called Plato, he tells his riders, is because he has a *plate* in his head. A piece of metal the size of a cake plate, holding things together. He fought in the Argonne Forest, which is how he got his skull blown off. But despite his injury Plato seems a happy enough soul.

From time to time he lets Clark or Willi drive his old dusty Nash while he strums his guitar and sings. Clark likes the sad prairie songs, the hobo songs, the songs about wayfaring strangers and poor boys a

189

long way from home, but Willi thinks he'll go nuts if he has to listen to much more of that hillbilly guff.

Foley Wells isn't a town, it's a landscape, a scrubland with oil derricks, the tall ones and the smaller kind that look like pecking chickens. The radio station there is a thirty-kilowatt shack-and-tower. Willi and Clark sit quietly in the studio while Plato puts on his cowboy hat, stands at the microphone, and does "Blue-Eyed Jane," "Ragged but Right," and "Silver-Haired Daddy of Mine." Afterward they drink liquor in the car parked next to the station. Well, Clark doesn't. Hard stuff is just wasted on him, he's decided. Willi takes a few swaps to be sociable, but Plato drinks one bottle and opens another, pints of Old Granddad. Finally he crawls off over a rock and sleeps in some weeds.

In the morning they take to the road again, heading for another radio station. Plato hasn't spoken a word since staggering back to the car after first light. The man looks miserable today, full of guilt and grief—like the mopes, Willi thinks, in all of his rambling gambler songs. Missing their old mothers and the girls they left behind.

The sky turns dark, and a dust storm kicks up.

After an hour or two of riding, Willi asks Plato to stop at a general store, he's famished. Ten miles later Plato steers off the road at a filling station with a small grocery attached. But as soon as Willi and Clark go inside to buy a loaf of bread, Plato takes off and leaves them stranded. Did he get tired of their company? Or just need to be alone with his lonesome blues? Whatever his reason, they are footing it again. Walking down a two-lane county road and talking, talking, talking.

Willi saying, "Not with *any* kind of stick, a *broom* stick. And a pink spaldeen."

Clark saying, "Gabby Hurnett," Willi saying, "Hank Greenburg."

Willi saying, "Three cards of one rank and a pair of another—that's a full house," Clark saying, "Does a flush beat a straight? It does, right?"

Willi saying, "There's nobody around—do you see anybody? So would you please just pick up that boulder and throw it? Humor me." Clark saying, "I don't *feel* like picking up any boulders."

And now off to their left a ball of oily black smoke—penetrated by a column of flame—foams high into the air. Somebody screams.

And Clark, who has been scuffling along next to Willi, suddenly isn't there . . .

In the days that follow, he obviously enjoys, even relishes, thinking about what he did at that oil field—put on a burst of speed to roll a boomer who'd caught fire and then grabbed up a well cap, tossed it over the well head, and sprawled across it till the flames all quit.

Apropos of nothing, he says, "How much do you figure that cap weighed? More than a ton? It's hard for me to gauge things like that." Or he says, "Guess I'm fireproof, huh? My hair, too." Or says, "We should've stuck around. I might've got some kind of reward."

Clark is definitely different. And Willi is not sure that he likes the change.

Dear Father,

As bad luck would have it, we found ourselves yesterday in a miserable place called Panterville where a murder trial was about to start. A colored man was supposed to have killed a white man, his boss, over the boss's wife. Or something like that, I'm not sure. I've seen race troubles since I've been gone, and back in Smallville too (remember what they did to Bill Hammer's face that time?), but it is most awful in Texas. Colored people keep they eyes down here and a great number of them stutter.

Anyhow, when we showed up in Panterville a Negro was going on trial and it seemed like the whole town was gathered outside the district courthouse trying to get in.

There were five Texas Rangers on the front steps. One of them was a captain and ~~him~~ he had a shotgun. The others had sidearms. We heard the captain say that he and his men were there at the order of the governor and their instructions were to see that the trial took place in a legal manner, so everybody should go home.

But nobody would. They just pushed closer. I wanted to get moving, but Willi wanted to stay so he could take pictures, which he did till some big farmer threatened to break his head. Then a shotgun went off twice inside the courthouse. A minute later they carried out two men ~~who's~~ whose chests were bloody from pellet wounds. The crowd turned rowdy and people started to throw rocks and then a fat old preacher threw an open can of gasoline through a broken window and suddenly the whole building was on fire.

Everybody got out of there except the prisoner. For safekeeping he'd been locked inside the district attorney's vault and now because of the fire nobody could get to it.

I ran inside and kept blowing hard to keep the flames away. I wasn't afraid of being burned, I just didn't want my clothes all ruined. But they got ruined anyway, by spark holes. I'm ashamed that I worried about such a thing at a time like that, but I did.

I had heard someone say the vault was on the third floor. It was and I found it and pulled off the door. But the prisoner was dead. don't know if the smoke got to him or what, but he was dead. His skin was red-hot in my arms. I carried him down the stairs and back outside.

Then a couple hundred people rushed at me and grabbed that poor colored man from my arms, they just snatched him away! You should have seen their faces. No, I wouldn't have wanted you to. They were like a pack of <u>dogs</u>. They were like that, exactly. And they tied that dead man, whose name I never got, by a rope to the bumper of a Ford car and dragged him around the public square. Then they cut him off the bumper and pulled him to a tree and hanged him.

They tortured and hanged a dead man, Dad. It was the worst thing I have ever seen.

And do you remember how when I was a boy and whenever I

stared at something too long it would start to smolder and even catch fire? Remember when I set those old magazines of Mom's on fire? I did that again yesterday, but on purpose.

Every single automobile and truck that I could find, I looked at <u>real hard</u> till the gas tank blew up.

Those people in Panterville they all just ran like hell, is what they did, excuse my language. But they ran like hell in all directions.

Willi must have seen something in my face because he dragged me away from there and back to the freight yards. And it's a good thing he did too, because otherwise I would have burned down that whole town, Dad. I <u>wanted</u> to.

I'm not sorry I did what I did no matter <u>how</u> much money those cars and trucks cost. I was glad and I still am as I write this letter to you. I guess I have a temper and should be a monk or a hermit! I have a bad temper, Dad, I do, and that could be a real disaster some day. People could hate me. They probably will. And if they can find nails that won't break, they might just crucify me.

   loving

Your son,

    ^

Clark

p.s. We have both had enough of this being on the bum and have decided to go to California to live and work. I will write again just as soon as we are settled.

p.p.s. It <u>was</u> wrong, wasn't it? Please don't be too disappointed in me.

PART THREE

—

THE SAUCER-MAN FROM TINSELTOWN

DIXON PUBLIC LIBRARY
DIXON ILLINOIS

Jealousy. The martini maker. Caesar Colluzo.
Ceil's hero. Smokin' Dynamite. Death of a henchman.

———

1

Despite Lex Luthor's savvy and sensitive draft report on the Harlem race riot, and despite his many contributions to both the unification of the transit system and the preparation of a new city charter; despite the federal loans and work projects Lex facilitated due to his agile handling of Harold Ickes, the notoriously ill-tempered Secretary of the Interior, and despite the fact that Lex's universal popularity has bolstered Fiorello LaGuardia's own flagging public approval—despite all of that, by the summer of 1937 the portly mayor of New York City has cooled significantly toward the affable young alderman.

He has snubbed Lex at City Hall, at Yankee Stadium and the Polo Grounds; seen to it that Lex was not included in group pictures of dignitaries taken during groundbreaking ceremonies for the World's Fair, the opening of the Lincoln Tunnel, and the dedication of the Triborough Bridge. He has left him out of strategy meetings, dropped him from steering committees. Arranged for him to be seated with cranks and boorish old coots at political banquets, no longer invites him to late-night games of Russian Bank at his family's apartment in East Harlem, and most recently he interrupted a budget conference to upbraid Lex for what he called his "incessant, irritating, tuneless, retardate *humming.*"

Does the mayor feel that Lex Luthor is becoming too popular? Is he piqued that Lex's low-altitude piloting antics at the Montauk Air Show eclipsed his own cornet solo that very same day with the Philharmonic at Carnegie Hall? Is LaGuardia angered by Lex's active lobbying efforts to be named either deputy mayor or city planning commissioner once the new charter is instituted? Or does he suspect that the alderman, observed on two occasions having drinks with Jeremiah Titus Mahoney, the Democratic candidate in the upcoming mayoral election, is hedging his bets, plotting disloyalty, possibly treachery?

Meanwhile, the handful of people in New York with some (but not full, not even close to full) knowledge of Lex Luthor's illegitimate enterprises are wondering if the mayor—self-styled racket buster and smasher of slot machines—has tumbled somehow onto the humming alderman's secret career. LaGuardia is no dope. He's a pain in the *tuchis,* a boil, a rat bastard, but no dope.

Lex, however, has no need to speculate: he knows *exactly* what's going on. "LaGuardia's a prude, that's *his* problem," he tells Caesar Colluzo one evening in the first week of August. Lex started in again ranting about the mayor just as soon as he switched off his short-wave radio, and then pressed a button, sending the receiving-and-transmitting station revolving back to its concealed niche behind the living-room wall. One of Lex's minor, but still lucrative, innovations in crime has been the establishment of a metropolitan wiretapping service, available to anyone willing and able to pay the price, and he just received his weekly update from a supervisor at the bootleg telephone exchange in Woodside, Queens. Along with a declaration of receipts, the woman— "Operative X12"—reported that yesterday afternoon at three-eleven P.M. Mayor LaGuardia was heard telling Robert Moses over the telephone that Lex would no longer be consulted regarding building contracts for the upcoming World's Fair. "He thinks I'm ostentatious for living in a place like this, and him still knocking around in that crummy little flat on the Upper East Side. He's so morally superior I'd like to strangle him."

Caesar Colluzo merely shrugs one shoulder.

"And it's driving him crazy that I'm a trendsetter. Have you noticed how many men are wearing tuxedos in the daytime ever since I started to do it? Have you?"

"No," says Colluzo, "I have not."

"Well, just look around and you'll see."

As Lex paces and Colluzo reclines on a claret-colored sofa in the library of Lex's new apartment in the Waldorf Towers, one of the phlegmatic Italian's latest robots—the prototype LR-1—handily mixes a pitcher of martinis. Thirty-eight inches tall, aluminum, noiseless, and with ball-bearings in lieu of feet, it scoops pimentoed olives from a bottle with a long-handled spoon and deposits one into each of two martini glasses. "Amazing," says Lex. "I've seen grown men with less dexterity."

Colluzo nods. "Yes, and he can pick up a dime, as well."

"That's wonderful. But can he pick up a *showgirl?*"

The Italian doesn't even smile. He is a slightly built, round-headed man in his early thirties with thinning black hair and the effete kind of mustache continental royalty affect, the sort that reminds Lex Luthor of two sardines on a collision course. As always Caesar is dressed in a tatty black suit, a white shirt, and a black string tie. The shirt buttons are yellow and brittle, and the frayed cuffs spill from his coat sleeves, ending just shy of his big knuckles.

When the robot delivers a martini in a frosted glass, Lex says, "Thank you." Then: "Can he hear me?"

"*It* is a machine, Mr. Luthor. It does not need your gratitude, nor can it respond to politeness. It cannot decode the *sounds* you make."

"The sounds I make," says Lex in a musing voice. He sips his drink. "Delicious!"

"I took the recipe from a bartender's guide I found in your kitchen."

"How resourceful of you." Finishing the martini, Lex smacks his lips. Then he clears his throat and changes his tone: "Fatty wants me to throw a public tantrum. But it's not going to happen."

Colluzo moves one shoulder again.

"I know when to turn the other cheek," says Lex, "and when to strike."

The robot glides over to the side of the chromium bar cabinet, and with a hard emphatic click turns itself off.

"But he'll get his eventually. I'll see *to* it."

"Why do you keep talking to me about the mayor? Do I care? I don't. I am an engineer."

"You're *my* engineer," says Lex. He glares but can't bring himself to grow angry at the little genius. Flinging himself down in a chair he lifts his feet onto the hassock and crosses his ankles. *My* engineer. *My* robot. *My* grand and perfect plan . . .

2

The scruffy little man was a fascination from the moment Lex first noticed him seated in a tiered lecture room at New York University a year ago this coming November. Lex was there in his official capacity to attend a seminar entitled "Public Works and Civil Engineering," and while the hall was crowded, so crowded that a number of attendees were perched on the steps or stood along the back wall, the chairs on either side of Caesar Colluzo remained unoccupied. Lex supposed it was because the little man (who *was* he?) was dressed like a ragamuffin, smelled of garlic, and seemed far more the knife-sharpening, organ-grinding, cart-pushing kind of Italian than he did the Enrico Fermi, Franco Rasetti sort. Lex was sitting two rows above and once his attention began to drift, as it always did during those sorts of things, he found himself staring down at Caesar with gathering absorption. He was astounded by the way Caesar's right hand never stopped moving as he jotted down every droning word the panelists uttered in an elegant stenography.

But that wasn't what caused Lex's real fascination. That came about when he realized that while Caesar Colluzo was taking notes with his right hand, he was simultaneously sketching and labeling diagrams in a separate notebook with his left.

Robots.

Caesar Colluzo was filling page after page of a red-covered note-book with sketches, diagrams, even preliminary blueprints for the kind of square-headed, block-bodied, tubular-legged robots that proliferated on the covers of science-fiction magazines and clanked across the floors of subterranean laboratories in Saturday-morning chapter-plays.

Lex decided then and there to learn more about this strange-looking little Italian.

And so he charged Paulie and Stick with finding out whatever they could. The first thing they discovered was that Caesar Colluzo was nei-ther a public official nor a city engineer, but instead was the most active, albeit unregistered, university student in the five boroughs of New York. In any week from early in the morning till late in the evening he sat in on classes—undergraduate, graduate, doctorate, post-doctorate, and always classes in the pure or applied sciences—at NYU, as well as at Hunter, Fordham, Columbia, Brooklyn College, City College, Queens College, even the College of Physicians and Surgeons. Taking copious notes with his right hand while sketching, revising, finessing, and providing schematics for a veritable fleet of man-shaped robots with his left.

This guy's a real cold shudder, boss, why you so interested in him?

Mind your own business, Paulie. Where's he live?

Some dump hotel, Forty-nine and Ninth.

Where's he get his money?

Money? He jumps every turnstile. Hides from the landlord.

How does he eat?

With his fingers.

Paulie . . .

He gets a roll and a cuppa every morning at six over at the Salvation Army.

Thank you, Paulie.

You want we should kill him?

Kill *him? Of course not, Stick. I* love *this guy.*

Lex didn't *really,* but he *was* mesmerized by him. And tantalized by certain possibilities that were becoming ever clearer in his mind.

Same as Lex, Caesar Colluzo was self-invented; he just hadn't pulled it off with anything near to Lex's high degree of polish. Born in Florence, he'd tell people; family impoverished by the Great War, he'd say; attended the Free University of Rome, he'd boast, where he received his first degrees, in theoretical physics, civil engineering, radiochemistry.

He attended the first international Solvay Conference in Brussels in 1927, Caesar would say, where he delivered a paper on quantum theory; Einstein applauded, Bohr applauded, everyone applauded. Immigrated to the United States in '28, he'd say, and took several more advanced degrees. He worked for the National Institute of Standards and Technology, he'd say, where he personally confirmed the existence of deuterium, an isotope of hydrogen. Then he spent a year, he'd say, working as a reliability engineer at the Picatinny arsenal in New Jersey. No, wait. First he worked at the arsenal, *then* he worked for the NIST. No, first he worked for NIST, then at the Westinghouse lab on the Televox automaton, and *then* he went to Picatinny. And then . . .

Caesar Colluzo's biography was a complete fabrication. It had taken Lex scarcely a week to dope out the real stuff.

He was born in Florence, all right—Florence, Pennsylvania. And yes, his parents *were* both Italians. A bricklayer and a seamstress. But the family name wasn't Colluzo, it was DiLappa. Caesar's birth name was Jacopo. He'd been in jail twice, each time for petty theft. And it was during his time in jail, apparently, while hiding from bullies in a surprisingly well-stocked library, that he first developed an interest in physics and chemistry, radio technology, and engineering in practically all of its branches (he wasn't particularly interested in building *buildings*). And where had his interest in robots come from? From *Metropolis,* of course. The German picture by Fritz Lang. Caesar Colluzo had fallen in love with the movie's female robot, the one who led the revolt of the masses.

Less than two weeks after the conference at NYU, Lex telephoned Caesar Colluzo, introduced himself, and invited him for drinks at the Waldorf.

Colluzo said, "That is very kind of you, I accept." Then, following a long pause, he inquired, "What exactly is an *alderman?*"

"Someone," said Lex, "who can make all of your dreams come true."

They met on a rainy weekday afternoon. Lex deliberately arrived early and sat at the bar with his briefcase on the floor leaning against his right leg. As he waited for Colluzo to appear he sipped a whiskey and watched in the back bar mirror as the fat English movie director Alfred Hitchcock entertained a table full of reporters. Hitchcock was waving an ice cream cone, his wife and small daughter sitting there with him at the table with tight smiles on their faces. With orotund delivery he was singing the praises of American ice cream, which he wouldn't trade for a steak-and-kidney pie, he said, or a broiled silversmith with carrots and dumplings, or even Kentish chicken pudding. It sounded rehearsed to Lex. Hitchcock was doing publicity for his new picture. The review that Lex had read in the *Times* made it sound good—but he just hadn't gotten around to seeing it. He hadn't gotten around to a lot of things.

All he seemed to have time for lately was city and criminal business, and at night he was too exhausted to do anything but go to bed and lie awake for hours, wondering why he had chosen to do what he'd done with his life.

When he was younger he'd operated by instinct, knowing before the age of fifteen that he needed to, was *fated* to, become a public figure as well as one of the most secretive men on the planet. But for the past year he'd wondered constantly just *why* he was doing it all. Why did he still work harder than anyone else in city government, the mayor included? Why take such pains with his wardrobe, with his persona? Why keep gobbling up, consolidating, *reinvigorating* the traditional New York rackets? Why keep launching new ones? Just because he could? It was an awful lot of work, and he no longer needed the money.

Perhaps he did, though. Perhaps he needed far more of it than he already had. Not for any *personal* use—he had no real love of luxury— but to underwrite something vast and historical. Something complicated and irrevocable. Some . . . grand scheme. The undertaking of, the commitment to. But a grand scheme to achieve *what?* There was the rub. Lex had no real idea what his goal should be. He was no longer interested in becoming mayor or governor, or the greatest racketeer since Vanderbilt and Rockefeller. The early appeal was gone, had vanished.

Nothing seemed *compelling* enough.

Was he having a moral crisis? Or just fed up to the gills?

But his long night of the soul ended the morning he first laid eyes upon Caesar Colluzo . . .

And now here came the little scruffy Italian, seemingly unimpressed by the Waldorf bar and the tuxedoed alderman who stood up immediately to shake his hand. What would he like to drink? Nothing. Well, perhaps a glass of seltzer. "You mentioned on the telephone about making my dreams come true. I'm curious, sir, how you might presume that I even *have* dreams. Or what they might entail." He really talked like that.

Smiling, Lex reached down and, while humming to himself ("How Deep Is the Ocean?"), picked up his briefcase. It weighed ten pounds and was filled with file folders and accordion folders stuffed with city ordinances and resolutions, revised budgetary figures, and correspondence that dealt with current labor negotiations, employee certifications, audits.

He undid the clasp, flicked through standing folders, then slid one out.

Colluzo's eyes widened when he realized it contained photostatic copies of roughly one hundred of his robot schematics.

"I don't understand," he said.

"No, I expect you don't," said Lex. He removed another file from his briefcase and passed that one to Colluzo as well. Then he took a sip from his drink. Straightened his cocktail napkin and carefully set down his glass.

Beside him Colluzo was staring with horror at the first of a dozen photographs inside the folder. Without looking at any of the others he snapped the folder closed.

"Just so you won't be kept in suspense," said Lex, "I'm very open-minded. Personally I don't care what a man does on his own time. What *two* men do. Of course, most people in the world are not quite so open-minded. Policemen and judges, for example. And prison guards."

"You are blackmailing me?"

"Engaging your services." Lex took back the file folder.

"To do what?"

"Build me a few robots," said Lex. "Isn't that what you've always dreamed about doing?"

3

"I wouldn't object to another one of those martinis," Lex says now, and Caesar Colluzo glumly snatches up the remote-control device—it resembles a model-train transformer—and presses a tablet.

At the same moment Lex Luthor's general factotum appears in the library: Mrs. O'Shea, a fiftyish Irish woman with a bubble of snowy white hair and a very slight brogue. She conveys a white telephone whose dial and disconnect buttons are made of 24-karat gold. Its cord snakes across the parquet floor, through the open doorway, and out into the hall. "It's that Polish woman again," she tells Lex. After putting the phone down on the table, she makes a tiny sneer at the LR-1, whose right arm lifts with a hydraulic hum to hover over the martini pitcher.

Mrs. O'Shea leaves the room.

Lex says, "Luthor," then patiently listens. "Ceil? Calm down, it's—*please,* Ceil, I want you to calm down. That's better. All right? Now I'll see what I can do, I'll try to stop by. I'll *try.*"

He ends the connection by pressing and holding down one of the buttons. Then he releases it and dials O. "I'll need my car, Henry. Ten minutes?" After he's pronged the receiver, Lex rubs a hand across his chin, his features composed into an unlikely expression, equal parts disgust and empathy.

When he strides toward the door, the LR-1, carrying a fresh martini, pivots and follows. Seeing it, Lex stops. So does the robot. Lex pinches the glass by its stem, raises and drains it. "I'll be gone for a couple of hours," he tells Caesar Colluzo. Then he sets his glass down on the flat surface of the robot's head and walks out.

4

Ceil Stickowski thinks Lex Luthor is the greatest, kindest, smartest man on planet Earth, and if you are prepared to argue that with her, she is prepared to slug with you toe-to-toe.

Ever since Herman went to the doctor in April complaining about shortness of breath and was diagnosed with terminal cancer, the alderman has taken care of all of the medical bills, the drugstore prescriptions, even the sick-room rental equipment. And he never fails to visit Stick every other day, usually in the late afternoon. He'll sit bedside and talk to Stick for a few minutes, then read to him for an hour. He's a prince, that Mr. Luthor!

In Ceil and Herman's time of crisis, Lex Luthor, God bless him, has even found a way for Ceil to make an income of her own. He's put her in charge of the mail-order catalogs. There have been two so far: the original Smokin' Dynamite catalog and the Smokin' Dynamite Summer Supplement. A third—the Smokin' Dynamite Fall Arsenal of Values—is ready to be printed, and a fourth, the last, a clearance catalog, is in the works. Because Ceil does all of the production work (layouts, photostats, pasteups), then oversees the print runs at a clandestine typography shop in Hoboken, Lex now puts another sixty dollars cash into Stick's pay envelope each Friday. She wishes he would give her the money she's earned in a separate envelope, one with her own name on it, but wouldn't dream of suggesting it.

When Mr. Luthor arrives at half past seven this evening, Ceil greets him pleasurably, taking both of his hands in hers and drawing him inside.

The Stickowskis rent a two-bedroom apartment on the ground floor of a brownstone in Turtle Bay, the rooms dark and sparsely, inexpensively furnished. Hung on the walls are framed pictures of scenic wonders—the Matterhorn, Arizona canyons, natural bridges. The only extravagances are a Stromburg-Carlson radio-phonograph in the living room and an African parrot named Zulu that Ceil keeps in a rattan cage out in the kitchen.

"I shouldn't have called, Mr. Luthor. I hope you'll forgive me but he seems so listless today and I guess I just—"

"It's fine, Ceil. I'm glad you called. Is he awake?"

"Last I checked."

Lex nods but makes no movement toward the bedroom. "I was wondering," he says, "about those proofs."

"Oh! They're all corrected. You can look at them before you leave, if you want."

"Why don't I do that?"

Ceil walks a step behind him as far as the bedroom. He goes in and leaves the door open. She remains outside. Lex starts to sit down in a chair but changes his mind and comes back and shuts the door.

As he does he gives Ceil a sympathetic smile.

In Stick's room Lex always feels conflicted and uncomfortable. He is sorry that Stick is dying, he truly is (the man was a most efficient triggerman), but wishes he'd just go ahead and *do* it, croak already. Let's get this show on the road.

Braced against three pillows in a hospital bed that rents for a dollar a day, Stick is pressing an oxygen mask to his face. It makes him look like a fatally ill bomber pilot.

On the nightstand, along with the medicine bottles, spoons, and crumpled tissues, are a thick wooden crucifix, two stubby white unlit candles, and a pygmy-size bottle of chrism.

"Priest been to see you?"

Stick nods yes while letting his hand drop away from the mask. The mask plops onto his stomach. He looks so tired and wasted that Lex feels drained of vitality himself just being near him. "Had Extreme Unction and everything."

"Excellent, Stick. Just terrific." He leans forward and pats Stick on the wrist. "Come up with any new ideas lately?"

"Wish I had, sir. But I think the medicine must be interfering with the old imagination."

"Well, don't worry about it."

Stick is pretty far gone in the head. Sometimes he'll hear quarreling voices and see crazy things: blue lizards that scramble over the walls and red bats that cling upside down to the ceiling, fish squirting out of his pillowcase to flop around in his bed, fall off, and die on the floor. It's the morphine.

But long before he started dosing with that stuff, Stick passed his days in bed dreaming up new criminal opportunities for Lex to pursue (restaurants, bakeries, trucking companies) and suggesting fresh variations on the old standbys of policy, extortion, and loan-sharking. Most of his ideas were pure cockamamie. One of them, however, was a real beaut.

Flipping idly through a pile of Sears-Roebuck and Montgomery Ward catalogs one day, it dawned on him that mail-order might be the perfect way to move a warehouse inventory of small ordnance—hand grenades, rifle grenades, smoke bombs, gas bombs, time bombs, dumb bombs, and novelty bomblets disguised as pencils, spaldeens, and lumps of coal—that Lex had acquired along with a score of bordellos in the aftermath of Lucky Luciano's imprisonment and Meyer Lansky's relocation to southern California.

Lex hadn't planned on becoming involved in the sale of incendiaries and small arms, but once he acquired that warehouse he got interested. With the U.S. Neutrality Act in effect, and an embargo on weapon sales to European and Asian belligerents, Lex decided to explore arms merchandising.

But, he decided, there might also be *American* markets for light and medium-grade explosives—corporations needed to stockpile that kind of thing in the face of labor strikes; strikers needed to do the same thing. It stood to reason. And there were the native fascist groups. And the communists too, of course, although they were notoriously bad credit risks. The Ku Klux Klan. Not to mention racketeers in other cities.

The problem was Lex had no idea how to unload the stuff. So for several months he'd done nothing. (The Italian government offered to buy whatever Lex could sell them, but they proposed delivery to a submarine off the southern coast of New Jersey, and Lex balked at that.)

When Stick mentioned his idea—beautifully printed, carefully distributed catalogs with a dozen postal blinds and automatic forwarding addresses to handle the direct-mail business—Lex got it immediately. It was simple and it was beautiful and it would work. You could, said Stick, probably set up a system where a dummy telephone number would switch incoming calls to an untraceable other number. Lex thought *definitely* could, not *probably*, and right away put Caesar Colluzo to work developing such a system.

It was also Stick who suggested there might be another market for these kinds of products scattered among ordinary citizens, and he proposed distributing the catalogs at gun shows and rodeos and stock-car races, at smokers and bachelor parties, bowling alleys and cabana clubs.

While Lex was fully prepared to recruit one of the chief copywriters at the largest advertising agency in New York (incriminating photographs, once again, would be involved), Stick proposed letting Ceil, who had done some editorial work as a young woman for a boosterism magazine in Putnam County, write all of the copy as well as lay everything out.

The first catalogs were mailed at the end of May.

Orders poured in almost immediately.

Lex considered his catalog business nothing short of an imaginative breakthrough in the annals of crime . . .

"Shall we continue with our story?" Lex says now, picking up the copy of *Northwest Passage* from Stick's bedside table. He opens it to the bookmark and glances at the page number: 159. Then he flips to the last page: 709. "We'll never make it to the end, Sticky," he says, keeping his tone light, almost joking.

Stick looks surprised and suddenly begins to gasp for air. He fumbles with both hands, searching after the oxygen mask. When he finds it and holds it over his nose and mouth, his chest relaxes.

Lex turns and examines the green oxygen cylinder.

Removing the mask from his face, Stick says, "Yeah, I'd like it if you just read a little, sir."

"Chapter . . . twenty-seven," says Lex after deciphering the Roman numerals. "'Rogers, it seemed to me, could go beyond the limits of human endurance; and then, without rest, buoyantly hurl himself against the fiercest opposition of Nature or man, or both. There was something elemental about—'"

"Boss, you can't imagine what it's like. It's awful."

"Knowing that you're a dead man?" Lex shuts the book around his index finger.

"I'm worried all the time."

"Ceil's going to be okay," says Lex. "Don't worry about Ceil. I'll see to it that she's well taken care of."

He has a cathouse in mind, a little place over in Chelsea. One of those that formerly belonged to Lucky Luciano. Like the whole string of them, it could use strong new management. Ceil has the starch, not to mention the heft, and the perfect madam's bosom.

"I'm not just worried about Ceil, of course."

"Of course not," says Lex. He heaves himself to his feet and tosses the book on the table. Stands with his hands clasped in front of him. "There's nothing afterwards, you know."

"What?"

"Once you die, that's it."

"Don't *say* that. Oh, don't say that, sir. Don't say things like that."

"I'd think it would be a comfort to you, Stick. Once you're dead you'll never know you ever existed. You're nothing."

Stick's eyes dart uneasily. On his chest the oxygen mask quietly hisses. "What about God, sir? What about heaven?"

"Think about it, Stick. Why would God surround himself in heaven with billions of idiotic human beings when he can have anything he wants?" Lex glances at his watch.

Stick begins to wheeze, his eyes bulge, and he claps the mask back onto his face.

"Why would he *do* such a thing? It's just not logical," says Lex as he turns off the oxygen flow; lefty-loosey, righty-tighty.

Stick is thumping his hands on the mattress and turning blue.

But taking one last grab at life he flings away the mask, struggles for breath, for energy, juddering his lips and finally managing to say, ". . . op Sandglass came to see me."

Lex turns the oxygen back on and Stick absorbs it, *gulps* it.

"*Richard* Sandglass? From the Detective Bureau?"

Stick nods.

"Came to see you?"

Stick nods again.

"You two pals or something?" Leaning over the bed, Lex takes the mask from Stick's hand. "You pals with a cop?"

"He pinched me twice as a fly dick. Both times when I was Jimmy Walker's bootlegger. We're not *pals* but he feels sorry for me, I guess. More than you can say for Paulie."

"Forget Paulie."

"He never comes to visit me!"

"I said forget Paulie. We're talking about Richard Sandglass. Who *didn't* come by here just to cheer you up. What'd he want?"

"First you got to promise you won't turn off that oxygen tank again."

"Fair enough." Lex sits back down on his chair. "What did he want?"

"He said he was sorry to hear I wasn't going to get better and told me that a deathbed confession has the weight of sworn testimony."

Lex feels a sharp cramp in his abdomen and looks down at his hands lying flat on his thighs. Not a tremble. But his fingers have turned cold. "So far as a cop like Sandglass is concerned you're a legger who went legit after Repeal. Why would he care about your deathbed confession?"

"He wanted me to tell him what I knew about you. What I did for you."

"And you said . . . ?"

"'Take a hike.' What *else* would I say? But he says you're nothing but a crook passing himself off as a politician. No offense, sir. I'm just repeating his words."

"And when were you going to tell me about all this?"

Stick closes his eyes. "Leave me alone, sir. You don't know what it's like facing what I'm facing. Every second is precious. Don't spoil it."

Lex thinks about that, weighs it, and finally nods. Case made. He picks up the Kenneth Roberts novel, finds his place. "There was something elemental about him," he reads, "something that made it possible for men who were dead with fatigue to gain renewed energy from him, just as a drooping wheat-field is stirred to life by the wall of wind that runs before a thunder storm." Lex pauses, glances up, and meets Stick's gaze. They both smile.

Lex resumes, "We'd no sooner made camp that night . . ."

5

From where she is sitting in the kitchen Ceil can see Lex Luthor step out of Herman's room and gently close the door.

While he picks up the phone and makes a call, she puts water on for tea, then drapes a towel over Zulu's cage. The parrot screeches in protest.

A few minutes later Lex walks into the kitchen.

"I bet Herman was glad to see you."

"He was. These the blues?" he asks picking up the proofs for the Fall Arsenal of Values. He flips through several pages. Headings read: "The Crown Prince," "the Medley," "the Salvo," "the Hoopla." All of the copy is illustrated by photographs of rifles and hand grenades, bomblets, cluster bomblets, stench and stink bombs (there's a difference), infernal bombs, and gravity bombs, everything offered at sharply reduced prices. There are special offers on rifle dischargers, deep discounts for ordering large quantities. Lex finds a typo: *Combo*, in *Combo Pak*, is spelled *Comba*. When he points it, out Ceil puts a circle around it with a red grease pencil, scores out the "a," draws a line, and carets in an "o."

Then: "Ceil, I want to talk to you about an opportunity you might be interested in. But we'll wait till after the funeral."

"The funeral?"

"He's gone, Ceil. That was Stick's doctor I just called. He'll call Mahoney's."

"Mahoney's?"

"The funeral parlor."

Lex promised Stick he would leave the oxygen tank alone and he did. He was a man of his word. He used a pillow.

It wasn't as though he expected Stick to betray him to Richard Sandglass, but why take chances? And besides, Stick's illness had dragged on. Lex did the man a favor.

Ceil reaches a hand to her forehead and leaves it there, pressing. "I should go see him"

"If you absolutely need to," says Lex, "but otherwise I wouldn't." As he is putting on his hat and coat he tells her, "By the way, you've done an excellent job on the catalog. Very excellent, indeed."

Charlie Brunner makes a purchase. Prehistoric life.
Recent news of Lois Lane. A strange visitor.
Alger in Kansas City. Skinny gets even.

———

1

The Smokin' Dynamite Fall Arsenal of Values is printed on August 9, 1937, between bootleg runs of *How to Win Friends and Influence People* and *Gone with the Wind.* (That was Lex's own brainstorm, producing cheap copies of best-selling books for the English-language markets in South and Central America. Booming business.) The catalogs are printed in Hoboken, New Jersey, with a counterfeit union bug as well as bogus state and federal licensing notices. They are then put into cartons, and the cartons trucked to a direct mailer in Newark who runs the catalogs through his machines, attaching labels. Reboxed, the catalogs are sent by train to Brownsville, Texas, then by truck to Mexico and mailed. Thus they re-enter the country and disappear into the U.S. postal routes.

Before the end of August the orders start pouring in.

One of them comes from a first-time customer in Hollywood, California, named Charles V. Brunner.

Brunner is a thirty-five-year-old trumpeter with the Bob Crosby Orchestra, a very decent Dixieland-style swing band despite the bandleader's complete lack of musical talent. But young Bob is good at fronting talent and he has name recognition, being kid brother to Bing.

Currently the band is playing an extended engagement at the Palomar Ballroom in Los Angeles. That's where Brunner picked up the Smokin' Dynamite catalog. It was lying around the dressing room in a messy pile of slicks and pulp magazines. The handsome painted cover caught his attention: in the style of James Montgomery Flagg at his most genially patriotic, it showed Uncle Sam on the porch of a log cabin accepting a parcel from his friendly mailman on the rural route; the Smokin' Dynamite logo appeared on the upper left-hand corner of Uncle Sam's parcel. Once Brunner realized what the catalog was offering, he found himself wholly absorbed in the array of products.

The revenge idea popped into his head practically full-blown the same instant he turned a page and came upon the double spread offering a wide selection of "infernal devices."

A *time* bomb. *That's* what he could do, he could blow her up with a time bomb.

For the past several weeks Brunner had been wondering just what the hell he was going to do about his wife's infidelity. She didn't know that he knew, that he'd *seen* them together. Charlie Brunner was biding his time but he had to do *something*. And it was the catalog that made him decide upon his course of action. He would kill her. Her and the boyfriend.

The model Brunner chose was called the "Trinitro-Delux." Three sturdy red cardboard tubes, TNT filler, fuse, safety clips, copper wires, and a Bulova "silent-tick" alarm clock. All for under thirty bucks, postage included.

He paid with a money order.

The Trinitro-Delux is delivered in a sturdy carton wrapped with brown paper—and ironically, since it comes on a Saturday, Skinny carries it in from the mailbox. "You got something," she says tossing the parcel on the coffee table and giving Brunner a sickening jolt because he knows immediately what's inside. But he needn't have worried—it was banged around a lot worse than that in the mails. The materiel is well packed in excelsior. "What'd you get?"

"None of your damn business," says Brunner, getting up from the couch and taking the parcel with him down the hall to the bathroom.

"Be like that. See if I care." Skinny flips him off behind his back.

Almost since day one the Brunners' marriage has been miserable and quarrelsome. A man should know better than to marry a woman with a shape like Skinny's. Pour a physique like hers into a nurse's uniform and watch out. Trouble, capital T. And Charlie Brunner has that, all right.

But at least he knows what's going on. He even knows where they've been doing the dirty: in a cheap little bungalow on Vine Street. And when: every Tuesday afternoon. Brunner followed Skinny there twice, loitering around but unable to make himself go bang on the door. He didn't want to be the ridiculous cuckold, the public fool, like one of those guys from the *Decameron* or the *Canterbury Tales.* He didn't want to make a scene. He considers himself quite an alligator. With a reputation to protect.

After he quit the Goodman orchestra (Benny was a monster to work for!) and joined Bob Crosby's outfit, he recorded a number of sides with the band for Decca, then traveled with the guys to Chicago, Boston, and finally New York City, playing four weeks at the Hotel New Yorker followed by six at the Hotel Lexington's Silver Grill.

Since he was in town, Brunner went and lived with Skinny Simon again. Why not? It was better than sharing a hotel room with one of the guys in the band. So they'd had their big reunion, and that was fine, but then one thing led to another, same old story, and before you knew it, Brunner was marrying the broad down at City Hall and bringing her back out to California with him. Big mistake.

But one he intends to rectify now.

On the twenty-eighth of September 1937, Charlie Brunner delivers his carefully assembled and packaged time bomb to the stoop of bungalow 9 at the Haciendas on Vine bungalow court. The Trinitro-Delux is rigged to explode when the package flaps are opened. And if they aren't, the bomb will go off in twenty minutes.

2

But Skinny Simon (now Skinny Brunner) doesn't meet Willi Berg at his bungalow this Tuesday afternoon. Because today is special, a celebration day, and they've agreed to meet at noon at Rancho La Brea on Wilshire Boulevard east of Fairfax. After they have a stroll around the famous bubbling tar pits and then walk into Hancock Park to look at the prehistoric statuary, they'll go grab lunch. Well, no, they won't just "grab lunch," today Willi is taking her to a nice restaurant. Which is why he's disappointed when Skinny shows up in her nursing whites. He understands why, but *still.* She is supposed to be down at the Kernville camp today, so it might've looked suspicious if she left home in anything but her uniform. Even so, Willi would have liked Skinny to dress up a little. Not that *he* has. He's wearing black whipcords, canvas shoes, and a threadbare gray suit jacket over a black shirt with snaps and white piping at the breast pockets.

Skinny has been living in L.A. less than three months, and this is her first visit to the tar pits. Willi has been a resident of Hollywood for eight months, but he's never been there, either. The tar is amazing (though it looks more like murky water, and the stench of congealed oil is pretty brutal), but they can't really concentrate on the tour; they're both too eager to sit down on a bench and look at the contents of Willi's manila envelope. So they do.

The envelope contains his contributor's copy of the new Odelle's of Paris and Hollywood lingerie catalog, which features pictures of Skinny all the way through it modeling peek-a-boo brassieres and frilly corsets, garter belts, bustiers, nylons, and negligees for the full-figured woman.

Skinny laughs as she turns through the coated pages, attracting the attention of several tourists, a few of whom peek at the open magazine and are startled by what they see. "These are great," says Skinny.

"Well sure," says Willi, then he draws out a business envelope from the inside pocket of his coat. "And let's not forget this."

"Oh God! Did they really pay you?"

"Of course they paid me. I said this was legit, it's legit. Say, doll, that guy at Odelle's thinks you ought to find an agent. Just by the way."

"What guy?"

"The *guy*. That hired me. The art director. He says you ought to take this"—tapping the catalog—"and go find yourself an agent."

"I don't know, Willi . . ."

"I'm just passing on what he said. He also wants to know if you're interested in any glamour work. I told him to ask you himself."

"You didn't give him my home number, did you?"

"No. Or your name, either. But what? You're never going to tell Charlie?"

"I will, I will." Skinny frowns and takes another pass at the catalog. She points to one picture. "I always thought I had a mole there."

"You do," says Willi. "I think it's sexy, but they wanted it off." Then he looks past Skinny and frowns. "Let's walk. Those people over there keep staring."

"What people?"

"Working that juice stand. Don't look."

But of course she does, looking directly at the couple in the "Ice Age Drinks" hut, a man and a woman, both sloppily overweight in cook whites and paper hats. They do indeed seem exceptionally interested in Willi Berg and Skinny Simon, and don't glance away when Skinny meets their eyes. "Okay," she says, "let's walk."

"Better safe than sorry."

"How do you stand it, Willi? Being on the run?"

"Most of the time I don't even think about it. And besides I got a secret weapon. If I'm ever pinched. Would you look at *that!*" he suddenly says, striding over to a cement mastodon planted in the shallows of a man-made lake. "Those babies were big!"

"What do you mean, secret weapon?"

"If I told you, it wouldn't be secret."

They walk on past statues of giant ground sloths, giant bears, giant vultures, giant rats. Twice Willi tries to hold Skinny's hand but she won't let him. It makes her too nervous.

She wishes their reunion had stayed platonic. Really. Even if her marriage is a mess. On the other hand, it's been so much fun seeing him again. And it was so incredible bumping into him by accident two months ago. What were the chances of *that?* Coincidences, in Skinny's experience, usually mean trouble, not delight. But that coincidence was sheer delight: Skinny volunteering at the Kernville migrant camp, Willi showing up there one day to snap some pictures after he'd dropped off his roommate at the nearby Prudential Studios. Willi Berg! With red hair! She recognized him instantly. It was great catching up (yeah, yeah, she was married, can you beat that?), great spending time together, and more than great posing for Willi's camera after he landed that catalog assignment. The person who probably doesn't think it was so great is Willi's quiet pal Clark Kent. He probably resents it like hell being kicked out of his own apartment every Tuesday afternoon so that Willi can take Skinny's pictures. Not that he's ever complained.

"I got a letter from Lois yesterday," she tells Willi now. "She's working for the *Daily Planet.*"

"No fooling. Good for her."

"She mentioned you."

"She did?"

"Yeah, that she hasn't heard from you in about a year."

"It hasn't been that long. God, maybe it has."

"And there's something else."

"She's got a boyfriend."

"You don't mind?"

"I've been gone for two years. And it's not like we were so perfect together. Who's the lucky guy?"

"A cop."

"Well, that's great, that's just swell!" Willi seems genuinely shocked, instantly bitter.

"She says his name is—"

"Not interested. Look, can we talk about something else?"

They stop to marvel at the giant camel, both saying they didn't know there'd been *camels* in the United States forty thousand years ago, but as they start to walk on again, discussing the quickest way back to Wilshire, a woman somewhere close behind them begins to shout: "That's him, that's him, arrest the bum, that no-good bum, *that's him!*"

Willi swivels his head around and knows instantly that he's caught and there's no point in trying to run: four uniformed cops are approaching obliquely, the closest one not even ten feet away. They all have revolvers drawn.

"That's him, *that's* him, that's the crummy *shamdeh un cherpeh!*"

Skinny squeezes Willi's arm, but a cop shoves her away and grips Willi himself. "Sir, could you come with us?"

As he is hustled away past the statues of gigantic rats, Willi glances at the fat woman from the juice stand now giving him the finger. "You should rot, you should fry!"

Ida?

Oh my God, it's *his sister!*

"*Ida!* What're you doing in California?"

"If you talk again," says the cop, pinioning Willi on his right, "I'm going to smash your teeth in with my stick. Are we clear about that?"

Thrown into the back of a pie wagon, into the stench of old stale vomit, Willi starts taking measured breaths trying to calm down.

All right, Clark, you can rescue me now.

3

Somehow he slipped into her apartment while she—and everyone else at home in the court this Tuesday afternoon—ran outside to find the source of an explosion terrific enough to bring down shelves, crack mirrors, shatter windows (none of hers, thank goodness), and heave prints from stuccoed walls. How did he get past her—past everyone—without being seen? What'd he do, crawl? Maybe so, maybe he crawled behind the hedges that bordered the sidewalks. Whatever he did, however he did it, he was standing in her living room fighting an inclination to stagger when she got back. Had she left the door open? Had he walked into the first open door he came to—or had he come specifically to her door?

He looked dazed. At first he couldn't speak—he tried but couldn't. He was shoeless and his dungarees were in tatters. The pocket rivets were melted and so was his belt buckle. All that remained of his shirt was its left sleeve, part of the yoke, and a wide ribbon of fabric that lay flat on his chest like a battle flag. She peeled that off him before she even walked him across the floor and sat him down. She didn't know his name so she called him honey or sweetheart or doll.

She said, "Honey, what *happened?*"

She said, "Sweetheart, did you smell gas or . . .?"

She said, "Doll, you really need to get to a hospital."

"No," he said, "they won't know what to do."

They won't know what to do? Was he nuts? A feeb? Or just rattled?

She sat down opposite him in a chair, folded her hands in her lap, and cocked her head.

He smiled apologetically.

That was half an hour ago.

Now she hears still another siren, maybe another hook-and-ladder, maybe another cop car. Then a jarring *whoosh* as yet another big hose is turned on down at the far end of the bungalow court. And is that crash, that crunch, that splintering from another ax?

Outside the air is densely smoky, so thick she can't see twenty feet through her front window to the opposite bungalow. She snaps the curtains closed with a noisy clack of wooden rings.

Her name is Diana. Diana Dewey. Well, it is and it isn't. She was christened Gladys Murrah but changed it to Christie Winsom when she landed her first job in pictures playing Harry Carey's pigtailed niece in Monogram's *Headin' West.* That was in 1928. The following year she changed her name again, that time to Ann Blaine, maintaining it throughout her five-year stay at the Mascot Studios on Las Palmas Avenue, where—costumed always in skintight riding pants—she co-starred with Tim McCoy, Tom Tyler, Joe Bonamo, or Rin Tin Tin in a dozen western and jungle-adventure serials, a few of which were recut later and released as five-reel features.

But Diana Dewey is what Harry Cohn at Columbia Pictures decided he wanted her called two years ago when he okayed her admission to starlet school—a permission he never would have granted had he known she was twenty-seven. (She just *looked* twenty-three.) But then she caught the grippe, contracted bronchial pneumonia, and her voice changed. It turned so husky it sounded like her throat was lined with carborundum, making her useless for pictures. But even though she washed out at Columbia (she got plenty of offers to smooch, none to act), she kept the Diana Dewey name. It was on her apartment lease and her health insurance, and she was tired of traipsing to court and filing papers.

A petite, athletic-looking woman, the type press agents would describe as "sportaletic," Diana has sleek black hair parted in the middle (a relatively new coiffure that replaced her head of cutie-pie curls), dark eyes, cherry-red lips (natural, not paint), and a white but healthy complexion. She wears steel-rimmed almond-shaped glasses.

Turning away from the window, she looks across her living room now at the young man seated eerily still, glassy-eyed and practically naked in the smaller of her two loveseats.

His hands clutch at his flat stomach.

"Sugar, there's probably an ambulance outside right now."

Again he shakes his head: no hospital, no ambulance, no doctor, no treatment. *Please.* "I'll be all right."

"How do you figure that, sweetie?" He doesn't reply, and Diana drops it. How do you figure *that?* How do you figure *this:* by all rights this narrow-faced boy should be nothing but ash and bone chips, yet here he is plopped in Diana's loveseat acting like he's suffering from acid indigestion. Well, no. Something a little bit worse than that.

This isn't the first time Diana has seen him. The first time was at Grand National Pictures in April, then a month later he turned up on the Republic back lot. He was one of Yakima Canutt's stuntmen: she watched him leap from a burning hayloft into the saddle of a galloping horse and topple from a cliff in Bronson Canyon. In July she saw him speeding down Melrose toward Western on roller skates. Good-looking, she thought, but no Gary Cooper. More like Paul Muni but without the devils. Or Cagney with jet-black hair and minus the smart-aleck bug. At least that was Diana's take on him from across the commissary or the street: what could she know or tell for sure?

When she realized a month ago that he was living only fifteen doors away, Diana felt the kind of juicy thrill in her solar plexus that she hadn't felt in a very long time. No denying it, she had the eagers to meet him. In recent weeks she managed—finagled—to be out and about the courts when he likely would be coming or leaving, and they'd exchanged smiling hellos on several occasions, the smiles growing steadily gladder and friendlier, although twice he'd been with his room-mate, a redheaded masher who always gave Diana that *look,* that *leer,* that insulting up-and-down once-over, usually punctuated by a wink. Him she didn't like. The kid, though. There was something about the kid that she liked. And it wasn't just his trim acrobat's physique; every other gee in Hollywood had one of those.

And now here he is.

His eyes are closed. His breathing is . . . shallow. Unnervingly so.

And now his hands separate and drop away from his stomach, revealing a lateral gash no wider and no longer than a toothpick.

As Diana stares, a thin line of blood trickles out and fills in his navel.

4

Earlier today Alger Lee drove the Ford pickup from Smallville to Kansas City, Missouri, leaving the Kent farm before daybreak and arriving at Union Station by eleven. Wanting to allow himself plenty of time he's allowed himself too much and ends up sitting on the platform for nearly an hour and a half.

When the train from Detroit pulls in at last, Alger searches for his mother and Claude Clemments in the hubbub of reunions and passengers in a hurry but can't find them. He stands there puzzledly with his hands in his pockets looking down the length of the train, past the coach cars and the Pullmans, sighting toward the caboose. He notices a number of shabby boys and men dropping from grab ladders and catwalks, picking up their bindles and darting across cinders and the maze of track. When he looks the other way, toward the locomotive engine, suddenly there is his mother and Mr. Clemments hopping off the narrow ledge between the coal tender and the baggage car. They wave.

It is a funny, complex moment for Alger Lee: he expected his mother and stepfather to arrive here like—normal people. Expected them to ride the cushions from Michigan to Missouri, not the blinds! And now he feels embarrassed going down off the platform and meeting them alongside of the tracks. In some nonverbal part of his mind Alger realizes that he's different now than he was the last time he saw his mother, that he's changed in significant ways.

He hugs his mother and shakes hands with Claude Clemments and leads them to where he parked Mr. Kent's truck. Their trousers and flannel shirts are peppered with tiny burn holes, their faces are smudged with soot. They keep flexing their hands, trying to get some feeling back into their fingers after so many hours holding on to bars of slippery metal. They have only one hobo sack between them, which Alger's mother carries slung on a shoulder by its loop cord.

The moment Mr. Clemments sees the truck he kicks a rear tire, curses the name of Henry Ford (he still has scars from strikes at both the Dearborn and Rouge plants), but declares the machine a thing of beauty. "That model's a 32 closed-cab on a double-T chassis," he tells Alger. Then Mr. Clemments pulls open the driver's door.

Alger expected this. What he didn't expect is his instinctive response. "I'll be driving us back to Smallville, Mr. Clemments."

"I don't *ride* in any vehicle when I'm the only man. I *drive* it."

"But see there, Mr. Clemments? You're *not* the only man," Alger says with a toothy smile.

As he motors across the bridge into Kansas, his mother keeps tapping his right knee, keeps saying how good it is to see him again. Is she clenching her eyes so they won't start to leak? Alger decides that she is.

"I can't tell you how happy I was to get your letter, son."

"I would've wrote you more but I didn't have an address."

"I know that and I'm sorry. But we did a lot of moving. Mr. Clemments has not had an easy time of it—have you, Mr. Clemments?"

Mr. Clemments, thin as a rake and with a long columnar neck raddled with veins, does not reply. He continues to watch the scenery as it flows past, the billboards for toothpaste, for Sunday worship, for Burma Shave.

"Mr. Clemments can't work in a car factory anymore, not since that last time he got hit in the head. He has a ringing in his ears now, you see, and it's just too much."

"He'll enjoy working on the farm then," says Alger, uncomfortable talking about Mr. Clemments as though he's not in the truck.

"I used to know the Kents," says Alger's mother after a while. "Your dad worked for them. But I don't remember Mr. Kent too well."

"Even if you did, Ma, you wouldn't recognize him now. His heart's giving out bit by bit. Every day it's a little weaker. He can't use the stairs anymore so I brought down his bed and put it in the parlor."

"They had a boy as I recall."

"Clark."

"And where is he?"

"Hollywood, California. Clark's in Hollywood."

"What's he doing there? He in pictures?" She isn't serious; she means it as a joke.

"As a matter of fact, he is. But you don't notice him. He's doing what they call stunt work, jumping off roofs and cliffs and like that. For cowboy pictures mostly. That's what he said in his last letter."

"Why ain't he home helping out with the farm?"

"He's just . . . not. But it's all right, he's been gone almost two years now, and Jon and me have managed just fine. Till recently."

"Jon?" Mr. Clemments is suddenly interested in the conversation. "You call the man Jon? To his face?"

"Sure I do, Mr. Clemments. We work together every day. I live in his house."

"Till the first time he forgets where he left his damn billfold and says you took it." Mr. Clemments snorts.

"I'm sure Alger knows what he's doing," says his mother.

They ride the rest of the way in silence.

As they are approaching the Kent farm, Mr. Clemments mutters, "He just better not expect *me* to call him Jon!"

"Oh, Mr. Clemments," says his wife, "don't be like that."

Alger stops the truck and cuts the engine. Gets out and runs across the county road, scoops mail from the RFD box. Returning to the truck, he flicks through it hoping to find an envelope addressed with Clark's handwriting. But no. He dreads seeing Jon Kent's face cloud and close when he has to tell him there's nothing from Clark, no letter again today.

Alger releases the brake and steers the truck into the driveway.

5

As soon as Skinny reads in the Wednesday papers that it was a *time bomb*—

"Hiya Nappy, hey Gil, either of you seen my hubby?"

—she knew Charlie did it. The son of a bitch!

"Hi Bob. Dean. Matty, you seen Charlie? 'Kay, thanks."

She hadn't known about the explosion at Willi Berg's apartment till she saw a picture of the damage in the *L.A. Times.* At first it didn't register. It took her several seconds before the page-one photo turned suddenly into a place she knew well, had been *inside* of once a week for the past half a dozen . . . Tuesdays.

The article said the bomb exploded at roughly one-fifteen in the afternoon.

Tuesday afternoon.

And all the while she thought Charlie didn't know!

She took a cab to the rehearsal studio downtown.

"Eddie? Charlie in there?"

"Sure is, sweetheart. How you *been,* we haven't seen you in—hey! You can't go in there!"

Skinny does, though, and finds her husband sitting on a toilet reading the *Times* himself.

Withdrawing the little silver derringer from her coat pocket, she sticks out her arm and touches the barrel to Charlie Brunner's forehead.

"You tried to kill me!" she says.

Brunner says, "Don't!"

His pathetic plea doesn't keep Skinny from squeezing the trigger.

Jail time. An interview with Captain Gould.
The seamstress of Poverty Row. Clark's talents are discussed.

———

1

It's going on five P.M. and the felony block is as quiet as an opium den. Willi isn't even sure how many of the other cells are occupied. Three or four would be his guess, but since he was processed in here yesterday none of his neighbors have shown the smallest inclination to communicate with him or with anyone else. Which is good—he was afraid the place would be a Bedlam, like in the movies. He was terrified he'd have to share a cell with some maniac.

As he pokes another Camel between his lips the iron door at the end of the tier swings open and a jail deputy—a freckle-faced blond who looks like he ought to be jerking sodas at Currie's ice cream parlor—comes in and walks directly to Willi's cell. "Stand up, turn around, and put your hands behind your back."

"What for?"

"I have to cuff you."

"Oh, for the love of Mike," says Willi ditching his smoke.

On the way down the block, their heeltaps echo loudly. Willi glances into all of the other cells. He guessed wrong: just two other prisoners. Neither of them look at him when he passes.

"Where we going?"

"Captain Gould wants to see you."

After riding an elevator down several flights and going through two more locked iron doors, Willi is delivered to an office in the basement.

Captain Gould is the spit-and-polish type, deeply tanned and thick-bodied, his waist going to flab. His uniform looks just off the hanger. Hands in his trouser pockets, he stands behind a conference table situated lengthwise down the room. On the table: a lidded gray cardboard box and a zipper-style briefcase with peeling varnish. "Sit."

Willi toes a chair away from the table and then awkwardly perches on the edge of its seat. His upper arms threaten to cramp but he'll grind his back teeth to a fine powder before he'll complain about the handcuffs.

Gould stares at him for thirty seconds, then withdraws his hands from his pockets. They're huge and the backs are covered with thick monkey hair. Picking up the lidded box, he comes and stands behind Willi's chair. Willi's whole body tenses.

"Collins!" says Gould, and the deputy appears like a genie. "Unlock the prisoner's handcuffs."

"Yes, sir."

As soon as they're off and the deputy has departed, Willi rubs at the grooves in his wrists. Gould takes the lid off the cardbox box. Flinging it aside, he tips the box forward, spilling on the table hunks of charred metal, part of the blackened face and radium dial of an alarm clock, scorched paper, bits of wire, bits of twine. "See this? It's what left of the guinea football that blew up your apartment."

Deliberately going for the socko effect, he then scoops out a palm's worth of ash. "And this is probably all that's left of your roommate."

Willi suddenly has a vicious headache and it's hard to think above and between its steady pulse. The apartment? Guinea football? *Clark?* Wait a second. Hold on.

". . . what I think, Willi? I think somebody tried to blow *you* up. Either that or your roommate blew himself up building a bomb."

"No."

"No?"

"Clark doesn't know anything about bombs. Are you sure he was there?"

"That's what the neighbors tell us."

"Well, he's not dead. I can tell you *that*."

Gould shakes his head. After a tiny hesitation he moves on: "Who blew up your place, Willi?"

"I don't know."

"Take a guess."

"You ever hear of a guy in New York named Lex Luthor?"

"No."

"He's a politician. And a crook. And the guy that framed me. *He* coulda sent the bomb. To get rid of me. He coulda found out where I was living and . . ." Willi trails off, his scenario sounding implausible even to him.

Captain Gould returns to the far end of the table and unzips his briefcase. What now? Brass knuckles?

Instead, he takes out a carton of Camel cigarettes, which he slides down the table to Willi. "A little gift from Meyer Lansky."

"What?"

"He read about you in the papers. And thought you might be needing a little pick-me-up. Just make 'em last, Willi—you could be here for a couple of weeks."

For a moment Willi thinks he might take the high ground and refuse the gift. But to hell with the high ground. He isn't about to pass up two hundred smokes for a principle. Besides, he sort of liked Meyer Lansky.

And he has the impression that Captain Gould sort of likes him, too. Otherwise Willi might be leaving here right now with a few busted ribs, a hamburger face, and a mouthful of blood.

Clark, he thinks. For crying out *loud.* Come get me!

2

On her way back from Republic Pictures, Diana is in a black mood: the producer she expected to be working for throughout the autumn, perhaps till the end of the year, was fired yesterday (an ill-advised practical joke, with injuries, at the studio canteen), and now his latest chapter-play, *Saucer-Man from Saturn,* is officially scratched from the production schedule. Instead, Herbert Yates is going to crank out another Zorro serial, and they already have costumes on hand from the first one.

Ever since she washed out as a picture actress, Diana has been designing and sewing, fitting and altering costumes for the Poverty Row studios and conglomerates in North Hollywood. It's not what she ever wanted to do, God knows, but you get what you get and you do what you can. And she takes pride in being damn good with a Singer machine.

But she'd been counting on that Saucer-Man job! Now what?

After she gets off the bus on Vine Street, Diana stops into a grocery store and picks up two cans of pork and beans and one can of corned-beef hash, canned beets, and a package of saltine crackers. Earlier she planned on preparing something special this evening for dinner—mushroom steak or pork chops—but hash and beans are just about all she has the spirit for now.

Coming through the door she flings her green felted beret on the wall peg and tosses the Saucer-Man costume, still in its plastic bag, over an arm of the bigger loveseat. She walks into the kitchen and puts down the grocery sack. "Clark!"

"Up here."

When she comes back out into the living room and peers up, there's Clark on the narrow balcony leaning over the banister. "How'd it go?"

"It didn't. They scrubbed the picture. What do you have on?"

He looks down at himself and grins: pathfinder moccasins, the jodhpurs from an African-safari shoot, a mailed shirt worn by a mer-man from an undersea kingdom, a domino mask, and a cowboy hat. He found everything crammed in with dozens of other wardrobe costumes on a push-boy in Diana's sewing room. "What, you don't like it?" He unties the mask, pulls it off his face, and drapes it over the railing. He's trying to be cute.

"Come down and keep me company in the kitchen."

He does immediately, sitting at the table and watching as Diana nimbly shapes the hash into little nests and then warms those in the oven. After ten minutes she removes them and fills them with hot pork and beans and puts them back in. She sets the table, fans the crackers out on a plate, and dumps the beets into a bowl. She finds an opened bottle of Italian Swiss Colony wine in the Frigidaire and pours two glasses. Wryly she clinks hers to his. Even in the harsh overhead kitchen light Diana looks beautiful. Gloomy today but still so beautiful.

"Maybe you can sell the same costumes to some other picture," says Clark as they wait for the pork and beans to warm through in the hash nests.

"I'll be all right, honey, don't worry about me. What about you? You feeling better?"

"Yeah." He touches his stomach, the wound area, even presses it. "Much."

She nods slowly, thoughtfully, then getting up, she grabs a pot holder and opens the oven door. Using a spatula, she slides a nest onto Clark's plate. Another onto her own. "Help yourself to beets," she said. "Bon appétit."

Before starting to eat she removes her eyeglasses and puts them aside. "What?" she asks.

"What do you mean?"

"You just frowned."

Clark shrugs. "Nothing."

"No, tell me."

"I like you with your glasses on."

"You're crazy. They make me look like a sweatshop girl."

"No! They make you look even more beautiful than you—" He can't believe he just said that! Color floods his face.

"Thank you, Clark, that's very sweet." She puts her glasses back on. "Better?"

"I'm sorry, I didn't mean—"

"*Thank you,* I said. Now let's eat."

They do.

"Clark . . . ?"

"Uh-huh?"

"It's Friday."

"Yes . . . ?"

"You got blown up on *Tuesday.* That's just three days ago."

"The bungalow got blown up, not me."

Diana's expression—almost-but-not-quite afraid, the fear mitigated by confusion and awe—is the same one he's been seeing again and again over the past two years. He saw it only last week at the Prudential lot after he'd fallen off the back of a galloping horse and slid under the left rear wheel of a stagecoach. Rolling over Clark's abdomen, the wheel shattered into great wooden chunks. The wagon pitched over, dragging the team of horses with it, injuring two of them. But Clark just got up apologizing—apologizing!—even before the production crew reached him.

"Clark?"

He starts clearing plates from the table.

"Clark, we have to talk."

He runs hot water in the sink, shakes in a little detergent. "What about?"

"'What about.' About *you.* About how—"

"I think I might be from another planet."

He looks timorously over a shoulder.

Diana laughs. "You too? What's the name of your planet? Mine's Tennessee."

*Stormy night. Skinny in transition. Meyer Lansky
again. The problem with capes. Bronson Canyon.*

———

1

Diana and Clark listen to the rain crash against the bungalow roof.
They are lying together fully dressed on her bed. Impulsively, he
reaches over with two hands and removes her eyeglasses. She smiles . . .
until he fits the side wires around his own ears. Then she bursts into
laughter. Again.

"What do you think?"

"They make you look very . . . intelligent."

"You think?" He rolls off the bed to go and stand in front of the
bureau mirror. "Really?"

"Yes," she says. "Really. Now come back to bed, superman."

"Because if there's one thing that I wish I was it's—*what* did you
call me?"

Later, after Diana falls asleep no longer in her clothes, Clark watches
her for hours. He wants to wake her up and do it again. Do it all over
again. But what if she gets mad? He doesn't want her to think he's a guy
with no self-control. He wants to touch her breasts. He doesn't. Wants
to kiss her mouth. Doesn't. Instead he picks her glasses up from the
table and puts them on in the dark.

Intelligent?

Really?

2

Skinny Simon sits at the open window of her hotel room looking out at the rain, relishing the breeze, smoking Chesterfield Kings, wondering what next. After Nevada, what next? Take the Super Chief back to New York or stick around here, become a lingerie model? A model! She's a nurse, for God's sake. Yeah, but is that inborn, is that *innate*, like eye color? When you come right down to it, nursing is a job, you do it for pay, same as modeling brassieres. And it's much harder work. Draining work. Every time Skinny returns to that migrant clinic in Kernville she discovers that another little girl or boy she saw the previous week has since died from a ruptured appendix or diphtheria. That takes its toll. At least when you're a model nobody dies.

At a crash of thunder Skinny jumps, then giggles for being skittish. She turns on the radio, leaves the dial at Rudy Vallee, lights another cigarette. When she finds the energy she'll call the hotel kitchen and order up room service. It's too bad about Willi. She wishes she could do something. What, though?

3

At the Palomar Ballroom, Charlie Brunner (Skinny's "gun," of course, was only a novelty lighter) doesn't realize that it's raining out till he looks down from the bandstand around ten o'clock and sees wet hair on dancers crowding the floor. So far tonight he's made a lot of chart errors, missed his solo cue twice. Because all he can think about is Skinny and how she can put him in prison. He blew up a *house*, maybe *killed* somebody! He could rot in San Quentin! She promised she won't tell, won't make trouble for him if—*if*—he leaves her alone, agrees to a Reno divorce, agrees to *alimony* and then actually *pays* it. But can he *trust* her?

Women.

4

Captain Gould, off duty, stands watching it rain through the sliding glass doors of the pool room at an exclusive men's club in the San Fernando Valley. Wearing a robe of white Turkish toweling, he raptly gazes at the bazillion animated rings on the swimming pool water outside.

Behind him a man steps naked from the sauna. He is extremely white, pot-bellied, fleshy. He has a long circumcised penis. "Did you have an opportunity to pass on my gift?"

"I did indeed, Mr. Lansky."

"Thank you."

"Glad to do it. So. Did the two of you know each other back in New York?"

Lansky doesn't choose to reply. He raises a hand instead, languidly. "This rain! Maybe it'll bring down the temperature."

"Just more humidity."

"Pessimist." Lansky wags a finger. "Pfui on pessimists. They get you killed."

"I thought it was the optimists did that."

"You thought wrong." He starts to go, shuffling off back toward the showers.

"Mr. Lansky. Who is . . . Lou Dexter?"

"I have no idea."

"He's a politician in New York. The Berg kid—"

"Lex Luthor?"

"That's it. What do you know about him?"

"Why are you asking? The Berg kid *what?*"

"Said he didn't kill anybody. That he was framed by this Lex Luthor, whoever he is."

"He's an alderman. And the kid's right. Which is too bad for the kid."

Meyer Lansky pads away.

Gould resumes watching the rain plink rings in the swimming pool.

5

By morning the rain has stopped, the skies are clear, and it's a glorious rinsed day in Los Angeles.

Diana wakes to find herself alone in bed but then hears Clark directly below in the kitchen: the refrigerator door closing, a cabinet door opening. She smiles and stretches.

After showering, she dresses in black slacks and a green blouse and goes downstairs. At the kitchen doorway she stops dead in her tracks. "Today, my friend, I am definitely going out and buying you some real clothes."

Clark has put on that Saucer-Man costume, the blue tights with the red trunks, the yellow belt, a red **S** inside a black shield appliquéd to the chest. He turns from the stove where he's using a whisk to scramble eggs. "Fits good," he says.

"Like a glove. You could get arrested for indecent exposure."

She has embarrassed him and he loves it. "But I got a question. What's the **S** stand for—*Saucer-Man* or *Saturn*?"

"Take your pick."

"Okay," says Clark, "but why would they even *have* the letter **S**—if they're from Saturn? I mean, do they write in English there?"

She sticks out her tongue and says, "Shut up and feed me, mister."

Using a spatula, he shovels the eggs—slightly watery, a little charred—onto her plate and his. "There's toast. And coffee. Anything else?"

"Only you."

He blushes again. Then, reaching behind him, he sweeps aside the long red cape before sitting down at the table.

"Personally I never liked capes," says Diana, watching Clark finally just hang it over the back of his chair. "But they always want villains and spacemen to wear them, don't ask me how come."

"I think they're great. Way better than neckties."

Diana takes a sip of her coffee. Smiles again. God, she feels like a smiling fool. Last night was so—

"Listen," says Clark, "I've been thinking."

"Always a dangerous thing." When he frowns, Diana adds, "Don't mind me. Thinking about what?"

"I have to go get Willi."

Diana smiles—again! The guy is completely adorable. Too bad he's nuts. "Clark. Sweetheart. You can't just go bust your pal out of jail."

"But he's innocent!"

"So you told me. You *still* can't do it."

"No," says Clark. "See, that's the thing: I can. I really can."

And suddenly Diana is no longer smiling.

6

Clark sits on a cliff at Bronson Canyon, a short distance from Hollywood. Legs dangling, he stares at the green lagoon fifty feet below, then out to the rough, undulating, boulder-strewn wasteland beyond, where most of the Poverty Row studios film their western chases. He's worked here a dozen times over the past seven months, has in fact leapt from this very cliff, pretending to be shot.

Clark was pretty awkward at first. Yakima Canutt kept saying he didn't know how in hell Clark hadn't broken his collarbone, at the very least, toppling off that Indian pony, the driver's box on that Wells Fargo stage, that promontory. In time, though, he got better—so good he was bombarded with offers of work, too many for Clark's liking. But it sure was nice making money.

Not that he has any of it now. He kept all of his savings at home, and now that his home is gone, blown to smithereens, his cash is gone, too.

After breakfast Diana went out and bought him some new clothes—the shirt and trousers, socks and shoes he's wearing now. She also gave him a hundred bucks. He promised to pay her back as soon as he could. She said don't worry about it. No, he said, he *wanted* to. She nodded, not smiling, and because he was so crazy about it she made him a gift of the Saucer-Man costume, acrobat's cape and all. She stuffed it into a string bag and threw in a pair of shiny red boots that belonged to another costume from another picture she worked on, *Santa Claus vs. the Gila Martians.*

He left her bungalow a short time later.

He purses his lips now and sighs, rattling the dusty leaves on a yucca tree some forty feet away. Two of them break off and flutter to the ground.

The idea of rescuing Willi makes Clark sick to his stomach. He may never have experienced the majority of natural aches and activities— he's never hiccupped, never had the sniffles, he doesn't need to shave more than once a month—but he knows about feeling nauseous and he knows about headaches and he knows about strained nerves. And right now he knows about all of those things all over again.

What if somebody gets hurt or killed while he's trying to break Willi Berg out of the L.A. County Jail? He'd feel so guilty, such Methodist guilt! What if they put him in jail for life and his lifetime is two hundred years! (Yeah, but—how could they *keep* him there?)

Without Willi around he doesn't have anyone to fret to. He used to fret to his mom, hardly ever to his dad. But even with them he felt they couldn't understand how strange, how lonesome it is being one of a kind. Being singular has always made Clark feel as though he's not quite genuine, that he's a made-up character in a story. And that's hard. Especially since he's not smart the way that he feels he should be, all things being equal. Intelligence to match his physical powers: is that too much to ask?

Maybe he should start wearing glasses.

Getting to his feet, Clark looks out across the canyon, a landscape that always seems to him both magical and personal since it is identical to the one, it *is* the one, that he used to see in western serials and African-safari movies on Saturdays at the Jewel. He notices a crevice in a rock formation and can imagine the Lone Ranger or the Laughing Caballero ducking inside while dodging a hail of bullets.

Tucking his elbows against his ribs, he crouches, trembles, and leaps. When he lands on a boulder down below, the soles of his new shoes give him no traction. Swooping both arms for balance, he flings off his string bag and sends it whizzing a hundred feet down the canyon. Clark hops to the ground and retrieves it. Then decides to jump from here to that shelf of granite down there and does, kicking up alkaline dust behind him. Leaping from outcrop to boulder to boulder to outcrop, he makes his way ever farther down the canyon. He doesn't notice when yet another long jump becomes a very *high* jump, but all of a sudden he's rising straight up into the air, the clouds. A small tickling electrical charge starts pulsing around his body, his velocity becoming so extravagant so quickly that his shirt and trousers and shoes all seethe from the friction. Without conscious thought, Clark tucks his head toward his left shoulder, makes a fist with his left hand, and his body immediately follows that direction. A few dozen starlings burst apart just moments before he passes through the flock.

He *can* fly!

But now he's plummeting. A moment later he hits the ground and keeps going, shredding his clothes, burrowing deeper and pulverizing bedrock before coming to a stop twenty feet underground at an oblique angle.

Clawing his way back to the surface, Clark pulls himself from the hole he made and sits on the edge of it, covered with dirt and earth-worms and beetles.

Whoa.

He gets up at last and dusts himself off, locates Diana's string bag tangled on the branch of a low, stunted tree and starts to hike back toward the cliff by the lagoon. He hasn't gone twenty feet when he stops again. He looks at the rags on his body, he looks at the bag in his hand, then looks around for a cave he remembers being catapulted, literally catapulted, from during a mine explosion scene in *Law West of the Pecos.*

Even though there is nobody around to see him, he'd feel funny stripping down and changing clothes right out here in the open.

A secret investigation is revealed. The Ghost Gang strikes. A new beau for Lois. Mrs. O'Shea and the dangerous caller. Jailbreak. A defrocked priest.

———

1

"Mr. Mayor," intones Dick Sandglass, then he stops and sips from a glass of water. Begins again: ". . . Mr. Mayor," trying for a looser sound, "there is a ghost gang operating in this city and . . ." Try it *again*, he thinks, and *this* time without the melodrama. "*Sir,* I have proof in this envelope here that a secret gang of criminals is operating in this city—a *ghost gang,* if you will, and . . . And . . . ?" He makes a face, all chagrin, then sticks out his tongue, razzing himself in his bureau mirror.

After looping a Windsor knot in his maroon tie and fitting the knot against his throat, Sandglass pulls his suit jacket from the bedpost and puts it on, smoothing the front, shooting the cuffs. He studies himself again, squaring his shoulders. "Mr. Mayor . . . Mayor LaGuardia, thank you for agreeing to meet with me tonight. Sir, there is a ghost gang operating in Greater New York that has been systematically eliminating all of its criminal competition." Damn, he sounds like Tom Dewey. Or Lowell Thomas. *Relax.*

The mayor has agreed to see Dick Sandglass under the conditions the detective proposed to the mayor's secretary: on the weekend, absent any staff, and with no record of the meeting entered on any appointment calendar. Tonight, seven-thirty, the mayor's apartment.

It's twenty past six.

"Mayor, for two years and completely on my own time and at my own expense, I have been collecting evidence which I believe proves the existence of a . . . let's call it a *ghost gang* operating here in our city."

Still not right.

Firing a cigarette, he goes and flicks through half a hundred shellac recordings cataloged alphabetically, finally selecting "Ring Dem Bells" by the Duke Ellington Orchestra with a Cootie Williams vocal. He slaps it down and cranks up the Victrola, sets the needle carefully in the lead-in groove. Sitting directly in front of the horn, Sandglass lets the music hit him square in the chest. Soon he's drumming on his thighs right along with Sonny Greer. He thinks of a woman he knows, a singer, but quickly puts her out of his mind. And thinks of Lex Luthor, then of Mayor LaGuardia and their meeting tonight.

His hands quit drumming.

It's quarter of seven.

"Mr. Mayor, I have with me this evening damning proof that a man trusted by the citizens of this city, trusted by you yourself, sir, has abused that sacred trust and . . . and has been positioning himself to become absolute king of the New York rackets. And that man, I am sorry to tell you, sir, is none other than—"

"That's when shots ring out from behind a curtain and you fall dead, Pop."

"Hey kid, when did you get back?"

"Few minutes ago." Spider Sandglass stands in the bedroom doorway with his arms crossed and a smile on his face. A paintbrush-size hank of black hair flops across his forehead, the rest glistens with Brylcreem. He needs a haircut. He needs better posture. He needs a job. Ah, leave the kid alone, thinks Dick Sandglass. He's *trying*.

"Go on, Pop, it sounded good. Who's the mystery villain?"

"You don't think I sounded like, I don't know, some guy in the movies?"

"No, was great. Very professional."

"Thanks."

"No really, you sounded great. Before you know it you'll be chief of police."

"Or wearing cement shoes in the Atlantic Ocean."

"Don't even joke, Pop."

"Who's joking?"

Spider changes the subject. "You want something to eat?"

"You kidding? With the butterflies in *my* stomach? You go ahead, though. There should be some chicken left."

"I finished that."

"Well, then you'll just have to look and see what's there."

Spider has been living with his father for three, going on four months now, since he got out of prison with time off for good behavior. He was only supposed to stay here briefly, just till he found some work, but so far he hasn't. Yeah, and who's going to hire an ex-con? Lay off, thinks Sandglass. He's your kid and you love him. And he loves you. Maybe.

When Dick Sandglass goes down the short hall five minutes later to say good-bye, he first asks Spider, "How much of what I was saying did you hear?"

"There's a ghost gang in town. Where'd you get that?"

"What, 'ghost gang'? You don't like it?" His attention is partly diverted by a song on the radio. Ben Pollack, maybe. Or Jean Goldkette. "You don't like 'ghost gang'?"

"It's a little corny."

"So I won't use it." Sandglass walks over to the icebox, puts his file down on top of it next to the radio, and then twists up the tiny volume knob. He can't help it, he's just a music nut. "Thanks for telling your old man he's corny." And his first guess was right: it *is* Ben Pollack and His Park Central Orchestra. "Buy, Buy for Baby." Belle Mann on vocals.

"I was only kidding, Pop. It's great. I can see it." Lifting one hand, Spider separates his thumb and first finger by six inches. "*Ghost Gang*, headlines this big."

"You staying in tonight?" asks Sandglass. Spider is repeatedly dipping his hand into a box of Kellogg's corn flakes. "Can't you get a bowl for that? You ate out of a box in prison?"

Spider doesn't bother to answer those questions. "You really going to see the mayor?"

"Yeah, I really am."

"Ever meet him before?"

"Once, when he was a congressman. Hey, I got to run. See you when I get back."

Already Spider has turned his attention back to Ed Sullivan's column in the *Daily News* spread out on the kitchen table. He doesn't see the old man go out, but ten seconds later, for some unknown reason, he feels it necessary to glance up at the wall clock. When he does he notices that his father left the envelope he was carrying on top of the icebox.

Sir, I have proof in this envelope here . . .

Theirs is a front-facing apartment on Second Street just off the Bowery, and Spider flings up the kitchen window to see if he can still catch his father.

"Hey, Pop!" he hollers down five stories just as a black Hudson pulls to the curb in front of Dick Sandglass and two men run up from behind him, probably from the next doorway, grab his arms, pinion them both, then drag him across the pavement and fling him into the back of the big car.

Standing at the window in shock, holding the fat envelope in his right hand, Spider Sandglass knows with utter certainty that this is the last time he will ever see his father alive.

2

Back in mid-July Lois Lane found herself in possession of two press tickets to the Sunday matinee of a struggling Broadway show. She went—why not? there was nothing else doing—but she went alone. Everyone she'd asked to come along said no, thanks. The reviews for

Never Too Tired, yet another society comedy by David Nero and S. B. Dillon, had been universally stinko. By intermission she was agreeing with the critics. Even Frank Conlan and Ilka Chase couldn't save the damn thing. Who cared about Mainline Philadelphians anymore? Whether they got amnesia or committed adultery? When people were starving, out of work, living on the bum, that stuff seemed worse than trite, it seemed tasteless. Maybe she wouldn't even stick around. She didn't *have* to see it through to the end. Was there some law? She was waiting on line at the lobby bar thinking maybe she wouldn't bother getting a drink, she'd just go home, when a man behind her said, "Your name is Lois, correct?"

She turned and, yes, she knew that she knew him, but couldn't place him: a tall, good-looking blond in his middle twenties, that chiseled Nordic look except for the spray of mick freckles on his cheeks. He was wearing a gun-club-check jacket and dark blue slacks. When she noticed his shoes, though—his black boatlike shoes—Lois placed him easily: he'd been the cop sitting guard outside Willi Berg's hospital room two years ago. He'd made her leave her purse with him, which she hadn't minded doing since he was cute and seemed genuinely apologetic.

"Oh hello!" she said, adding, "I'm sorry, but I've forgotten your name."

As soon as he told her, she thought, Lois Jaeger, because that kind of thing, sounding out her possible married name, had been instinctual with her since she was twelve. Just an old stupid habit. It wasn't like she was looking to get married, she had a career, thank you very much. Lois Jaeger. It wasn't *bad,* though, and neither was he.

When Ben Jaeger asked how she liked the show, Lois wrinkled her nose. He laughed: his sentiments exactly. Then he asked her if she wanted to go for a drink, even an early supper.

Why not?

Until their fourth date, when he took her to see the Giants play (first time anyone she knew ever suggested doing *that*), Ben Jaeger never brought up Willi Berg's name. She had been expecting him to, of course, and the fact that he had not led her to wonder with increasing unease if she were being used somehow to run Willi down. But at the Polo Grounds that afternoon Ben suddenly mentioned his boss Richard Sandglass, saying that Sandglass still hoped Willi Berg would come back to town, voluntarily resurface. Sandglass, Ben told her, might be able to help Willi out of his jam.

Lois said, "Are you asking me to pass on a message? Because Mr. Sandglass has already asked me to do the same thing."

"It's lieutenant," said Jaeger. "*Lieutenant* Sandglass."

"Yeah? And if I want to call him mister, I will. You didn't answer my question."

"Are you saying you're in touch with him still?"

"I asked you first."

"I'm not some fly dick, Lois, going out with you to catch a crook, if that's what you're suggesting."

Lois nodded vaguely and gazed out over the astonishing green turf of the outfield, the whiteness of the base bags, listening to the whooping roll of the pipe organ over the P.A. system. "Yeah, I guess that's what I was suggesting."

"Well, I'm not."

"And I'm not in touch with Willi Berg, either."

"Damn, I've wasted all this time!"

She poked him in the ribs, and they watched the rest of the game, Giants 4, Washington Senators, 3.

Ten weeks of twice-weekly dates later: early Saturday evening, October the first. After taking in the new Van Gogh exhibition at the Museum of Modern Art, Lois and Ben walk down Sixth Avenue for a while. Then Ben checks his watch and says he really should make a phone call—does Lois mind? It will only take a minute. He just needs to "check in." He doesn't say with whom.

And now he's talking excitedly to someone he calls "Spider" from a booth at the rear of an Irish bar just off Times Square. The air is full of tumbling steam and heavy with the odor of boiled cabbage. He says into the telephone receiver, "It'll be all right," and Lois tugs on his belt loop, asking, "What? What's the matter?"

Ben's face is ghastly pale when he hangs up. "Lois, I'm sorry, you're going to have to get home by yourself."

"Why? What's going on?"

He shakes his head.

"*Ben.*"

So he tells her, "Something might've happened to the lieutenant. I'm going to his apartment."

"Let me come."

"No."

They push their way down the length of the crowded barroom, Ben leading, clearing a passage, Lois tagging close behind.

Outside on Broadway near the corner of West Forty-eighth Street, Ben steps off the curb and hails a Checker. He puts Lois in while looking over the cab roof to see if he can spot a patrol car to commandeer. Then he bends down, leans into the taxi, and kisses her. "I'll call you later."

Lois has taken out a note pad, already flipped through several pages, and says to Jaeger, "Richard Sandglass, 28 East Second Street. Need a lift?"

"Lois, don't. This is serious. I'll *call* you."

Lois tells the hackie, "Twenty-eight East Second, that's right off the Bowery."

Up until fifteen seconds ago she considered Ben Jaeger her boyfriend, and not because they've gone all the way, because they still haven't, not *all* the way, but because she knows his birthday—October the fifth—and for weeks has been trying to think of the perfect gift. Now, though, she's less sure. Maybe he's *not* her boyfriend.

"And driver, put on some speed."

3

"Pop just said he was going out. That's all he told me."

"He never mentioned he was going to see the mayor?"

"LaGuardia? No."

"Spider, did you recognize either of the men?"

"No. Two guys. Hats, coats."

Ben Jaeger rubs a hand across his forehead, then palms it over the top of his head, flattening his hair. "What kind of hats?"

"Hats. Men's hats."

Lois, who is sitting with them both at the kitchen table—she arrived at the Sandglass apartment a full ten minutes before Ben did—smiles now at Spider and asks him, "How was he dressed, your dad? Was he wearing his uniform?"

"No, his good suit. His only suit. Pop used to call it his funeral suit—you know, because it's black and he only wears it when he's going to wakes and funerals."

Jaeger says, "Lois, I'm asking the questions, all right?"

Lois shrugs but wants to kick him.

"Spider, this is important," says Ben. "Did your father take anything with him—a big envelope?"

"I don't know," says Spider reaching for a carton of breakfast cereal, then looking down into it, checking if there are flakes still left. "I didn't see any envelope." He stares past Ben through the open kitchen window. "No," he says, "I don't remember seeing any envelope."

4

Mrs. O'Shea's husband, Denholm, is languishing in state prison at Sing-Sing, has been for the past three years, and will be for the next forty-seven. Denny O'Shea killed a union organizer on the West Side docks—deliberately went after the guy, chased him for a block, then chopped off his head with a shed cutter ordinarily used to trim cabbage. He went down for depraved homicide.

Afterward Mrs. O'Shea found employment at the Straubenmuller

Textile High School on West Eighteenth Street. She supervised the kitchen, maintained the on-premises fabrics museum, and devised a streamlined accounting system that saved the arithmetically challenged principal hundreds of hours of headaches. Just about a year ago, however, an audit of the high school's finances revealed that Mrs. O'Shea had embezzled Straubenmuller out of nearly twenty thousand dollars, which she'd used to buy a summer home in Deal, New Jersey.

Lex Luthor heard about the crime during idle chitchat with an old-time ward-heeler in the district.

The following afternoon Lex visited Mrs. O'Shea in the House of Detention for Women in Greenwich Village and made her a proposition: in return for his covering her debt to the city and ensuring that all criminal charges against her would be dropped, she would come to work for him. She started to answer yes immediately, but he raised his hand and stopped her. "No, listen to me first," he said. "If you come to work for me, you have to know something."

"That you're a criminal. Yes," she said, "I guessed as much. I understand what that means, Alderman, and I accept your offer."

Lex never forgave her for that, for having "guessed as much." And how had she guessed? Of course, he asked her.

"It takes one to know one," she said. Then she said, "Do you remember the first time we met?"

"The first time we've met, madam, is today. Right now."

"Perhaps I shouldn't have said *met*. The first time you *saw* me."

He was waiting with one eyebrow lifted.

"You saw me at the high school's Christmas Bazaar last December. You were there shaking hands, I was manning the silent-auction table." She took out a cigarette but he told her to put it away. She laughed. But did as she was told. "I saw you ask the principal who I was."

Lex suddenly grinned. "You're right. I did. I said, 'My God, that woman over there just gave me a start. She looks exactly the way my mother looked at fifty.'"

Mrs. O'Shea's face drained.

She never would—or ever did—quite forgive him for that . . .

This Saturday evening while Lex is away having dinner with Joseph P. Kennedy and Gloria Swanson, Mrs. O'Shea avails herself of the Waldorf premises—bathes in the master bath with the solid-gold taps, fixes a chicken sandwich and a potent Manhattan, and then gets comfortable on the sofa in the living room, settling in with the Nero Wolfe novel she's currently reading. She hasn't gotten far, three or four chapters, and is looking forward to finishing it tonight.

Then the telephone rings.

Mrs. O'Shea checks her wristwatch—ten past eight—and considers letting it ring out, but it could be her lord and master checking in.

"Luthor residence."

"Let me talk to the alderman."

"I'm sorry, the alderman is not at home. And for your information, whoever you are, when you call someone you should say who's calling. That's just common courtesy. Who is this, please?"

But whoever it is—it sounds like a young man—says, "I'll call back" and breaks the connection.

He calls back ten seconds later.

"Where's he gone to? When's he coming home? Do you have a number where I can reach him?"

"Didn't I just instruct you in telephone etiquette?"

"Lady, don't start."

"I'm hanging up right now. You're just plain rude."

"No, wait! My name is Steven Sandglass! Is this *Mrs.* Luthor?"

"This is Mr. Luthor's personal assistant."

"Can you tell me where he is? I need to talk to him—tonight."

"Mr. Sandglass, I'm certainly not telling you where the alderman is. Just what exactly is the nature of your business with him?"

"The nature of my business? The nature of my *business,* lady, is that I want my father back. Your boss kidnapped my pop, and if he's hurt him I swear to God all the stuff in this envelope I have right here in my hand is going straight to the mayor. And I'm not bluffing!"

"What are you talking about?"

"I want to speak with Lex Luthor tonight."

"That's not going to happen."

"Then the next time you see him, he'll be in jail."

Mrs. O'Shea takes a sip from her Manhattan, switches the receiver to her left ear. "Listen to me—what did you say your name was?"

"Sandglass, Steven Sandglass, but people call me Spider."

"And how old are you, Mr. Sandglass?"

"What's that got to do—?"

"*How* old?"

"Twenty-four."

"Then people shouldn't be calling you Spider. Now listen to me— are you listening? If you would like to live to be twenty-five, I wouldn't go around making these kind of threats, not to me, not to Alderman Luthor, and not in the city of New York."

"I want my father back. And then he can have the file. I'm calling back in an hour, and Lex Luther better answer this phone."

"Don't you dare hang up your phone."

"Who are you, telling me what to do?"

He hangs up.

Mrs. O'Shea replaces the handset, then stands up from her chair, plants her hands on her hips, and glares at the telephone. "You ring right back, do you *hear* me?"

The phone rings.

"Don't you *dare* hang up on me again," she says after she's snatched up the receiver again.

"Mrs. O'Shea?"

"Oh, it's *you*."

"Yes, it's me. Has Paulie phoned in?"

"No," she says, "he has not."

"Any other calls?"

"No, sir."

"Then who was it that hung up on you?"

"I do have a personal life."

"Oh? How nice for you. But Mrs. O? Do not conduct it on my telephone."

"Good night, Mr. Luthor," she says and presses the disconnect toggle.

Then she looks at her book and shrugs. *The League of Frightened Men* will have to wait.

Then the phone rings again.

5

In Los Angeles, where it is just a few minutes past five in the afternoon, Captain Gould is staring at a big hole in the exterior wall of a cell on the felony block of the county jail, while behind him a guard is saying there were a dozen reports of a guy in tights and a cape floating around outside, looking into one cell after another until he found the one he was looking for. *This* one.

Gould turns around. "Did you say a *floating* man?"

"Yes, sir, and he had a big red **S** on the front of his shirt."

On his way out of Willi Berg's cell, Captain Gould notices an empty Camels packet lying crumpled on the painted cement floor.

6

Earlier this evening at dinner, Joe Kennedy told Lex that while Hitler was clearly a lunatic, Nazism was a sound, even a *scientific* response to the world economic crisis and the very real threat of international communism. He said there were executives and leaders in Germany, both in the Reich and in private corporations, that wide-awake Americans could feel altogether comfortable dealing with. "I'll gladly arrange for any contacts you might wish to make," he said. Lex said he did appreciate the kind offer and would definitely take him up on it. He was, he said, most interested in raising investment capital. Kennedy leaned across the restaurant table, eager to hear more. Lex smiled, paused significantly, then said, "I'm involved in something that you, yourself, may like to own a piece of. Considering that it's certain to be the next . . . essential thing."

"You mean television?" said Kennedy.

Lex pursed his lips, retracted them; leaned back in his chair, spread his hands, and said: "Robots."

"I love robots!" said Gloria Swanson.

"Of course you do," said Lex. "*Everyone* does."

And that included Joseph Kennedy, who could see to coughing up at least a quarter of a million dollars.

Altogether an excellent evening. Very excellent.

When he arrives back at the Waldorf just before midnight, Lex is in an expansive mood. But the moment he steps into the foyer of his suite in the Towers his face drops. The nine framed linoleum cuts by Reginald Marsh (rainy street scenes) have been removed from their hooks and are stacked on the floor. Impaled now on the brass picture hooks are photostatic copies of several incorporation documents along with private laboratory reports whose subject, he sees upon closer inspection, is fingerprint matching.

Slowly he follows the trail of documents down the hallway. Just outside his office, photographs are tacked up around the doorframe the way some people display Christmas cards. They are pictures, many looking as though they were taken from behind potted palms, of Lex Luthor huddled in conversations with Mussolini's first cousin, with investment bankers Prescott Bush and George Herbert Walker and a representative of a Berlin chemical factory, with two mafia godfathers and a notorious madam.

The door to Lex's office, usually shut and locked, is partly open.

He pushes it the rest of the way with his fingertips.

Mrs. O'Shea is seated behind the desk. She has on a glen-plaid business suit, a white shirt, and a gray tie that Lex recognizes as his own. In front of her is a delicate hand-painted coffee cup on a saucer. A matching cup is lying on its rim on the white pile rug near a brown stain that still looks wet.

Also lying on the rug is the rigid body of a young man in his early twenties. His eyes bulge and his clenched teeth are flecked with dried foam.

"Have a seat, Lex. We need to talk."

"And this young man is . . . ?"

"Steven Sandglass. He said you kidnapped his father."

"Steven Sandglass."

"Yes. But called Spider by his friends. He brought over a certain envelope he thought you'd be interested in."

"Ransom."

"So he was hoping. Now won't you have a seat?"

"Poison?"

Mrs. O'Shea blinks, then sits up straighter. "I convinced him I was shocked. Assured him that his father was still alive—he's not, is he?"

"No."

"Then I offered him a cup of coffee."

"And now there's a dead body in my office." Lex stands near it, looking down. "What am I supposed to do about it?"

"You'll figure something out."

"I could, you know, remove all of those documents from the wall and call the cops. You poisoned your faithless young lover. He was about to dump you. It'll be a scandal but I'll survive."

Mrs. O'Shea's face goes slack. She stands up behind the desk. "You wouldn't."

"Why not? What's the alternative?" He takes out his linen handkerchief, stoops down, and lays it over the coffee stain. He picks up the cup and sniffs. "I asked you, what's my alternative course?"

"You call Paulie and he takes the body off the dumbwaiter in the basement, we get a professional carpet shampoo, and from now on I'm a full partner."

"No," says Lex. "I believe I'm still inclined to my suggestion. With the added element that you killed yourself afterward in fear of disgrace and the electric chair."

"Try and make me."

"He didn't want money?"

"Apparently just his dad returned unharmed."

Lex grins and finally sits down on one of the upholstered chairs along the wainscoting. "You know what's funny?" says Lex.

"No, what's funny?"

"I don't even know your first name."

"Helen. It's Helen."

He stretches out his legs, crosses his feet over his ankles, and stares at Spider Sandglass. "Helen," says Lex. "Well, well."

7

Before he was defrocked for giving VD to a tenth-grade parochial high school girl and then looting the poor box to pay her off not to squeal, Carl Krusada was one of several young good-looking curates at St. Rocco's, the church Paulie Scaffa and his father attended. Because Carl was the youngest priest there, he'd been assigned to hear confessions in the church for two hours every Sunday evening. Nobody else at the rectory wanted to do it because most of the really good radio programs came on then. There was never much traffic in and out of the confessional on Sunday evening, and Carl used the time in between penitents to read; he'd long since given up reading his daily office and was working his way through the Studs Lonigan trilogy.

He was just a few pages into *Young Manhood* when he had his first visit from Paulie. That was eighteen months ago.

"If you think it's funny, I don't, and neither does my dad," Paulie said through the confessional's mesh screen. "What are you thinking, making a man of his age kneel at the altar reciting two hundred Hail Marys. That ain't right. You having your fun or something?"

Carl was stunned—he'd never had anyone speak angrily to him during confession before, and he'd certainly never had someone criticize him before about the severity of his dispensed penance. "How dare you! Who do you think you're talking to?"

"I *know* who I'm talking to, which is the problem, you stupid jerk. Who could take you serious?"

"Paulie? Paulie *Scaffa,* oh Christ, I didn't recognize your voice! That's *your* old man? Tell him to quit reading *Spicy Detective.*"

"You tell him. But from now on out it's two Hail Marys, two Our Fathers, and a good Act of Contrition. I want a *civilized* penance from here on out, Carl, 'cause if I find out different . . ."

"Okay, okay. Maybe I was out of line. Maybe I was fooling around, busting the old man's chops. But I didn't know it was *your* dad, Paulie."

"Let's just forget it."

"In fact, why don't you send him back in here right now, I'll give him a reduced sentence."

Paulie chuckled. "Nah, that's all right. Starting next week. So, you work this shift every Sunday?"

"Every Sunday."

"Then maybe I'll talk to you again."

"You always come with the old man?"

"Yeah, he don't want to let it go more than a week at his age. You know."

"Sure, sure. Say, what've you been doing?"

"I can't talk about it but it's good."

"You ever see any of the guys from the neighborhood?"

"Nah."

"Ronnie Squitieri joined the Carmelite order."

"I heard that. You guys. The Depression ain't gonna last forever and when it's over you're still gonna be priests."

They laughed.

That was a year and a half ago and since then Paulie Scaffa and Carl Krusada have forged a genuine friendship, something they'd never had back in grammar school. They went drinking, to the ballgame (the Yankees and the football Giants), even deep-sea fishing. Then Carl had to go and give the clap to a schoolgirl, the poor shmuck. And while Paulie Scaffa in no way took responsibility for Carl's problems, he *had* felt badly when it turned out Carl picked up his dose from a chippy working a house that Lex Luthor owned and that Paulie recommended, even going so far as to give Carl a handful of brass coins exchangeable for services . . .

Paulie comes home this morning to find Carl asleep on his living-room sofa. The phonograph needle is lisping in the lead-out groove and the moment Paulie turns off the Victrola, Carl wakes up. "What time is it?"

"Around three."

"In the *morning?*"

"Yeah, the *morning.* Some people *work* in the world." Paulie walks into the kitchen and shakes the coffee pot. A little sloshes inside so he lights a match, then a burner, and reheats it.

Carl slumps in and sits down at the table.

"I walked your dad over to St. Rock's. They got Forty Hours Devotion going."

"That was brave of you." Paulie reaches down a cup and a saucer from a low shelf, gets out the condensed milk. Then he takes out a packet of Herbert Tarrytons and lights one. "You wouldn't believe how tired I am."

"Whatcha been doing?" Carl opens the top of a box of lemon-filled cupcakes, the dozen Paulie has a standing order for with the Dugan bread man every Thursday.

"Let me have one of those. If you really must know," says Paulie exhaling smoke from his nostrils, "I was carting some kid's body out to a crematorium over the South Beach section of Staten Island."

"Some kid?"

"This thing's hard as a rock," says Paulie knocking his cupcake against the metal edge of the table. "Why don't you remember to put this kind of thing in the icebox, is that too much to ask? I have to eat stale cupcakes?"

"Sorry, Paulie. You know, I bet if you heated it in the oven . . ."

"What, I want hot filling?" Then he makes an anguished face.

"What?"

"I just remembered I was supposed to call the boss when I was fin-ished. If he makes me go out *again* . . ."

"Didn't you used to have a guy working with you?"

"Yeah, and let me tell you, that was better. Much as Sticky ticked me off, that was better. We could take turns doing things for Mr.—for the boss." He pours his coffee, adds sweetened milk, and carries the cup on its saucer back into the living room. Carl follows him. "What'd *you* do all evening?"

"Listened to records," says Carl.

"While I'm taking a body to the crematorium."

"You said it was a *kid?* How old a kid?"

"Twenties. I killed his father last night."

"Paulie."

"What? What, 'Father Krusada,' what's the matter? You disapprove?"

Carl rubs a hand around the top of his head. "Did I say I disapproved? A man has to make a living."

"Glad you think so. Now, if you'll excuse me," says Paulie, "I have to call the boss."

"Yeah, sure," says Carl.

Paulie sets down his coffee and sits on the hard chair next to the telephone table. He picks up the receiver but then notices Carl still standing there. "You mind giving me a little privacy?"

"Yeah sure, but . . ."

"What?"

"Is your . . . do you think your boss is ever gonna hire somebody to replace that partner you had?"

"Why?"

"I'd like to apply for the job. If it ever opens up."

Paulie stares at him for a moment, then shrugs. "Yeah, sure, why not. I'll mention it."

"Yeah?"

"I said I would."

"Hey . . . that's real white of you."

"Anything for a pal. Now get out of here."

Why did he *ever* offer the guy a place to stay till he got back on his feet? He not only takes care of his old man, he also takes care of his crazy friend. Paulie figures he's probably built up such a reserve of sanctifying grace, doing so many good deeds, that he could shoot *twenty* cops and still get into heaven. He dials the phone and when the boss answers, he says, "All done. That kid is *smoke.*"

8

Usually on Mondays, Mrs. O'Shea takes the train to Ossining and visits Denny at the prison there; she brings him his weekly cigarette-money and a dozen nickel chocolate bars, Nestlés, which she pronounces "nessles" and he pronounces "nest-lees." Then they both lapse into awkward silence for half an hour.

But today her first conscious thought is that she won't be visiting her husband this particular Monday. And perhaps never again. Who knows? She throws off the comforter and rolls out of bed, Lex Luthor's bed, then steps quickly to the bathroom and jumps into the shower. She keeps the water as hot as she can bear it and scrubs and scrubs at herself. Then she begins reducing the cold water till the spray is entirely hot water and her body burns painfully. Then she twists off the hot tap. Stands there dripping, breathing heavily, her shoulders and meaty chest bright cherry-red, even beginning to blister in places.

Back in the bedroom Mrs. O finds one of Lex's royal blue bathrobes and puts it on. There are no slippers that fit.

She flings open the office door and then stops abruptly. Dressed in a midnight blue tuxedo, Lex is seated behind his desk. He has on a pair of headphones and is scribbling madly on a pad of yellow foolscap. When he sees Mrs. O he frowns, then holds up a warning finger: be quiet. He writes more. Mrs. O half turns her head to the left and, not expecting to find anyone else here, she flinches: Caesar Colluzo, that garlic-eater she can't abide, is perched rigidly in one of the chairs, his black hat on his lap.

Stationed beside him is yet another of his shiny tin men, another of those creepy robots, this one larger than the others she's seen, less tubular, leaner. The others were unnerving but ridiculous; this one frightens her. It seems to be turned off. But how can you really tell?

Mrs. O's attention is diverted by a loud click: Lex snapping a toggle on a small radio receiver.

He removes his headphones and tosses them down.

Then he looks at Mrs. O, at Caesar Colluzo. "Apparently," he says, "I am now the focus of a very classified secret criminal investigation."

"How do you—?"

"Helen, I was just read the transcript of two intercepted telephone calls, one outgoing, one incoming, from the mayor's private line." He picks up a pencil, begins tapping it. "I gather that Fatty has spoken with the late Lieutenant Sandglass's young sidekick and has chosen to believe what he says. Even without documentation."

"What does this mean?" asks Caesar. As always he seems disgusted—and Mrs. O is furious that he asked the same question *she* was about to ask. "Now what?"

Lex grins and leans forward. "Oh, I'll think of something," he says.

PART FOUR

—

ANYTHING FOR HALLOWEEN?

Ablutions. The General Slocum. *Clark Kent meets Lois Lane and discovers that first love is fleeting.*

1

For nearly a month Lois Lane has been spending most nights with Ben Jaeger, but now she is ready to sleep by herself again.

Ben Jaeger seems not just different, which he definitely is, but *replaced.* The sweet boy-cop has become a cynical and angry cop-cop. He sulks and glowers and still mourns his beloved mentor Dick Sandglass. As part of his mourning ritual Ben even plays on Lois's Victrola the lieutenant's blues and hot jazz records, which he "retrieved" from the Sandglass apartment on Second Street. If she has to listen to Mildred Bailey or Bessie Smith *one more time,* Lois thinks she'll scream.

As a member of the D.A.'s special "task force," Ben has become obsessed by the criminal investigation of Lex Luthor. Lois feels sorry for the new Ben—she does, she's not heartless and cold, it's just . . . she just doesn't much *like* him. And if she doesn't like somebody when he's vertical, she won't like him any better when he's horizontal.

Using the hand shower in the tub this morning, Lois decides she really *has* to do something. And what she has to do is end it. When Ben comes back here tonight (he was already gone when she woke up half an hour ago) she is going to talk to him. *If* he comes back tonight.

The Luthor investigation is not going well.

And speaking of that . . .

Lois steps dripping from the tub and blots herself dry with a Turkish towel, uses another to wipe steam from the mirror, then raises the window several inches to let out the steam, let in some cool autumn air. According to John Gambling on the radio, it's supposed to be sunny and warm today with highs in the upper fifties.

. . . Speaking of Lex Luthor, she'd better put the speed on. In half an hour she has to meet with someone who called her yesterday at the *Daily Planet* on behalf of Willi Berg. Someone named Clark.

After sprinkling talcum powder on her throat and chest and the back of her neck, after she rubs it briskly all around, Lois goes and selects her underwear, then sits down on the side of the bed to roll on her gunmetal stockings. And there, tangled nearby in the sheets, are Ben's skivvies. Fruit of the Loom. She flicks them on top of her own dirty laundry, piled next to a small neat stack of *Planet*s she intends to go through with scissors whenever she finds the time. The papers are recent editions containing stories Lois wrote. SUICIDE, 54, WAS JOBLESS 6 YEARS. DRIFTER HELD IN KNIFE SLAYING. LL LAWYER CALLS MISSING SAND-GLASS FILE 'INSIDIOUS MYTH.'

Lois imagines she'll eventually grow tired of culling and filing her clippings, but for now it's still exciting. She's a reporter!

And if this reporter doesn't shake a leg she is going to miss her appointment down in Tompkins Square Park. She finishes dressing (black skirt, white blouse, patent-leather pumps), brushes her hair, and dabs on the slightest coat of lip paint with a fingertip. Finally she's ready to grab her swagger coat, stick on a beret, and go. Well, almost ready. First she has to make the bed. Crazy or not, it's a ritual she performs every day.

As she plumps one of the pillows, Lois notices a grease stain on the sham, her nice percale sham—Ben's hair creme. She *told* him to stop putting on so much Brylcreem; even wished out loud he wouldn't use any at all. It's kind of endearing, though. Ben's vanity over his gleaming hair. He can be so . . . well, he can be so *cute,* and always with the

Schrafft's candy—even at his mopiest he brings her candy or a pint of chocolate ice cream. Oh God. The truth is she *does* like Ben, still does, and really it's not his fault things haven't worked out. It's just . . . okay: there's no *chemistry*. And Lois is beginning to think she wants to fall in love.

She's never been "in love," not with any of the boys back in Monticello, not with Willi Berg and not with Ben Jaeger. At least she *hopes* not. Because if *that* was love, all she can say is there are *far* too many beautiful songs touting such a measly emotion.

Lately she has begun to worry about herself—especially after scoring so poorly on *Glamour* magazine's "How Romantic Are You?" take-it-yourself quiz. Her score (94 points out of a possible 200) put her in the Cold Fish category! What, just because she's never gone rink skating with a man or necked in a gazebo during a summer shower, never dressed "sylph-like" for her "best beau"? Nertz! She's romantic, she *is*, she cries when the guy and the girl embrace finally and eternally at the end of serious movies, she cries even harder when one of them becomes fatally ill. She *is* ready to fall in love.

Today is Friday, the twenty-ninth of October 1937.

2

Beginning in the 1830s, a large German immigrant community known as Kleindeutschland thrived on the Lower East Side of Manhattan. The focal point of the community was Tompkins Square, bordered on the north by Tenth Street, on the south by Seventh Street, on the east by Avenue A, and on the west by Avenue B. On the morning of June 15, 1904, 1,331 Kleindeutschlanders, all of them parishioners of St. Mark's German Lutheran Church and most of them women and young children, boarded an excursion vessel for a picnic outing to the northern shore of Long Island. The *General Slocum*, an enormous wooden boat with three open decks, two side paddlewheels, and coal-fed boilers, departed from the Third Street Pier shortly before nine-thirty and steamed up the East River. Minutes later, as she was passing Blackwell's Island, flames engulfed her forward part. By quarter of ten, the boat was completely afire and foundering in the treacherous waters of Hell Gate. The ill-trained crew discovered that practically all of the fire hoses—decades old and original to the vessel—were rotted. When their nozzles were turned on, the canvas burst. There were insufficient lifeboats, the cork filler had crumbled in the lifejackets, and practically none of the passengers could swim. At least 1,300 people died, either burned to death or drowned.

Virtually every family in Kleindeutschland suffered a loss, and the funerals, one following the other around the clock, lasted for more than a week . . .

On his second day in New York City, Clark Kent happened upon a small monument erected to the memory of the *General Slocum*'s dead. He was taking a stroll around his new neighborhood when he saw it—a small bronze of a boy and a girl watching a steamboat—tucked away at the northernmost end of Tompkins Square Park. He read the plaque and was horrified. He pulled his brand-new eyeglasses off his face and rubbed his eyes. For the rest of the day he couldn't get that awful tragedy out of his mind. He returned the next day and the next. Each time he did he found himself thinking identical thoughts.

This morning, for the fourth straight day, Clark is back at the monument thinking about what he might have done, what heroism he could have performed, had he been around in 1904.

For one thing, he could have plucked women and children out of the East River. A lot of them. And rescued still others from the decks. Or cracked a water tank off its base on the roof of some tall building, then emptied it onto the flames. But wait a second. *Could* he have done that? Could he *do* that if something comparable happened today? Or tomorrow? Is he strong and agile enough to manage such a thing? Such things. Could he still fly while carrying a water tank? And could he grasp the tank with one hand while he socked holes into it with the other? What if he tried—and dropped the whole damn water tank over a city street, crushed a dozen people? Oh God.

"Are you Clark?"

A slender brunette is tapping him on the shoulder.

"Lois?"

"Sorry I'm late."

"That's all ri—"

"Is Clark your first name or your last?" she asks in a clipped alto.

"First." Her thick hair is the color, he thinks, of milk chocolate. And so shiny! "Did you come by yourself?"

"I'm a reporter, not a cop."

"I was just being care—"

"Is Willi in New York?"

"Yeah, we're living . . ." But Clark breaks off and vaguely swings his left arm behind him: in that direction, somewhere back there.

"When did he get here?"

"We *both* got here four days ago. No, five." Clark nods toward Avenue A, toward St. Mark's Place. "How about we start walking?"

Two Greek Orthodox priests join Clark and Lois on the curb, their long wiry black beards reminding Clark of that character in *Popeye*, Mr. Geezil, the hot-tempered guy who hates Wimpy to pieces. Clark notices one of the priests ogling Lois, especially her ankles and calves, and feels like punching him in the nose.

At last there's a break in traffic. Clark and Lois rush across Avenue A, then continue west on St. Mark's Place past stoops and tenements, dodging fatigued-looking women pushing baby strollers or dragging small children, weaving around sidewalk clusters of young Jewish men in skullcaps, older Slavic men in shabby suits smoking brown cigarettes and arguing politics. Stalin is good, Stalin is bad, Stalin is this, Stalin is that. As they're coming up on a grocery store, someone inside begins to shout: "Did you pay for that? Stop! Thief!"

A lithe and lean thirtyish-looking man leaps through the open doorway, a loaf of Silvercup bread squeezed in each fist. His lips are skinned back over yellow teeth and red gums, making him seem both feral and unstrung. He dashes in front of Clark and into the street, then takes off sprinting in the direction of Cooper Union. The grocer runs outside, swears a Yiddish oath while glaring at Clark, who looks down at his shoes and hurries on—Lois saying as she trots after him, "So. You a bleeding heart or were you just afraid the guy'd bop you with a loaf of bread?"

"People are hungry."

"That's true, some people are. But what about that poor guy who owns the grocery store? People keep stealing his bread whenever they're hungry, pretty soon he'll be hungry himself. Or don't you see it that way?"

"What are you, a Republican? The guy was *hungry.* I'm supposed to grab a hungry man and send him to jail?"

Lois smiles. "So he was hungry. He needed to steal *two* loaves of bread?"

Clark grunts. "Maybe he's got a big family."

"Oh, for the luvva—"

"Okay, *okay,* so he was a thief, I should've tripped him," says Clark, and if someone were to walk up to him now and ask, How's Diana? he most likely would say, Diana? Diana *who?*

3

Lois says, "Fifth floor, huh?"

"Two more flights."

"Fifth floor, huh?"

The tenement is quiet for a change, but as always cooking odors (last night's, last week's, last year's, last century's) are heavy and oppressive in the stairwell. On the fourth-floor landing they meet one of the housewives who live in the building, the young and stout Mrs. Palubiski. She glances at Lois and gives Clark a sly Old World wink. He blushes.

With Lois following him along the hallway, Clark takes out his door key.

Two clogged ashtrays sit on the kitchen table and the air is sour with the stench of tobacco smoke.

"Well?"

"He *was* here."

"Look, Kent, this—"

Rushing up to her from behind the door, Willi throws his arms around Lois and squeezes.

Casually, she drives an elbow into his stomach, then whirls around and with a blazing smile slaps him with her right hand. "Hello, Willi. It's been a long time."

"Maybe not long *enough*," he says rubbing the blotch on his cheek. He laughs and shuts the door and puts on the chain. "Shall we . . . get reacquainted?" Gesturing to a chair at the kitchen table, he says, "Coffee, cuppa tea? Clark has some Yoo-hoo."

"What are you doing in New York?"

"Couldn't that wait a minute?"

"No."

He looks at her levelly and then laughs again. "Okay. All right. The plan was, I'd hook back up with you and you'd hook me back up with Dick Sandglass . . ."

"You've heard?"

"We heard," says Clark. "But not till we got here and saw what's in the papers."

Lois doesn't take her eyes from Willi's face. "Perfect timing."

"Yeah," says Willi. "That's what me and Clark've been saying." He pauses to light a cigarette. "Dick Sandglass was a good guy."

"There've been a lot of rumors circulating that he was anything *but* that."

"Luthor's doing."

"Oh, I agree," says Lois, "but they're doing their damage."

Removing a pencil and a small notepad from her coat pocket, she takes a seat at the kitchen table. "So where've you been since you . . . got out of jail?"

"Mexico. For about three weeks." He reaches over and crushes out his Camel in an abalone shell. "Seemed like a good idea to go where nobody was looking to arrest me. And kind of take stock. Figure out what next."

"And you decided to come back here and see Dick Sandglass."

"*You* and Dick. The both of you. But yeah. That's what we decided."

"Why didn't you do this a *year* ago?"

Willi shrugs. "We weren't ready yet." He looks drolly—or is it critically?—at Clark. Lois doesn't seem to register the plural.

"Well, let's get down to business," she says. "First, I want to know how you managed to break out of jail. *Then* we'll talk about the situation here." She flips through her pad—full of quotes she jotted during her long interview yesterday with Manhattan D.A. William C. Dodge— till she finds a fresh page. "Do we have a deal?"

"Are you *sure* you're the same Lois Lane that I used to know? Come on, Lo, it's *Willi!*" He sounds amused, looks annoyed. "'*Do we have a deal.*'"

"*Do* we?"

Willi scratches at his throat. "Yes," he finally says, "we have a deal, Miss Lane."

4

There is no refrigerator in the apartment, so the Yoo-hoo drink that Clark goes and gets for himself from the cardboard carrier is room temperature. Following instructions on the cap, he shakes it well before opening, then sits down at the table. The place came furnished with that table, three shaky chairs, a boxy sofa covered in worn chenille, and a painful cast-iron bed, the flophouse kind that Clark and Willi slept on occasionally during their vagabond days. When they moved in they flipped a coin to see who took the bed. Clark lost, got the sofa and the much better deal.

Lois is saying, "Okay. Somebody put a hole through the wall of your cell. A guy in a red cape. Care to enlighten me?"

"Superman," says Willi with an unlit cigarette in his mouth.

"Excuse me?"

"His name is Superman, and he's a buddy of mine and Clark's. Red cape and blue tights. Superman."

"With no hyphen," Clark puts in. He's flip-flopped over this—hyphen, no hyphen—and has decided finally: no hyphen. "Superman is one word."

Willi throws Clark a look pointed enough that he stands up and wanders off through an archway into the poky living room. Going to the window, he looks down into a courtyard full of loose garbage and sodden old mattresses, then across the air space to a heavyset woman framed in her bedroom window. She is stretching a shirt over an ironing board, sprinkling on water from a 7-Up bottle. She's wearing only her slip and Clark is curious, even thrilled, despite the woman's age and bulk.

Not to be caught looking, he takes a few steps back, then peers through a narrow crevice between tenements and watches people passing along the sidewalk on St. Mark's Place. Small people. And not just small *people,* small . . . witches, cone-hatted witches, and a horned red devil, a princess wearing an Alice-blue gown and a sparkly tiara, a blacksmith, a cop, *two* little cops, a cowboy, a cowgirl, a pilot, a soldier, a sailor, a fairy with gauzy wings, and a pint-sized magician in a top hat and opera cape.

Children from the nearby parochial school on their way home for lunch on the Friday before Halloween.

Smiling, Clark strains to look closer, his irises bulging slightly and his pupils narrowing, turning to lozenges, till he is seeing telescopically: the dirty knuckles and chewed-back fingernails of the World War soldier; where the batting is taped to the wire armature of the fairy's wings; the *Mutt & Jeff* cover of the comic book clutched in a hand of the tiny blacksmith.

Meanwhile, in the kitchen Lois asks, "You met him in a *boxcar?*"

Moving his lips, Clark matches Willi's reply word for word: "Somewhere in Oklahoma. And the three of us decided to bum it together."

They discussed it a lot, "The Story," rehashed it and rehearsed it— first down in Mexico, then during the seemingly interminable flight from Sonoito to Albuquerque to Omaha to Philadelphia to New York City. (Willi squirmed a lot, embarrassed to be carried scooped up in Clark's arms across the United States. He complained nonstop: he was nauseous, he was freezing, couldn't Clark fly *lower,* where the air was a little bit *warmer?*) Once they were holed up in their apartment they covered every detail of The Story they could think of and agreed that when the time came Willi would do all of the talking, he could be the storyteller. It made sense and felt safer.

Obviously the first thing anyone was going to ask was how Willi escaped from the Los Angeles County Jail, so it ought to be Willi who answered, especially since—*especially since*—Clark would be in no position to speak with authority. After all, he hadn't *been* there. Had *not.* Clark hadn't had anything to *do* with that, it was—

"Superman," says Lois, and Clark can hear derision and downright disbelief in her voice. No big surprise. "And what's Superman's real name?"

"That *is* his real name."

"You call some guy *Superman?* Is that what you're telling me?"

"That's what I'm telling you, right. We'll say, 'Hey Superman, get a load of that sunset. Hey Superman, check out the sweet trick in the bobby socks.' Look, toots, scoff all you like but I *did* get out of jail and there *was* a hole in the damn wall afterwards and a lot of people *did* see a guy dressed in a blue union suit and a red cape flying all over the place. Scoff on, Lo, but you *asked.*"

Clark smiles, then squints till his vision becomes normally binocular again.

Across the courtyard the woman stands her iron on its heel rest, plucks her smoking cigarette from an ashtray on the windowsill, takes a short puff, and then turns to say something to a man who sits bolt upright suddenly on the bed.

Lois is saying, "So you, the four-eyes from Kansas and this . . . Superman from Oklahoma—"

"I don't know if he's *from* Oklahoma, Lois, we just *met* him there."

"—you all just wandered around together for *how* long?"

"Little over a year. Him, Clark, and me, correct."

There it is. The gist of The Story: it hasn't been just Willi and Clark, it's been Willi and Clark and . . . Superman. The lie is simple, easy to keep straight. Two become three. One becomes two. Will it work? Can it?

Now Willi is telling Lois how their pal Superman capped an oil well fire ". . . while Clark and me stood there with our mouths wide open." And the funny thing is Clark can visualize the scene at the boomer site as if he *had* been standing right next to Willi, just watching. It gives him an unpleasant tingling at the pit of his stomach. But it's also exciting, the prospect of living not one life but two different lives. *If* he can pull it off.

Across the courtyard in the opposite apartment the man and the woman are quarreling. He grabs her hair in a fist and shakes her.

Now the little girl in the fairy costume, the same kid Clark saw just a minute ago down on the street, walks into her parents' bedroom. She can't be much older than eight.

". . . So when I got pinched," Willi is saying, "I knew he'd get me out. He took his sweet time about it but he finally came through. Our pal Superman."

Lois says, "And who bombed your apartment, Willi?"

"I was thinking Lex Luthor."

"You think he found out where you were?"

"What, that's not possible?"

Clark draws in a sharp breath as the little girl in the opposite apartment flings up a defensive hand when her father pivots and charges at her.

Throwing up the casement window, Clark bites hard into his bottom lip. Pulls off his glasses.

The man raises his right arm—but in the instant before he can deliver a blow, the edge and palm of his big white hand turn bright red and break out in blisters. He screams and stumbles from view, probably heading for a sink and cold water.

On Second Avenue and Stuyvesant Street, the steeple bells at St. Mark's-in-the-Bouwerie begin tolling the hour.

Clark puts his glasses back on.

5

"Lex?" Mrs. O'Shea grips his elbow gently, barely touches it. "It's noon, don't you think you might want to get up?"

He rubs his forehead with the tips of his fingers. Fully awake now. Alert. Refreshed. "Has Hadorn called?" Philip Hadorn: Lex Luthor's personal attorney and one of the best in New York City. Two years ago he poisoned his first wife in order to marry his secretary—an undiscovered, unpunished homicide that Lex spent twenty thousand dollars (midnight exhumation, laboratory forensics, college tuition for all five children of a certain druggist in Chelsea) proving beyond the shadow of a doubt. But the proof will remain locked inside of a safety-deposit box so long as Hadorn provides Lex with expert legal counsel—pro bono, of course.

"He phoned around ten, yes. But I didn't wake you since he was still waiting to hear from Dodge. He thinks it'll be today though."

Lex tosses off his sheet and blanket. "Excellent."

Twenty minutes later he is sitting at the kitchen table and reaching for a carton of Wheaties when Mrs. O'Shea comes in with the telephone. "Hadorn," she says.

Brusquely, Lex takes the receiver. "Well?" He listens, nods, speaks softly, and hangs up. Passing back the phone, he says, "Done."

"No chance they'll suddenly change their—"

"It's *done*," says Lex. He throws back his head and laughs. "Call Paulie Scaffa and tell him to grab that other monkey and be over here in twenty minutes. Then call the papers."

"Yes, sir."

"And say I'll be happy to meet with reporters today at one o'clock . . . no, make it one-fifteen. In City Hall Park."

"Why not at City Hall?"

"The park, Mrs. O. At the statue of Civic Virtue." He picks up the Wheaties carton and fills his bowl. A square white packet drops out. He plucks it up and nearly tosses it aside. Instead he tears off a corner and shakes free a small green toy, a rocket ship exhibiting a star-ringed decal transfer that reads: "Solar Scouts."

Behind Lex, Mrs. O laughs.

Lex is silent for a long time just looking at the toy. Then he gets up, no longer hungry. "I think you have some calls to make," he tells Mrs. O'Shea. Carrying his coffee cup on its saucer, he walks down the hall and into his office where he sits behind his desk, rolls a sheet of paper into the typewriter, and begins to draft remarks for his upcoming press conference.

——

1

While Clark uses up the last of the spiced ham and sliced bread fixing three sandwiches, Willi has both elbows planted on the kitchen
table and his face squeezed between his hands. "Tell me it ain't so—
please."

"Wish I could," says Lois.

As she has just finished explaining, the special investigation of Lex
Luthor announced four weeks earlier by Fiorello LaGuardia has splut-
tered into a metropolitan farce, generating titters on the street, skepti-
cism in the press, and gag cartoons in *The New Yorker*.

Each and every locale that the late (and lately much maligned)
Richard Sandglass planned to identify as housing one or more of Lex
Luthor's felonious enterprises turned out to be completely and unim-
peachably . . . legitimate. The alleged brothels in Greenwich Village,
Chelsea, and Turtle Bay, as well as in the outer boroughs, were just
rental apartments, single-family dwellings, and licensed nursing
homes. (The administrator of one of those hushed residences, a still-
grieving widow named Ceil Stickowski, was *not* amused when the
premises were invaded one morning by a squad of uniformed policemen.) In Hoboken the "counterfeit printing operation" was only a laundry and dry cleaner's. No munitions were found stockpiled in a

warehouse on Staten Island; instead, it was filled with Persian rugs. And there was no telephone call–tapping station on Blofeld Street in Queens, merely a permanent-waving establishment.

The originals of incorporation papers and real estate transfers—documents Sandglass presumably had photographed with a spy camera—turned up either missing or telling a very different story than the one the slain police lieutenant would have claimed they told.

And so on.

"How did Luthor *do* it?"

"I already told you. He got hold of the file that Dick put together."

"But how did he manage to *undo* everything? So quickly?"

"He was ready for this," says Lois. "Or at least prepared for it."

"Wasn't there a copy?" says Clark. He slides one plate down in front of Lois, another in front of Willi. "You said there were photographs—where are the negatives? Didn't he keep the negatives?" He takes a bite from his own sandwich.

"If he did—"

"*If?*"

"Listen, farm boy, quit talking when I'm talking. And don't talk with food in your mouth." She glares. "If he *did* keep a copy, nobody's found it."

"Did they search his apartment?"

"Of *course*. Ben went through the whole place the same night Dick Sandglass was murdered."

"Ben? *Ben* did?" That's Willi: with a smirk. "This wouldn't by some chance be the cop you're dating?"

"How do you know who I'm dating?"

Willi folds his arms. "*Is* it?"

"That's none of your business—but yes."

Clark figures he'd better step in or else the conversation might quickly go awry. "But maybe he didn't keep a copy at home. Maybe someplace else? What about a safety deposit box?"

"If he rented one, nobody's found a receipt."

"So *now* what?" Willi again: no longer smirking.

"Well," says Lois, "there's always 'Superman.'" She takes a mincing bite of her sandwich.

"He's real, Lois."

"Uh-huh."

"He *is.* You'll see."

"I can't wait."

But Clark is thinking that he sure can. *He* can wait. Gladly. Because no matter how strong he is or how fast or how far he can see, he is still a farm boy, as Lois rightly called him, a twenty-year-old wheat from Kansas who never figured out the mysteries of the slide rule, who can't fathom electricity or the principles of music theory, much less radio transmission, and who is utterly mystified by the atom, the X-ray, and the salinity of the ocean. So just how is a guy like *him* supposed to take on and best somebody like Lex Luthor, a grown-up, a millionaire, a *genius* who evidently can snap his fingers and make whatever he wants or doesn't want vanish into the air?

In Clark's mouth his bite of sandwich tastes like mucilage.

"Do you have any mustard?" Lois lifts the top off her sandwich to frown at the spiced ham.

"Gee," says Clark, "no."

When she pushes her plate aside, rejecting lunch, Clark—on top of everything else he's feeling, worrying about, even *suffering* at this particular moment—is all of a sudden ardently and utterly in love.

2

The special task force assembled to investigate Alderman Lex Luthor commandeered office space in the sub-basement of police headquarters on Centre Street. Ordinarily by seven A.M. the place was packed with uniformed and plainclothes cops, accountants, clerk-typists, and assistant D.A.s. But when Ben Jaeger arrived that Friday morning at quarter of eight he walked into an empty room. Several desks that had been crammed in there only last night were gone, both rolling blackboards had been wiped clean, the telephones were disconnected (he tried three of them), and even the electric percolator was cold.

On the desk he'd been using, Ben discovered an envelope with his name on it. He picked it up and for more than a minute stood holding it in both hands before he took a long breath and tore open the flap. He'd half expected reassignment orders—to a potsy beat in Totenville or Inwood. But it was simply a handwritten note telling him to report immediately upstairs, Room 411.

Twenty minutes later Ben was saying, "Yes, sir. I understand that, sir, but if you—"

He listened and nodded, said, "Yes, sir" again. And: "I know, sir, and I'm grateful. But, Mr. Mayor, if you could just—"

Once more he stopped, squinting against tears that sprang into his eyes, and listened. "Of course, sir. I can see how that's probably . . . best. Thank you, sir."

He unpinned his shield from the breast of his tunic and placed it on the desk, his fingers reluctant to withdraw. But finally they did. Ben nodded to the mayor of New York City, the commissioner of investigation, the commissioner of police, and the Manhattan district attorney. Nothing more was said. He opened the door and walked out. Downstairs in the locker room he changed back into civilian clothes. When he turned in his uniform and brogans, the property clerk told him he had to pay a dollar-ten for dry cleaning and twenty-five cents for new heels. Those were the rules. "You can take it out of my last paycheck," said Ben. He left the building and walked from Centre Street over to Canal, and along Canal only as far as the first saloon.

3

Willi Berg stands on the roof of the tenement, smoking another cigarette and looking west down St. Mark's Place. And there's Clark, trotting after Lois Lane, catching up to her—the dog. And now they're walking together, stopping. Lois walking again, Clark watching. Catching up with her again. His old girlfriend and his best pal. His *only* pal. Some pal. You'd think he might've *asked* Willi if it was okay before he started flossing with Lois.

That hick's got some crust.

Not that Willi is still *interested* in Lois, that's all done, that's ancient history.

But *still.*

He coughs, clears his throat, and reaches again for his packet of cigarettes. That's not what he wants, though. What he wants is a life. His real life. His old life. His Willi the Great life.

And despite being a hick, Clark is the guy to get it for him, get it back, especially now that Dick Sandglass, dammit, is dead. Simple as that. For two years Willi has been using Clark for a bodyguard, his ace in the hole, and maybe that was crummy, maybe it was even chicken-shit, but so? So what? It was self-preservation. Besides, he'd been good for Clark—got him out of the sticks, didn't he? Showed him the big, wide world, or at least part of it. And hasn't he encouraged Clark to practice every day, to inventory all of his crazy ripening talents and fig-ure out what he could do with them? Lift that, toss that, boil this. See where I'm pointing? What's on the other side? And don't give me any baloney about eye strain—*just tell me.* Willi had done, was still doing, a lot for Clark Kent. So what kind of thanks does he get? Big lug tries to steal his girlfriend!

Well, *former.*

But *still.*

Even though he doesn't want another cigarette he lights one any-way and wonders what the hell is he going to do for the rest of the day.

There are no magazines, no books in the apartment, and he's fin-ished with the morning dailies. The only thing on the radio till the late afternoon are soap operas for women, and it would take a lot more than boredom, it would take brainsickness, before Willi Berg would consider tuning into *Pretty Kitty Kelly* or *The Road to Life.* Hold on, though. Not so fast. Thinking of women—but not, he hopes, soap operas—has just reminded him that Mrs. Palubiski said only yesterday that he ought to drop by sometime. They met on the roof, right over there. Mrs. Palubiski, *Christina,* was hanging sheets, Willi was doing calisthenics. Come visit, she said. She could offer him coffee or a ginger ale. Or if he preferred something stronger, she also had that. She owned a phonograph and half a dozen Bing Crosby sides. Ted Lewis stuff, too, and Benny Goodman. His version of "Moon Glow." And she had "Stormy Weather" by that colored girl—Ethel Waters. He told her his name was Ace and prayed she wouldn't ask him for his last name because he hadn't made one up yet. She had not. Instead she'd asked him could he dance. No? She could teach him. Days were long, yes? *Too* long. And her husband, she let drop, never came home before six-thirty, quarter of seven.

Willi is thinking now, what the hell. He's still miffed at Clark—pfui to you, pal, and to you too, Lois—but what the hell. Just . . . what the hell.

Till he got his life back he still had to live.

4

The barber shop is below sidewalk level on Broadway just above Canal. The barber is Italian, in his fifties, small and short—he wears lifts on his shoes. As he wields a comb and scissors now around Ben Jaeger's head he keeps saying, "Hold still or I cut your ear."

Ben is drunk, very drunk, sliding down and shifting around in the chair, rolling his head, snoozing off and then flinching awake.

"You don't keep still, I cut your ear."

"Sorry, paisan." Ben sits up and squares his shoulders, looks straight ahead at a wall of framed and autographed celebrity photographs: Don Budge, Clyde Beatty, Eddie Arcaro, Joel McCrea.

On the radio Little Jack Little's recording of "I'm in the Mood for Love" is playing. Dick Sandglass had no use for Little Jack Little—he's one of those lightweights, like Rudy Vallee or Paul Whiteman. Ben remembers how Sandglass would tease him for being so crazy about Bing Crosby: *You got no taste, kid. One of these days, when I got a year or two, I'll teach you how to listen.* And now Ben is remembering the names of some of the drummers that Sandglass admired (Jo Jones, Gene Krupa, Stan King), the ones he'd booshwash about while they were tailing Lex Luthor at three in the morning or taking sneaky photographs of brothels in Queens and Brooklyn, a warehouse out by New Dorp beach, a print shop in Hoboken. Ben remembers how Sandglass would solo on the steering wheel with his index fingers, on the dashboard with a couple of pencils.

"You okay?"

"Sure, sure," says Ben. "I'm fine."

"You don't *look* fine."

The barber continues to work on the right side of Ben's head, carefully snipping.

"I'm in the Mood for Love" finishes playing and is followed by a gong and then by an announcer who comes on to read the one o'clock news in a high-hat baritone. To end insurgency in the Holy Land, he says, British authorities today are burning the homes of Arab terrorists. The barber lowers the volume. Emperor Hirohito, says the announcer, has again declared that Japan will continue its war in China until victory is achieved. Local news and weather in a moment, says the announcer, but first this important word from Kreml Shampoo—it removes dandruff and checks falling hair because it's made from an 80 percent olive oil base.

"That stuff's no good," says the barber.

"No?"

"Not so good, no."

The announcer resumes his sonorous reading of the news: "Embattled alderman Alexander Luthor has . . ."

"Hold *still!*"

"Shhh!"

"—alled a news conference for one-fifteen this afternoon at City Hall Park."

With half of his hair barbered and the other half not, Ben Jaeger is out the front door before the snooty broadcaster can finish observing a rhetorical pause.

"A major announcement is expected."

5

Lex Luthor arrives at City Hall Park at seven minutes past the hour. When his limousine turns off Broadway and passes the old triangular post office he tells Paulie Scaffa, "Drive around. I shouldn't be early."

"Sure thing, boss."

Carl Krusada sits up front with Paulie. Carl is wearing his cleric's suit but not a Roman collar.

A number of reporters already congregated at the statue of Civic Virtue spot the big Lincoln and dash madly away from the monument's dry basin and into the street. "Alderman! Alderman!" Before Lex can tell him to, Paulie speeds up. He turns off Park Row onto Frankfort Street, heading east and rolling parallel to the elevated railroad and the plaza entrance to the Brooklyn Bridge.

"Just for that," says Lex, "I think I'll show up late."

Beside him but not touching, Mrs. O smiles.

"Paulie, why don't you go on over to Water Street?"

At twelve minutes past one Lex climbs from the back of the car. He glances around making certain no reporters have followed. Only a few blocks away is the bustling Fulton fish market, but over here the cobblestone street and broken sidewalks are deserted. Identical low brick buildings, former tanneries dating back to the early nineteenth century, face each other across Water Street. Lex uses a key to let himself into the most decrepit-looking one.

Inside is a long, freshly plastered room lighted by fluorescent tubing on the ceiling. Against the south wall stand more than a dozen robot prototypes, the original LR series, each partly disassembled. Against the north wall, stacked three deep, four high, and numbering over a hundred, are square and softly lustrous metal boxes. Except for the suitcase-style leather grips mounted on the lids, they resemble doorstep milk boxes, the kind provided to customers by local dairies. In a crate nearby are an equal number of small, flat radio-transmitters in Bakelite housings. Positioned against the east wall and taking up nearly its full length is an electrostatic generator with crackling sparks jumping from electrode to electrode.

At a semicircular work table centered in the room, Caesar Colluzo is bent over a circuit board no bigger than a playing card. He is apply-ing solder. A twist of smoke rises and breaks when it touches his fore-head. Scattered across the tabletop are various transistors, plug fuses, miniature vacuum tubes, a radio-frequency oscillator, pipes of different lengths, and a few small black cubes equipped with terminals and ground wires.

"Well?" says Lex. He strolls over to the wall of metal boxes, lifts the hinged lid on one, peeks inside, and shuts it again. "Any progress?"

Colluzo swivels around on his stool and—quite out of character—he smiles.

6

When Lois asked where was the closest place with a public tele-phone, Clark said there was a candy store just a block and a half away—then offered to walk her there. He didn't want her to—you know. Walk *past* it. "Why should I?" said Lois. "Is it disguised as a Chinese laundry?"

"Just let me walk you."

"No, that's all right."

"No, I insist."

"So do I," she said, and left.

He waited ten seconds then followed her down and out to St. Mark's Place. Falling into step beside her, Clark couldn't help but admire her profile. He liked her chin, he liked her throat, he liked the way that her eyebrows arched. She didn't pluck them, did she? It didn't look like it.

"Can I ask you something?"

She stops but looks in a hurry. "What?"

Seeking the courage to ask her out, Clark doesn't find it. "I used to be a reporter for the *Smallville Herald-Progress,* that's in Kansas, and I was wondering if you could help me get a job with *your* newspaper."

She rolls her eyes (he likes those, too) and resumes walking.

"I'm serious!"

She stops again, this time to laugh.

"You don't have to do that."

Lois shuts her mouth, then opens it, then shuts it.

"You could've just said no, you can't help me. But you didn't have to laugh in my face."

"Oh my," she says.

"Yes," he says right back. "Oh my."

"I apologize. I'm sorry."

Maybe she is and maybe she isn't. He can't tell. "Thank you," says Clark. Then he points. "The candy store. Now you can make your phone call." He turns around and starts back down the block.

"Kent."

He hates it whenever somebody calls him by his last name.

"I practically just got hired myself," says Lois. "I don't have any clout."

Two little boys Clark might have seen an hour ago from his window, one dressed as a pirate, the other as a cowboy, scoot around Lois into the candy store.

"But for what it's worth, my editor has this standing offer: If you scoop everybody else and bring him a story that makes the front page, he'll hire you on the spot."

"Yeah? That how you did it?"

She makes a face. "I graduated from journalism school. First in my class."

"Oh."

"Yeah—'oh.'" She walks into the candy store just as the two boys in Halloween costumes walk out chewing on braided sticks of red licorice.

Clark is still waiting when she comes rushing back out and points beyond him, saying, "I need that cab!"

In a moment Clark has sped twenty yards up the street and is keeping pace with the Checker, thumping a hand on the roof. Just short of the corner of St. Mark's and Third Avenue the cab finally stops. Clark pulls open the back door and waits for Lois to arrive at a trot.

"You have some legs, mister."

He grins but wishes she'd start calling him Clark.

Climbing into the back of the cab, Lois says, "Tell Willi our friend the alderman is having a press conference right now."

"That where you're going?"

"City Hall Park," she tells the hackie.

"Can I come with you?"

She closes the door and the Checker pulls away. At the corner it turns right and disappears.

By the candy store clock it's one twenty-five when Clark plucks a pamphlet-style tourist map from the spinner rack and turns to the index, runs a finger down the list. City College, City Court, City Hall . . . City Hall Park. H5. The counter lady barks Hey! it's not a public library. So he buys the map for a dime and several deckle-edge penny postcards. Then he plonks down another penny and helps himself to two sticks of red licorice.

7

Lex Luthor arrives back at City Hall Park at twenty minutes before two—Lois checks her watch when he steps from his limousine. A dozen of her colleagues do the same. It's an odd salad of general assignment and wire reporters, political writers and police-beat veterans, even some chatter columnists. Winchell is present, and Runyon, Bugs Baer, Ed Sullivan. Thirty, forty newsmen altogether, including photographers. Lois is the only woman—"news hen," is what the others all call her—but that's no problem. She can hold her own. She's disappointed Dorothy Kilgallen isn't here. Lois still hasn't met her and is dying to.

Kilgallen, she heard, is in Europe, sent by Hearst to interview Hitler, an assignment Lois cannot imagine being up to herself. Yet.

Lex quickly makes his way toward the enormous marble statue of Civic Virtue, nodding this way and that but not smiling, not joshing or pointing or shaking hands the way that he usually does at public events. Nor does he pause to hum a snatch of a popular tune to get a cheap laugh and butter up the pen-and-pencil men. He goes and stands on the rim of the fountain basin with his arms folded across his chest, displaying confident balance. Behind him is the giant marble figure of a muscular sword-wielding young man, naked but for an inexplicable scrap of seaweed that covers his privates.

Lex withdraws a sheet of onion-skin paper from his tuxedo jacket.

"Gentlemen," he begins, ". . . and Miss Lane," he adds with a chilly smile, "thank you all for coming. For the past month, as you know, I've been the subject of something called a 'special investigation.' From the start I have proclaimed both my outrage and my innocence. This afternoon I have the great pleasure to inform you that Mr. Dodge's *task force,* a task force assembled at the instruction of Mayor LaGuardia, has completed its work and that I have been found completely innocent of any wrongdoing of any kind.

"I'm relieved, of course, but more than that I'm *sorrowful.*" He doesn't look it. "Sorrowful that despite all of my efforts on behalf of the citizens of Greater New York I could have had my reputation impugned and my freedom imperiled by a series of wild accusations made against me by two members of our city's otherwise superb police department. Officers corrupted by their association with known criminal elements."

Lois opens her mouth.

Standing twenty yards away and half hidden behind a Dutch elm, Clark watches her close it again. He listens to her heart pound. Nothing to it, he's discovered. You look, you focus, then you filter out everything else and hear what you need to hear. Or want to.

"*One* of these officers," says Lex, "the *instigator* of the attack against me, was murdered several weeks ago by his own cronies in the narcotics trade. I am speaking of course about Lieutenant Richard Sandglass. But we need concern ourselves no longer with *him*. Almighty God will handle Lieutenant Sandglass, if He hasn't already, and save our courts the expense."

"Alderman—just what *proof* do you have that Lieutenant Sandglass was involved in the narcotics racket? Or anything else illegal?" It's Lois, her face unprofessionally red.

"Miss Lane, I'm not finished."

"No, but we're all supposed to quote you tomorrow and *that'll* be the proof."

"If I may continue . . ."

Her fellow reporters are glaring at her. Most of them. The others smirk or laugh outright.

"A just God, as I say, will take care of Lieutenant Sandglass. In the meantime, I take satisfaction in informing all of you that the lieutenant's partner in mischief, in crime, in calumny—Benjamin Harold Jaeger—was dismissed from duty earlier today. I am fully confident that charges will be brought against Officer Jaeger at the proper time."

That staggers Lois. But she quickly recovers. "Alderman, I'm asking you again, what *proof*—"

But already Lex has turned to his left and is addressing Walter Winchell, who just asked how you spelled Jaeger.

Consulting his typescript, Lex says, "J . . . A . . ."

"E-G-E-R!" booms a rapid voice from the back of the crowd. "My name is spelled J-A-E-G-E-R, and yours, you murdering son of a bitch, is spelled L-I-A-R!"

Along with everyone else, Clark turns and looks. Ben Jaeger's bright yellow hair is shorter, much shorter, on one side of his head than it is on the other. And he's drunk. *That,* thinks Clark, is Lois Lane's *boyfriend?*

Although it seems likely Ben Jaeger—tromping through the crowd with his arms thrust out like Karloff's Frankenstein—will hurl himself momentarily at Lex Luthor, Lex himself never budges. Nor do any of the press brigade try to impede or restrain him. They all merely step clear like it's none of their business. No, Clark realizes, not *that*—like stepping clear *is* their business. Which Clark supposes is true.

It just isn't true for him.

But before he can do anything—what, exactly, Clark has no idea—Lois Lane tosses away her pad and pencil, shouts Ben's name, and lunges in front of him. She grabs his wrists. For a moment he struggles. It looks as though he'll twist free and send her reeling. Then he just . . . quits.

With her right hand still clamped to his wrist and her left pressed gently now to the small of his back, she leads Ben away.

From a distance of fifty or sixty yards Clark hears her murmur, "It's going to be all right, honey, it's going to be okay."

Honey.

For two or three seconds Clark's heart doesn't beat.

The reporters are laughing now because Lex Luthor has just said, "Walter, did you get that spelling?"

Clark steps away from the tree and walks over to where Lois dropped her pad and pencil and picks them up.

Lex has noticed Clark, is looking down at him with an amused expression.

Clark coolly stares back.

And Lex's smile falters. He remembers his typed remarks and consults them. "I have"—he clears his throat—"just one more thing to say before I let all of you gentlemen go about your business."

From the edge of his eyes he glances back over at Clark.

Clark is still staring at him.

"Now that this malicious *investigation* has been concluded and my good name restored . . . I am announcing today my resignation from the Board of Aldermen. Effective immediately."

Lex waits for the hubbub to quiet down. While he does he looks back over to the spot where Clark was standing. But Clark is gone. He seeks him elsewhere in the press crowd, but no. He's just—gone.

8

Shortly after the big clocks on the colonnaded municipal, state, and federal buildings grouped around Foley Square have marked two o'clock with perfect synchronicity, Clark finds Lois Lane sitting on the steps of the Supreme Court building with Ben Jaeger.

He followed her talcum scent and the jangly meter of her heart.

"I thought you might need this," he says holding out Lois's notepad. If she doesn't ask for it back, he intends to keep the pencil still in his pocket. It's just an ordinary yellow Ticonderoga Number 2 pencil, it doesn't say *Daily Planet* on it or anything, but still Clark thinks he'd like to keep it. Little memento. The day we met.

Lois is astonished to see him but more astonished—jolted—by the sight of her notepad. "How did you—? What are you *doing* here?"

Clark smiles and shrugs. Has he ever *been* so happy?

Ben, meanwhile, regards him with chilly suspicion. "Lois . . . ?" He cuffs the edges of his red eyes. After he blots away their shine, he narrows them.

"Ben, this is, um, Clark Kent."

Ben waits for a little bit more than that—Clark Kent *who?*

"Clark came by the *Planet* yesterday looking for a job. I gave him some advice."

Ben Jaeger isn't buying it, not entirely. But after giving Clark the quick once-over, he reaches up to shake hands. "Ben Jaeger."

He grips Clark's hand aggressively, too firmly and for several moments too long.

Clark resists the impulse to crunch his right back.

Really crunch it.

"Good to meet you," he says.

"Good to meet *you*," says Ben.

A momentary change in his heart rate tells Clark he's lying. Or at the very least being insincere.

"You still haven't said how you got *this*," says Lois. She waggles her pad.

"I was there. I saw you drop it. I picked it up. Oh." He points. "Hope you don't mind, but I took some notes for the parts you missed."

Lois and Ben exchange an uncertain glance, then she hastily flips through the pad.

Her eyes open wide. "This is *true?* He actually resigned?"

"That's what he said."

"Ben, do you hear this? Luthor just quit as alderman."

Ben Jaeger gets to his feet. "But why would he do that? Why not just stick around and *gloat?*"

"And what's he planning to do now?" says Lois.

Without another word to Clark—it's as though they've completely forgotten he's here—they cross Foley Square together and continue north on Lafayette Street into the dense hard shade cast by the Criminal Courts building.

Clark's bliss is gone.

But at least she didn't ask him for her stupid pencil back.

Willi gets the blues. Berenice Abbott.
Trick or treat. Ceil visits the Chrysler Building.
The Next Essential Thing. Soda's Place.

———

1

It's Halloween and Willi Berg has the blues. He should go jump in the river and drown. He has his pick of two, the East or the North, but the way that he's feeling he can't get out of *bed,* much less pick a *river.* He doesn't have the energy. He sighs a lot and stares at the crackled ceiling, counts paint blisters. Clark keeps popping in. Can he get Willi something? He means a Pepsi-Cola or a cup of coffee, a bite to eat, but Willi says, Yeah sure, how 'bout my life back? In fact he doesn't *say* it, just *thinks* it; he's so far in the bushes that it seems pointless to speak. He just wallows, too blah, too whipped even to smoke.

While the news of Lex Luthor's vindication surely played a major part in his gathering despair, as did the fact that Saturday came and Saturday went without another visit from Lois Lane, what really plunged Willi into full-blown wretchedness was a one-sentence plug in Ed Sullivan's Saturday column for a new exhibit of Berenice Abbott's photographs at the Museum of the City of New York.

Back in 1932 Willi had gone there to see Abbott's first one-woman show and was amazed by her pictures of Manhattan's bridges and piers and ferry slips, its car barns and railroad stations, hotels, theaters, flophouses, and skyscrapers. Except that they didn't have any dead bodies or abandoned babies in them, and nobody in handcuffs, Abbott's pictures, Willi felt, could easily have been *his.* And they were hanging in a fancy museum. Her prints made Willi feel special, like he was onto something, maybe something permanent, but for sure something more meaningful than a first-use fee. He loved her stuff.

Last night Willi tore Sullivan's column from the paper and circled the item, found a tack, and stuck it to the kitchen wall—all done before it dawned on him: he couldn't go to see Berenice Abbott's new exhibition, was he nuts? He couldn't just waltz into a *museum,* he's a wanted man! That was a bad moment. But things got worse. He examined his predicament and his spirits crashed.

For two years he's been drifting, and his name is no closer to being cleared than it was on the day he woke up in Roosevelt Hospital. He is still floating, still drifting. Worse, he is still running. He used to have a career, he used to *do* something, *be* somebody. He used to be Willi the Great.

Now he's Willi the Lamster. Hiding out with the cockroaches, flopping a married woman for something to do, and counting on a freak from Kansas to be his lucky charm, his guardian angel. His way back.

He crawled into bed last night at eight. Now it's seventeen hours later, going on one o'clock Sunday afternoon, and Willi is still in bed with a creaky back and a full bladder. By his count there are two hundred eighteen, two hundred nineteen, two hundred *twenty* discrete paint blisters on the ceiling. And six different places where plaster is missing and you can see the lathing.

There's a knock on the apartment door. Willi's mouth turns dry.

Clark sticks his head into the bedroom. "Don't worry, it's just some kids trick or treating."

"How do *you* know?"

Clark squints at him in amusement.

Oh. Right. Those eyes.

After Clark has gone and dispensed penny candy into several open paper sacks, he returns to Willi's bedside. "Why don't you get up? It's a beautiful day."

"Leave me alone."

"Want to play Parcheesi?"

"Beat it."

With a shrug, Clark goes back to the kitchen. Soon Willi can hear him fiddling with the midget radio. He selects the Metropolitan Opera broadcast, which in ordinary circumstances Willi would tell him to turn *off*. But the way that he feels now he just can't be bothered. So he folds his pillow around his head to block out some tenor's booming aria.

A minute later Clark is back again. "I'm going to wash some clothes in the tub, anything you need done?"

"No!"

Ten minutes later Willi hears him walking around on the roof, hanging his wet laundry on one of the clotheslines strung up there.

Another half an hour goes past and by this point Willi knows if he doesn't pee soon he's going to burst. With reluctance he sits up and swings his legs to the floor. His joints and cartilage pop when he stands, then he stumbles because his right foot has got pins and needles. He's still wearing yesterday's clothes.

Limping into the kitchen, he finds Clark dressed in his Superman costume. But it's been newly accessorized with one of Willi's size-34 black belts cinched around his waist. The belt is narrow and braided and has a dull pewter buckle.

"What do you think?"

"The belt's got to be wider."

"I think so, too. But *in general*—you like?"

"Yeah, it's not too bad."

Clark beams.

"I got to take a leak," says Willi heading for the door. The toilet's down the hall.

When he comes back he lets Clark fix him a cup of tea. Sitting down at the kitchen table, he flicks a finger through a clogged ashtray until he finds a butt with a good inch left. He lights up while Clark is sprinkling loose pekoe into a tea ball. "You think a belt looks good, though, right?"

"Yeah. Terrific. But get your own."

"I will. And I'll get one that's a little wider, like you said."

There's another knock on the door.

"More kids," says Clark picking up the sack of candy.

"Hey! You can't open the door dressed like *that.*"

Clark glances down at himself. "Why not? It's Halloween," he says and opens the door to a trio of boys in Brooklyn Dodger uniforms. In unison they say, "Anything for Halloween?"

But then their mouths all fall open.

"Holy smokes!" says one of the boys, the tallest and the one wearing basketball sneakers, not regulation cleats. "Who're *you* supposed to be?"

"Me?" says Clark distributing wax lips, chocolate babies, and bubble-gum cigars. "I'm the Saucer-Man from Saturn."

The kids traipse off laughing and Clark shuts the door. "I just had the greatest idea," he says striding purposely into the bedroom and pulling the sheet off the bed. He begins ripping it into long strips.

"Clark, what do you think you're doing? Hey!"

"You want to go to that museum, right? Let's go today. Let's go now."

"You're nuts. I can't go to any museum."

"I know *you* can't," he says bending over Willi and wrapping one of the strips around the top of his head. "But what's to stop the Invisible Man. It's *Halloween,* Willi, don't you get it? Trick or treat. *Dress up.*"

When he catches on, Willi laughs—but then makes a wincing face and crabs, "*Looser,* for crying out loud, you wanna *smother* me . . . ?"

2

Like everyone else, for the past seven years Ceil Stickowski has admired the tall and graceful new Chrysler Building with its helmet-like spire, its dramatic setbacks and decorative stainless-steel eagles.

But being a New York City native she never would have considered going there just to see it. Tourists do that, it's a dead giveaway, and Ceil would have felt disloyal to her city's culture of indifference had she ever strolled into the lobby without a compelling reason. Today, however, she has an excellent—a very excellent—reason.

After the taxi drops her off on the corner of Lexington Avenue and Forty-second Street she throws back her shoulders, glances to both sides, and then enters the building.

Oh my lord! The lobby is finished in spectacular marble, and there is a revolving display of Chrysler motorcars, both classic and new, that she would like to spend some time admiring, but she isn't here to gawk. She is here on business. And for it to be transacted on a Sunday afternoon, she thinks, it must surely be very special, very important business indeed. She has no idea what that business might be; all she knows is that Lex Luthor has requested her presence and that is good enough for her.

She feels self-conscious and trivial when she joins four middle-aged men also waiting for an elevator. Their immobile faces all share that poreless quality, that shell-pink glow you find only in the pampered well-to-do. They carry leather briefcases unmarred by the pettiest scratch or scuff. Lawyers? Possibly. But *corporate* lawyers. Or executives. Bigwigs. When the elevator comes they stand back and let Ceil precede them in. The marquetry is gorgeous, like nothing she has ever laid eyes on before. She struggles to keep her face bland and unimpressable. But wow. Some veneer.

Ceil has not seen Lex Luthor since the evening her poor husband died. She's talked to him on the telephone several times, however, their longest conversation being the one they had a week after Herman's funeral. (Mr. Luthor, bless his soul, paid for everything, including a granite headstone with a polished area for Herman's name and dates.) During that particular conversation Ceil readily agreed to take over the running of one of Mr. Luthor's "entertainment establishments" in Chelsea, and while she initially felt some misgivings about the work, she was in no position to turn it down. The salary was generous. Besides, Lex Luthor was the finest man she'd ever known. If he asked her to do something, she would do it. She made only one demand. Well, it wasn't a demand exactly, she'd never demand anything from Lex Luthor. It was more in the nature of a request. She said she hoped there would be no colored girls working on the premises. And she said colored girls, that was the term she used, she wasn't being *derogatory*. Even so, Mr. Luthor chided her. "Colored girls are human beings too, Mrs. Stickowski. Just like yourself." She said of course they were, she understood that, it was just— "But rest assured, Mrs. Stickowski, the girls in your charge will all be white." She was upset, feeling that she'd disappointed Mr. Luthor, who was surely more advanced than anyone alive in his social attitudes and his sympathies.

Ceil enjoyed operating the house, a four-story, seven-bedroom brownstone on West Twenty-third Street. And she felt motherly toward the girls, who were mostly Scotch-Irish. And they all behaved themselves. They followed instructions, had regular physician check-ups, and avoided dangerous narcotics. You could ask them to do anything, with anyone, and they did it gladly. It was a pleasant time in Ceil's life and a good way to get over the loss of her beloved husband.

So it was awfully perturbing when, just a month ago, she received another call from Lex Luthor, one that lasted only a few seconds. He merely spoke the code word she'd hoped never to hear. He said, "Blue," and at once Ceil followed the protocols. Immediately upon hanging up the telephone receiver, she hurried downstairs to her office and drew out cash packets and open airplane tickets from the wall safe. She next emptied the house of clients, then summoned her girls to the front parlor, gave them each a thousand dollars and a plane ticket. They were packed, kissed good-bye, and gone by taxicabs in under an hour. Before they had even left the premises a crew of carpenters arrived, then a team of movers who carried in a dozen hospital beds and carried out the canopied and sleigh beds, as well as the long mechanized bed that did double duty as a torture rack. By morning the first patients were delivered, a contingent of destitute geriatric felons gathered from lord only knows where.

A manager is a manager, Ceil knows, and it really shouldn't matter what she manages, but a nursing home just doesn't have quite the zest of a cathouse.

When the elevator operator announces, "Forty-seventh floor," Ceil is surprised to discover that it is also the destination of the four men sharing the car with her. An attractive slender woman with piled white hair and dressed in a royal blue dress stands waiting in the corridor. She holds a clipboard. Behind her on the wall, to the right of the entrance to a reception area, Ceil can see where the name of a former tenant—company name and logo limned ghostly by adhesive—once was fastened. There is no signage for a current occupant.

The woman presents a formal smile and pulls open the glass door by its tubular handle. "Gentlemen," she says, "go right in, please." Is that a brogue Ceil hears? The woman halts her with an expression both mild and despotic. Ceil takes a breath and holds it. "Mrs. Stickowski? Would you mind coming with me?" Leading Ceil down the corridor, she adds over a shoulder, "I'm Helen O'Shea, Mr. Luthor's personal assistant."

Ceil Stickowski nods, having already noted two things: first, Helen O'Shea hesitated ever so slightly before saying "personal assistant," as if not entirely sure that's what she is; and second, Mrs. O'Shea has a flat fanny. And no hips to speak of. And her ankles are thick. All right, that makes four things. Ceil doesn't like the woman at all.

At the end of the corridor Mrs. O'Shea turns left and brings Ceil to an unmarked door. She knocks once and without waiting opens it and ushers Ceil inside.

Besides Lex Luthor, there are several other men in the office—at a table, on a sofa—but Ceil registers only their presence, nothing else. Her attention is drawn to and monopolized by her generous benefactor. Ceil expected to detect some physical evidence of the strain he must have suffered over the last month, was afraid his mood and demeanor would in some way reflect the bitterness he has to be feeling about it all now. But no. Mr. Luthor seems relaxed and cheerful. And if Ceil is not mistaken, he's spent some time recently under a sunlamp: his face—his entire head—is tanned to an agreeable tawny bronze.

Hands clasped behind his back, Lex is standing at a picture window that looks into the conference room next door. The men Ceil came up with in the elevator are seated in there now at a long mahogany table with another half dozen men of identical mien. Each is reading through his own legal-looking document or signing it with a pen that must've cost a hundred dollars. The window, Ceil assumes, is a mirror on the conference-room side. Thanks to Herman she knows about such things.

"Mr. Luthor," says the awful Mrs. O'Shea, "I've brought—"

"*Ceil!*" he exclaims. "Wonderful to see you again!"

He makes her feel as alive as a young animal. Give her a gun, a club, a pair of scissors, and gladly she will pick off whomever he says. Herman was so lucky!

"It's good to see you again, sir."

Beaming, he walks across the office with a rhythmic stride. She thinks he might greet her with a hug but he does not. He waits for her to put out a hand—because that's what a gentleman does—and then he grips it in both of his. "Thank you for coming."

"I'm only too glad." She hesitates, not certain whether she ought to make any reference to his recent troubles. But finally she decides it would be rude not to. "Congratulations on how everything has . . . worked out." Was that the wrong thing to say—congratulations?

"Thank you, Ceil. But it's all in the past—as though it happened *years* ago."

She can't help being surprised. He's so resilient! "Well, I'm not voting for LaGuardia on Tuesday, I can promise you *that*."

He laughs. "That's very loyal of you." Then he says, "Excuse me for a moment," already turning to Mrs. O'Shea stationed alongside of the door. "Mrs. O, would you go and collect those confidentiality statements? And make sure they're all properly initialed throughout and signed."

"Yes, sir."

"And Mrs. O? After you've done that, we'll be ready to serve cocktails."

She nods curtly and exits.

Taking Ceil by the hand, Lex conducts her across the office, a huge space carpeted in dark green spongy broadloom. In the carpeting are the impressions where a long desk and several bookcases once stood. On the walls are the outlines of missing paintings or framed photographs. "I want to introduce you to some associates," says Lex.

Three men who seem all of an age—late twenties, early thirties— are huddled around a solid heavy table littered with pads of paper, squares of oak tag, pencils, black crayons, alphabet stencils, brushes, and bottles of India ink. There are half-eaten hamburger sandwiches, too, and cardboard coffee containers. Mounted on the ledge of an easel standing catercorner to the table is a large poster that reads: INTRODUC- ING . . . THE MARVEL OF 1937! An area below the press type is ridged and smeared with rubber cement and flecked with bits of paper where a picture was pasted on and then removed.

The men look exhausted, ashen, near collapse, and their good clothing is disheveled and wrinkled, speckled with coffee and ketchup and mustard and ink stains. Shirtsleeves rolled up, collars open, neckties unknotted or missing. Their suit coats are draped over the backs of their chairs. What strikes Ceil is the absence of smoke in the air and filled ashtrays, cigarette packets and books of matches. The picture—Men Working Under A Deadline—seems incomplete without those things.

Lex introduces her to the men, but Ceil is so engrossed in registering their haggard faces (and also in trying to read, upside down, some of the stenciled lettering on the oak-tag boards) that she doesn't catch their names. She does, however, hear Lex explain to her that the "fellows" were employed formerly by the Young and Rubicam advertising agency as, respectively, chief copywriter, chief copy tester, and the executive in charge of market research. "But I convinced them," he says, "to come work for me."

The men, Ceil thinks, don't seem at all pleased by their new situation.

"And of course you know Paulie Scaffa," says Lex.

He is sitting with another man, a small olive-skinned man, on the sofa off in a far corner and partly concealed behind a stack of doorstep milk boxes—well, Ceil guesses they're not *really* milk boxes, but that's what they *look* like.

"Paulie," she says hearing the coolness in her voice. "How are you?" She will never forgive him for not visiting poor Herman when he was so ill. Simple human kindness, is that so hard to muster? The big baboon. He certainly hasn't learned anything from Mr. Luthor's example, has he?

"Nice seeing you again, Ceil."

She could swat Paulie when he doesn't so much as get up from his seat.

But at least his companion shows some manners. When Lex says, "And this is Caesar Colluzo, my chief engineer and bottle washer," the little man promptly stands and bows his head. Then he sits back down and refolds his arms across his chest.

"Ceil, won't you take a seat?"

"Thank you, Mr. Luthor," she says as he steers a roller chair around behind her.

"Now, Ceil, I asked you here because I need your help."

"Mine?" She lays a hand flat on her chest above the hivelike swellings of her bosom. "Certainly I'll do my best, but . . ." She feels light-headed. She will fail. Disappoint him. Oh dear God.

"I'm going to show you something, and you have to promise you won't say a word about it to anyone."

"Of course. You can trust me, Mr. Luthor."

"I know that." He pats her on the shoulder like Daddy used to do whenever she'd bring home a good report card. "Paulie?"

Immediately Paulie Scaffa gets up from the couch. Lifting one of those milk-box-things by a leather handle on its lid, he conveys it across the office. The box doesn't appear to be heavy. The trio of advertising men, responding to a scowl from Lex Luthor, clear a space for it on the table.

"And may I have a remote control, Caesar? *If* you don't mind."

From the inside pocket of his ill-fitting sport coat the little Italian removes a flat piece of black plastic, about the same dimensions as a Hershey bar, and passes it to Lex. "Now, Ceil, what I am about to show you is—well, I think of it as the next essential thing." (Because of the way he says it, Ceil imagines capital letters: Next Essential Thing.) Lex pauses for dramatic effect. "There are some who believe that the next essential thing, the product that every human being simply *must* possess, will be a thing called television. But they're wrong. Dead wrong."

He aims the piece of black plastic in the direction of the milk box. Then he carefully presses the buttons on it in a prescribed sequence.

A moment later Ceil gasps.

After the lid opens, a post of gleaming nested metal shoots two, two-and-a-half feet straight up from the box. Immediately the post begins to reconfigure itself. Narrow rods unfold from a dozen grooves. From the rods come other, slimmer, more articulated rods, which in turn are grooved with channels, and from which . . .

Ceil covers her mouth with both hands. It's like a gigantic Swiss army knife! But instead of a couple of blades and a nail file, a screwdriver, a toothpick, an orange peeler, a tweezers, and a key ring, it contains, neatly and miraculously within itself—

"A mechanical man!" she exclaims.

When completely unfolded and self-assembled, it is twenty-seven inches tall.

It steps from the box onto the table. With its red eyes blinking, its arms moving forcefully up and down, its fingers clicking as they clench, its knees bending, legs pumping—thunka-thunka-thunka-thunka—it does a kind of martial parade-in-place.

"Mr. Luthor, you've built a mechanical man! How wonderful!"

He presses another sequence of buttons and it stops marching. Then: another sequence and suddenly it is broadcasting *Tristan and Isolde* over the WCBS radio network. Another sequence and then it's

WNEW, Martin Block on *Make Believe Ballroom* introducing the Andrews Sisters' recording of "Bei Mir Bist Du Schoen."

"What a marvelous—"

"It's not a toy, Ceil."

"Oh, I wasn't going to say *that,* sir."

But yes, yes she was: that's *exactly* what she intended to call it.

"It's the next essential thing."

"I can see *why.*"

No, she really can't, but—well, if Mr. Luthor says so, then surely it will be.

"This is our very basic model," he tells her. "In addition to being equipped with both commercial and short-wave radio it contains a library of classic novels—"

Another sequence of buttons and a mellifluous, albeit clearly artificial voice intones, "Happy families are all alike; every unhappy family is unhappy in its own way."

"—and of course it can . . ." Lex reaches over, picking up a pad of foolscap from the table. He flips the top sheet over, finds what he's searching for and then squinting to decipher handwriting not his own, he continues, "it can do—let's make that *perform,* shall we? It can *perform* a multitude of household chores—run the Bissell, fire the furnace, feed the dog, clean the cat box." He grabs a pencil, strikes out the word "do" and writes "perform" directly above it.

The three advertising men look blankly back at him.

He consults the pad again. "Our luxury models are not only taller, but smarter—they can prepare meals, from plain fare to a five-course banquet." Luthor frowns. "Five-course banquet? How about we say *fine dining* instead? From plain fare to *fine dining.*"

One of the admen leans forward and puts his elbows on the table and his face between his hands.

Ceil meanwhile notices that the little Italian man is doing a slow burn but trying to contain it: his lips keep moving in and out as he fixes Lex Luthor with a baleful stare.

What is going *on?* And why, Ceil asks herself, is *she* here?

Now Lex points behind her with the pad of paper and says, "*Those* are the luxury models."

Ceil turns and what she sees jolts her again.

In the conference room a pair of six-foot-tall mechanical men are gliding around the table with pitchers and cocktail shakers, ambidextrously filling glasses with martinis, Manhattans, Rob Roys, and whiskey sours.

The gentlemen assembled there, whose demeanor hitherto seemed so worldly and rigid, look as wonderstruck now as little boys at their first circus.

"Ceil . . . ?"

She's been staring, open-mouthed. "Excuse me, Mr. Luthor. I'm just . . . flabbergasted."

"Excellent," he says, "very excellent. It's the reaction I was hoping for. And the one I expect from *everyone* in due time." As he says that, Lex pointedly looks at one of the advertising men, the one introduced to Ceil earlier as the director of market research.

"Mr. Luthor," says Ceil, "you said something about needing my help, but I don't see . . ." Her stomach is tied in knots. "Perhaps . . ."

"It's quite simple, dear lady. I need your expertise."

"Sir?"

"These gentlemen," says Lex indicating the admen, "have been working on a campaign to launch this marvelous creation of mine, to introduce it to the world. Well, first to New York and *then* to the world." He picks up a different pad of paper. "But they're still not quite . . . on target." He reads: "'It's a pet . . . it's a pal . . . it's a *plant waterer?*' No, still not quite. But they're making progress. In the meantime . . ."

Ceil lifts her eyes to Lex, now resting his left palm on top of the mechanical man's square head.

"In the meantime one crucial question remains: what do we *call* this marvel of 1937?"

"Call it?"

"You referred to it as a mechanical man. But that's hardly *catchy*, is it? Our friends here in the ad biz keep urging me to call it simply the Luthor—as if it's an automobile. The Chrysler. The Studebaker. The Luthor. But it's *not* an automobile, Ceil."

"No," she says. "It's the next . . . essential thing."

He beams at her. "And our friend Mr. Scaffa, taking his cue from Mr. Walt Disney, wants me to name it *Rudy*—as if it were a *cartoon character.* Mickey Mouse. Donald Duck. Rudy Robot."

"Or Robby," says Paulie, back on the sofa. "Robby Robot could work just as well."

Luthor quirks up one side of his mouth in dismissal.

"But it's *not* a cartoon character, Ceil."

"No," she agrees.

"And Mr. Colluzo over there," says Lex, "wants me to call it the Caesar!"

Because Lex laughs, Ceil does too. Although her tension turns it into something of a bray.

Sneaking another glance at Caesar Colluzo, also back on the sofa, Ceil can see high color rising in his throat, his cheeks. Both hands are clamped between his knees. He looks capable of homicide.

"All ridiculous names," says Luthor. "Completely inappropriate. But the problem has become suddenly grave, Ceil."

"Grave, sir?"

"*Extremely.* Because I have a roomful of investors next door with millions of dollars at their disposal, millions that I intend to use for the manufacture of millions of robots. *But what do we call them?*" He taps the basic robot's head. "What do we call *it?*"

Ceil's stomach folds in half. Why is he telling *her* this? Surely he doesn't think—

"Quite a problem. But then it dawned on me. Who is better at this very thing than Ceil Stickowski?"

"Mr. Luthor, I don't—"

"You, dear lady, are going to christen the next human necessity. Come up with the next household name. Right here. Right now. *You.*"

"Me?" Her hands are clamped around the armrests. "But Mr. Luthor, I don't know anything about—"

"Don't be so modest—Mrs. Smokin' Dynamite Fall Arsenal of Values!"

"But, sir, I didn't—"

"Who could ever forget your Crown Prince, your Medley, your Hoopla, your Salvo, your *Trinitro-Delux!* Wonderful names, all of them—names so good, so *perfect* they emptied out an entire warehouse, Ceil."

"But that was Herman, Mr. Luthor, *Herman* came up with all of those names. I just pasted up the catalogs." Oh dear God dear God dear God . . .

"Please." Luthor holds up a hand, palm toward Ceil. "Stop. I don't appreciate false modesty." And his abrupt change of expression underscores that: his eyes turn stony and terrifying.

In front of Ceil's face appear red and black threads that drift and sizzle. She feels as if she might faint.

Luthor bends down and speaks softly into her ear. "So what do we call it? I'm expected next door in two minutes, Ceil. I need a product name. Give it to me."

"Sir, please . . ."

"A name. The perfect name."

"Mr. Luthor, I swear to you, Herman made up those names for the catalogs. He enjoyed it! He had nothing else to do!"

"Ceil. I think I know what Herman was and was not capable of."

"He did the word scramble every day in the paper. Herman was very good with words. It was a hobby!"

"Oh Ceil, he was a common thug. He couldn't even *spell medley.*"

It's as if Lex Luthor just struck her in the stomach. She can't catch her breath.

"Ceil, the perfect name, please. We have less than two minutes. *You* have less than two minutes."

Ceil turns her head and looks at him dead on.

And she knows—instantly she knows that her husband did not pass from his cancer.

Oh my God.

"Ceil? I'm *waiting.*"

She shakes her head.

"Still waiting. The name that tens of millions of people will utter day after day for the next hundred years. I'm *waiting.*"

His hand touches her elbow, creeps slowly up to her shoulder toward her throat.

Herman, she prays. Help me!

She closes her eyes.

She opens them and looks at the mechanical . . . thing, that steely robot standing motionless on the tabletop. It seems to her now anything but benign. It's something nasty, something dangerous. Something wicked. As nasty and dangerous and wicked as . . .

She mumbles something.

"I didn't hear you, Ceil."

Her eyes move to his face. "I said . . . call it the Lexbot."

For a long time Lex remains crouched beside her, his hand painfully squeezing her shoulder.

Then he chuckles, his hand falls away, and he stands up.

"The Lexbot," he says. "The Lexbot. *Lexbot.*"

Ceil is weeping, openly sobbing.

"The *Lexbot.* Did you hear that, gentlemen? It's the Lexbot, the marvel of 1937!"

Ceil's shoulders move helplessly up and down.

"Very good," she hears him say, then watches him type L-E-X-B-O-T on a cramped keyboard attached to a small die-cut device. He yanks down hard on a side lever, and out shoots a small lozenge of metal. He holds it up between his thumb and forefinger. "Lexbot." Then tossing down the metal tag as though it were a nickel for a newspaper, he says, "Thank you. Ceil. Mrs. O'Shea will show you out when you've composed yourself."

Ten minutes later, as that horrid white-haired Irisher leads her from the office, Ceil glances through the one-way mirror and there is Luthor—not *Mister* Luthor, *Luthor*—gesturing expansively at the head of the conference table while the moneymen all write checks and the two robots, the two *Lexbots,* replenish their cocktails.

3

In addition to the torn sheets wrapped around his head, Willi's disguise—his Halloween costume—includes dark glasses, leather gloves, and a black trench coat. Everyone they pass on the street or ride with on the IRT local identifies him immediately. Hey, look! It's the Invisible Man! Whenever someone laughs or makes a friendly crack, Willi responds in a lousy British accent, playacting Claude Rains.

On the subway they see other grown men and women in costume—a black knight, a pilgrim, and a bum with a crushed hat and a wine bottle sticking out of his coat pocket. Oh. No. That *is* a bum.

A couple dressed up as Abraham Lincoln and Mary Todd swing on straps all the way down the length of the car to invite Willi and Clark to a masquerade party on West End Avenue. Oh come on, *please?* It'll be fun! You fellas look great!

Clark takes delight in how completely *emancipated* Willi seems to feel. Behind that linen wrapper he is laughing his head off. Why, the crazy nut even walks straight up to a transit cop when they get off the subway at 103rd Street and just for fun asks him if this is the right station for the Museum of the City of New York! "Up those stairs, boyo, and left to Fifth." The cop grins at Willi's getup, then tucks his double chin, taking a long scrutiny of Clark, giving an interrogative grunt. "And himself behind yeh? Who's your caped friend there supposed to be?"

"The Saucer-Man," says Willi. "From Saturn."

Clark taps the toy ray gun stuck under his belt; if you turn a key on its side it clacks and sparks. He bought it earlier at the candy store on St. Mark's Place. In that same place he also bought a black celluloid mask identical to the one the Lone Ranger wears. He's wearing it for two reasons. It matches his belt, his boots, and the background color of his chest appliqué, giving his appearance a unified, even fashion-savvy touch. And it makes him appear like a genuine Halloween reveler. A guy on his way to a party.

An enormous five-story building faced with red brick and trimmed with white marble, the museum is—according to the free booklet Clark picks up—"the city's attic," a palatial depository of dioramas depicting events from the purchase of Manhattan Island to the construction of the Empire State Building, and galleries crammed with historical furniture, portraits, costumes, documents, and memorabilia. But Willi makes it clear that he's not interested in any of "that old junk." He is here for only one reason: to see Berenice Abbott's photographs.

As they follow arrows to the proper gallery, Clark keeps stopping to admire things—a Dutch sleigh, a tallyho coach, the figurehead from an old clipper ship. He is powerfully affected by it all but couldn't say why.

Following Willi down a long hall he notices a pair of open doors leading into a raked auditorium. Just inside the entrance a sign is still posted for a two o'clock lecture long since over: "From There to Here, From There to Home: The Immigrant Experience."

"Would you get a *move* on?"

"I'm *coming*," says Clark.

From there to here, from there to home.

His red cape sailing out in back of him, he puts on a little speed—just a *little*—and ends up beating Willi to the exhibition gallery.

"Think you're funny? Well, you're not."

Clark slings an arm around Willi's shoulder and together they go inside and look at pictures of the city. Willi's city. And maybe, Clark thinks, his city too.

The name of the exhibition is *Metropolis*.

4

It was a mistake to name her joint "Soda's." From the night it opened, people have been walking in expecting fountain service, wanting a strawberry milk shake, a chocolate malt. The name, and especially that fancy gold script she'd had painted on the front window—just a bad idea, a mistake. This here is a *club*, she has been saying for almost a year, telling squares, telling high school sweethearts, telling little kids tapping on the door with two bits apiece squeezed in their sweaty mitts. This here is a *jazz music club.* They always want to know so why's it called *Soda's?* And some people are downright *nasty* about it, like it's *her* fault they can't get a large root beer. Why is it called Soda's? She'll *tell* them why: because that's my *name.* My name is Soda Wauters.

She was *Edith* Wauters before she joined Harry Seltzer's Carbonated Rhythm Orchestra. It was a joke, of course, but the name stuck. What the heck. She likes it.

This afternoon in her club—formerly a "billiard hall for Coloreds" on South Orange Avenue in Newark, New Jersey—she sits alone drinking at the bar. Tipping the bottle of Seagram's Pedigree whenever she notices that her glass has somehow gotten itself empty. Outside, neighborhood children pass by in pairs and bunches dressed up for Halloween. When Soda cabbed over here earlier from her apartment near Five Corners she brought along a twenty-four-count box of candy cigarettes, and for a while, the first hour or so, she got up and dispensed goodies whenever some trick-or-treaters tapped on the door. But even before the candy was depleted she quit answering, no longer trusting her legs. She is a large woman—nearly two hundred pounds—and if she falls she is liable to fall hard.

The club is closed until tomorrow night, and she just might sit here drinking till then. Who's going to stop her? This is her joint.

Last night she had a gang of musicians she knew drop by on their way home to New York from a recording session for RCA Victor in Camden. She was glad to see everybody, and they were all genuinely congratulatory about her club. But almost to a man they asked her, Why so glum, chum? Doc Wershow even joshed her saying, "You ain't no blues singer, honey, you just a big ol' canary, how come you wearin' that long face?" She told him, she told everybody, she was just tired.

She's tired, all right. Of everything.

It is half past three now as she tips the Seagram's bottle again, avoiding her eyes in the mirror.

She's never going to see him again. It's been more than a month now, and it's—he's not coming back.

The first time she saw him was in late June, a weeknight. He was sitting at a table by himself, and Soda was doing a set with the house band. She was, she recalls, singing "I'll Get By." He wasn't especially good-looking—*not the kind of man that girls think of as handsome,* she thinks now and smiles—but he *had* something. And from across the room she could identify that something as decency. He looked about fifty and was dressed in a dark gray tropical worsted suit. Don't be no copper, she thought. Please.

Soda didn't talk to him that night. Or the next time he came in, either. Or the time after that.

But the time after that she bought him a drink. And no, he wouldn't insist on beer if the lady was buying. Seagram's Pedigree? He invited her to sit down. Told her he loved her voice and how she could put a song across. For the next forty-five minutes they talked about band singers. Helen Ward, Ruth Etting, Annette Hanshaw, Connie Boswell. He knew his stuff, the man knew about popular music, that was for certain, and took delight in all of her stories about musicians she'd known, still knew. She told him about the times she'd had stage fright and the times she'd sung better, in her own humble opinion, than Billie Holiday on her best day. She talked about grilling steaks at a backyard cookout with Lester Young, playing horseshoes with Red Norvo. The man seemed to take delight in hearing *anything* Soda wanted to talk about, including her two marriages.

"Now you," she said, meaning now you tell *me* something. "Wait, though. You're not a po-liceman, right? Tell me you're not?"

"That wouldn't be good?"

"That wouldn't be good."

"And why is that?"

She smiled, ran a finger around in circles on some bar spill. "My daddy was a copper."

"Sounds like a song."

"It wasn't no song, honey. So. You ain't, are you?"

He shook his head.

"Now we're cooking," she said.

"Are we? I'd like to think so."

"I'd like to think so, too."

By that time, they were sitting together on the day bed in Soda's private office at the rear of the club.

"So what *do* you do, honey?"

But with a small sad smile he shook his head again. "Can you wait on that one?"

"You on the lam?"

"No, I can swear to you that I'm not on the lam."

"Married?"

"No."

She kissed him.

"You're the funniest guy I ever met."

"I doubt it."

"You a musician?"

He hesitated for a second, then said, "No."

She kissed him again, and that time he kissed her back.

He returned a week later and sat at his regular table and drank his usual beer and a half. When she'd finished both of her sets and the crowd thinned out she sent over a bottle of straight bourbon.

He stayed till the club shut down at two, then helped her upend chairs on the tables. He sat behind the drums and picked up two brushes and accompanied her while she sang "What Kind o' Man Is You?"

He stayed the night.

Soda fell in love and he didn't. Or maybe he did, she couldn't tell.

But he was always decent to her, oh my God was he decent to her.

He was the nicest and the tenderest man she ever had met.

Told her his first name but not his last. "In time," he said. "All in good time."

But time had run out and her sweet lovin' daddy was gone. Said, "I'll see you tomorrow," then never came back . . .

The rim of the shot glass is touching Soda's bottom lip and there it stops.

Jesus, Mary, and Saint Joseph.

The *package.* That fat envelope with the red flap string he left with Soda the last time they were together. Saying, "Honey"—by that time he was calling her that—"Honey, could you do me a big favor and keep this in your safe?"

As soon as she is sober enough to walk back to her office and her fool head is clear enough to remember the safe combination, Soda is going to take a *look* at that envelope, and maybe, just maybe, find out Richard's last name.

Some other things, too.

The black cube. Clark shows off. Phone tap.
Scene of the crime. Ciao, Caesar.

———

1

By the time the gentlemen from the Ford Motor Company, the DuPont Corporation, the Union Banking Corporation, the L. Henry Schroder Banking Company, and the investment firm of Brown Brothers/Harriman leave the conference room late this Sunday afternoon, all of them are tipsy and swaying and utterly convinced that Lex Luthor's robots, God blesh 'em, make the world's most perfect martinis. The men have become enchanted by the machines as well as by their profit potential. Television. Feh! Lexbots are next!

In combination they pledged a total of twelve million dollars for the construction and outfitting of three Lexbot factories.

"Congratulations," says Mrs. O.

Still seated at the head of the conference table, Lex is turning a small black socketed cube around and around with the fingers of his right hand. "Thank you." He sets the cube down in front of him and picks up a remote-control device. When he presses a sequence of buttons, one of the two luxury Lexbots in the room steps away from the wall and glides to the table. "And tomorrow," he says, "I'm expecting to do equally as well. Even better."

In the morning Lex is scheduled to meet with executives from the August Thyssen Bank, the Dresdner Bank, German General Electric, and Braunkohle-Benzin A.G. In the afternoon he is seeing representatives from Fiat, Centro Stile Zagato, and the Pontifical Court.

During the next several weeks he expects investment capital to roll in with almost ridiculous ease.

As he realized the day he first saw Caesar Colluzo doodling on a pad in that lecture hall, nobody can resist a robot. Nobody.

Mrs. O watches Lex get up and open a small panel in the back of the machine. He snugly fits the cube inside. Shuts the panel. Then he walks over to the long mirror on the wall, reaches up, and pulls down a blackout shade.

"If you don't need me anymore . . ."

"Now or entirely?" He stabs in another sequence of buttons on the remote-control device.

". . . I'd like to go home."

"You do that, Helen. Have Paulie take you in his car. And tell Caesar I want to have a word with him upstairs." He glances at his watch. "Ten minutes."

"And what about the admen?"

"Order them more coffee and sandwiches." He cocks his head at Mrs. O'Shea. "Leave."

"Yes, sir. Congratulations again." She hesitates, then: "Lex, I think we might have a problem with Ceil Stickowski. I didn't like the way she looked at you when—"

"Don't worry about Ceil. Just go."

She closes the door firmly behind her.

Lex presses a red button.

From the Lexbot comes a low rasping sound that turns into a hum, then a beep, and suddenly the twelve-foot-long table is hurled across the conference room. It smashes against the far wall, blasting cracks through the plaster.

The door re-opens, and Mrs. O sticks her head back into the room. She is pale. She looks at the table, its surface now scorched and blistered. Here and there tiny flames struggle in patches of varnish, then wink out.

Giving a snort of glee, Lex manipulates the remote-control again. The Lexbot swivels and moves noiselessly back to its carrying case, steps into it, and stands motionless. With yet another poke of Lex's finger at a button, a gray one this time, it disassembles itself, turning back into a gleaming metal post. The top section of the post slides down, nesting in the section below it. When the top of the post is flush with the ledge of the carrying case, the lid slaps shut with a satisfying click.

Lex repeats the process for the second robot.

"Mrs. O? One last thing. Tell Paulie to grab these and carry them down when you're both heading out. He can drop them off at Water Street."

With a curt nod he walks out.

Mrs. O remains in the doorway, frowning. As she turns finally to leave, the conference table—its four legs as charred and friable as if they've spent hours burning in a fireplace—suddenly crashes to the floor.

2

"Is this Lois Lane?"

She doesn't recognize the caller's voice. A woman's. "Yes . . ."

"The reporter?"

"Yes."

"I hope you don't mind me calling you at home, Miss Lane. I called the *Daily Planet* but you weren't there, and they wouldn't give me your exchange. But it's in the directory, you know."

"Yes, I know. Who is this?"

"Miss Lane, I'd like to speak with you about Lex Luthor. I read your stories in the paper and I think we should talk."

"And your name is . . . ?"

"I'm sorry, it's Ceil. Ceil Stickowski? Mrs. Herman Stickowski."

"*Sticky's* wife?"

"His widow, Miss Lane. Do you think we might get together?"

Lois says, "Could you hold on for just one second?" She lays down the receiver and then goes and gently closes the bedroom door where

Ben Jaeger is asleep in his undershirt and skivvies. She returns to the phone and says, "Of course we can get together, Mrs. Stickowski—tonight?"

3

While the Invisible Man is making his tenth circuit of the special exhibition gallery, the Saucer-Man from Saturn, who by this time has had his fill of Berenice Abbott's photographs, drifts back out into the corridor and strolls around the museum by himself. Walking from room to room, floor to floor, cursorily inspecting displays of eighteenth- and nineteenth-century furniture, costumes, theater posters, and the like. George Washington's boudoir slippers, Alexander Hamilton's comb and brush. A re-creation of John D. Rockefeller's bedroom, circa 1880.

The elastic band on Clark's black mask is uncomfortably tight. And the mask itself feels constricting, makes his cheeks sweat, feel slimy, and his eyebrows itch. He doesn't know how the Lone Ranger puts up with it.

He goes into the gift shop and purchases a few postal cards. The cashier smiles at his costume. "Shouldn't that be a **Z** on your chest?"

"Pardon me?"

The cashier points to the red **S**. "I thought you spelled Zucchini with a **Z**."

"Zucchini?"

"Aren't you supposed to be one of those Zucchini brothers that get shot out of a cannon?"

Strolling back into the main hall, Clark finds a cushioned bench. For a while he watches people, mostly families with small children. Some of the children are dressed for Halloween. None of the adults are.

He finds himself thinking about Diana Dewey. He can recall everything about her, but what he *especially* recalls is her croaky voice. It was adorable. *She* was adorable. He misses her, wants to see her again. But now he is suddenly thinking about Lois Lane. He's never met anyone like her before. Ever. In his whole *life!*

But now he's thinking of Diana again: making him soup and tea, applying sticking plaster to the only cut he's ever had . . .

Diana.

Only twenty years old and already Clark is like one of those no-good, two-timing rambler types that Plato Beatty used to sing about. He's like Blackjack David! He's disgusted.

Yes, but still he wants to see Lois Lane again. Soon.

To clear his mind of both hankerings and reprimands, he licks the point of his pencil, selects a postal card with a picture of a clipper ship on the front side, and begins composing a note on the back to his father. Hi! How are you? I am fine.

He pauses, glancing up to further gather his thoughts. That's when he notices a series of portraits in heavy gilt frames on the wall across the lobby. With a narrowing of his eyes and the smallest mental *oomph*, he can read the identification plates affixed below the oil paintings. It's a gallery of the English governors of New York.

Clark licks his pencil point again and turns his attention back to the postal card.

But almost immediately he glances back up again. Running his gaze down the line of portraits, left to right, he stops to focus on the portrait of Sir Danvers Osborne, Baronet, appointed 10 October 1753.

Like the rest of his fellow royal governors, Sir Danvers looks haughty and mildly cross.

The problem is—and Clark hopes this doesn't mean he is inordinately finicky—but the problem is the picture frame: it's crooked. Not terribly crooked, just out of alignment with the others along the wall.

Clark wants to go over there and—adjust it.

Which would probably set off bells and end up in his being ejected.

Well, if it doesn't bother the guards, if it doesn't bother the *curators*, it shouldn't bother him. And it really is none of his business. Crossing one leg over the other, he returns his full attention to the postal card. The weather is good but getting chilly. The buildings are—

The Invisible Man finally appears. "You ready to go?"

By now it is late afternoon. The temperature has fallen sharply and there's a nippy wind. But that doesn't bother Clark, and Willi has his trench coat. They decide to walk for a while, turning south at Fifth Avenue and heading back downtown.

"So I guess you enjoyed that show," says Clark.

Willi says, "Yeah."

"What were your favorite pictures?"

Willi shrugs.

"Mine were the up-close bridge ones, just the girders? And that newsstand with the million magazines."

"Yeah, they were good."

"You okay?"

"I'm fine."

"You don't *sound* fine, you seem . . . I don't know. You *sure* you're okay?"

"I'm *fine. God.*" Willi stops to light a cigarette, cupping his hands but still going through four matches.

"Hey, you know," says Clark. "I was thinking. If you have to smoke, you should consider switching to a brand that gives you coupons. We could save them up for something—like a bridge table or something."

Willi lifts his dark glasses and shoots Clark a dirty look through his eye holes.

Without any conscious thought or decision they enter Central Park at Ninety-ninth Street onto a footpath that winds past baseball fields and running tracks.

"What're you thinking about?"

"Nothing," says Willi.

"You're all mopey again."

"I'm not mopey." He picks at the cotton strip below his bottom lips and irritably tugs it down. "Why do you always have to talk all the time?"

"I don't."

"So don't."

"Fine, I won't."

"Great."

Ten seconds later Clark says, "Hey, come here," and pinches hold of one of Willi's coat sleeves, pulling him off the path onto a graveled running track. "Just stand here." He releases Willi's sleeve and stands beside him, two feet apart. "Race you."

"I don't want to—"

"I won. You lost."

"What?"

"I just ran all the way around the track—didn't you see me?" He laughs and punches Willi in the shoulder playfully. "Wanna race again?"

"You're full of it, Kent. You didn't run around any track—you're not *that* fast."

"Who says? Watch."

Clark is here, then not here, then here again.

"I took it a little slow that time, so you'd believe me. What do you think?"

Willi clamps a hand around the lower part of his face, squeezes the wrapping till it gathers. He walks back to the footpath. Keeps going.

Clark is twenty yards ahead of him, arms folded, the picture of patience.

Willi goes around him, cuts across the transverse road at Ninety-seventh Street, and strides across South Meadow with the high wall of Croton Reservoir on his left.

"Willi! Hey! *Up here!*"

Willi grudgingly stops.

"Up here!"

But while he knows where Clark is, knows that he's standing (strutting, actually) on top of the reservoir, Willi refuses to lift his eyes. He merely shakes his head and resumes walking.

Half a minute later, as Willi trudges along beside Children's Playground, he comes upon Clark seated on a bench with one leg crossed over the other.

"What'd I do? Did I do something wrong?"

Willi gives an exasperated sigh and flings himself down on the bench beside Clark. "I'm sorry. All right?"

"You don't have to apologize. Just tell me what's wrong."

"What's *wrong?*"

"I mean what's wrong *now?* Did something happen at the museum?"

"Those pictures were great, weren't they?"

"Yeah, sure. So?"

"That's what I want to do. That's what I want to do *again.* But I can't. And I won't ever."

"That's not true."

"Oh, you're so sure? How am I supposed to get my life back?"

Clark says, "I thought that's what *I* was for."

Willi removes his dark glasses and sticks them in his coat pocket. "You willing to snatch Lex Luthor and threaten to throw him off the Brooklyn Bridge?"

"Maybe."

4

"I hope you don't mind me calling you at home, Miss Lane. I called the *Daily Planet* but you weren't there, and they wouldn't give me your exchange. But it's in the directory, you know."

"Yes, I know. Who is this?"

"Miss Lane, I'd like to speak with you about Lex Luthor. I read your stories in the paper and I think we should talk."

"And your name is . . . ?"

"I'm sorry, it's Ceil. Ceil Stickowski? Mrs. Herman Stickowski."

"*Sticky's* wife?"

"His widow, Miss Lane. Do you think we might get together?"

"Could you hold on for just one second? . . . Of course we can get together, Mrs. Stickowski—tonight?"

"Would nine o'clock be too late? I know it's silly, but I have some programs I like to listen to."

"Nine o'clock, then. And where would you like to meet?"

"My house? Would that be all right?"

"More than all right, Mrs. Stickowski."

"Ceil."

"Let me just grab something to write with, Ceil, so I can get your address."

Mrs. O'Shea presses a finger on the hook and holds it down for a count of three, then releases it.

She doesn't need to hear any more of the recording: she knows perfectly well where Ceil Stickowski lives.

Releasing the telephone button once more, she is reconnected with the phone-tap supervisor on duty that evening (the rerouting station has been relocated from the split-level home in Corona, Queens, to a liquor store basement in Bensonhurst, Brooklyn). "Thank you again."

"Certainly."

"You can erase it now."

"Of course."

Mrs. O hangs up. For a minute she stands mulling in the living room of Lex Luthor's apartment (hers, too!) at the Waldorf-Astoria. She picks up the phone again and dials. Lets it ring ten times before hanging up and dialing a different number. "Paulie? Do you have any idea where Mr. Luthor is?"

"No. Why? Something the matter?"

She glances at the small clock on the mantel.

It's a few minutes past seven.

"I need you to drive over here now and pick me up."

"What's going on?"

"Paulie. Hang up, get into your car, and drive over here—now."

"Since when did you start giving me orders?"

"*Now*, Paulie," she says and hangs up.

5

It is full dark and cold enough to see your breath when Clark and Willi exit Central Park at Grand Army Plaza. Clark's eyes flick toward the bronze and gilt equestrian statue of William Tecumseh Sherman, to the Fountain of Abundance, then to the Plaza Hotel. He stares at the heavy traffic moving along Central Park South, at the sign on Bergdorf-Goodman. Nearby are hansom cabs with bonneted horses standing placidly in their traces. Liveried drivers huddle in groups sipping coffee from cardboard cartons, eating soft pretzels slathered with yellow mustard, talking and laughing but spotting each couple that passes—"How's about a nice romantic Halloween drive through the park? Better than flowers, better than—ach, *what* were we talkin' about?"

Clark gazes at everything. "Bet you wish you had your camera with you *now*, huh?"

Willi makes a face. "Close your mouth, you look like a rube."

"I *am* a rube!" He laughs. "And seeing as how I'm wearing a black mask, blue tights, and a red cape, I should worry how I *look?* And I won't even mention how *you* look." He nudges Willi with his elbow, does it again, again.

"Cut it *out*, would you?"

As they are crossing the street, a gust of wind sweeps under Clark's cape, balloons it up behind him and into the face of a fat man in a box-plaid swagger coat. It knocks off his hat. Stammering apologies, Clark snatches it from the street before it can roll away, hands it back. The man looks at him, at Willi the Invisible Man, and lumbers on.

"I'm still not sure about this stupid cape."

"Maybe you oughta shorten it."

"But I like it long."

"Then shut up already."

The young, fashionably dressed men and women hurrying up or down the steps of the Plaza remind Clark of that Gatsby novel he read in coal tenders and sidecars moving through New Mexico and Arizona. And he realizes that for the first time all day his and Willi's costumes are failing to elicit amusement. Even the doorman gives them a contemptuous look.

In front of the Hotel St. Moritz a woman is climbing out of a long white limousine.

"Willi! I think that's Myrna Loy! It's Myrna Loy."

"You're nuts."

"I'm not, it's her."

"She doesn't even *look* like Myrna Loy."

"It was her."

"Was not."

"Was too."

They cross Sixth Avenue and continue west, Clark's eyes darting, lifting, opening wide, his lips moving as he recites to himself the names of all the skyscraper hotels they pass: the Barbizon, the Hampshire House, the Essex.

Willi says, "I'm freezing."

Clark shrugs and walks over to the curb—better vantage—and checks out the façade of the New York Athletic Club, counting stories: . . . nineteen, twenty, twenty-one.

"You don't feel the cold? At all?"

"Well, I feel a change in the air. But nah, I never feel cold. Or hot."

"You're lucky, you know it?" Willi crosses his arms and repeatedly slaps his hands against his upper arms. "Must be nice."

"What, not feeling the cold? I guess."

"I'm talking more . . . in general. In general it must be nice not having any of our, you know, frailties."

"No, hey no. I'm not so different, come on. I'm not."

"Do you have to brush your teeth?"

"I do it."

"Yeah, but do you *have* to? You get cavities?"

"This is stupid. You think I'm not a human being or something?"

"Ever get a blister? Wear a pair of shoes that don't fit and get a blister?"

"That doesn't mean anything. That's being human, getting a blister? What about that bomb? *That* didn't hurt?"

"A normal person would've been blown to bits."

"I didn't say I was normal, I said I was human."

6

"Pop. Pop, lookit! Is this amazing or what? Poppy, you looking?"

No, Paulie Scaffa's father is not looking: he has dozed off again in what used to be Paulie's favorite chair till the old man moved in and claimed it. Every night, every blessed night he just plops down there and won't get up. Okay, it's close to the radio, he can reach the dials, but Paulie has offered to *move* the radio, even offered to bring it into his father's bedroom. Wouldn't that be nice? He can stay in his room, he won't have to get up at all except to go to the bathroom. But Mr. Scaffa made a face and muttered under his breath. He is *always* muttering under his breath, the old—

Being a good son is the hardest work in the world. What's harder? Doing the right thing is very, very difficult. Sometimes it disrupts everything, makes your life a living hell. But what can Paulie do? The smelly old guy *is* his father . . .

"Pop, don't you want to look at this? I think you'll get a kick out of it."

After dropping off Mrs. O'Shea at the Waldorf Astoria, Paulie drove down to Water Street, like the boss said, but instead of leaving both robots there he left only one, took the other home with him. He figured the old man would enjoy seeing it. When Paulie was eleven his pop bought him an Erector Set, but he couldn't assemble even the most rudimentary bridge or Ferris wheel, so the old man claimed it for his own and played with it for years.

"Pop, look!"

Paulie has some difficulty now recalling the proper sequence of buttons (he's never used the remote-control device before, just watched

Mr. Luthor), and all that he manages to do is start an ominous clicking noise inside the box. The lid won't open.

Finally, though, it does.

But once the metal pole rises up (a lot more slowly than it ought to), he can't make the Lexbot assemble itself. Which is the best thing about it, in Paulie's opinion.

Now he's jabbing buttons randomly, frustrated that he's such a klutz, annoyed that his father isn't responding. Doesn't he have the common courtesy to wake up and pay some attention to his only son? But why should *tonight* be any different?

When a loud crackling sounds from down inside the box, Mr. Scaffa finally opens his eyes.

"What the hell you doin'? What's that thing? Why'd you bring that thing inside?"

Oh, right: *now* he wakes up. Just in time to see Paulie looking *stunato.*

"It's a robot, Poppy, wait'll you see."

"What're you tellin' me, *robot?* What do you bring that in here for? Where's Carl? At least he can play canasta."

"Hey Pop, look. It opens up and turns into . . ." Paulie scowls, jabbing more buttons, the palm of his right hand so slick the remote-control housing is sliding all over the place.

The box, sitting on the living-room rug with its two-foot steel pole sticking out, begins to vibrate so tremulously that it bounces several inches to the left, then vibrates further, in a half circle.

"*Te spach el cul!*" says the old man.

"Yeah? Same to you, Pop!"

Mr. Scaffa chops downward with his hand in disgust and dismissal. "Put that away, I want to listen to Edgar Bergen. Barbara Stanwyck's gonna be on. I like her knockers."

"How you supposed to see her knockers on the radio, Pop?"

"What do you know what I see?"

The telephone rings. Paulie answers it.

It's Mrs. O'Shea, his second-least-favorite person in the world.

"I need you to drive over here now and pick me up."

"What's going on?"

"Paulie. Hang up, get into your car, and drive over here—now."

"Since when did you start giving me orders?"

"*Now,* Paulie."

She hangs up in his ear.

"I gotta go back out, Pop."

"Good! Put on the radio before you leave."

"Yeah, sure."

Paulie looks at the remote-control in his hand, at the open box on the floor, at the gleaming metal pole, the unassembled Lexbot. This is positively the last time he's going to do anything nice for the old bastard, it's just not worth it.

He tosses the remote-control on the telephone table.

A moment later Paulie's father utters a loud cry as the Lexbot, shooting out appendages and subappendages, builds its own bulk, assembling itself at twice the speed it ordinarily does.

Paulie doesn't like the sounds it keeps making.

"Turn it off!" his father shouts.

"It's a robot, Pop—see? Isn't it great? Everybody in the *world's* gonna own one."

From the robot comes a deep unpropitious hum.

When the high back of the armchair bursts apart, spewing upholstery batting, the old man flings himself forward as though ejected, and in that way—although he bangs his elbow and sprains an ankle when he hits the floor—Mr. Scaffa saves himself from serious injury. A moment later the entire chair erupts into flames.

Despite his son's presence of mind in grabbing a throw rug and beating out the fire, he calls Paulie every insult he can think of in Italian, from a jackass to a condom.

Paulie isn't listening though. He merely goggles at the tall Lexbot in his living room.

Since when, he wants to know, was it supposed to do *that?*

7

Walking down Broadway, Clark can't help grinning at all of the vaudeville and radio theaters they pass, the first-run movie houses, the restaurants and night clubs, the legitimate theaters lining the side streets. The Continental, the Hollywood, the Capitol! Lindy's! Jack Dempsey's! The Cotton Club! The Paradise! The Gaiety, the Fulton, the Shubert! He calls them all out and exclaims whenever he sees a famous actor's name on a marquee: George M. Cohan! Katherine Cornell! Fanny Brice! Orson Welles in *Julius Caesar!*

For half an hour they wander around Times Square with its statues and fearless pigeons, its juice bars and wide-windowed clothing stores, its ticket offices, haberdashers, lunch counters, and novelty concessions. The Loew's State (Errol Flynn in *The Perfect Specimen*), the Paramount (Cary Grant and Irene Dunn in *The Awful Truth*), the Rialto (Eddie Cantor in *Ali Baba Goes to Town*), the Astor Hotel, the New York Times building—spot news spelled out up high in letters that crawl around its four glazed terra-cotta sides. IDAHO FIREWORKS BLAST TOLL REACHES TEN . . . ITALY, GERMANY VOW MUTUAL AID IF ATTACKED . . . LAGUARDIA PREDICTS BIG WIN ON TUES-DAY . . .

Clark is dazzled. By the electric lights and the walls of ever-shifting colors, by the blinking signs for chewing gum, beautiful girls, razor blades, by the pulse of inexhaustible energy, by the crowds, by the *crush.* He stares at and reads everything—even a small plaque affixed to a wall of the Knickerbocker building saying Enrico Caruso lived there once when it was the Knickerbocker Hotel.

"Would you come *on?*" says Willi. "I want to show you something. Let's walk."

At the out-of-town newsstand Clark asks if they carry the *Smallville Herald-Progress,* but the newsie just laughs.

Five minutes later Willi plants himself in front of a padlocked accordion gate pulled across the front of a pawnshop. "This is what I wanted to show you."

"This is *that* pawnshop?"

"Yeah. The sign used to say Chodash's."

Now it says: Manhattan Hock—We Pay Cash For Gold.

Clark peers through a chink in the grating, studying the guitars, knives, pocket watches, and harmonicas on haphazard display in the window seat.

Narrowing his eyes, the pupils turning to vertical slits, he takes in the wardrobes and bureaus and china closets on display inside, the rolled-up carpets, feathered quilts and crewel bedspreads, the steamer trunks and Chinese screens. Musical instruments—saxophones, cornets, trumpets, banjos, violins—hang from hooks on the wall. A big brass National cash register. The glass-fronted showcase, deep shelves behind it that climb to the pressed-tin ceiling. "You think that Luthor guy still owns this place? Think it's still a front?"

"Where'd you learn about *fronts?* And how should I know?"

"I bet he does."

After a soft clink Clark rolls the gate back just enough to squeeze through.

"What're you *doing?*"

The pawnshop door swings open.

Clark smiles over a shoulder at Willi.

Then he's gone.

Now he's back—pulling the door shut, sliding the gate back, grinning broadly, and passing Willi Berg a bulky 4 × 5 Speed Graphic camera. Flash gun attached.

"You're nuts!" Willi swings the camera over his head like it's a baby. "You are completely and totally nuts! And I'm gonna kiss you!"

"Don't, okay? Let's just get out of here."

"I can't believe you *did* that!"

"Let's *go!*" Tugging Willi by a sleeve, Clark springs forward. But suddenly he is yanked backward—the hem of his cape snagged on the folding gate.

Willi sets his camera down to free it.

"Don't rip the fabric."

"I'm not gonna rip the fabric. Jeez."

When the cape is free they take off, prank-giddy and laughing shrilly as twelve-year-olds.

Clark can't bring himself to tell Willi that he left a twenty-dollar bill back on the ledge of the cash register.

He hopes twenty dollars covers it.

8

The moment Caesar Colluzo, carrying a battered-looking satchel, walks into the small office that Lex maintains on the fifty-second floor of the Chrysler Building, his eyes dart to the file folder on the desk blotter. His eyebrows inch up but otherwise his facial expression remains the same as always: blandly furious.

"You seem a little surprised, Caesar," says Lex. "Didn't I promise you I'd have it?"

"You'll excuse me, sir, if I don't trust you."

"No. No, I don't believe I will excuse you. I'm a man of my word. You've given me what I asked you to deliver—and now I'm delivering you this." He taps the folder and then opens the cover. Inside are slightly more than a dozen photographic prints, face down as a courtesy. There is also a strip of negatives. As well as a banker's check made out to Caesar Colluzo in the amount of five hundred thousand dollars. "I'll be sorry to see you go, Caesar, but a deal is a deal. The machines"—as another courtesy he doesn't refer to them as Lexbots— "are magnificent."

"Of course they are." Since he came into the office and stopped, Colluzo has not moved one step closer to the desk.

"Shall we have a drink? I'd like to propose a toast."

"No, thank you."

Lex sits back in his chair, pressing his palms together, steepling his fingers. "You're more than welcome to stay on."

"I think not."

"I thought not, too," says Lex. He shrugs. "Well then. Shall we make the exchange and bid each other farewell?" He gets up and comes around from behind the desk. "Everything is in there?" he says pointing to the satchel.

"Everything."

"And naturally the schematics, et cetera, are all authentic?"

"Would you know if they weren't?"

"You'd be surprised, Caesar. So why don't you just wipe that little sneer off your face." He reaches behind him and without looking picks up the folder. Holds it out.

With a dubious scowl Colluzo walks up and takes it. He hesitates for a second before passing off the schoolbag.

"What are your plans now, Caesar, if you don't mind my asking?"

"I *do* mind. And my plans are no business of yours."

"Not entirely true. I'll remind you of those nondisclosure forms you signed. They're quite binding."

Colluzo shrugs. "Good night, Mr. Luthor. And good-bye."

"Five hundred thousand dollars is no paltry sum."

"Compared to what you'll earn from my machines?"

"This has never been about earnings, my friend."

"Oh no? Then what *has* it been about?"

Lex's eyes flash briefly and he smiles. For a moment he thinks he just might take Caesar Colluzo into his confidence. Why not? At this stage, why not? But finally. no. Much better to keep his plans to himself.

By summer, by Lex's lowball estimation, there will be at least ten million Lexbots in circulation worldwide, each one, thanks to the little black cube, under his absolute command. Recording conversations, filming activities in the boardroom, the bedroom, the Situation Room, the nursery, memorizing alternate ledgers, secret codes, secret formulas, secret kisses, secret deals. The labels of prescription-drug bottles, the combinations to wall safes.

Oh yes, and the list of things just goes on.

And by this time next year a hundred forty million Lexbots! Playing music, playing cards, doing dishes, doing homework, doing the taxes, driving limousines and the family Ford. Keeping people company. Lighting their cigarettes and (although it would not, of course, be suggested in the Owner's Manual) probably stimulating their genitals.

And they said *television* was going to be the "next essential thing"!

Lex could have Hitler strangled in his sleep. Or Albert Einstein. Or Cordell Hull. Blackmail everyone from bootblacks to prime ministers, from Bing Crosby to the Pope. Loot the Crown Jewels, bankrupt Warner Bros., sink the *Normandie*.

And in a couple of years—a Lexbot for every ten people on earth.

That's when he could *really* pull out the stops.

Kidnap a thousand babies, *ten* thousand, in one fell swoop.

Assassinate every male over the age of—what? Eighteen? Twenty-one? Thirty-five?

Or just let the robots run amok: *all together now, one, two . . .*

He says now to Caesar Colluzo, "I think we're done."

They leave together through a dark reception area and then step out into the empty corridor. The elevator is to the left, about twenty feet away.

They walk there in silence.

"By the way, Caesar, that appointment you made for next Thursday at Westinghouse?" Lex presses the elevator button. "It's been canceled."

Colluzo's mouth tightens. His tongue appears, disappears. "How did you—"

"Oh, please. No more robot building for you, I'm afraid."

The elevator doors open.

There is no car behind them, just cables.

But Caesar Colluzo doesn't notice that—too busy glaring at Lex Luthor. Who grins all of a sudden, reaching out with his left hand to snatch the file folder. With the flat of his right hand he shoves Colluzo in the chest, as hard as he can.

Carl Krusada appears from behind the fire door and joins Lex at the lip of the elevator. Together they look down.

Finally the doors close.

"Good work, Carl. Did it give you any trouble?"

"Not really, sir, no."

"Excellent," says Lex. "Very excellent."

Lois & Ben & Willi & Clark. "Herman says hello."
Mrs. O vs. Mrs. S. Panic in the street.

————

1

In Lois Lane's apartment, Ben Jaeger is stretched out on the sofa, haphazardly flipping through a back issue of *Life* with hunting spaniels pictured on the cover. "Lo, what're you doing? Feel like getting something to eat? Lois?"

No answer.

He kicks off his shoes, crosses his ankles.

Jumps up and goes to the window.

Then he pivots around and marches straight to the radio, snaps it on. Turns it off.

Starts to pour a drink but changes his mind.

Goes back to the window. Back to the sofa.

He jumps up again and just stands there.

Ben figures he's going crazy. If he doesn't think of something pretty soon to salvage his reputation, his job, and—come on, pal, admit it—his girlfriend, he is definitely headed for the nuthouse.

The telephone rings.

"Lois, you want me to answer that?"

No reply.

Ben scoops up the receiver.

When he says hello there's a click and the line goes dead.

As he is turning away from the nook, an address scribbled hastily on a notepad catches Ben's eye.

On at least two occasions he drove Lieutenant Sandglass to that same address in Turtle Bay and waited in the car while the lieutenant went inside to speak with Herman Stickowski on his deathbed. Thirty-ninth Street between Second and First.

Grabbing up the pad, Ben crosses the living room into the bedroom. "Just where the *hell* are you going tonight?"

Lois is taking her peacoat off a hanger in the closet. "To work. It's what I do, Ben, I work. Do you mind?"

"Who gave you this address?" He holds up the telephone pad.

"I'll thank you to leave my stuff alone." She grabs the pad. "Now why don't you go sulk some more, you're so good at it. Meanwhile, I'm going to work."

2

Heading down to the Lower East Side, they keep to Seventh Avenue until Thirty-second Street, then cut east and pick up Broadway again where it angles sharply in below Herald Square. At the corner of Twenty-ninth and Broadway, Clark draws himself up, faces east, and frowns. "You hear that?"

"What?"

Clark flips the black mask up over his forehead. "I just heard Lois."

"What?" Willi looks up and down Broadway. "You got that skirt on the brain." He walks on.

"She doesn't live around here, does she?"

"As if you don't know."

"How would I?"

Willi turns around. "I must've told you."

"Never."

"There." He points down Twenty-ninth Street. "She lives right over there."

Tugging the mask back down over his eyes, Clark turns east.

"What'd she say? You heard her say something—really? What'd she say?"

"That she's going to work."

3

"How come? You're asking me how come I want to go with you to see Sticky's wife? Damn, Lois, this could be it. What we're *looking* for."

Ben stands blocking the door.

"Get out of my way."

"I can't believe you weren't going to tell me that Ceil called."

"Ben, you've been acting like a jerk. And I don't need some jerk messing up my interview. Okay? I know what I'm doing. I can take care of myself."

"Oh yeah? And what if it's a trap?"

Lois tucks her chin, shuts one eye, and beams him a withering ray with the other. *"A trap?* Who do you think you are, Doc Savage?"

4

"Who the heck is Doc Savage?" says Willi. And Clark almost tells him. But then he holds up a silencing finger to listen some more.

They are standing on the sidewalk opposite Lois Lane's apartment building.

Clark says, "She's going to see somebody named Ceil who lives someplace called Turtle Bay—"

"That's just east of here, runs uptown."

"Who's Ceil?"

Willi shrugs.

"She's Sticky's wife."

"Sticky?" Willi grabs Clark's arm. "Lois said *Sticky's* wife?"

"That's what she—*hold on!* They're coming down."

Willi tugs him up the steps of the apartment house behind them and into the unlighted vestibule.

Moments later Lois and Ben come out and turn left, begin walking toward Madison Avenue.

"Let's go," says Willi.

"Who's Sticky?"

Willi is out the door and down the steps, turning to his right and moving fast.

"Who's Sticky?"

"The guy that mighta shot me. Now come on if you're coming. Shake a leg, Saucer-Man."

5

Ever since the cathouse she'd managed was converted into a nursing and convalescent home, Ceil Stickowski has been taking Thursdays and Sundays off. Before then she worked a seven-day week, happily so. She liked her girls, she liked the clientele (for the most part), and keeping busy in a charged atmosphere was the perfect way of coping with her widow's grief. She still missed Herman. But once the girls were shipped off, the furnishings changed, and the place filled up with codgers and lungers and paraplegics, Ceil needed regular breaks, days away from the odors of illness and age, the wails of senility. She had no trouble finding student nurses from St. Vincent's and Bellevue to run the place twice a week.

One of those, a cute little Puerto Rican named Rosa, telephones Ceil at home this evening at precisely twenty-seven minutes past eight, as per instructions. Between then and half past, *The Chase and Sanborn Hour* breaks for commercials and the NBC-Blue station identification. It has been a quiet day, Rosa tells Ceil. Ike the Plug's son came by and took the ninety-four-year-old former lush worker out for Sunday dinner, and Sal the Swan's diarrhea seems finally to be under control. Rosa has done inventory, she says, and it looks to her they can stand to order mercurochrome, shoelaces, abdominal binders, canasta decks, mahjong tiles, and at least two new toilet-seat elevators, especially since Mr. Boiardo (the former Lemon Drop Kid, scourge of Five Points) refuses to stay on his diet, no matter what anyone—

"Honey," says Ceil. "Listen to me. Is there any way you can come back and work tomorrow?"

"Tomorrow? You mean Monday?"

"Tomorrow is Monday, sweetheart, yes. Is there any way you can do that? Because I won't be coming in, and I need someone there I can trust."

"Well . . . I have a nutrition class in the afternoon. But I could work till then. Are you ill, Mrs. Stickowski?"

"No, no, I'm fine. I just . . . won't be in tomorrow."

Or ever again, Ceil has decided.

She doesn't know what will happen once she's told the hen from the *Daily Planet* everything that Herman told her—but whatever it is, she's ready for it.

Lex Luthor would have killed her this afternoon if she hadn't come up with a name for his stupid robots. She saw it in his eyes. And seeing that look she realized that somehow he'd killed her husband last summer. He'd killed Herman. Ceil just . . . knew it.

"Rosa? Thank you so much, sweetheart. I have to run."

Ceil hangs up the phone and hears Don Ameche's suave voice turning the microphone back over to Edgar Bergen. In the kitchen the oven timer starts to ding, which means the Toll House cookies she baked to serve to Lois Lane are done.

Transferring the cookie sheet to a trivet on the counter, Ceil listens to Charlie McCarthy rib Edgar Bergen about his garish necktie.

In his cage the African parrot watches her. All of a sudden he says, "Herman says hello, Herman says hello, Herman says hello."

"I know he does, darling," says Ceil.

"Herman says hello, Herman says hello!"

Herman taught Zulu to say that so that Ceil would know he was thinking of her on those long days and nights when he was away from home working for Lex Luthor.

Herman was no saint, but as a hubby the man was peerless.

She goes back into the living room and sits down to wait.

When she thinks about what she is about to do, a sharp pain just below her sternum takes Ceil's breath away.

Maybe she won't answer the door when Lois Lane arrives, maybe she'll return to work tomorrow. After all, she *did* name that robot, everything is okay now, and Lex Luthor will go on paying her a generous salary: she can continue living the way she's been, a radio and telephone in every room, subscriptions to whichever magazines she cares to look at. New hats and shoes whenever the impulse sweeps her.

No.

She saw something in those eyes today that scared her half to death.

Just as she is getting up to go put the coffee on, her doorbell rings. Ceil glances at her wristwatch. It's only quarter of nine and she *told* that girl to come by *after* nine.

The bell sounds again.

Ceil walks back into the kitchen and plugs the electric percolator into the wall.

Then, rubbing her palms against her skirt, she goes and answers the door.

Mrs. O'Shea stands in the vestibule.

"Good evening, Ceil," she says, then punches her viciously in the face, a blow that shatters the cartilage in Ceil's nose and sends her staggering backward. Before Ceil can recover from the shock, Mrs. O is upon her, both hands locked around her throat, killing her . . .

6

Mrs. O was angry enough when it took Paulie Scaffa more than twice the time she estimated it should have to drive from his flat to the Waldorf-Astoria, but when she found out *why*—

"Who gave you permission to bring one of those things home with you?"

"I didn't think there'd be a problem." Paulie tried to control his own anger by speaking through gritted teeth and squeezing the wheel and driving hunched way over it. And he wouldn't look at Mrs. O.

"Where is it now?"

"In the luggage compartment."

"Is it back in its—"

"Yes, it's back in its box. But you're missing the point. What the hell did it do, you see what I'm saying? It blew up my chair. I thought these things were supposed to . . . mix drinks and play music."

Mrs. O didn't respond.

"So I'm thinking maybe there's something wrong with that stupid guinea's machine. Some flaw, like. We should tell the boss."

"How on earth did he ever find *you?*"

"Lady, you give me a pain in my neck."

"Do you think you could put on a *little* speed? It's already eight-thirty, thanks to your robot demonstration. I want to be in and out before her company arrives."

"I thought you called the skirt's house and she was still home."

"I'm *assuming* she was if her boyfriend was there. But I can't know for sure."

It was twenty minutes before nine when they turned off Second Avenue into East Thirty-ninth Street.

"There!" said Mrs. O. "That's the house."

"I know the house, lady. I only been inside it two thousand times." Paulie parked and set the brake. Mrs. O put a hand on his knee before he had the chance to open his door.

"You can wait here. I'll go in."

He looked at her incredulously.

"You brought me all the way from *Brooklyn* so *you* can do the job? Why didn't you just take a taxi?"

"Because taxi drivers can be questioned about fares."

"Then you coulda walked!"

"I'll be right back."

"You got a weapon?"

"I don't need one."

"Ceil outweighs you by fifty pounds!" He pulled up his shirt and removed a .45 caliber automatic from the waistband of his trousers. "Take this."

"I don't *need* a weapon, I said."

She slammed the door, hesitated a moment at the foot of the stoop, then squared her shoulders and walked up the steps. Opened the street door and went into the vestibule.

Paulie shook his head. Then he leaned over in the dark automobile and thumped his right hand along the top of the instrument panel searching for his cigarettes and matches. He found them, but only after accidentally tapping the Lexbot's remote-control device, which he'd tossed there when he left home.

That gave him a little twinge.

But nothing, thank God, moved in the luggage compartment.

7

Kneeling squarely upon Ceil's chest, Mrs. O removes one hand from her throat and snatches hold of her hair.

Now she is both strangling Ceil and hammering the floor with the back of her skull.

Summoning what little strength she has left, Ceil slaps at the floor with her left arm, fingers scrabbling till the tips scrape against the leg of a small drop-leaf table. She pulls the table toward her, then whirls it down like a club. The curved edge of a leaf opens a deep gash above Mrs. O's right eye. A crosspiece slams against her mouth, lacerating her top gum line, knocking out teeth. The drawer shoots free and slams into her forehead with force enough to brand it with the tiny fleur-de-lis design on the pewter knob.

Mrs. O is stunned.

And Ceil is quick.

She is on her feet, bracing herself against the Morris chair and shaking her head to clear it.

Anger burns up the back of her neck. She's never felt this furious, this crazy-furious—probably the closest she ever came to it before was thirty years ago: age fourteen, in the eighth grade, a rainy day in April when she failed three tests, forgot her lunch, and then was called, without provocation, a "dumb pollock" by Geraldine Walsh, hands down the stupidest girl in her class.

Before this minute, *that* was the angriest Ceil has ever been.

She kicked Geraldine Walsh, too, when *she* was down on her knees.

Although not nearly as many times as she kicks Mrs. O. Or with anything close to the ferocity.

Geraldine Walsh ended up with four broken ribs.

Ceil has no way of knowing how many of Mrs. O's ribs she breaks but she hears bones crack and that is satisfaction enough.

Face flushed, her breathing labored, she takes a step back, intending to land one final, perfect, and incapacitating blow to that sobbing *bitch.* But when she lashes out with her right foot, somehow she turns it. When it strikes flesh, an acute and stabbing pain flares through Ceil's ankle and radiates to her groin.

Even with a broken foot, even with her nose swollen, Ceil laughs as openly and boisterously as she does at Laurel and Hardy when a house crashes around them or a piano bounces after them down a hundred and fifty steps.

She laughs and then collapses into the Morris chair. Her ankle is purpling and her foot seems on fire inside her shoe.

Mrs. O pushes with her hands, managing to lift the upper half of her body. Her lips are balloonlike. Blood streams from her mouth.

Her eyes find Ceil's.

"Think you're great?" says Ceil. "Think you're so great? Guess what, girly, *you stink!* You stink on ice!"

It's what Ceil Wojcicki, aged fourteen, had screamed in the face of Geraldine Walsh thirty years ago, and it seems just as apt tonight with this other, older Irisher.

"On *ice* you stink!"

There are droplets and thick strings of blood clotted in Mrs. O's white hair.

She tries to speak.

"What? I can't hear you! You want to say something, speak up, you mick piece of—"

"Ceil, I'm surprised at you! You know what Mr. Luthor thinks about that kind of talk."

Paulie Scaffa is standing now in the arched entryway to the living room. He looks at Mrs. O down on the floor, raising his eyebrows when he sees the bloated ruins of her lips and the red circle impressed into her forehead, the tiny image of a lily inside of it. Then he looks at Ceil in the chair and notices the raw scratches on her face, the broken nose, the bruises on her throat. He clucks.

At last Mrs. O manages to say something clearly. "Kill her, Paulie."

"Oh? I thought *you* wanted to handle this."

"Kill her!"

He takes out the .45 automatic. It is silver-plated and looks brand-new.

Ceil's eyes widen. "Paulie, no. Please, Paulie. You were Herman's partner, don't hurt me, please. Herman loved you!"

"I wouldn't go *that* far, Ceil. But we got along okay."

"Kill her, Paulie! Shoot her!"

"Paulie, please. You ate Thanksgiving dinner here, how many times? Please!"

"Ceil, I hate to tell you this, but I never really liked you that much."

Mrs. O makes a gurgling sound and pink froth appears between her lips.

She's laughing.

Paulie turns the gun on her. "You think that's funny? Here's something even funnier. I don't like you either."

He swivels his wrist and trains the gun back on Ceil.

Then right away he turns it back on Mrs. O.

"I don't like either one of you, if you wanna know the truth."

8

"Herman says hello, Herman says hello!"

Paulie considers shooting the damn parrot too, but that would just gum up his brilliant idea.

He is almost sorry Mrs. O is dead because he *really* wants to rub his idea right in her snooty face.

He shot her first. Once in the stomach so it hurt, then once—at close range—between the eyes.

Ceil looked stunned, but you'd also have to say *relieved*. Paulie could understand *that*.

She thought because he'd shot Mrs. O he wouldn't shoot her.

And if that made her last few moments less terrifying, Paulie was glad to do it. He didn't like Ceil but he didn't *hate* her. He wasn't a *bad* guy. If the way he'd played this gave her some comfort, cause to hope, he was glad to do it.

He smiled at Ceil when he walked over and stood next to her chair. Stooped a little and frowned at her broken nose. "That must hurt," he said. "We'll have to see about getting *that* fixed up."

He put the automatic to her right temple and gently squeezed the trigger.

And then he lifted her right hand, pressed her pinky, third, and second fingers around the grip of the .45 and her index finger through the trigger guard. When he let her hand fall, the gun dropped where it might have fallen naturally to the floor.

He is quite certain the cops and the press will flag this as a Forbidden Love Turns Fatal thing.

There hasn't been one of those in the news for a while.

One murder, one suicide. And one *hell* of a brawl beforehand.

"Herman says hello, Herman says hello!"

"Hello to you too, Herman," Paulie calls to the parrot. "I sent you your lovely wife, hope you appreciate that, pally."

He turns out all the lights.

The only thing that worries Paulie now is how Mr. Luthor might react.

Ceil had to go, Mrs. O was right about that. So no problem there.

But will the boss be angry that he also shot that white-haired—

As soon as Paulie shuts the outside door and it locks behind him he wonders if Ceil had even *been* right-handed. What if she'd been *left-*handed.

Ah, she was right-handed. Forget about it.

Then he realizes he probably shouldn't have turned off all the lights.

Screw it. Ceil might've done it before blowing out her brains.

She was a woman, right? You made allowances for their screwy behavior.

He lights a cigarette. A man and a woman are standing across the street in deep shadow, and Paulie figures them for a couple on a date. He hurries down the steps to his automobile.

But as soon as he starts to get in, everything turns bad.

"Paulie! Wait up—I need a word with you," says Ben Jaeger coming into the street at a jog.

And there goes Paulie's beautiful Lesbian Sweethearts angle.

He is so chagrined—it's like some moron piping up after you've worked your way through an entire joke and spoiling your punch line—that he yanks out a revolver and shoots Jaeger twice in the chest.

He jumps behind the wheel, keys the ignition, releases the hand brake, lets out the clutch.

Glancing into the sideview mirror he sees a woman—has to be that Lois Lane—run out and stoop down beside Jaeger.

She looks toward the car and her eyes meet Paulie's in the side mirror.

That decides it.

He steers away from the curb, then twists the wheel, making a U-turn but sideswiping a boat-size Cadillac 60 parked on the opposite side of the street.

The Caddy's chromium door handle sails out in front of Paulie's hood, gleaming like an ingot when it arcs across the headlights.

Paulie shoves the transmission into reverse, backs up, and then guns the engine.

But less than ten feet away from its targets, the car stops with such precipitate suddenness that Paulie slams against the steering wheel, hard. Something breaks inside of his chest.

The front tires are spinning, the rubber burning, great chunks splatting off to bounce freely down the street.

The rear wheels are still spinning too, but they're no longer touching blacktop.

Paulie lurches again as the car tips forward.

Reflected in the rearview mirror is a man wearing a Lone Ranger mask.

Paulie doesn't know *what's* going on. But whatever it is, it's not good.

He twists around in his seat and something sharp inside his chest pierces something soft. Which bursts and starts to leak.

He manages nevertheless to extend his right arm and fire his revolver three times.

The rear window shatters.

There is now a big hole punched through the bridge of the guy's black mask. And two angry red welts on his forehead.

But he's still there *holding back the damn car!*

Now it rises at a steeper angle, now it crashes down. Paulie's cigarettes spew from their packet, his matchbox striking him in the face, ricocheting off. And that Bakelite remote-control device lands plop in his lap.

Snatching it up, Paulie haphazardly pushes buttons. Red green, green black red, black gray black, green red, red red black . . .

And despite his being the button pusher, Paulie Scaffa is just as surprised as the masked guy behind him when, in the wake of a loud juddering vibration, the luggage compartment lid bursts suddenly open.

9

Clark Kent is more than just passingly familiar with robots.

As a boy, he read all of L. Frank Baum's Oz novels, and from his introduction in *Ozma of Oz,* Tik-Tok the Clockwork Man became Clark's favorite of all of the series characters.

In high school he was a voracious reader of the "scientifiction" stories he found in dime pulps at Pinky Wargo's cigar shop on South Main Street. And while he read every story in each chunky issue that he purchased (his mother said to do any less would be a waste of good money), the types of stories Clark liked most were about either alien invasions or robots. In his opinion John W. Campbell wrote the best robot yarns, although he had to admit that Edmond Hamilton and Harl Vincent wrote some pretty good stuff too.

And of course a good many of the movie serials that Clark enjoyed as a young teenager had nifty robots shuffling through them—*Phantom Empire, Flash Gordon, The Undersea Kingdom.*

So, yes, Clark Kent is more than just passingly familiar with robots.

Even so . . . when the automobile's luggage compartment twangs open in his face and he is confronted by a genuine all-steel robot, a robot that assembles itself as it sprouts up and up from a square box, Clark's first thought is to misconstrue the Lexbot for the latest advance in dairy technology.

He mistakes it for an automatic milking machine.

His fingers are curled under the rear bumper and he is still holding the street coupe lifted a foot and a half off the ground.

The rear tires spin futilely.

The engine is straining.

Or maybe it's not the engine at all.

Maybe it's *that* thing.

It is. The whining noise definitely comes from the robot. The whine changes abruptly to a sibilant whistle. That's followed by a loud clap, a flash of red light. And Clark is blown out of his boots (literally) and sent hurtling backward toward First Avenue, *across* First Avenue, headed for the East River. His cape snapping and billowing and tattered, he shoots down East Thirty-ninth Street at a velocity in excess of a major-league fastball.

The acetate mask sails off his face and spins away.

His blue jersey is scorched black at his solar plexus.

Half of the threads that have kept the big red **S** sewn into place have dissolved into ash, and the appliqué flaps and flutters like a shingle in a gale.

Just before Clark smashes into and pulverizes part of the rocky bluff below and to the south of the Tudor City apartments, and before he is stunned into unconsciousness, he becomes aware of a tremendous explosion.

Somewhere.

Lois sees the cape-man. Faith and Carl Krusada.
Clark's breakdown. Willi clicks a few. Trapped.

———

1

Lois will always remember—and each time with the same troubling mixture of shame and self-regard—that immediately after Ben Jaeger was shot, two bullets in his chest, the first thing she did was glance at her wristwatch: six past nine by the radium dial.

Former New York City police officer Benjamin Jaeger, who resigned last Friday in the wake of the controversial Lex Luthor criminal investigation, was killed Sunday evening when a gunman suddenly opened fire—

Shot. He was *shot* Sunday evening.

That's all Lois knew for certain, all that she'd witnessed: Ben was *shot.* What kind of a reporter is she, jumping to conclusions? What kind of a person?

Afraid to move, certain she couldn't, Lois broke from the sidewalk's protective shadows and ran into the street.

When she dropped to her knees beside him, Ben was laboring to breathe, struggling to lift his head.

A pinkish foam bubbled through his lips.

"Just lie still, okay? 'Kay, baby? Don't try to get up," she said, then stupidly (she *knew* it was stupid, so why was she doing it?) Lois forced a hand under Ben's shoulders and elevated him slightly.

He gasped but then gulped a breath. Breathed out, breathed in again.

So maybe it hadn't been stupid.

At the hard slam of a car door, Lois looked up. The gunman (Ben had called him Paul; *Paulie*) had slid under the wheel of his two-door—*what?* What make was it? A Hudson, a Gen? DeSoto? Her glance shifted to the cowl of the automobile where the chromium hood ornament—an Art Deco winged locomotive—identified it as a Nash-Lafayette. (Only last month a police-beat reporter had told her to be a "smart girly" and memorize grilles, bumpers, hubcaps, and hood ornaments, it might come in handy, you never know. She'd done just that.) A Nash-Lafayette 3-window coupe, 1936. Okay, but what *color?* Too dark to tell. It looked black but could've been green, it could've been maroon, could've—

She met Paulie's eyes in the outside mirror.

Lois scuttled crablike around behind Ben, tried dragging him toward the curb. She hadn't gotten far when the continental heel on her left pump wobbled and snapped off. She sat down hard in the street, legs splayed. Ben toppled against her chest and into her arms.

The Nash made a wide, careless U-turn, slammed hard into a parked Cadillac, stalled, started again, then backed up and roared straight at them.

Lois flung an arm across her eyes.

This couldn't be happening.

But it was.

Then it wasn't.

The engine sound changed from a brash throb to a high-pitched caterwaul. Tires screeched and the air thickened with oily smoke, the fetor of heated rubber. When she lowered her arm Lois was pelted with stinging chunks and morsels of tire tread, and the Nash's fender-mounted headlamps glanced off the street surface and beamed obliquely over her head.

And now . . .

Motor howling, overdrive in clear distress, the street coupe not only has come to a dead stop, it's raked like a seesaw, the rear section elevated, the front end and waterfall grille sloped acutely down.

Lois checks on Ben, who has lapsed into unconsciousness, and then looks back toward the Nash. The glare-and-dark is disorienting, her eyes water, everything shimmers, refracts, but still—her vision registers something red behind the car, something pennantlike, *flaglike* billowing up, snapping and swirling above the roof.

The back end of the Nash crashes down, the undercarriage kindling sparks and the shock coils twanging. The motor falters before growling back into full power.

Inside the car Paulie-in-silhouette twists around.

Then: more gunfire (*three shots,* Lois notes for later, now that "later" seems at least a possibility).

Glass pelts the street like drenching rain.

Bracing a hand on the ground, Lois secures her balance. As she stands her skull throbs and her legs tremble with the aftershocks of panic. Her focus narrows till she is certain this is no dirty trick of poor light and heavy shadow, no stress-created illusion . . .

(*An eyewitness at the scene reported seeing . . .*)

(*This reporter personally observed . . .*)

Half clouded by exhaust smoke, a man in a weightlifter's squat is crouched in back of the Nash, holding onto the narrow bumper. Chips of window glass wink in his dark hair, cling to his shoulders, and spangle his—cape; it's a *cape,* not a pennant or a flag, *a red cape.* Billowing out behind him, lifting, floating down, lifting . . .

The long sloping lid to the luggage compartment springs up, blocking her view.

What are those *sounds*?

Before she can isolate them with nouns and adjectives (piercing whistle? hissing whine?), the luggage lid tears violently from its hinges and somersaults high into the air. Instantly there is a loud sizzling noise and all of the house fronts and grillwork and wrought-iron fences, the leafless trees and parked cars, the garbage cans set out for

Monday-morning pickup, are illuminated by an arc of red and yellow-green fireworks that spume from the Nash's boot.

And the cape-man is gone.

Behind Lois the luggage lid strikes paving with a metallic clatter, bounces, bounces, and hits a curb, spins up, wheels serenely, and crashes through someone's front window.

Flames lick an ornamental pear tree before they envelop it.

Canted to her right, her weight on the foot in the broken shoe, Lois just stares.

A hand clamps firmly down on her shoulder, spins her.

Willi Berg thrusts a press camera at her. "Here," he says, "take this."

She already has it.

"Now run for it, kid—run!"

He shoves her away from the Nash, toward the curb.

Then he scoops up Ben Jaeger in a fireman's carry.

Farther down the block, another tree, this time an English oak, bursts into flame. The front stoop and enormous bay of a Gilded Age house explode into chunks of brownstone, glass, sash, sills, weather-board, and jamb.

Suddenly Ronald Colman's mellifluous voice recites the first sentence of Lois Lane's favorite childhood novel: "My father's family name being Pirrip, and my Christian name being Philip, my infant tongue could make of both names nothing longer or more explicit than Pip."

Lois turns her head and what she sees now spinning around and around in the street looks like the bastard child of an Electrolux and a knight in shining armor.

"So I called myself Pip," booms Ronald Colman's voice from a round mesh loudspeaker in its chest, "and came to be called Pip."

A low brick wall explodes, a lawn fountain, a post lantern, a wall lantern, a Ford cabriolet.

The Nash-Lafayette.

"*Lois!*"

Finally she runs for it.

2

While Carl Krusada was in the seminary he knew he was nothing but a phonus-balonus, an imposter-postulant whose professed piety and religious "vocation" were just means to an end, the end being safety in a world gone smash: a roof over his head, three squares a day, and clean clothes on his back (although the clothing, God knows, left something to be desired).

When the Depression *really* hit, back in 1930, and there were no jobs and scant prospects of any turning up soon, Carl panicked and seized the first opportunity that came to mind (actually it first came to his mother's mind, and she relayed the thought).

He did well enough at the seminary, primarily because he was a good dissembler, but also because he was talented at memorization. That's a chasuble, that's an alb, that's a cruet, that's a Pastoral candle. *Dominus vobiscum. Et cum spiritu tuo.* Nothing to it.

Following his ordination and his surprise posting to the same parish in Carrolton, Brooklyn, where he'd been baptized, confirmed, and educated through high school, Carl discovered that he didn't hate what he was doing, despite doing it under false pretenses. Although he disobeyed as many rules as he followed (fish on Friday? *Every* Friday?), he liked being told what to do, enjoyed being a servant of a kind. He didn't really believe in God but he completely believed in serving the Lord. It was hard to explain, not that he tried explaining it to anyone, but it made sense to him.

Being a parish priest was okay: he played a lot of basketball with the boys at St. Rocco's, always had time for an afternoon nap, and he got to hear confession. Hands down it was the most interesting of the sacraments, although it quickly destroyed any lingering illusions that Carl still held regarding human beings.

As he chauffeurs Lex Luthor this evening, Carl regales him with tales from the confessional box (the beloved old barber who sold pornography, the Cub Scout den mother who laced her husband's eggs each morning with atropine), and Mr. Luthor nods and smiles at everything. (Naturally Lex initiated the conversation; Carl wouldn't have dreamed of initiating anything when it came to the boss.)

For almost three hours they've been motoring around with no destination. Midtown. Uptown. Harlem. Inwood. Now on the drive back down Broadway, Carl is saying, "This guy used to come in every few months, local committeeman that everybody liked 'cause he was always taking baskets of food and stuff to the poor. He'd come in, kneel down and go, 'Bless me, father, for I have sinned, it's been ten weeks since my last confession. I had impure thoughts fifteen times, I lost my temper five times, and I strangled another prostitute last Thursday.' You know how the *Daily News* would print all those scare stories about the White Glove Killer? I *talked* to the guy."

"Human beings," says Lex.

"Oh yeah, we're something else, we are."

"Yes, you are," says Lex.

He asks Carl for the name of the White Glove Killer, and Carl gives it to him, watching as Lex jots it down in a small notebook.

After being "dismissed from the clerical state," Carl briefly considered soldiering, almost joined the French Foreign Legion. He checked and you really could do such a thing! But he never got around to filling out the paperwork. And how lucky was *that?* Otherwise he wouldn't have ended up with Mr. Luthor.

Once Paulie Scaffa helped him land this job, Carl realized that abiding service was his one true and legitimate vocation. Previously he'd pledged his allegiance to the wrong god.

Now Carl has it straight, and Lex seems to recognize his devotion, his reverence toward him, his worship of him.

Well, sure: now it's Carl Krusada, not Paulie Scaffa, driving Lex around in the big Lincoln. Carl, not Paulie, that Lex had orchestrate that little elevator-shaft accident back at the Chrysler Building. And it's Carl, not Paulie, whose tales of human perfidy amuse Lex so much, cause him to smile, chuckle even, and crinkle his eyes.

At twenty-two minutes past nine—Carl checks the dashboard

clock—Lex decides he's ready to head back to the Waldorf. "I've thought my thoughts," he says, "and now I could use a little dinner. It's been a most satisfactory day."

"I'm glad, sir."

"The Lexbot."

"Perfect name."

"By this time next year there'll be one in every household. Probably several."

"Won't that be something."

"And I'll be announcing a no-interest guaranteed loan program this winter so that even the most unfortunate among us will have *at least* one of his own."

"I can't wait to get mine."

"Don't be naive. Believe me, Carl, you don't want one. I wouldn't let you *have* one."

"Sir?"

"You're too valuable."

"Thank you, sir." Carl is thrilled that Lex thinks he's so "valuable," but . . . *Why* won't he let him own a Lexbot? And why is it "naive" for Carl to *want* one? He wishes he could ask.

Lex sits back against the plush upholstery. "Do you know what I was doing while we took our nice cruise around the city?"

"No, sir."

"I was making a list. Of who's to get the first hundred Lexbots that come off the assembly line. They'll all be gifts. To prime the pump."

"And did you finish your list, sir? All hundred names?"

Carl can almost feel a drop in the air temperature. He shouldn't have asked such a direct question; is he *crazy*? Know your place, Krusada, he tells himself. Know your place.

When Lex speaks again, nearly a minute later, he seems to have forgiven Carl's impudence. "All hundred names, yes. And Number One goes to the president of the United States. Number Two I'll give to his ugly wife. Every Lexbot will have its own serial number, of course."

"Is that right?"

"LaGuardia, I've decided, will have Number Nine."

"Even if he loses the election on Tuesday?"

"He won't, Carl. Number Nine goes to Fatty. Shirley Temple gets Number 48. Clark Gable, 32. Deanna Durbin, 46."

"Deanna Durbin!" says Carl. "I have a little crush on her!"

As the limousine progresses downtown, Lex rattles off several more famous names from Hollywood and politics (Louie B. Mayer, Robert A. Taft, Earl Browder) as well as from the worlds of business and high finance, athletics, education, fashion, literature, the arts, publishing, broadcasting, and the sciences, both abstract and applied— among them Henry Ford and Carl Hubbell, John Dewey, Coco Chanel, Margaret Mitchell, Frank Lloyd Wright, Henry Luce, Westbrook Pegler, and George Washington Carver.

"George Washington Carver, sir? But he's a Negro."

"I don't discriminate, Carl. All human beings are the same to me."

"Yes, sir. May I ask a question?"

"You may."

"If the president and the first lady get numbers one and two—who gets Number Three?"

"Adolf Hitler."

Carl hadn't expected *that*. He'd been thinking maybe Ernest Hemingway or Bing Crosby.

"The Lexbot will be an *international* phenomenon, Carl."

"Yes, sir, of course."

"And Number Four will go with my compliments to Signore Mussolini, Number Five to Comrade Stalin, Number Six to General Franco, and Number Seven to King George. Or maybe I'll reverse that, Six to the Sixth, eh?"

"That's a lot of free merchandise you'll be handing out. Sir."

"You have to spend money to make it, Carl."

"I can just see it now, sir—ten, fifteen pages in *Life* magazine. Everybody showing off their brand-new Lexbots. At lawn parties and so on."

While the limousine is stopped for a red light, Lex reaches into his topcoat and takes out a small black socketed cube. He bounces it lightly in the palm of his hand.

3

Clark's impact with the granite bluff not only rendered him sense-less and blank but also left him wedged in a crevice of his own making. New pebbles and pulverized rock steadily pepper his head and sieve down on his face and shoulders.

The south-facing windows of the Tudor City buildings are all lighted now, moon faces in nearly every one. Traffic on First Avenue has come to a complete stop, with drivers peering through windshields and riders jumping out to point at Clark. It's like that terrible morning in third grade when Clark dozed off, a cheek pressed to his arithmetic workbook, then woke amid a babble of silvery laughter to find his classmates gleefully surrounding him. He burst into tears. Later, when he informed his mother that he could never, ever, go back to school, she told him, "Clark, you just can't be so sensitive."

After disengaging himself, Clark slides down the face of the rock, lands flat-footed, finds his balance, and starts to walk. Is he limping? He's limping! Although it doesn't persist very long (ten steps and the favoring vanishes), it's nonetheless unnerving.

People call to him. Shout. He ignores them and crosses First Avenue, squeezing between the front fenders and rear bumpers of two or three automobiles, his breathing labored, his head woozy.

On Thirty-ninth Street he steps around metal scraps, hunks of tire, and a car bonnet. He stumbles over a massive piece of a brick wall, crunches more glass with every step, tearing his athletic socks to ribbons.

He fixes his gaze on that whirling dervish twenty feet away and doesn't know what to do.

But coming closer to it, at least the fog in his head grows fainter, his breathing becomes less shallow.

Clark can feel it all returning, his vitality, his talents.

Then his legs cave and he falls to his knees.

When he lifts his eyes the robot is right there.

Then he's hurtling backward again, smashing through a bay window, tumbling through an interior space, a living room, passing upside down beyond an archway and into a foyer—smacking the wall hard enough to both explode plaster and splinter lathing.

He drops to the floor, whacking his rib cage on a radiator valve.

Propping a hand on its warm coils, Clark uses the radiator to give him leverage and get him back on his feet.

He totters through the archway into the well-appointed living room. It glitters with broken glass. Going light-headed again, he puts out a hand and clamps his fingers over the back of a Morris chair.

Slumped in the chair is a dead woman with a small hole in one temple. A wide ribbon of blood runs from it down past her ear and underneath her jaw, where it breaks into two separate thinner ribbons that disappear finally behind the sopping collar of her white-and-rose housedress.

Another dead woman is splayed out bloody on the floor.

In the street something else blows up. Across the street rooftops are in flames. A fire truck clangs. There's gunfire. Another explosion.

Clark looks from one corpse to the other.

Taking his time, he walks carefully across the living room and sits in an upholstered chair. Leans forward and looks at his hands.

They're shaking.

He clasps them, pins them between his knees.

He thinks about Donny Poore and that Negro prisoner cooked to death inside a vault.

He remembers the *General Slocum* and feels sure he would've dropped the water tank before he'd flown it to the excursion boat.

They'd all have drowned anyway.

For two years he's been trying to grow up, pay attention, make himself ready . . . and do you know what?

It was a joke.

He wonders if there is a back door he can use.

Getting up, he looks around (but not at the dead women), then walks through a doorway into the kitchen.

A parrot is squawking in its cage.

He smells burnt coffee.

There are dishes drying in a rack and a plate of Toll House cookies on the table.

No back door.

Clark pulls out a chair, sits at the table, and glances mechanically at the glow-in-the-dark clock in the back panel of the electric range. It reads nine-twenty-three.

"Herman says hello, Herman says hello!"

Picking up a Toll House cookie, Clark regards it closely as though inspecting it for imperfections. His mom used to make these: butter, sifted flour, baking soda, salt, chocolate morsels—anything else?

"Herman says hello, Herman says hello!"

He puts the cookie back on the pile.

Folding his hands in his lap, he stares at the new-looking white Kelvinator with the basket-shaped motor on top.

Diana Dewey had a new refrigerator, too. He doesn't think hers was a Kelvinator though. But maybe.

He remembers Diana's raspy voice, her crooked smile, the silky texture of her skin.

"Your mother says hello, your mother says hello."

"Hello, Mom."

"What are you doing just sitting there, Clark?"

"I'm not sure, Mom."

"Don't you think it's pretty selfish?"

"No, I guess I don't."

"Clark Kent!"

"I'm sorry, Mom. But I don't know what to do."

"Herman says hello, Herman says hello."

Clark turns and looks at the parrot, then he turns back and looks at the Kelvinator.

The clock on the electric range reads nine-twenty-three.

"Son, do you plan on sitting here all night?"

"Probably not. Just till everything goes away outside."

"Clark . . ."

"I don't know what to do!"

"Give yourself a little credit, son. Your vanity will do you in if you don't."

"My *vanity?*" Clark laughs. "Me, vain?"

"Herman says hello, Herman says hello."

"Mom?"

"Herman says hello . . ."

"Mom, come on, quit it," he says pulling on his tattered sleeve, poking a finger through a burn hole in an elasticized cuff, slack now and droopy. "Mom?"

"Clark, are you scared?"

He considers the question for a moment.

"Yes, ma'am, I suppose I am."

"That's good."

"That's *good?*"

"I wouldn't want to think your father and I raised a fool."

"No, ma'am."

"Now get off that silly chair and go do something. Doesn't matter what. Just do something, Clark."

When he leaves the kitchen the glow-in-the-dark clock on the electric range reads nine-twenty-three.

Passing through the living room without glancing at either of the dead women, Clark goes and stands in the bay window. A hook-and-ladder screeches to a stop, firemen dropping from it, unwinding canvas hoses and dragging them toward hydrants. Several cars, skeletons now, still burn. Another just *whumped* into flames. As far as Clark can see, all of the house fronts, brick and brownstone, are scorched black, and every other window looks blown out.

About twenty, twenty-five feet away from where he stands (but raising one foot now to the window seat, bracing it there, jiggling it nervously), the robot continues its monotonous spin. Pencil-thin streaky light shoots from its head and the ends of its fingers. Clark lifts his other foot onto the windowsill and crouches, arms winged back like a competitive swimmer.

The instant he springs, the air is raked with submachine-gun fire. Volleys of bullets strike him and recoil, further shredding his tights, his trunks, his cape, and snipping off the final stitch fastening the wedge-shaped emblem to his chest.

The big **S** goes skimming away just as Clark plows fists-first into the robot, digging knuckles into its plated chest, lifting it off the street, and carrying it with him over the roofs of the police cars (everyone ducks) and down toward First Avenue.

But that's not where Clark wants to go—he can see a crowd gathered there—so he bears down with his weight, and both he and the robot (Clark on top) crash into the street. Tumbling half a dozen times, Clark collides with a lamp post, his lower vertebrae taking most of the impact. The lamp post snaps near its base and slams across the pavement.

Angling as it goes, the robot skates on its back down the street, then strikes the curb and sideslips across the pavement, toppling over a low metal railing and down a flight of steps to the basement entrance of a brownstone. It clatters and clatters and finally bashes against a door.

Clark picks himself up and shakes his head.

Despite all the sirens and the roars of hose water and flames, the staticky grumble of squad-car radios, it seems all of a sudden very quiet and still.

Then: "You in the leotard!" Edges crackling, the voice comes amplified through a bullhorn. "Down on the ground with both your hands in back of your neck—now!"

From the bottom of the areaway comes a low scritching sound followed by a soft whir and then silence.

From behind Clark come the racking of shotguns.

He slightly turns his head, looks over a shoulder.

A dozen policemen, at least a dozen, are pointing their weapons at him across the bonnets and boots of radio cars.

"This is your last warning, circus boy! Get down on the ground!"

With a vague hand gesture, much the same one a good host would use during a party if a guest offered to get up and fix his own drink, Clark continues on across the pavement.

The cops don't shoot him.

But a bluish white light flashes.

Clark closes the short distance to the top of the areaway and then peers down the steps.

Popping a molten pimpled bulb from his camera's flash attachment, Willi Berg smiles up at him.

Looking jailed, Lois Lane stands just inside the basement behind a decorative wrought-iron security gate.

A couple in bathrobes and pajamas flank her, peeking cautiously out. The man is armed with a pewter candlestick, the woman with a coal shovel.

Willi takes another flash picture of a badly dented, partly crumpled steel cylinder, maybe eighteen inches long, that lists in a corner, half buried in a clump of dead leaves.

The cylinder sporadically emits crackling blue sparkles.

Willi calls up, "Check out the mechanical monster."

"What happened to it?"

"Your guess is as good as mine. Oh. Um, *Superman*, I want to introduce you to my good friend Lois Lane. Lois, this is Superman I was telling you about. And that's Mr. and Mrs. Pierce. Dave and Sally were kind enough to let us in during the fireworks."

Clark goes down a few steps, nodding hello to all but never taking his eyes off Lois Lane. She's going to recognize him. Of course she will. He'll never pull this off.

But then she says, "Superman, huh? What's your *real* name?" and Clark feels the giddy joyful pleasure of a practical joke successfully perpetrated. Remembering to lower his voice, he says, "Let's talk about that some other time, shall we, Miss Lane?"

Clark feels cocky enough to swagger but then, catching his own reflection in a lit-from-behind basement window, he is mortified: his hair sticks out and his face is streaked with grime, his clothes are in complete tatters, and where his emblem used to be, minuscule knots and twists of black thread shabbily outline its tricornered shape.

His boots are gone and he has white socks on.

No wonder Lois Lane doesn't recognize him! Who would?

Like a futuristic whoopie canister, the cylinder suddenly springs open and reassembles. A shaft of ruby-red light cuts a neat furrow, a dandy's central part, through Willi's thick hair, singeing it down to his scalp. It also passes between two bars of the iron gate and strikes the blade of the coal shovel, which then smacks Mrs. Pierce in the face, knocking her flat on her back.

Simultaneously the reconstituted robot's articulated fingers close around Willi's trachea and squeeze.

Clark drives his left fist through the robot, back to front. It comes out tangled with circuitry and spaghetti wires. He yanks it back inside, flexes open his fingers, and just—grabs. Anything he can find. And when he withdraws his hand, he pulls out still more insulated wire, more circuits, a spool of celluloid film, a tangle of paper tape punched with slots, and a small black socketed cube.

Willi is rubbing his throat, coughing and gasping.

Clark has had enough of this.

Plucking the gutted robot off the ground, he bends, crushes, twists, countertwists, and otherwise compacts it till it is roughly the size of a grapefruit. A small ellipsoidal plate mark dislodges itself and hits the bottom step with a bright *ting!*

Willi picks it up, and with Clark leaning over his shoulder they inspect it together. Stamped into the metal plate is a nine-numeral serial number, plus this information:

LEXBOT Sidekick S-40

LUTHOR Corp.

Assembled in the United States of America

Soda in turmoil. LaGuardia gets testy.
Boastfulness and diffidence. "Deep Elem Blues."

———

1

Dialing from her office at the club, Soda Wauters asked the operator to put her through to City Hall, New York City, only to be told to lie
down and sleep it off, lady. And the operator strongly suggested that in
the future Soda try speaking *civilly* over the telephone. What? She'd
been civil. *What?* She'd said *what?* Called the operator *what?* She'd
never—

But maybe Soda had, it was hard to remember. She was drunker
than she'd been in a long while.

She considered calling one of the big dailies in New York but was
afraid she would only get that same hateful operator again. Ditto for
calling a cab. So she left the club around seven-thirty and waited on
South Orange Avenue for a Public Service bus.

While she did, she got violently sick over the gutter.

Eventually she found herself in Newark's Pennsylvania Railroad
Station, following red arrows to the Hudson-Manhattan Tubes. Despite
those she wandered around for half an hour, or maybe it just felt that
long, till a transit cop nearly arrested her for public intoxication.

But rattling the bulky envelope in his not-unkind face, Soda told
him she was on a *mission,* she had to catch the tubes because the man
that she loved—the man she'd met and briefly but unconditionally

loved, *a po-liceman of all things,* had entrusted her with special documents intended for hizzonner the mayor of New York City— *these.*

"Sure, lady, sure," he said. "Why don't I help you walk over to Nedick's and we'll get you a cup of coffee?"

"I'm sure he's dead!" she wailed.

"Who?" The cop looked sorry he had ever paid her any attention.

"The man I loved. He stopped coming around and now I'm sure he's dead. And I have to get these papers and pictures to the mayor of New York City. *Don't you get it?* That's why he left them with me!"

When the transit cop took Soda firmly by an elbow she almost struggled. But something told her to be still and shut up, the right thing to do because at last he led her to the correct platform.

She paid her twenty-two cents, boarded a train, and promptly dozed off. She rode all the way into Manhattan and to the end of the line . . . then all the way back under the East River, through Jersey City, across the Hackensack Meadows, to Kearny, where she woke up, and then to Newark again.

She changed trains and willed herself to stay awake.

Although Soda had never been to City Hall before (it never crossed her mind that the mayor might not be there on a Sunday evening—he *lived* there, didn't he?), she knew it was downtown, not far from the Woolworth Building, so she meant to get off at the first stop in lower Manhattan: Cortlandt Street.

But somehow she missed it and got off at the *second* stop: Church Street. Good enough. She'd find the place. She *had* to. She was determined to deliver the envelope, and to deliver it tonight.

After Soda had taken it from her safe this afternoon she pored over just enough of its contents to get the gist.

There was a "ghost gang" operating in New York City, and her Richard (his last name was Sandglass, she discovered: "respectfully submitted, Richard Sandglass") had rooted it out, gotten the goods on all of those dirty crooks like a G-man in a Warner Bros. picture. Why hadn't he *said* he was a cop? Because she'd practically told him *don't be one?* Or was she flattering herself?

Alexander Luthor, a name that kept appearing on page after page, meant nothing to Soda because she never read the papers. Why read a newspaper when you had a phonograph? Newspapers could only make you feel bad-sad, but songs could make you feel *good*-sad. No contest.

Now, after Soda has dragged herself up the stairs from Hudson Terminal and is standing on the pavement in front of two bridged skyscrapers on Court Street, she is struck with a pang of terror: it's dark, it's cold, the streets are empty. And turning dizzily in a circle, she can't locate the Woolworth Building. She is lost in a canyon of tall buildings, her stomach is churning, her temples are throbbing, her cheeks are wet and chapped.

Soda's instincts tell her to walk south; in fact, she heads due west, believing it's south, and shortly finds herself on Greenwich Street. Stepping off the curb, her left ankle buckles and she goes down, whacking both kneecaps. The envelope sails from her grip, skims into the street. She gets up again—hosiery torn, knees bleeding, embedded with grit—and limps after it. Why is she doing this? Why did Richard come into her club? Why did she ever send him a drink? Why did he smile the way that he did?

She can't do this.

She's lost.

She's fat and lonely and her heart is broken and she can't do this, she's lost.

Clutching the envelope horizontally, she folds it around her face like a mask and stands there.

Just stands there.

2

"Are you ever going to take these things off? I'm not a criminal, I'm a reporter!"

"There's a difference?" says the cop who just leaned into the front of the radio car to grab a long-barrel flashlight, a notebook, and a fountain pen from the dashboard.

"Please. Can't you take them off?"

Lois holds up her wrists fettered by handcuffs that are not just heavy but painfully tight, grooving her flesh. She cocks her head, looking miserable. "Come on, be a good guy."

He slams the door and hikes away up the middle of Thirty-ninth Street, sidestepping debris and splashing through hose-water puddles.

Lois pounds her handcuffs against the steel grating that separates the front and back of the police car, then clashes them harder against the side window.

Of all the things she has to worry about (being handcuffed, being scooped, Ben's condition, the way "Superman" stared at her and the way it made her feel), what primarily troubles Lois at the moment is this: she deliberately remained behind that locked security gate and let Willi Berg go back outside to inspect that robot-turned-cylinder.

She is appalled at herself, deeply ashamed.

Lois stayed behind the iron gate because she was scared.

Six or seven years ago, when she was still in high school, Lois went on a weekend camping trip with her father. (Her mother, as usual, didn't accompany them; too many insects, too many *sounds* at night.) It was midsummer in the Adirondacks; they were hiking a rocky hillside, Lois in the lead. She felt strong, nimble, full of health, and took a wholly conscious, unkind pleasure in the way that her father grunted and puffed and picked his way slowly along behind her.

As she found the last footholds to boost herself to the summit, she heard a clacking sound she ascribed to heat bugs. Planting the knee of one leg and swinging the other up and over the rim, she dragged herself onto the flat, sun-warmed surface of the granite rock only to discover, two feet away, a coiled rattlesnake. Its wedge-shaped head feinted and its tongue flicked. Lois froze in terror. Her mind shut down, went blank, so blank she never saw the snake slither away.

When her father arrived, she had already beaten her fists bloody against craggy rock. He had to grab her wrists to make her stop. Then it took Lois ten minutes to calm down enough to say what happened. He could understand her terror but not her anger. That just unleashed further anger. Didn't he *see?* Couldn't he get it? What was the *matter* with him? She was so scared that *she'd done nothing!* "And just what do you think you were supposed to do?" he asked her. Go back! Run! Find a rock! No, no, no, he said. *No.* She'd done the right thing. *Nothing* was the right thing *to* do. Scared was good. Scared was smart. She could've fallen, she could've fallen *on him!* If she'd moved, the snake would have moved faster. Didn't *she* get it? Scared was *good.* He put his arm around her shoulders, tried pulling her close but she flung herself away. "Scared is good," he told her one last time, and let it drop.

Scared is *not* good! Lois thinks again now, sitting in the back of a squad car. Scared is just . . . scared.

And weak.

She stayed behind that iron safety gate because she was weak. Period.

And if there is one thing Lois Lane despises above everything else it is being, and being seen as, weak.

She turns to strike again at the side window with her handcuffs but sees a flying wedge of police- and fire-department officials flanking a short, rotund, furiously gesticulating man in a flapping overcoat and a black sombrero.

Lois palm slaps the glass and the bracelets beat percussion.

Pausing in midgesture, midbellow ("And I want—"), Fiorello LaGuardia glances irritably around.

Turning to one of the two police commissioners accompanying him, the mayor asks a quick question, nods at the reply. Then he says something else, and twenty seconds later Lois is sighing with relief as a key turns and her handcuffs snap open.

When the mayor says, "Good evening, Lois," she feels an instant puerile gratitude that he called her by her first name. They've never spoken before, although she has attended half a dozen of his press conferences, even asked him a few questions, one of which ("Are you at all

embarrassed to have sponsored Lex Luthor's entrance into city politics?) he called "impudent."

"Good evening, Mr. Mayor. And thank you." She makes a big show
of rubbing her chafed wrists. "At least *some* people know how to treat
members of the press."

"Don't push it, Miss Lane," he says, eyes snapping. "You were
involved in a very damaging series of events here tonight, and for all we
know you're partly responsible. *Are* you?"

"Of course not!"

"What do you know about that infernal device? Are you *smiling?*"

"I'm sorry, Mayor. 'Infernal device?'"

"That's funny?"

"It was a robot."

"So they tell me. What do you know about it?"

"It was in the luggage compartment of a car"—she ought to have
said: a 1936 Nash-Lafayette 3-window coupe, now scrap metal, now
shrapnel—"driven by the same person who shot Ben Jaeger."

"And that's all you know."

"That's it."

Lois doesn't deem it necessary to inform the mayor about the small
obloid metal tag that Willi passed to her and that is concealed now
inside the left cup of her white cotton Gamble's brassiere. He can read
about it like everybody else in tomorrow morning's *Daily Planet*.

"And what can you tell us about this—strongman?"

Commissioner Blanshard—or maybe it's Valentine, she always gets
those two men confused—leans forward and whispers into LaGuardia's
left ear.

"I've just been reminded there's a team of weightlifters in town from
the Soviet Union. Did you happen to notice if this fellow spoke Russian?"

"Mayor LaGuardia, he's not just some run-of-the-mill muscleman,
he can *fly!* Ask your cops. They had him surrounded and he just—"

"I'm having a difficult time believing all this."

"Welcome to the club."

Again one of the police commissioners speaks quietly into the mayor's ear. LaGuardia frowns. "Are you certain?"

The commissioner says that he is.

"Miss Lane"—apparently "Lois" was a one-time-only form of address—"you saw this flying man escape . . ."

"I don't think he was *escaping*. I think he was just *leaving*."

"The police ordered him to stay."

Lois shrugs. "If it hadn't been for him, Mayor, there wouldn't be a single house standing on this block right now. But have it your way. Yes, I saw this flying man *escape* . . ."

"Taking another man along with him. A photographer."

"Well, he had a camera, but I don't know if—"

"Who was he, Miss Lane?"

"You know, Mr. Mayor, if I may change the subject for just a moment. Right as we speak there's a wonderful man in the hospital with two bullets in his chest, a police officer that you *personally* scapegoated because you wanted to get all of that nasty Lex Luthor business out of the way before the election—"

"Miss Lane: *who was the photographer?*"

"I don't know."

"Yes, you do. And so do we."

"Then why ask?"

"Put her back in the car," says LaGuardia.

Lois immediately stretches out her arms, presses her fists together: the martyr.

"That won't be necessary," he says. "But don't tempt me." He turns away, sloshing off (lord! he remembered galoshes) through water that still rushes down the street in torrents.

3

"Can I get you more toast? We doing all right with that bacon, sir?"

"Nothing more for me, Carl, thank you. But why don't you try calling Paulie's house again?"

Since their arrival back at Lex's apartment in the Waldorf Towers, Carl already has telephoned the Scaffa residence three separate times, each time at Lex's curt prompting. The first time, Mr. Scaffa said only that Paulie was out. The second time, he said that Paulie had received a telephone call and *then* went out. And the third time, he said that Paulie was *still* out, that he'd gone out after receiving a telephone call, and that so far as Mr. Scaffa was concerned the worthless *stunad* should *stay* out.

He also mentioned something about Paulie trying to kill him with a jack-in-the-box, but Carl didn't bother reporting it to Lex Luthor since he figured it was simply another instance of the old coot's senility.

"There's no answer at all now, sir. Mr. Scaffa usually goes straight to bed on Sundays right after Edgar Bergen."

What is going *on?* Lex wants to know. Mrs. O'Shea wasn't at home when he returned—and not a note. Paulie's gone out—where?—and is unreachable.

"Mr. Luthor?"

"Leave," he says.

"Yes, sir, but can I do anything else before I—"

"Just leave. Now! Get out!"

"Yes, sir." Carl Krusada looks crushed. His face has turned paper-white, and he stumbles against the coffee table in his haste to obey. "What time will you need me in the morning? Sir?"

But Lex doesn't answer, seems in fact to have blotted Carl from his vision and his consciousness.

What is going *on? Something* is. *What?*

At that precise moment a grapefruit-size ball of crumpled metal smashes through the French doors, twenty-seven flights above Lexington Avenue, shattering glass and whizzing across the living room to embed itself four inches deep in the silver-papered wall behind the wet bar.

4

"—that cop?"

"Yeah! Did you *see* that guy?"

"With the nose, right? That cop with the red nose?"

"Was he a riot or what?"

"Like he was gonna have a heart attack!"

"I bet he quits the force!"

"I bet they make him!"

"And that other one, you see him try to grab my cape?"

"He tried to grab your cape? Which one?"

"Big mustache?"

"He tried to grab your *cape?* Man, it's lucky he didn't end up hitching a ride!"

Clark rubs a hand around his jaw. "I was afraid I'd drop you."

"You were?"

"I wasn't sure I had a good grip. It all happened so fast."

"You had a *great* grip. *I* was afraid I'd drop the stupid camera."

They are on the flat tar-papered roof of their tenement on St. Mark's Place, Willi sitting on the parapet smoking while Clark pulls a pair of his trousers, a shirt, and black socks off a clothesline.

Stepping into his trousers, Clark tugs them over his ruined tights. He retrieves his eyeglasses from the little pocket he sewed into his cape and then stuffs in the tail. "It feels lumpy. Does it *look* lumpy?" He turns around so Willi can give his opinion.

"It looks all right. Makes your rear end look kind of big . . ."

"*How* big?"

"Relax. It looks fine."

Clark goes and sits next to Willi while he puts on his socks. "Can I borrow your shoes? And your belt?"

Willi makes a face. But okay: belt and shoes. Then he says, "Can I ask you something?"

"Hmmm?"

"Who are you right now?"

"What?"

"Who are you supposed to be right now? Clark or Superman?"

"I'm not *supposed* to be anybody, it's all just—"

"Because whether you know it or not you're still talking in that deep voice."

"I am?"

"You just changed it. But yeah, you were."

Clark wrinkles his forehead. "I guess I should watch that." He stands up. "So where *is* this place?"

Willi points downtown and to the west. "You can't miss it—it's got a big globe on the roof." He stoops and picks up his camera from the rooftop, ejects a used flashbulb, and lobs it casually over his shoulder. They hear it burst down in the courtyard. Then Willi snaps the film hatch shut. "I kind of thought we'd get a bigger reaction from the guy."

"What guy?"

"'What guy?' Luthor!"

"Oh. Yeah. Me too. Think we did a lot of damage? How much you think it'll cost to replace those doors?"

Willi drops the roll of exposed film into Clark's palm. "Forget about the stupid doors. And don't scuff the shoes."

Clark steps onto the parapet.

"And don't let anybody see you flying around in those clothes."

"I *won't*."

Clark doesn't move.

"Are you gonna do this or not?"

"I'm a little nervous."

"You just annihilated a *robot.* I think you can talk to the editor of the *Daily Planet.* Would you *go* already? I'm freezing to death up here. But wake me when you get back."

5

It's on the tip of Ben Jaeger's tongue, whose version of "Deep Elem Blues" they're listening to. But he just can't . . . "The Shelton Brothers? Gene Autry on vocals?"

"Nice try, kid. But no cigar. Les Paul, recording as Rhubarb Red. Decca, 1936."

"I'll never have your ear, Lieutenant."

"Sure you will, you just have to pay attention."

Of all the places Ben has been most comfortable in his life, been most himself, Lieutenant Sandglass's living room is right at the top. He never thought he'd be here again. But here he is. Except for the obvious absence of photographs and photostats, the accumulating contents of their Lex Luthor dossier piled on the coffee table and the sofa cushions, on any flat surface, the room doesn't look any different than it did during all of those evenings Dick Sandglass and Ben Jaeger spent here together. Growing more excited with each piece of the story they fit into place.

The furniture is the same, there is still that crack in the window. The same rug, the radiator with the perforated cover. The record collection is still here too, hundreds of thick varnished disks in their paper sleeves, cataloged in alphabetical order.

Tieless but otherwise dressed for a wake or a funeral in his one black suit, Dick Sandglass sings along with the recording: "Oh sweet mama, your daddy's got the Deep Elem Blues . . ."

Ben leans forward. "Lieutenant? There's something I need to tell you."

"Can it wait for a little while?"

"Sure, that's fine."

Sandglass smiles. "When you go down to Deep Elem," he and Les Paul sing, "put your money in your socks, them Deep Elem monsters, they will throw you on the rocks."

Monsters? Ben always thought the lyric said *women,* them Deep Elem *women,* they will throw you on the rocks.

But there you go. It just goes to prove how little he pays attention. He doesn't pay enough attention to *anything.* That's his problem, his weakness. One of them.

During the next refrain Spider Sandglass comes in from the hall. He barely acknowledges Ben. "Do you need the car?" Spider asks his father. "I'd like to take it out for a spin."

Ben notices that a fine trickle of sand or powder is spilling from the bottom of Spider's trouser legs. He tracks the stuff across the floor.

"Actually, I do need it tonight," says Dick Sandglass. "Ben will be leaving in a short while and I have to run him back." He smiles at his son. "Do you want to take a ride with us?"

"No, that's okay."

When Spider turns and goes back out, Ben leans to the side in his chair, mesmerized by the steady sifting of that fine white powder drizzling out behind him.

Sandglass catches Ben looking. "He can't help it, that boy was *born* messy." They both laugh. "But in the end that hardly matters. It *doesn't* matter. He's a good boy, a good son. I was so proud of him. You would've been too, Benny." Sandglass pushes himself out of his easy chair and lifts the armature off the recording, sets it carefully on its prong. "Come on, I'll give you a lift back."

"If you don't mind I'd like to stay a while longer."

"Sorry, kid. Time to go."

"But we still haven't talked."

"So we'll talk in the car."

Dick Sandglass's Dodge coupe never used to have a radio in the dashboard but now it does, a good one too, with a brilliant yellow dial light and excellent sound.

By a real coincidence the song playing as they drive away from the Bowery and through the half-deserted streets of the old Fourth Ward is another version of "Deep Elem Blues."

Sandglass removes his right hand from the steering wheel to poke Ben in the shoulder with a finger.

"The Blue Ridge Ramblers?"

"I'll give it to you this time, but it's the Blue Ridge Ramblers recording as the *Prairie* Ramblers."

"You don't have to give it to me. I didn't get it right, I messed up."

Ben notices a small deckle-edged photograph clipped to the driver's sun visor. Leaning forward, he examines it: a heavyset pretty woman in a chiffon dress standing on a bandstand singing at a microphone, lost in bliss. "Who's that, Lieutenant?"

He grins. "None of your beeswax."

They are motoring through the Jewish District now, on Orchard crossing Delancey, crossing Rivington, crossing Stanton, then crossing East Houston and taking First Avenue north past the numbered streets.

"You wanted to tell me something," says Dick Sandglass. "This is probably the time."

"I just wanted to say how sorry I am. You picked a lousy protégé."

"You think?"

"I know."

"No, you don't. Excuse me, Benny, but you don't. You did the best you could. So did I. But sometimes . . ." He shrugs. "We're only people."

"I let you down, Lieutenant."

"Cut it out."

While they're stopped at a red light, Ben glances through his side window and notices, inside a Nash-Lafayette stopped parallel to the Dodge, a stocky dark-haired man seated behind the wheel with his face buried in his hands. His shoulders jerk up and down. He's sobbing. In the back seat a slender, attractive white-haired woman is tapping the tip of an index finger against a small red hole in the center of her forehead. Then she runs the fingertip around and around her pinched lips, rouging them.

Ben thinks: Oh.

So this is—

The light changes to green and Dick Sandglass drives on, but the Nash-Lafayette stays where it was. Twisting around in his seat, Ben looks through the rear window: the traffic light behind them has turned quickly back to red.

"We're all people, Benny, and our fundamental nature is to screw up things like you wouldn't believe. Most of the time. But would you want it any different?"

"Are you kidding? Sure I would!"

"No, you wouldn't. Trust me."

"I only wanted to say I'm sorry and I hope you forgive me. We worked so long to bring down that—"

"Okay! I heard you say you're sorry, and if you think you need my forgiveness, you got it. All right?"

Ben nods.

"So that's finished. And so far as that bald-headed monster is concerned, kiddo, we did our part, we did our best."

"But it wasn't enough."

"Cry sake, *we did our part.* And other people did theirs, whether they know it or not. Nobody does it all by himself, Ben. Do your little part and hope for the best. That's our motto."

"Whose motto?"

"People's, Benny. Human beings. And here's where you get out."

They've pulled curbside and the car idles now in front of one of the newer buildings of Bellevue Hospital. The sign chiseled above the entrance reads: THE PATHOLOGICAL BUILDING.

It's the city morgue.

Ben turns his head and finds Sandglass grinning. "Actually, *you* go in up there," he says pointing through the windshield at the main entrance to the hospital complex.

"What, you couldn't've parked closer?"

"Scared you."

"Did not."

"Did too," says Sandglass.

In the space of a single breath Ben's expression changes from delight (he can't *believe* the lieutenant just teased him, he *never* did that before) to deep melancholy. "Lieutenant. I hope you know just how much I—"

"No schmaltz, kid. Just get out of here and do the best you can."

They shake hands and Ben starts to open his door.

"Oh. Kid. Wait up."

Sandglass stretches out his right arm and Ben Jaeger moves in and lets himself be hugged. But then he winces. And realizes that he's dressed now in a hospital gown. Peering down its open neck, he discovers surgical dressings on his chest crisscrossed with adhesive tape. "See you, Lieutenant."

"Not for a while, kid."

When the Dodge turns down Thirtieth Street and disappears, Ben walks barefooted to the main hospital entrance and goes inside. Rides the elevator to the sixth floor, Intensive Care. As if directed by a homing device, he negotiates the pea-soup-green hallways and side corridors, weaving around orderlies and nurses, physicians and suited administrators who pay him no attention. At last he comes to the Post-Op ward. Checking a clipboard on the counter at the head nurse's station, he learns that his room is 6115.

But as he turns the last corner, Ben shudders and comes to an abrupt stop.

Straight ahead stands Lois Lane, her stockings full of holes, both shoes missing their heels, her coat encrusted with dried blood.

She is speaking animatedly to a blond nurse who looks vaguely familiar and is built like Mae West.

Ben's heart speeds up, then spasms, then sinks.

He is tired suddenly. Exhausted.

Slipping past Lois and the nurse, Ben enters his room, slides under the sheets. A midget radio on the night table is turned on with the volume low.

The song playing is "Deep Elem Blues."

Les Paul recording as Rhubarb Red, Ben says to himself. Decca, 1936.

Perry White. Skinny returns. **The** *Daily Planet.*
Lovesick. Conversation on the nut bench. A scoop at last.
Superman and Lex Luthor.

———

1

Less than a minute after she is dropped off at Bellevue Hospital, Lois tosses a nickel into one of the pay telephones, pulls closed the bifold door, and rids her mind of everything except first graf, second graf, third graf.

When she is connected to the *Planet*'s City Room she says, still tickled to say it, "Get me rewrite; this is Lois Lane."

"Hold on."

First graf: New York's latest marvel em-dash call him a miracle em-dash appeared last night in the form of a super hyphen man with the strength of twenty comma make that fifty comma Goliaths cap-G comma the speed of—

"Lois? Perry White."

Recently hired away from the Cleveland *Plain-Dealer,* Perry White is the paper's new managing editor, and so far they haven't hit it off so well. He thinks she's careless; she thinks he's stodgy.

"Perry, I asked for rewrite!"

"If this is about that pandemonium on Thirty-ninth Street, relax, we got it covered."

"But I was *there!* I know what happened at every—"

"I'm pretty sure we do, too." Then he breaks into a soft chuckle. "Say, do you happen to know a guy named Clark Kent? He's using you as a reference."

"What? He's *there?*"

"Sitting right in front of me. Would you care to say hello?"

"Perry, kick him out! I don't care what he's telling you, he wasn't anywhere *near* Thirty-ninth Street!"

"See you when you get here."

He breaks the connection.

"No! Perry! It's *my* story, I was there! *Perry!*"

She clubs the telephone receiver against the metal armrest, then keeps it up till the door folds open beside her and a lobby guard asks, "Something the matter, miss?"

Storming past him, Lois very nearly leaves the hospital without first going upstairs to check on Ben.

She's not coldhearted, though. Steamed, yes, stunned and brutally humiliated, check—but *not* coldhearted.

Sixth floor, Intensive Care.

Flashing her press card, she races past the head nurse's station, then reluctantly has to backtrack and meekly ask for Ben's room number.

6115.

The attending nurse is just stepping out into the corridor when Lois arrives in such an overwrought state that she doesn't recognize her old pal and former roommate till Skinny Simon lets out with a strictly forbidden whoop of surprise.

"Honey! Your coat! It's covered with blood."

"Don't worry, it's not mine, it's his," says Lois, meaning Ben Jaeger's. "How's he doing?"

"Better than he should. What's he to you? The news?"

Lois shakes her head. "Kind of a boyfriend. But not really. What are you *doing* here, I thought you were in California?"

"I was. But here I am."

"How's Charlie?"

"I'm not sure, but my guess is pretty nervous. It's a long story. How are *you?*"

"At the moment, Skin, not so great. I nearly got run down by a car and incinerated by a robot. And now I just found out I was scooped by a four-eyed farm boy from Kansas."

"A *robot?*"

"That's a long story, too. But I got to run. Where're you staying?"

"A hotel for the time being. Need a roommate?"

"I might. Call me. Or maybe I'll see you back here. Tell him I came by, all right?"

"Sure. Hey, am I imagining things or is he the same cop that used to stand guard on our mutual friend that time at Roosevelt?"

"Same cop, yeah."

"Cute." Then Skinny adds, "I mean, not at the *moment.* But otherwise."

As Lois hurries back down the hallway (You could have at *least* taken a *peek* at Ben, she berates herself), Skinny Simon calls, "Hey! I saw Willi out in Hollywood! He took pictures of me in my underwear!"

Lois glances sourly over a shoulder.

No, she really doesn't need a roommate.

2

Not long after Joseph Pulitzer II sold the once-great but long-ailing New York *World* to the Scripps-Howard company in 1930, it was merged with the *Evening Telegraph* and moved uptown, leaving only two dailies in operation along lower Manhattan's legendary Newspaper Row: the *Sun* and the *Planet.* The *Sun's* editorial and business offices, as well as its printing plant, are housed in the Stewart Building near City Hall Park on the northeast corner of Chamber Street and Broadway. The *Planet,* at Spruce and Nassau streets, exclusively occupies a sixteen-story building made of brick with a front facing of polished granite designed by Richard Morris Hunt. A revolving sidereally precise gilded globe of the earth seems, in light both natural and artificial, to be suspended wondrously in midair twenty feet above the rooftop.

While the *Daily Planet* remains located in a neighborhood that is a relic of the newspapering past, its grand old building with its light-filled offices, below-ground printing plant, and spacious marbled lobby (supposedly modeled after a ballroom in the Versailles palace) are all turbines of activity and nervous energy at any time of the day or night.

For example, here it is late on a Sunday evening . . .

The giant rotary presses' rumbling can be heard as far away as a quarter mile, and dozens of delivery trucks, big Federals, are lining up along three sides of the building, waiting for tomorrow's first edition, the night-owl, to come trundling out to the loading docks in bound wet bales. Around in front, taxicabs come and go, dropping off and picking up reporters, photographers, freelancers, press agents. Delivery men from a score of different Jewish delicatessens and late-kitchen restaurants hustle inside, lugging pasteboard cartons packed with bialys shmeared with cream cheese, corned beef sandwiches, coffee and beer and celery soda.

Plenty of cops around, twirling their billys, trading quips with the boxing writers, checking out the pins on the society-page editor, seeing if there are any hot tips to be cadged from the track reporters.

The lobby is bedlam tonight, unsavory-looking men dashing for the elevators, punching the buttons impatiently, smashing into the riders who seem propelled out of the cars when the doors finally unseal. Carny Oates, who has operated the candy and cigar concession for three decades, has seen his share of nights like this one, big-news nights—war, peace, the stock market bust, the Lindbergh snatch, the Ruth Snyder fricassee, the Will Rogers smash-up, the Morro Castle, the Hindenburg, John Dillinger down.

He's been trying for the past hour and change to get the lowdown on what's going on, hailing practically every pencil-and-pad man he's seen race by, even the ones who aren't his regular customers, but nobody has stopped. Business stinks. Carny relights his stogie, blows out the match. Then he snaps to attention when a cop-house reporter veers over and scoops up a handful of cheap Florida cigars and a box of Chiclets. "Hey! Wilson, what's going on?"

"Benny Jaeger got shot."

"The Luthor patsy? No kidding! Who by?"

"I heard it was a robot."

"What?"

"Gotta run, Carn." And he does.

A *robot?*

Carny is still puzzling over that when a heavyset woman appears in front of him, red-faced and very bright-eyed, clutching a fat envelope and reeking of alcohol. And because Carny Oates has no truck with soakers, no truck at all, he glowers.

"Where do I go if I want to report something?"

"Depends on what you want to report," says Carny. "You want to report a giant octopus in the harbor, you go wait on that bench," he says pointing to a disheveled man seated over there, clutching himself as though he's freezing; that's Mr. Spencer, who drops by three times a week to report an octopus-sighting in the waters between the Battery and Governors Island, although he'll admit it's possible it could have been a giant squid, even a German submarine. "And if you want to report cannibalism among the Hebrew citizenry, you can go sit down on that bench," says Carny, using his cigar to gesture at a rail-thin gray-haired woman seated ramrod straight on a different bench against the same wall. "And if you want to report a pink elephant, sister, why'n't you just walk around the corner to McCutcheon's bar and tell it to the fine patrons you'll encounter there?"

The fat woman blinks at him, seems as though she might burst into tears, then turns abruptly, stumbling when an ankle buckles, and walks purposely across the lobby to one of the uniformed guards.

Carny Oates grins when the guard takes the hippo by an arm and steers her right over to Mr. Spencer's bench, plonks her down there, and wags a finger in her face.

Glancing at a clock he keeps on a shelf, Carny sees that it's already midnight—time for a break. He parks his Be Right Back sign in the brass change bowl and ducks under the counter. He is doing some deep-knee bends when he sees Lois Lane trot briskly across the lobby. "Hiya sweetheart," he calls. "What do you have to tell old Carny to brighten his lonely night?"

She ignores him and heads for an elevator.

3

Clark Kent is sitting in Perry White's glass-enclosed office talking to both White and George Taylor when Lois flings the door open without knocking. It bangs against the wall and she barges in. Clark jumps to his feet. The perfect gentleman—that rat!

"Well, hel-lo," says George Taylor. "You don't look any the worse for wear." He smiles and gives her a quick head-to-toe. "Okay, maybe you do."

"I nearly got myself killed for this story. It's mine—not his!" she says pointing like an accuser from a witness box. Him! *That's* the man!

Clark says, "Lois, please, I wouldn't—"

"Shut up, you! George, I told him you'd give him a job if he came in with a front-page story and now he's trying to swindle you. Swindler! He wasn't there! He wasn't there!"

Taylor turns to Clark. "Were you there?"

"No, sir. But—"

"Shut up, kid," says Taylor, and turns back to Lois. "He wasn't there. But he never said he was. However, and just in case this might be *news* to you, at least fifty other reporters *were*. Including a few of ours."

"But I was there first!"

"Did you phone it in?"

Lois clamps her jaws, grinds her teeth, and breathes in through her nose with such aggression it sounds like water boiling. When she can speak again she says, "Just do not hire that—*farmer*. He's a fraud!"

Perry White has had enough. "He well may be. But are *these?*" he says grabbing a batch of damp prints from his desk and swacking them into Lois's hand.

She riffles through them as a phantom buzz starts deep in her ears. The car, the cape. The robot. The robot again, that time blurred, speed dramatically smudging its shape. Then *him*. Then him again. Him again. His hair like a bomb flash, his gymnasiast clothing in such tatters that he looks almost comical and the print like a production still from a Hal Roach comedy. Him *again.* The big red **S** dangling by a thread or two. Him again, him again.

Willi's pictures.

Lois tosses them all back on the desk. *Willi's* pictures. What is she going to say now? Does she have to talk? She puts a hand up to her lips. Can't she just leave? Where's a phone? She needs to call her father.

"I want a sidebar," she says, "for the red-eye edition."

Both Taylor and White stare at her.

For all she knows Clark Kent does, too.

But she can't look at him.

"A sidebar," says Taylor. "Convince me."

Then as her two editors look on in amazement (only Taylor blushes), Lois undoes her top buttons, sticks a hand inside a brassiere cup, and plucks out the small metal plate mark she's kept hidden there for the past two hours. She holds it up, pinching it between her thumb and first finger so that her hand won't tremble. "We finally got Lex Luthor dead to rights."

Struggling to keep her breathing natural, she passes over the plate mark to George Taylor.

His eyebrows go up, as do the corners of his mouth.

"Kent," he says, "you'll have to excuse us. See the paymaster on your way out, he'll settle up. And Kent?"

"Yes, sir?"

Lois cringes at how suddenly hopeful he looks. Pitiful.

"Tell your shy friend if he wants a job he's got one. Otherwise we'd be happy to look at anything else he'd care to show us."

"Yes, sir," he says quietly and looks as if he might cry.

"Nice meeting you, Kent," says Perry White showing him to the door.

"You too. And you too, sir," he says back to George Taylor. "But I was wondering . . ."

"Kent, we're really busy now," says Taylor.

"Of course. I'm sorry. But if, well, if anything *does* come up in the way of a job for me . . ."

"Get us a front page story of your own and I'll *give* you a job. All right? Now beat it."

As Clark is stepping through the doorway looking melancholic, looking very young, a copyboy ducks underneath his arm, scoots around him and, with near-triumphant brio, slaps down a copy of the night-owl edition on Perry White's desk.

The war-declared-size headline screams: IT'S SUPERMAN!

4

He's embarrassed and sore. *Angry.* And heartsick. More heartsick than angry. But that's stupid. How can he measure, how can he gauge? He's upset. Mostly about how she treated him.

She really thought he'd sneaked around behind her back to scoop her. That he's the kind of a guy who would *do* such a thing. Is capable of it.

She hates me.

Clark is standing at the paymaster's window, two floors below the City Room. Third in line. It's twenty minutes past twelve by the wall clock. Yesterday seems like it took a whole *week*, this past week seemed like a month, *two* months. What if every day, every week seems as long? A person couldn't stand it.

He doesn't want to plow into robots all the time. That much he knows. He wants to go to work in the morning like regular people. Have a desk, drawers full of rubber bands, his own typewriter. He wants to talk to guys at the water fountain. *And* girls. One in particular.

Although at the moment she's the last person on *Earth* he'd talk to.

A farmer.

And just what was so wrong, Clark wants to know, with being a farmer? Do you like green vegetables? Do you like fruit? Do you like *bread?* Do you like Cream of Wheat? Then quit insulting farmers.

There is nothing wrong with being a farmer.

But Clark wants to be a reporter. And he wants to work *here.*

She hates me.

"Son? Step up, step up," says the paymaster. He sits on a stool behind a banker's grille. Has on a green visor and almond-shaped spectacles, wears old-fashioned garters on his shirt sleeves.

Clark passes him the voucher he got from Perry White.

"Signature here. And initials there," says the paymaster indicating with a fountain pen two places on the form. And now he counts from a sheaf of bills, counts again, a third time. "Three hundred twenty-five and no cents."

Three hundred twenty-five *dollars?*

Clark is amazed by the amount, almost stunned, he's never—

"Stand aside," says the paymaster. *"Next."*

"That's all right," says Lois Lane, "I'm just waiting for Hayseed Harry."

"Excuse me," says Clark brushing past her, stuffing the money into his pocket without counting it—something that would've earned him his mother's severest reproach.

"Clark! I was only kidding. I'm *kidding.*"

He pushes through a pair of plate doors and crosses the hall to the elevators.

She catches up to him. "Forgive me?"

He presses the call button.

"I'm sorry—okay? I just thought you'd, *you know.*"

"Stabbed you in the back?"

"Yeah!" She smiles.

The elevator bell rings, the doors slide open. He puts a hand out to stop them from closing right away.

He doesn't want to leave.

"I really am sorry."

He says, "Okay. Thanks." With a shrug he turns to go.

"Clark! Wait!"

He turns quickly back around.

"I want to interview your friend."

He looks at her.

"Superman. Can you arrange it?"

Clark steps into the elevator car and without turning around punches the button.

It cracks into fifty bits of hard plastic that sprinkle to the floor.

All the way down Clark stares at his vague unhappy reflection in burled walnut.

Crossing the lobby he is waylaid by a very large woman (he was taught it's impolite to describe people as fat) who galumphs along beside him and clutches his sleeve with a manic intensity that makes him flinch. "Can you help me?" she says. "Are you a reporter?"

"I wish!" says Clark.

"All right, lady, that's the last time you get to bother anybody tonight." A uniformed guard is dragging her away before he's even finished speaking. "Out you go!"

Clark says, "That's all right, we were just having a conversation. It's okay, really."

"Then she's yours, mister." The guard turns a hard look on the woman. "And no more trouble, you."

"What trouble?" she says. "This is supposed to be a newspaper? I should've picked another one."

"We all wish you did," says the guard.

"Aren't you the rudest thing! I only picked *this* one because I found a copy in the back of my cab." She turns to Clark. "I thought it was like a sign. Finding a copy of the *Daily Planet* in the back of my cab. So I came here. I should've picked another paper."

"I'm sorry you feel that way, ma'am," says Clark as if—as if what? As if he is personally distressed, even mortified, that the poor woman might leave here with an unfavorable opinion of the *Daily Planet.* Why should he care? "I'm not sure I can help you, but if I can, I will."

The guard looks at them both. "Quack, quack," he says, spinning a finger at his temple as he walks off. "Quack, quack, quack!"

The fat woman looks at Clark in a sidelong way. "Thank you."

"I'm not a reporter," he says. "To finally answer your question."

"Well, that's what I need. But they don't make it easy for you. It's easier to get into Fort Knox."

When she laughs Clark realizes two things: she's very pretty and she's not drunk, no matter how cloying the alcohol smell that conveys with her.

"I'm not a reporter *now*," says Clark. "But I *used* to be." He is unsure why he feels a need, and he definitely does, to prolong this encounter. He feels sorry for her, yes. But that's not it. "Would you like to sit down?"

"I'm Edith Wauters."

"Clark Kent."

"Good to meet you, Clark. Sure, we can sit. I'm exhausted."

She leads him to a long varnished bench occupied by a man with thick snarled hair. His coat and trousers are filthy, his shoes are caked with tar, and he is tapping an envelope against one knee. Edith Wauters curtly nods to him, then tells Clark, "Have a seat. Nobody here except us squirrels, right, Mr. Spencer?" Then she explains, "This is where they store the nuts."

Spencer takes umbrage. He brandishes his own envelope. "I have proof!"

"We all have proof, darling. Just nobody wants to see it." She turns back to Clark and sighs. "I've been on quite an odyssey. Do you know what time it is?"

"About twelve-thirty, I'd guess."

"Originally I was going to see the mayor. But I decided that probably wasn't such a great idea."

Spencer says to Clark, "Would you like to take a look at these?" He has a collection of snapshots in his hand.

"No, thank you." Then he says, "Miss Wauters? You were going to tell me why you needed a reporter."

Edith lowers her head, twisting it to one side, and her demeanor hardens with alarming quickness. She curls her fingers around the sides of her envelope. But she doesn't say anything.

Seizing the opportunity presented by the woman's silence, Mr. Spencer leans around her and tells Clark, "There's at *least* one octopus out there in the harbor. But I could be seeing different ones."

"Have you really seen an octopus?"

"Oh yes! Many, many times. And it's enormous!"

His systolic pressure spurts like a thermometer dipped into boiling water.

He's lying. Mr. Spencer hasn't seen any such thing, he's simply made it up. Which Clark finds sad.

And he is suddenly afraid the more he discovers about people in the world the sadder he will become.

Edith is stroking her envelope now, repetitively, almost fondly, as if it were the flank of a lap dog. "When I give this up, that's it, he's gone. But that's why he left it with me. Just in case."

"Somebody gave you that? Who did? What is it?"

Just *listen* to me, thinks Clark. All that's left is When, Where, and Why?

I could *do* this. I really could.

Because, he thinks, I honestly don't want to go around beating up robots night and day. Raising blisters on the back of a bully's hand.

Carrying dead bodies down the courthouse steps.

"Edith? What's in the envelope?"

"First, I have to tell you something else. My name is really Soda. Well, it's not *really*, but it's who I am. Silly name, isn't it?"

"Not at all."

"I'm a singer."

"A singer! Well, I'd love to hear you one of these days."

"I'm a night watchman," says Mr. Spencer. "Pier A. Not anymore, but I used to be. They let me go after there was a barge collision. They said I fell asleep. But I didn't. I couldn't have. My eyes are always open. Last night I saw an octopus!"

"Mr. Spencer," says Edith-now-Soda, "for the love of God, would you shut up?"

"But it could've been a squid."

"The envelope," says Clark.

"When I give it up, he's gone."

"Maybe not." Clark has no idea what she's talking about.

She unwinds the string and pulls from the envelope a sheaf of papers punched with three holes and bound together with brass fasteners.

To: The Honorable Fiorello LaGuardia/From: Richard D. Sandglass, Lt. NYPD.

"Edith . . ."

"Soda."

"Is this the man who gave you the envelope? Richard Sandglass?"

"Why, do you know him, too?"

"I never met him, no. But I know who he . . ."

"Was?"

Clark nods.

Her lips push out, pull back in.

He puts an arm around her and she leans against him. He says, "I'm so very sorry for your loss."

Because that's how his parents taught him to express condolences to the bereaved.

His mother also told Clark that he could add, "He (or she) is in a much better place now."

But he never has, he doesn't now, and he probably never will.

He and Soda sit together on the nut bench for half an hour.

It is ten minutes past one when they take an elevator to the City Room. Clark, who feels he already knows the lay of the land, confidently directs her to George Taylor's office.

They barge in.

It is five minutes before two when both George Taylor and Perry White take turns shaking Clark's hand and welcoming him as a new employee of the Daily Planet Company.

They are starting him off at a weekly salary of thirty-five dollars and sixty-four cents. (Why sixty-four cents, Clark has no idea and is too happy and excited to ask.)

And it is two o'clock when he picks up Soda Wauters from the little staff lounge tucked away behind Perry White's office. She has finished crying, but each of her handkerchiefs is balled up and stuffed under a blouse cuff, just in case.

Clark puts her in a taxi, hands the driver a ten-dollar bill, and tells him, "Take the lady to Newark." He smiles at Soda through the closed window, mouths, "Thank you," mouths, "I'll see you," then touches his ear and mouths, "I want to come hear you sing." Lightly he slaps a hand on the roof of the cab. He watches it roll away.

Clark removes his glasses, looks at them, then breathes on the lenses, polishes them with his shirt. After he puts them back on he starts walking, just walking, crossing Nassau Street, crossing Park Row, walking through his city.

He is too excited to sleep.

5

It is a quarter past six Monday morning.

"I knew you'd show up. It's the only reason I've stayed around. Can we get you anything? Soda pop? Glass of milk?"

"They replaced the windows already."

"Just that you'll know, so you don't make the same mistake in the future, they're called *French doors*. And why wouldn't they be replaced already? This is the Waldorf-Astoria, boy. They believe in service here. Look at that wall! Plastered, painted, better than ever. And I dare you to find even a *sliver* of glass in the broadloom."

"I shouldn't have done that."

"No? I thought it was marvelous, myself. Carl, here, is inclined to your position."

"I'll pay for the damages."

"He's offered to pay for the damages, Carl! Thanks for the offer, but it won't be necessary. Please, though! Sit down. Get comfortable. Carl, why don't you put on a record?"

"I don't want to listen to any records. And I'll just stand, if you don't mind. I don't want to soil the furniture."

"You do look like a chimney sweep, pardon my saying! When you came in just now, I said to myself, this poor fellow looks like some cross between a chimney sweep and Peter Pan. Do you recall Peter Pan came in that way, too? By a little balcony and through the *French doors?* Didn't he? Surely you read *Peter Pan.* Was he barefoot, as well? You do realize you're barefoot, don't you?"

"I'm just here to—"

"There's a picture of your boots in the *Mirror.* So that explains the bare feet. And the missing patch. Or was that supposed to be an *insignia?* They ran a picture of that as well. I *know* why you're here. And we'll get to it. Are you in a big hurry?"

"Not especially. But I'm expecting the police any minute. To tell you the truth, Mr. Luthor, I'm surprised I got here first."

"Well, you're a pretty speedy lad. Says so in all the papers. Have you read them? I have. Carl was kind enough to bring them. Oh! Will you stop glaring?"

The living room is the largest Clark has ever seen and furnished like the ones in those lavish MGM pictures about rich people who quip and quarrel and do the Continental. There is a gas fireplace, but it's not turned on. A glass-topped coffee table. Early-edition newspapers are scattered on top. Only the *Planet* has a picture of Clark on its front page, the rest just have pictures of incinerated automobiles, demolished house fronts, his boots, and his insignia. Also on the table are half a dozen black socketed cubes, identical to the one that Clark ripped out of the robot when he tore out its wiring.

And in the center of the table, between the cubes and the news-papers, is the crumpled robot.

Set down there like that it reminds Clark of a sculpture he saw recently in a *Life* magazine photographic essay entitled "Your Guess Is As Good As Ours . . . Abstract Art in Today's America."

Lex is seated on the larger of the two sofas.

The other man, Carl, is seated in an armchair but looks ready to spring to his feet at any moment. He has a nervous pallor.

Lex looks healthy, tanned, rested. And he's grinning.

"If you intend to keep up the vaudeville act, by the way, you *have* to get a replacement costume. I'll see what I can do. Something in asbestos, perhaps? I have resources."

When a beeping starts in the wall, Lex goes and presses a button under the fluted edge of a piecrust lamp table. Instantly it whirls away and is replaced by a short-wave radio set with both headphones and a microphone on top. He puts on the headphones, adjusting them over his ears. "Excuse me, won't you?" Flipping a toggle, he leans close to the microphone. "Yes?" He listens, he frowns, he sighs. "All right." Then after a pause he says, "Don't contact me here again after, let's say"—glancing at the mantel clock—"half past six. Excellent. Very excellent." He flips the toggle back to its original position, throws down the head-phones, brings back the piecrust table. "Where were we?"

"I need to tell you why I came here. And then I need to go."

"You can't *go.* We've just *met.*"

"I came here—"

"To meet me."

"No."

"Of course you did. But under the ruse of telling me that a dupli-cate copy of the dreaded 'Sandglass File' miraculously turned up last night. Well I'm sorry, boy, but that's old news. Telephones were calling telephones were calling telephones were calling *me* before the *Planet* called the cops. *Now, sit down and quit fidgeting!*"

He's fidgeting?

Out in the hallway a telephone rings.

"Carl, get that. I expect it'll be the police. Tell them I can't speak to them now."

Carl leaves the room.

Speaking with a deliberate, confidential air, Lex says, "He used to be a priest. But he lost his faith. Or perhaps he never had any. Till now. Now he believes in me. Give him time and he'll believe in you, too. He'll believe in the both of us. As will everyone else."

Carl returns.

"Was I right?"

"Yes, sir. They want you to come down to Police Headquarters right now."

"And if I don't?"

"They're going to come here and arrest you at seven o'clock this morning."

"Which means they'll be here by twenty of. If not sooner."

"You think?"

"Oh, Carl, Carl . . ." He winks at Clark. "Carl, why don't you go into my bedroom and bring out my luggage?"

"Yes, sir."

"And set it down by the door."

"Yes, sir."

"I'm not going to let you leave," says Clark.

"Don't be silly."

"*I'm* going to leave, but you're going to jail."

Lex's eyebrows lower. "What's that accent? Nebraska?"

Clark flinches.

"Missouri? Kansas? Off some farm, I'd wager."

Clark swallows.

"I know that you're trying your very hardest, boy, but I have to tell you: it's just not working. You still sound like a yokel."

A warmth starts to rise in Clark's neck, moving up from under his jaws, suffusing his cheeks, climbing through his temples, crawling into his scalp, making it prickle. He doesn't trust himself to speak again.

Lex reaches over and touches the grapefruit-size ball of crumpled metal. "But it's all right that you're stupid. You'll have me for brains!"

With great difficulty—cords standing out in his neck, face turning red, a vein rising, quivering above an eyebrow—Lex hoists up the compacted robot. He staggers to one side but manages to push it through the air at Clark.

Who catches it, snatching it tranquilly, as though it weighed no more than a dime-store pink ball.

Calling in from the hall, Carl says, "Is there anything else you need me to do right now?" He sets down a pair of strapped leather suitcases.

"Actually, there is. Why don't you go stand outside on the balcony?"

"The balcony?"

"Through the *French doors,* there. The balcony."

"Yes, sir."

"You can keep an eye out on the street, let us know when any police cars arrive. Could you do that?"

"Yes, sir."

Paler than before, Carl steps out on the balcony.

"I'm sorry we keep being interrupted," Lex says to Clark.

Whose face still feels warm. Does it show?

"That was a wonderful idea," says Lex indicating the compacted robot in Clark's hand. "But there'll be other ideas. As you'll come to realize the longer we're together."

"Together." Clark has to smile; half smile.

"I'm going to save you a lot of time, boy. Spare you the step-by-step stages of development I had to pass through to get where I am. I regret none of it, of course, since it all led me here. But there's no reason that you should go through it. Why repeat? And as stupid as you are, boy, you *must* realize you have nothing in common with them."

"Them?"

He points to Carl, using him as an example. *"Them."*

Clark smiles at the metal ball, then pegs it abruptly at Lex, missing his head by half an inch. It smashes through an oil painting of a girl in a red hat watering flowers, and sticks into the wall.

Lex turns and looks, looks back at Clark. "One hundred fifty thousand dollars. Sotheby's," he says. "You need to learn self-control. I'll teach you."

Clark has to say it. He *has* to. It's sizzling on his tongue, pushing at his lips, and he just *has* to say it: "You're crazy."

"And you are so obviously stupid. But I'm willing to be patient with you."

"And what are we supposed to do together exactly? I mean, after you've taught me everything—rule the world? Go bother Hitler, why don't you, and leave me alone."

"Mr. Luthor!" says Carl from the balcony. "There's about . . . five, six—there's seven cop cars pulling up down front."

Luthor rises from the sofa. "Take me out of here. Now."

"You *are* crazy."

"I won't bother asking you now who injected you with what, there'll be plenty of time for all of that later." He brings his palms together. "But one *look* at you and I can see you don't have the brains to survive. *I* have those, boy."

Clark says nothing.

"Mr. Luthor!" says Carl. "They're in the building!"

Luthor comes and stands three, four feet away from Clark. "You need me."

"Why?"

"You *know* why. Come on, boy."

"Don't call me that. Don't call me that again."

Carl steps back into the room. "Mr. Luthor, are we gonna go or what?"

Without taking his eyes from Clark's face, Lex raises an arm and points to the balcony. "Get back out there, Carl, where I told you to stay."

"Yes, sir."

The doorbell rings.

"Take me from here. *Now.*"

Pounding begins. "Police! Open the door!"

"Take me from here now and I'll give you the world."

Clark says, "Shall I let them in or will you?"

"You really *are* stupid."

"Then I guess that makes two of us."

"Carl!"

Carl steps back into the room. His face is ashen.

"You trust me, Carl, don't you?"

"Yes, sir. But, Mr. Luthor, what do we—?"

"If you trust me, Carl, if you *believe* in me . . ."

"Mr. Luthor, what do we *do?*"

"Police! Open the door now or we kick it in!"

"Mr. Luthor!"

"Jump, Carl."

"Mr. Luthor!"

Clark looks from one to the other, from Carl to Lex, from Lex back to Carl.

"Jump! And I promise you won't die!"

"Mr. Luthor!"

"Jump!"

And Carl does.

Steps back out onto the balcony and simply flings himself over the rail.

By the time Clark catches him he's already passed the ninth floor.

And by the time he delivers him back to Lex's apartment and lays him down on the longer of the two white sofas, Carl's heart has stopped.

Clark shakes him and pounds him on his chest, angrily, furiously.

Not again!

He drops to his knees and presses his forehead against the couch cushion.

"Up! On your feet!"

When he looks around, Clark finds himself, for the second time in only a few hours, confronted by armed policemen.

Others are moving swiftly through the apartment.

"Not in here!"

"Not back here!"

Not anywhere.

Lex Luthor is gone.

So is his luggage.

"You!" says one of the officers fishing handcuffs from his belt with one hand, grabbing Clark's wrist with another. "Behind your back."

Mutely, Clark does as he's told and is handcuffed.

"Let's go." The cop grips him by his left arm. "Move it."

But Clark plants himself, refuses to budge.

The cop tries dragging him. Another cop comes over, takes hold of Clark's right arm, and they *both* try dragging him.

Finally they stop trying and step back.

"You're under arrest," says the first cop, "and I am hereby ordering you to submit to our custody. Do you understand what I'm saying to you?"

"Yes." What's he think, Clark doesn't speak English?

"And are you willing to comply with my lawful command?"

Clark thinks about it.

"No," he says, and twitches each fist in an opposite direction, snapping the handcuff links. He thinks to apologize but does not. Then he walks to the windows—the stupid French doors. Nobody tries to stop him. Going out onto the balcony, Clark estimates how much leg thrust he'll need to clear the top of the Park Lane Hotel across the street.

And then he flies away.

6

Lex Luthor escaped from his apartment by means of a concealed wall panel.

Of course.

Going directly to the other, smaller apartment he maintained under a different name at the Waldorf-Astoria (next door to Cole Porter's), Lex changed his clothes, changed his appearance (sweeping maestro wig, Vandyke beard, pin-striped suit), then left the hotel and walked calmly over to Grand Central Terminal, where he took a sleeper on the New Haven & Hartford line.

From Connecticut, Lex takes another train, to Ohio. After withdrawing a briefcase full of cash and negotiable bonds from a long-term locker in Toledo, he pays a visit to a general science teacher at a small land-grant college in nearby Bowling Green. Great mind. Deplorable social habits.

By the following day Lex has persuaded the man to begin work developing a virtually indestructible fabric as well as an evaporation ray and a precipitation ray. One that might dry up the ocean, one that might drown the whole world.

Then Lex takes a hotel suite and sends out for the latest prospectus from the Radio Corporation of America and everything available concerning the creation of fully electronic television, which everyone knows is the Next Essential Thing.

He likes having options. As usual, he plans for both the long-range and the short-view, and in every plan that he makes he includes Superman.

Always.

He hasn't felt this alive, this engaged, since he shot those three gunmen in his mother's cemetery.

Life is good.

PART FIVE

—

FIRST-NIGHTERS

The cast takes a bow. Clark is (again) plagued by doubt.
Return to Smallville. Nicely-Nicely.
The conclusion is reached.

———

1

Our version of the story draws toward its conclusion a few minutes before eleven o'clock on Friday, the fourth of February 1938, with the sniffling and sobbing of a first-night audience at the Henry Miller's Theatre in New York City. The show just finished being performed is another of those sceneryless dramas currently in vogue, this one called *Our Town*. It was written by Thornton Wilder, who is not in attendance. When the cast reassembles on the forestage to take their bows, the applause is scattered—enthusiastic, even boisterous, but definitely scattered, because so many hands are reaching for hankies or otherwise being employed: knuckling up tears, rubbing red eyes, et cetera.

Frank Carew, the veteran stage actor who has been dispensing an equal mixture of cracker-barrel and mystical philosophy all evening in his role of the Stage Manager, is clearly taken by surprise. Until this minute and despite some well-received tryout performances last month in New Jersey, he had serious doubts about the play, especially that last act in the cemetery. Too gloomy? Too bathetic? Too long? He catches the attention of pretty Martha Scott, who plays poor doomed Emily, then reaches for her hand. She takes his and they bow together. The applause grows louder.

Martha notices a large man down in the fourth row, center orchestra, so inconsolably distraught that she wishes he'd stop burying his face in his hands and look up. Look here! she wants to call out, just *look*. I'm not *really* dead.

The weeping man (whom Martha Scott fails to recognize because she has yet to work in Hollywood) is Samuel Goldwyn, the powerful movie mogul. In the seat beside his, Beatrice Lilly blows her nose again, exasperated by the fresh tears that well up and spill over.

Several rows back sits Eddie Cantor. His bottom lip quivers but he couldn't be more welcoming of the bittersweet nostalgia that's filled him up. Recently he's lived with seething rage, brooding anxiety, out-and-out fear. The American Nazi Party has been threatening the sponsors of his Monday-night radio program with a boycott of their products by ten million Germans living in the U.S. Kike off the air! Kike off the air! And last week Cantor received the same swastika-embellished note every day in the mail: "Get out of Los Angeles, Jew, before you are carried out in a pine box." When he flew to New York, he told his friends, he told his wife, he told himself that he had pressing business matters there. Now he would like to fly to New Hampshire. He wants to live in Grovers Corner, the town in the play. But who is he kidding? The place doesn't exist. Say it did, though, just say that. Would they embrace a Jew there, even one who can sing and crack good jokes?

Eddie Cantor's is only one name in a lengthy list of famous names that Skinny Simon has jotted on her program. Throughout the evening, from her excellent seat in the loge, she has been craning her head, seeing how many celebrities she could spot. Walter Huston, Walter Winchell, Frederic March. Eddie Picaro the golfer. Fiorello LaGuardia (recently re-elected mayor) and his chubby wife. Two-Ton Tony Galento, the heavyweight boxer who trains on beer and hot dogs. Frank ("Bring 'Em Back Alive") Buck. Claudette Colbert. The list goes on. Oh! She's just spotted another one. Constance Bennett.

Unlike most others in the theater, Skinny is unmoved by this evening's performance. But that's only because she has seen it so often.

She attended as many rehearsals as she could manage, even though Ben Jaeger's part ultimately became a nonspeaking one (celebrant at the wedding, cemetery resident on a camp chair).

Jed Harris, the show's director, met Ben a week before Thanksgiving in a solarium at Bellevue. Harris was there for nervous exhaustion, Ben was nearly recovered from his gunshot wounds and multiple surgeries. Thinking Ben perfect for the role of George Gibbs (boyish looks, quick smile), Harris insisted he audition once he was released from the hospital. Despite no acting experience he did well enough to be called back twice, although the role finally was given to John Craven. Ben was disappointed of course, but grateful to Harris for the consolation job. He now thinks he might pursue acting as his livelihood.

Skinny isn't sure that she likes that idea. Although smitten by celebrities, understandably she is still wary of the "show business life" after what happened with her *first* husband. But if it makes Ben happy . . .

And she has to admit, he does seem happy tonight. Just look at the big goofus waving from the stage. What's he think, he's the star of the show? Men.

No, Ben Jaeger doesn't think he's the star; he knows he is only a wedding guest and a dead guy, but gosh! Things look so different from up here on stage. All those bawling playgoers! And the farther back they sit—mezzanine, balcony—the more perturbed they seem. Naturally Ben too has become immunized to the play's sentiment; how many times can a person get the shivers hearing good-bye to food and coffee, to new-ironed dresses and hot baths, and oh Earth, you're too wonderful for anyone to realize you? But still, being in a real Broadway show is great fun and beats the heck out of being a cop! So Ben enjoys himself, waving, grinning, blowing a kiss to Skinny. And as much as he would like to blow a kiss to Lois Lane, seated only ten rows away, orchestra left, he's afraid Skinny might notice. She can be jealous. But more than that he's afraid Lois might not appreciate it. When a thing is over, it's over. Whoever said that, brother, knew what he was talking about. When it's over, it *is* over. But who's that slickster she's sitting with? Ben doesn't like his looks, not one tiny bit. He's too old for you, Lois! Don't waste yourself on a guy like that! Oh, Lois, Lois, sweet Lois. He blows a big kiss in her direction.

Lois winks back, pressing out a tear that trickles down her cheek. Seeing that tear, John Gurney grunts with moral disappointment. He snaps closed his notepad and teasingly flicks it away. "Oh, for pete's sake, Lois, surely not you!" She slaps his hand, reaches around behind her for her coat. He told her during intermission that he intended to "crucify" this "pseudo-Chinese wreck of a play," and it is evident he hasn't changed his mind.

Since returning in December from Washington, D.C. (a victim of WPA politics), Gurney has been writing theater criticism (some, however, call it carnage) for the *Daily Planet* while teaching journalism again at Columbia. He invited Lois to speak to his class in mid-January, and since then they've gone out on three dates, four counting tonight although Lois doesn't know if she would—he just had an extra ticket. He didn't buy her dinner.

She doesn't know how she feels about dating Professor Gurney— *John!* He's handsome and worldly, not a cheapskate, and a very good kisser. And she does believe, sincerely believe, that a modern girl ought to have a wide variety of experiences with men, older ones included. Still . . . "Would you just listen to all this weeping and gnashing of teeth," says Gurney swiveling his head from side to side. Then he cups his hands to his mouth and says in a raised voice, "It's only a play, ladies and gentlemen, *a very bad play!*"

"Oh, will you shut up," says Lois. As she is sticking an arm into a coat sleeve she glances up, for about the fiftieth time this evening, to a rococo-embellished formal box that juts over the stage. But Clark Kent's back is still turned to her, not that she *really* wants to see his stupid mug (seeing it every day at work is bad enough!). And now that dyed-blond human hippo he's sitting with leans over and says something to Clark, blocking him entirely. One, Lois can't believe he spent the money it cost to buy those seats (at *least* twenty dollars!), and two, she can't believe he'd show up at the theater with that blowsy so-called jazz singer.

You don't think that Clark and she . . . that she and Clark? Forget about *Ulysses, that's* obscene. For a fact she knows Clark goes over to Soda (heaven help us: Soda) Wauters's little nightclub at least once a week, and Lois knows it for a fact because he's asked her repeatedly to go with him, even though she has made it abundantly clear she has no interest in dating him. No interest in Clark, period.

Now, if Clark's friend *Superman* (over the last three months it's gotten much easier for Lois to call him that) asked her out to a jazz club in Newark, you'd better believe she'd say yes. With that guy she'd go to a jazz club in Antarctica! Pick me up at eight and don't be late!

"You about ready to leave?" says Gurney. "I could use a drink."

But the cast has returned to the stage and is taking another series of bows while the audience gives them a second ovation—and Lois joins in.

2

Tonight just happens to be Soda Wauters's thirty-seventh birthday, and she cannot imagine a grander, kinder, sweeter, more *thoughtful* gift than this! She has never been to a Broadway opening before, and this particular show was extra-special because it was written by Mr. Thornton Wilder. At Christmas, Clark gave her a copy of *The Bridge at San Luis Rey* and she'd loved it. Loved what it said, at least what it said to *her.* She is no literary expert, of course, and certainly no big reader, but what Soda took away from Mr. Wilder's novel was this: everything is connected. And that includes every*body.* Everything and everybody is connected, and whatever happens, big or small, good or bad, happens for some reason. There are no accidents in the universe. It made sense. It comforted Soda. She even wrote a letter to Mr. Wilder to thank him for his wonderful book, and he wrote her back! Now she keeps his letter (". . . I cannot tell you, dear lady, how much your kind note has meant to me . . .") framed and hanging in her office at the club.

When she heard that Mr. Wilder had a new play previewing at the McCarter Theater in New Brunswick, Soda tried to get a ticket. But none were available. She told Clark how disappointed she was—and look what he did! Box seats on her birthday. She could kiss him! Instead she asks him now, "Are you all right?" and he nods.

But she's not too sure of that.

He's had a rough time of it lately, and since he came back last week from Kansas he's been quiet and moody. Tonight he's made every effort to be upbeat but hasn't pulled it off. And he can't sit still. Poor fidgety thing. Earlier she noticed him frowning, straining as if the actors weren't speaking loud enough (which they most certainly were), then suddenly in a whisper he said, "Do you hear a fire engine?" A fire engine? No, Soda didn't hear a fire engine. All she heard was the stage manager talking about how maybe once in a thousand times a marriage is interesting, and boy, could she relate to that! A fire engine? No, Soda didn't hear any fire engine. And the next thing she knew Clark was gone! Didn't get back till the intermission was nearly over. Hair disheveled, necktie askew, and if Soda didn't know better she would have thought he sneaked out for a cigarette. His clothes reeked of smoke. He'd gotten a charley horse, he said, and had to walk it out.

She lays a hand on his shoulder. "Clark, thank you again, so much!"

He nods.

"I loved it. Did you love it?"

He nods.

"Oh look, Clark! From here you can see the people backstage crowding around to peek out. You see them?"

He nods.

"See that skinny old man with the suspenders? Doesn't he look exactly like a guy you'd see in those Dick Powell musicals? 'Old Pop.' Doesn't he?"

Clark nods.

Soda takes a breath, applauds again as the little boy who delivered newspapers in act one and then was already dead (casualty of war) by act two steps forward to take another bow.

"Oh Clark, Clark! Look backstage, see where I'm pointing? Isn't that your friend Willi?"

Clark nods.

"What's he doing there?"

Clark shrugs, then leans forward and gently rests his forehead on the ledge of the box. Soda strokes his back in a wide circle . . .

3

Willi Berg is on assignment this evening for *Life* magazine, that's why he's backstage. Before tonight's performance he spent two hours snapping candids of the actors. Even though Willi doesn't particularly like Ben Jaeger, he nevertheless took three shots of the blond lummox. It rankles Willi that a guy like Jaeger—not a guy *like* Jaeger, *Jaeger*—ends up not only making time with Lois Lane but marrying Skinny Simon!

But Willi prides himself on being a professional and didn't let his feelings for Jaeger interfere with his work. He was civil to the jerk and took three pictures of him: eating a sinker, scratching his nose, sticking his tongue out in front of a mirror. And he took a ton of pictures of Martha Scott, and got her telephone number while he was at it.

During the performance, Willi ate a sandwich and played a few hands of poker with the electricians, listened to "Old Pop" tell a funny story about walking in on Ethel Barrymore with her clothes off, and then strolled around snapping pictures of stagehands, asking the ones who weren't smoking if they minded lighting up for his camera. He is amassing a collection of pictures that he hopes eventually to exhibit in an art gallery and later collect into a book. Both the exhibition and the book will be entitled *Smoking Metropolis.* To punctuate his people, he plans also to include pictures of leaves burning in gutters, buildings on fire, smokestacks, that sort of thing.

This is his fourth assignment for *Life* since December. So far he's photographed a Beaux-Arts ball at the Hotel Navarro, a solemn High Mass at St. Patrick's Cathedral (no flash bulbs permitted), and, notoriously, a feature called "The Birth of a Baby" that generated several thousand letters of "strong objection." Willi couldn't have asked for a better career boost! He was proud of that sequence of pictures, despite reservations about taking on the job in the first place. He didn't know if he'd have the stomach for it. Up till the moment he walked into the delivery room at Doctor's Hospital, either he'd been dreading the assignment or making crude jokes about it. Then he got to work and was awestruck. Afterward he held the swaddled baby; later still, he'd sent the mother and father a congratulatory card and the infant girl a flannel nightgown. Maybe he's getting old or getting soft. Anyhow, the pictures came out great.

"Aren't they *ever* gonna quit applauding?" he says now backstage, peering out from the wings, seeing the cast take still more bows.

"Ah, let the kids enjoy themselves," says Old Pop. "They deserve it."

"I guess," says Willi going up on his toes and checking out Martha Scott's fine little fanny. "What's the play about anyway?"

Old Pop looks at him, surprised. "Boy meets girl. They get married. She dies in childbirth."

"What's so great about *that?*"

Old Pop makes a face and walks away.

Willi picks up his camera and takes another picture of the cast taking their—what?—nine hundredth bows. As he lowers it he looks past the actors and sees Clark up in a fancy-schmancy box, arms folded on the railing, his face pressed against a forearm.

Poor guy. The poor guy.

He just hasn't been the same since he got back from Kansas.

4

Clark doesn't know what's come over him. But he just feels so sad, so hopeless and sad. He can understand the play making him feel sad—but hopeless? There was nothing hopeless about *Our Town*. It was neither hopeless nor hopeful, just a play about how things are, how things go, for human beings on the planet, in the solar system, in the universe, in the mind of God. You're born, you grow older, you live in a family, you go to school, you make friends, you get a job, you fall in love, you marry, you start another family, your eyes start to dim, your body fails, and you die. That's all. Grovers Corner was a lot like Smallville, but also a lot like the dozens of towns he and Willi had passed through, drifted into, drifted out of. He could recognize Grovers Corner too in the filthy shantytowns and terrible hobo jungles he remembered, and in Hollywood as well, and in New York. Even in Panterville. Even in Panterville.

And all of the characters, all of the *people* in the play—the doctor, the editor, the wife who pined to go to Paris, the melancholic choir master, the gossips, the milkman, the soda jerk, the geologist, all of them—Clark recognized them all, had met them all and knew them all, young as he was. Those ordinary, ordinary, fortunate ordinary people.

He loved them, lived among them, but was not of them.

How could he be?

Would *his* eyes ever dim? *His* body ever fail?

Would *he* ever die?

He looks human and he tries hard, as hard as he can, to behave as he believes a human being ought to, but it is only playacting. If he isn't human, though, what *is* he? He doesn't know, just as he doesn't really know anymore *who* he is—is he Clark Kent or is he this person called Superman? Only three months and he's lost his way, lost his bearings.

There is nobody to teach him what to do, how to act, how to feel about the actions that he takes. He is alone, more now than he's ever been. He hates it whenever he reads about himself in the newspaper or goes to the movies and sees himself in *The March of Time.* "Unique." "Unparalleled." "One of a kind." "In a class by himself."

Alone.

All by himself in the world, in the solar system, in the universe . . .

Lex Luthor, at least, seemed to get it.

But nobody else does.

Okay: Willi. But Willi is a big-shot photographer now, always busy. And when he isn't, he's off chasing showgirls, or drinking at the Stork

Club, hobnobbing with guys like Alfred Eisenstaedt and Ernest Hemingway. Not that Clark disapproves (well, he does, but it's none of his business), he just misses Willi's steady company.

And no matter how often he lets her know that he's interested in her, not just as a girlfriend (hopeless) but as a *friend,* Lois Lane spurns him.

When it comes to Lois, no matter what Clark does it's always the wrong thing. Like the time she checked into the Rockland State Hospital for the Insane to expose its deplorable conditions. She used an alias and faked a serious mental depression. She intended to stay for thirty days, but after less than a week she had insomnia and dropped fifteen pounds; she was diagnosed with incipient dementia praecox and confined to an isolation wing, denied visitors. When Clark came to see her and was told of her "deteriorating" condition, he promptly informed the doctors of her real identity and she was released. Lois was in such a bad state she had to spend the Christmas holidays in a private sanatorium. But when she came home, shortly after New Year's, she immediately phoned Clark and called him every name in the book of insults. He'd ruined her story, he'd humiliated her. He was jealous, that's all, jealous—because she was the better reporter, the *real* reporter, and he shouldn't even *think* of speaking to her ever again!

Clark bet it would've been a different story if *Superman* had gone busting in there and flown her out.

Sometimes Clark really hates Superman.

But how can he hate Superman? He *is* Superman.

Maybe *he* belongs in Rockland State Hospital for the Insane.

Him, but not Superman. Superman is doing just great. Growing stronger and more coordinated by the day . . .

Willi isn't around much anymore. And Lois won't give him a tumble. And . . .

And Soda Wauters? They're good friends, Clark enjoys visiting her, seeing her perform (whenever he drops by the club, she always sings "Someone to Watch Over Me" and dedicates it to Clark, which is very sweet, but hardly the case). But she's so much older than he is, and they aren't really what you might call confidants. She has never explained to him the nature of her relationship with Richard Sandglass, and for his part Clark has never told her about—well, he's never *told* her.

So who does he have in his life?

Lex Luthor.

In the third week of December a package arrived at the *Daily Planet* for Superman. Clark said he'd see that he got it, and did.

Inside was a beautifully made Superman costume.

"Asbestos," read the note. "As promised."

It wasn't actually made of asbestos. Willi did Clark a huge favor and had the costume (Clark meant to call it a "uniform" but it always came out "costume") examined by a DuPont chemist he knew; they'd met at juvenile court years ago and stayed in touch. The chemist wasn't sure *what* the fabric was, but whatever it was, it was virtually indestructible.

DuPont offered to buy the costume—*uniform*—and duplicate its synthetic fibers, but Clark said no.

Then he checked it over for hidden microphones and transmitting bugs, slow-acting poisons and so on.

The uniform—costume—*uniform* was clean as a whistle.

It seemed nuts to accept such a gift, much less wear it every day, but it also seemed wrong *not* to. Before the package arrived, Clark—again with Willi's assistance—had had two Superman costumes sewn for him by a seamstress Willi knew in midtown who did wardrobes for major Broadway productions. They cost over forty dollars apiece and each was quickly ruined. The first was shredded by state police machine-gun fire the night Clark broke into Governor Lehman's Albany mansion to bring him proof (discovered by Lois Lane) that a woman about to be electrocuted was, in fact, innocent. He'd saved Evelyn Curry's life, but the uniform was a total loss.

The second was torn to ribbons while he'd wrestled with Gargantua after the gorilla went on a rampage and mauled half a dozen circus clowns.

The Luthor-made uniform was identical to the one Diana Dewey had made, except that it came with a wide black belt and the red satin **S** appeared on a yellow, not a black, background.

Why had Lex Luthor changed it?

And why had he made the costume in the first place?

As much as Clark hated to admit it, though, it was a beauty. And it fit him perfectly.

Because of its provenance it did bother Clark to wear it, and of course he wore it all the time. When he wasn't off nabbing bank robbers—twice so far—or chasing after fire engines to see what he could do, he had it on under his street clothes. He washed it in the sink every Wednesday and Saturday nights. It didn't require any ironing.

Truly a miracle fabric!

5

Finally the applause has ended and the cast of *Our Town* is leaving the stage.

Around the performance hall, people are putting on their scarves, their coats and hats (well, the women are putting on their hats; the men, of course, will wait till they are outside).

The house lights are up.

"Lois, can we please go for a drink now? What are you *looking* at?" John Gurney puts his face close to hers and follows her gaze directly up to a box where a strapping-big woman in a gaudy yellow dress is leaning over a man who seems to have fallen asleep with his head cradled on his arms. "Somebody you know?"

She doesn't answer. Is something the matter? Is something wrong with Clark? Not that she really *cares,* but . . .

He *is* a colleague. (And he's turned out to be a very good reporter, not that Lois is ready to tell *him* that. Maybe she'll never be.)

"Let's get a move on, if we're going to have that drink. I still have to go back to the office and build that cross to crucify this miserable excuse for a—"

"Oh, will you just take a hike?"

With a ferocious glare, he snatches his coat and storms off, weaving up the aisle, uncivilly jostling the slowpokes, and then he's gone.

Good riddance.

Lois is glad she never told her father about John Gurney.

He would have been disappointed in her, would have told her, Oh, darling, you can do better than *that*.

And she can. She *knows* she can.

She's not a cold fish, no matter *what* that *Glamour* magazine quiz score supposedly revealed.

And she's not coldhearted, either.

Is something the matter with Clark?

Without planning to, she leaves her row and is now bucking the crowd, heading down the center aisle to get a closer look at what's going on up there in Clark's box.

6

"Clark? How's about we go out and have ourselves a hamburger sandwich? That would make this the *perfect* birthday. Want to?"

But he shakes his head no. He doesn't want to eat. He has no appetite.

Is he having a nervous breakdown? Is this what it feels like? When you feel like it's all just so . . . pointless? When you feel like you don't want to get up and get on with anything? He shouldn't have seen this play. But it's not that. He's been feeling these blues coming on for a while now, several weeks at least.

Clark doesn't know what to do, or how to do it. And what good is what he does, anyhow? There's going to be another world war, it's coming, everybody knows that—and what's *he* supposed to do? He can't stop it. And for every freighter he rescues from foundering in a nor'easter, another one goes down with all hands on board. For every fire he puts out (like the one this evening, over on West Sixty-first Street, that caused him to duck out during intermission), there are fifty others he doesn't know about. A hundred. A thousand. He lives here, but there's an earthquake there, a tornado. For every skier he digs out of an avalanche . . .

What's the use?

People are starving to death, is he feeding them?

People are being mowed down in the Spanish countryside, beaten to death on the streets of Germany. Lynched in America.

What's the use?

He doesn't know what he's doing. *Should* do.

And the more he thinks about it the less certain he feels.

During the most recent of F.D.R.'s fireside chats, the president expressed the wish that Superman would contact the White House, "drop by" for a visit, but Clark pointedly has ignored the request. What if Roosevelt orders him to join the army or something? He's afraid to meet the President of the United States. Who, him? Clark Kent, the B-student from Smallville, Kansas?

Why can't he be smarter? He's not stupid, but why can't he be *smarter?* He says such dumb things sometimes.

In early December he agreed to meet with members of the press, something he vows he will never do again! They bombarded him with the most ridiculous questions. Do you shave? Do you brush your teeth? Do you think most people are frightened of you? Are you a Democrat or a Republican? What do you intend to do about the gambling problem in this city?

The gambling problem?

Yes! Didn't Superman support Mayor LaGuardia's campaign against illegal gambling?

"Of course," said Superman.

"Well—what part do you intend to play?"

He hadn't thought about it but felt he should say something, so he said, "Well . . . I guess . . . I guess I'm issuing a warning to illegal gamblers right here and now. They'd better stop."

"Is that right? And what'll you do if they don't?"

Clark was inclined to shrug (which would've been bad, no doubt), but instead he answered the question (much worse): "I'll beat them up," he said.

The press had a field day.

S'MAN TO ODDSMAKERS: PACK UP OR POW!

"Clark," says Soda Wauters, "we should go, hon. Whyn't you let me sneak off to the powder room and you kind of pick yourself up, okay?"

He's not paying attention to her.

I don't know what I'm doing.

That's what he told his father last week, back in Smallville. "And I don't know what to do. I'm trying but it's not working. Can I come home?"

His father said, "No. No, son, you can't."

Clark visited home at Thanksgiving, then again at Christmas. Thanksgiving was good, mostly because Mr. Kent had some color in his face and strength enough to walk around, at least get from his bed to the kitchen, and he actually ate a little white meat, a bit of cranberry sauce, and seemed to enjoy it. And they'd had time to talk. Mostly they talked about Superman, who by then was a national phenomenon; *Life* had even run a cover picture of him leaping over the tower of the Empire State Building. (Willi was peeved when he didn't get the assignment; Carl Mydans got it instead.) Superman had actually been only a speck, but his (tinted) cape was captured in a highly dramatic swirl. Mr. Kent said he was proud of Clark; Clark told him that, so far, it was "kind of fun."

Christmas wasn't good. Mr. Kent had taken a sharp turn for the worse, and when Alger Lee met Clark at the door upon his arrival, he warned him to get ready for a shock. And it was a shock, a terrible one.

His father was dying.

Clark could no longer deny it. How could he? He could hear his father's sluggish heart, see the inflammation of the sac surrounding it, and the leakage from the mitral valve.

But Mrs. Clemments did her best to make him comfortable, sitting with him for hours and trying to be cheerful. Clark tried being cheerful, too. It was hard. There wasn't much opportunity to talk alone with his father during that visit, and for Clark just about the only thing at all pleasurable about the holiday was the unexpected gift from Mr. Clemments, a hand-carved box. It was the first time Mr. Clemments had displayed any friendliness. And he seemed genuinely thrilled by the Schrafft's chocolates he got from Clark. (Alger had told Clark at Thanksgiving, "Get him candy. You can't go wrong.")

When he left after Christmas to return to New York City, Clark had the terrible feeling he would never see his father alive again.

But he did.

A week ago last Monday, Alger phoned (the farm not only had a telephone now, but also electric light in nearly every room) and told Clark he had better get home just as soon as he possibly could. The doctor said Mr. Kent would probably not last beyond the weekend.

Arriving at the farm early on Tuesday morning, Clark found his father wasted and terribly weak, barely conscious. He sat quietly at Mr. Kent's bedside. He stayed there all day. Mrs. Clemments would come in and then go right out again. When Alger and Mr. Clemments returned from the day's farmwork, they washed and changed into clean clothes and then kept the vigil with Clark.

At last, just after nine o'clock, Mr. Kent seemed alert suddenly, weak but alert, and after beckoning Alger close, he whispered something into his ear. Then Mr. Kent touched Alger's face. Alger went quickly from the room. Mr. Clemments stood up. He and Mr. Kent exchanged a long steady look that ended with mutual slight nods. Then Mr. Clemments went out, too.

Clark sat down on the edge of the bed.

He started to speak but Mr. Kent, smiling gently, touched a finger to Clark's lips.

"I love you, son."

"I love you too."

"And don't worry. Don't fret. You'll be fine. Need I remind you of trigonometry? If you got through that, Clark, you can get through anything."

"But I feel like a big phony."

"We all feel like that, son. Just go on out and do the best you can."

"I'm *trying,* but it's not working. Can I come home?"

"No. No, son, you can't. It wouldn't be fair."

"To who?"

"To *whom,*" said Mr. Kent correcting Clark's grammar but not answering his question.

His funeral was lightly attended, in no small measure because of his presumed heathenism but also because he had brought three Negroes into his home. Clark spoke a few words he'd prepared. But halfway through his text what he was saying struck him as trite and borrowed, so he dispensed with the rest of it and just recited "The Broken Field," a poem by Sara Teasdale that he recalled his mother reading once or twice to his father. "My soul is a dark ploughed field / In the cold rain . . ."

He amazed himself that he didn't forget any of the words.

Jonathan Kent was buried in a plot next to Martha's in the churchyard.

That same night, Clark returned there alone and stood by the headstones under a black sky with a ribbon of cloud suspended across the cold ivory moon. He tried to think of something to tell them both with his thoughts. Finally all he could think of was good-bye. I love you, good-bye.

7

"Clark," says Lois. "Clark!"

All right, she thinks, if the silly lummox won't answer me, to hell with him!

"Clark!"

What's it any business of *mine* if something's the matter with—

"*Clark!*"

When he still doesn't rouse himself and peer down, Lois has an uncharitable impulse to raise her voice and call him "Nicely-Nicely," which she has done half a dozen times already at the *Planet,* in mockery. Although she is almost positive Clark doesn't know the reference (somehow, she can't imagine that farm boy ever having read Damon Runyon), she is 100 percent positive he gets the point of the needle.

Nicely-Nicely, the sickeningly sweet guy. Nicely-Nicely guys finish last. No thanks, Nicely-Nicely, I'm busy on Thursday. And Friday through Wednesday, as well. Candy? For me? Oh Nicely-Nicely, you shouldn't have! Especially since I wouldn't take it from you if you were the last candy giver on Earth! Hey Nicely-Nicely, is it true what I hear? Have you really seen *Snow White and the Seven Dwarfs* twelve times? Nicely-Nicely . . .

"Clark!" says Lois. "You okay up there?"

When she is not kidding herself (now, for example), Lois will admit she's been a thorough b-i-t-c-h to Clark Kent, and it's not something she much likes about herself.

Okay, but he's just so—nice!

And that's a problem?

Yes, that is definitely a serious problem.

It's also a problem that he is so obviously nuts about her, a *big* problem.

Take Superman: he's all business, and except for that one time on Halloween night, she hasn't seen as much as a trace of interest in those dark blue eyes, not a flicker. All business. Always: Miss Lane, Miss Lane, Miss Lane.

She's *told* him to call her Lois, *please,* but always it's Miss Lane.

They've been running into each other at least once or twice a week—at the fund-raising banquet for the Children's Aid Society; at that disastrous press conference when he threatened to beat up gamblers if they didn't behave; at a chemical-factory fire in Brooklyn, a hostage taking in Ozone Park, a train derailment in Yonkers. She just keeps running into him.

And he keeps saving her life. But it's funny about that. She can't remember her life ever being in any real danger *until* he showed up.

"Clark!" she says. "Hey Clark, you okay?"

Since that robot broil, he's plucked her out of the East River after she was trussed up, tied to an anchor, and rolled off the transom of a fishing boat (smugglers); he's caught her midplummet off Jenny Jump Mountain in New Jersey (escaped convict); he's lunged in front of her on Seventh Avenue, scattering machine-gun bullets (fur thieves); he's even rescued her from a four-hundred-pound gorilla that was galloping after her at the circus (Gargantua). And it's always been, Are you all right, Miss Lane? Are you sure you're all right?

"Clark!"

Clark, on the other hand, isn't the kind of a guy who's going to snatch you from the drink or catch you when you're falling but he *has* been, well . . . considerate—*too* damn considerate—in the aftermaths of her close calls. Appearing suddenly at pierside with a blanket, fashioning in the wilds of Jersey a splint for her sprained ankle, showing up in the Garment District with a thermos of Irish coffee when her nerves were still jangly, finding her a sweater at Madison Square Garden after her blouse was slashed immodestly to ribbons. And so on.

He calls her Lois.

And she calls him Nicely-Nicely to hurt his feelings.

She *does* have a cold heart, she *is* a cold fish!

No, it's not that, it's . . . she's fallen hard for Superman, as ridiculous and as impossible and as unwise as that is.

When she was growing up, her father told her dozens of times, "Lois, honey, a woman's reach should exceed her grasp, but the way that you reach is just plain nuts!"

As it was with Willi Berg, it is now with Superman. Lois can never have him, not *really*.

And as it was with Ben Jaeger, it is now with Clark Kent. She can have Clark. Any day she likes.

So of course she doesn't want him.

"Clark! Hey! Clark! I'm talking to you!"

How dare that Kansas cornball ignore her when she's trying to talk to him!

Without thinking about it she stands on one leg, bends the other one parallel to the floor, and pulls off her shoe. Then the former short-stop for the girls' high school softball team pegs it toward the box. After it bloops over the ledge she hears it clunk.

Clark's head pops up from his forearms. Half rising and leaning forward he looks straight down, dramatically startled, then immediately flustered, to discover Lois standing there. His face is shiny with tears. With evident embarrassment he whips off his glasses, drying his eyes against his shoulders. First the left, then the right.

He tries a smile now.

Lois just stares up, her arms and hands tingling oddly.

Without those thick old-man spectacles he looks so *different*. Almost like another . . .

She says, "Clark?"

8

And here, at last, is the point where our version of the story merges with all of the others, the point at which Lois Lane (with one shoe on and one shoe off) peers up at Clark Kent (whose glasses are once again back on his face) with a dawning but already deep suspicion that feels strangely gleeful, almost like affection. *(Clark?)* The point at which Clark Kent pushes a hand shyly, flusteredly (but actorishly, too) back through his thick hair and smiles at Lois Lane. *(Lois?)* The point at which he is filled up with and surrounded by a plain and yet intricate awe: he came maybe a trillion miles to be *here*. This moment, this point in time, this point in space feels both destined and deserved, earned and inevitable. He is in a theater on the island of Manhattan, in the city of New York, in the state of New York, in the United States of America, on the continent of North America, on the planet Earth, in the solar system, in the universe, in the mind of God—whatever that means. Somehow he got here. Somehow he did. And somehow Lois Lane got here, too. She has the loveliest eyes he will ever see and he wants to see those eyes every single day, forever. And if she won't love him, love *him,* he still will love her, love her all the more. And because he will— he will go on out and do the best that he can, like everybody else.

Just like everybody else.